Duck Prints Press Presents

SCHOLARLY PURSUITS

A QUEER ANTHOLOGY
OF COZY ACADEMIA STORIES

DUCK PRINTS PRESS

Duck Prints Press, LLC
Schenectady, NY

The stories in this anthology are works of fiction. The characters and events portrayed are a product of the authors' imaginations. Businesses, places, and incidents pulled from the real world or history are used in a fictional manner. Any resemblance to real people or events is coincidental.

Scholarly Pursuits © 2025, Duck Prints Press, LLC

"The Case of the Lost Grimoire" © 2025, Robin S. Blackwood
"Late or Never" © 2025, E. V. Dean
"Courtship by Marginalia" © 2025, Eliza J. Fitzwilliam
"Some Strange Alchemy" © 2025, Rhosyn Goodfellow
"beautiful and true" © 2025, Mare Griffen
"The Life Cycle of Leaf Sprites" © 2025, Zel Howland
"A Curatorial Puzzle of the Heart" © 2025, Robin Huntington
"Historians" © 2025, Indigo J. H.
"The Cat in the Library" © 2025, Bettina Juszak
"Caffeine and the Unsleeping" © 2025, Lucy K. R.
"Living Legends" © 2025, Nicola Kapron
"Partnered Up" © 2025, Cassia King
"$C_8H_{10}N_4O_2$" © 2025, Mina Kramek
"Family Meal" © 2025, Shannon Lippert
"What We Call Ourselves" © 2025, Lyonel Loy
"A Clockwork Warmth" © 2025, Jessica Mason
"Fair Winds and Fortune" © 2025, Maggie Page
"Queenright" © 2025, Lee Pini
"Escape the Stacks" © 2025, Vee Sloane
"Belonging" © 2025, Swev
"Writ of Evocation" © 2025, D. E. Towry
"Field Research" © 2025, Dei Walker

Wrap-around Cover Art © 2025, Liz Lee Illustration (https://linktr.ee/lizleeillustration)

Edited by boneturtle, E. Conway, Catherine E. Green, Rascal Hartley, A. L. Heard, Mikki Madison, Shea Sullivan, Nina Waters, and Rachael L. Young. Significant contributions also made by the Duck Prints Press editorial, art, and staff teams.
Cover text treatments by Aceriee.
Print manuscript formatting by Hermit Prints.
E-book formatting by Nina Waters.

Published by Duck Prints Press, LLC
Schenectady, New York
duckprintspress.com

ISBN (ePub): 978-1-962488-40-2
ISBN (PDF): 978-1-962488-41-9
ISBN (Trade Paperback): 978-1-962488-39-6

TABLE OF CONTENTS

COURTSHIP BY MARGINALIA

ELIZA J. FITZWILLIAM

Tags: college/university, f/f (background), first kiss, gay, library, m/m, magic use, modern with magic, mystery, past tense, period-typical homophobia, professor, romance, scientist, third person limited point of view, time travel

Felix approached the small, familiar archive with equal parts anticipation and dread. The wintertime weather matched his contrary mood, offering gorgeous late rays of sunlight piercing through a lingering fog and a cold chill. He'd spent the afternoon at his department's end-of-term party ahead of the winter break, wishing colleagues the best as they whizzed off to their holidays and gamely wading through congratulations as the news that his manuscript was off for final edits circulated the room. The party had run longer than he'd accounted for, and the lingering fizz on his skin from the festive illusion cantrips left him grateful for the bracingly cold air as he walked to the museum.

Inside, the Barrington Museum of the History and Science of Magic was a study in contrasts to the outside and Felix's own emotions. The warmth fogged his glasses despite their inlaid charms, and the excited chatter of parents and their school-aged kids taking refuge from the chill was festive and alive. Felix quickly veered off to the archive in the

1

much-quieter western wing. He waved his lanyard with its complex layers of imbued permissions at the various gates and doors as he walked through the warren of corridors until he reached the reading room, slightly winded.

The Barrington Archive, like many of the older buildings in town, was poorly retrofitted for its new purpose; its Victorian sensibilities clashed badly with the institutional chic of the major renovations of the late '80s. It took patience and practice to navigate successfully, which meant Felix usually reached his destination only after at least one turn down a misleading corridor.

The reading room was closing when he arrived: near-empty save for an unfamiliar young woman, bundled for braving the cold, standing at the desk with the banked impatience of one waiting for a friend to finish up. She was crafting an elaborate illusion as she waited, an idle but precise thing, layering the facets and features of the nearby Jadner Central Library. It was lovely work. Felix didn't want to interrupt her efforts, but the soft *snick* of the door closing behind him was loud enough to jolt her from her crafting, and she lost control of the spell. The sight of the spell's slow unravelling was both tragic and perversely comical, but her cheeks were already bright red with embarrassment, so Felix refrained from commenting on the spectacle of the slow melting of the edifices, like a tiered cake left to puddle in front of a roaring fire. He merely gave her the standard, somewhat awkward smile of greeting that was trademark among strangers making eye contact unexpectedly and mouthed, *Sorry.*

"Ah shit, didn't expect to see anyone," she said, waving off his apology. After taking in his scholarly appearance and the way he was wielding a staff lanyard like a warding bell, she asked, "Are you Risa's post-doc researcher?"

"I guess I must be," Felix said with a small laugh, because Risa liked to claim that any scholars who came through the archive were hers by association. "Felix Elmswarren." He offered a small wave between divesting himself of his gloves and stuffing them into his coat pocket.

"Felix!" Risa herself emerged from the office, interrupting the introductions. "I'm glad I caught you before closing up. I know Doctor Oakmoor gave you out-of-hours access, but I wanted to say goodbye before I headed off for the break."

"Hi, Risa," Felix said, bringing up a smile for the enthusiastic young archive assistant. "Great to see you."

"Did you have a chance to meet Dani?" Risa asked, gesturing to the other woman with a besotted smile that had Felix rewrite his understanding of their relationship from presumed friends to likely girlfriends.

"I have now," Felix said. "Nice to meet you, Dani."

"Likewise."

"I'm glad you've met," Risa said, pulling on her coat in a way that managed to not get it caught on her sleek black hair. "Dani's been hearing about the archive for so long without actually meeting anyone who works here that she's started to accuse me of making people up."

"It wouldn't be the first time," Dani cut in with a teasing smile. "I'm with the art school, so Risa telling me about her research and her researchers is as good as a podcast while I'm painting. But I am convinced she runs out of stories before I'm done and starts inventing people." Risa's own research, Felix knew, related to some grisly medico-magical files that the Barrington had boxes of, so he could imagine wanting to offer a lighter topic of discussion.

"Art school," Felix said, not brave enough to wade into a couple's teasing sortie. "That explains the illusion magic."

"Oh, did she show you her work?" Risa asked, all beaming pride.

"Felix startled me when he came in, so he got to watch my Jadner illusion collapse," Dani told Risa, who made a mournful sound.

"Tragedy," Risa said, pausing in her packing to pantomime tears.

With permission from Peter Oakmoor, the new head archivist, to come and go as he pleased, and with the need to balance his work at the array labs with this short-term research project, Felix had originally planned to stick to out-of-hours research. He hadn't been expecting to make a new friend. But when he'd first visited to get the lay of the archive, Risa had recognised him from an *Arrays and Runeology of the Early-Modern Period* course he had taught and took it upon herself to keep up to date with his progress. Enjoying her enthusiasm, Felix had increasingly arrived before Risa closed up.

"Here to do some work on your boy?" Risa asked before immediately adding, because it was an entirely redundant question, "I've got his journals set up in your usual corner. Plus, because you are my favourite researcher here"—she cheekily gestured to the empty room—"I left you the least scratchy of our blankets. The heating system should be good 'til midnight, but you know how it is…" The pipes and back-up heating spells in the building were infamously unreliable due to some undergraduate seminar gone awry in the '80s. Felix was moved by Risa's kindness, and thanked her.

Felix could see Dani looking between them with undisguised curiosity, likely trying to place *which* of Risa's researchers he was, so he offered, "I've been hired to work on the Nathanial Brightling journals." At her look of blinking incomprehension—but not disinterest—Felix ventured to continue, politeness warring with his desire to talk about Brightling. "He was a brilliant magical researcher in the 1820s, a specialist in arrays. He was a contemporary of Selkirk but was never part of that set." At the mention of Selkirk, Dani straightened in recognition of a *Name*. Very few students of any discipline could graduate without some passing familiarity with Selkirk. Alongside libraries, institutes, and buildings across the magical academic world, James Selkirk had given his name to the Selkirkian array standards that most students started out learning.

"Brightling disappeared early into his career, in the winter of 1827," Felix continued, "so he never became as well-known or influential as Selkirk, but he was doing fantastic work before he vanished. He even taught Barrington for a couple of years."

"That's why he's our favourite, and why we have the journals," Risa said with the possessive pride of a scholar who treated institutional ties the same way others did football teams.

"Exactly," Felix agreed with a laugh, still feeling a bit like a preacher in the church of Brightling. "I've been hired to make his work more accessible."

The Brightling journals were too array-heavy for simple scanning, so they had been neglected in the Barrington's push for digitalisation. Not that Felix could blame them. The Telmeai research group in the '90s had learned the dangers of digitally scanning arrays the hard way, when their labs had been stuck in time for nearly three months before a team of the best countercasters could layer together a nullification that freed the last technician. It was only when a private funder came forward with money specifically for the task that the digitalisation of the Brightling journals moved up the list of priorities. As part of his transcription, Felix would carefully copy out Brightling's arrays into a null field software for wider distribution.

"I'm also offering my insights as an arrayist." This part was the most interesting, and turned a week of work, depending on how fast Felix traced and typed, into something that he had been working at for nearly a month. It was fascinating work, but distant enough from his research to feel like a break. Felix's own dissertation, and soon-to-be monograph, studied the intersection of materials and array outcomes. The traditional ink and chalk were still favoured for their stability, but his work had qualitatively demonstrated a range of media from linen thread to lipstick had advantages in certain circumstances. This was a generally held truism, but nobody before Felix had systematically *proved* that suspicion. It was an academic contribution bound to be exciting for his small community of scholars and a somewhat wider group of craftspeople.

"He's been hired to transcribe the journals and assess the existing and unfinished arrays," Risa said, translating for her girlfriend whose brows had knit together in confusion at Felix's sparse explanation. "And, obviously, solve the great mystery of Brightling's disappearance."

"Oh?" Dani said, eyes bright with interest. "Do you have any idea?"

"I've got the final set of pages to read today; the last entry is dated to the day he disappeared. So time will tell." Nobody else working on Brightling's journals had come to any widely accepted conclusions, so Felix didn't love his chances of finding anything definitive. "But realistically, I think he was a brilliant, overworked, and overtired researcher who made a mistake when trying a new array and got stuck somewhere."

That dimmed their enthusiasm, and Felix felt like a prick. Though, in his defence, he hadn't mentioned how he had spent the past weeks obsessively fretting over the balance of Brightling's optimism against his evident loneliness, his brilliance against a clearly yearned-for respect from his peers. And even, if Felix had correctly read some coded asides about an intimate friendship gone awry, a queerness that *cannot* have been fun—or safe—in the 1820s. Still, he scrambled for something to say, not wanting to cast a pall over their evening; he had given his own up for a bad job. Felix had never felt grief for the end of a project before, but he didn't know how else to describe the heavy feeling today's work had created in him.

"But hey, let me show you something cool that I learned in the journals," Felix said, opening his bag and getting out his second-neatest copy of Brightling's runic symbology guide. "In the early 1820s, it was the fashion for students and magicians to come up with a sigil of their name, as a signature and for array work. Brightling came up with a more elegant template than the standard." Felix laid down the guide, pleased when both women peered over. He grabbed three of the scraps of paper left out for circulation numbers. "You start with letter groupings in your first name, and then you slowly pick up the rest of the letters of your full name, working in concentric circles, so it eventually looks like this." He demonstrated with his own name in a practiced flourish.

After some requisite *oohs* of appreciation, they set to trying on their own names. Dani was apparently a Daniela, and much better than Risa at getting the swoop between letter groupings. He commended their first attempts, but once it looked like they would set in to keep practicing, all prior rush clearly forgotten, Felix made to leave. A hushed conversation that Felix only caught half of suggested that they had met passing notes to each other in class, so Felix suspected he had triggered some nostalgic memory. Either way, Felix took the opportunity of their distraction to take his own name-sigil, make a quiet farewell, and sit down in his usual spot.

He then set up, positioning the archival pillow to cradle the last volume of Brightling's journals that Risa had fetched for him. Felix left his laptop in his bag for now and got out his notebook. He had already decided to focus on reading and note-taking rather than transcription today. Once everything was in place, he passed a small surge of magic into the painstakingly stitched array on his notebook, awakening the latent magic.

He'd come up with this transliteration array, his most useful creation, in his last year as an undergraduate. Overwhelmed by the speed of work during a final-year research seminar, Felix had hit his books and pulled his array together from base principles. The array, once powered, created a non-magically infused copy of each page of text as he worked (this, he'd discovered after the squirrel incident of 2015, was *essential*), which allowed him to gloss and annotate at will. It saved Felix hours of meticulously recreating the various arrays he worked with. He would still need to transcribe the Brightling arrays as digital inputs, but with his own copies, that painstaking work could be done in the comfort of his flat, rather than in the archive.

It had been this array, Felix suspected, that had won him the project. After they'd met in grad school, Felix's fast friend, and now Head Archivist at Barrington, Peter Oakmoor had become enamoured with the array, often begging Felix to make transcriptions for him as well. And so when a wealthy donor had approached the Barrington hoping to finally bring Brightling's work out of the archival depths, Peter had immediately contacted Felix. Felix figured it was about what Peter owed him for the hours spent helping with *his* transcriptions, but he had still taken Peter out for a pint in thanks.

For all the benefits of Felix's array, it had been no easy start. The first Brightling journals had been a struggle to gloss. At eighteen, Brightling had a tight, dense, almost impenetrable hand. Paper being expensive for a student, Brightling hadn't wasted an inch. It was tough going, so bad that towards the end, Felix had written in his notebook, crammed next to a copy of an array that Brightling had squished onto the last page, "Brilliant guy, absolute nightmare to gloss—if he doesn't chill out with the scribbling, I may have to try a new approach next journal."

Thankfully, by the time Felix had opened the next journal, Brightling had clearly decided he could afford the cost of paper and left more space between his writing. Brightling had continued to improve with each successive journal, offering increasing space between each of his jottings as the years went on. By his final journal, Brightling was leaving such inviting gaps that Felix felt almost rude not adding his own thoughts and commentary (in his own transcribed journal of course).

Although, with more space, Felix's commentary had veered from the practical and the academic to the increasingly personal. From adding, "Nice" and a quick doodle to Brightling's account of stumbling out of his rooms tired and seeing a fox "as surprised to see me as the reverse"; to contributing "fuck this guy, he sounds like the worst" when Brightling described a visit from famed magical innovator James Selkirk, where the man had been rude about Nathanial's ideas ("Jas. called upon me today, ate my best biscuits and intimated it would be better for all if I were to vacate the labs to let a more deserving scholar occupy. Will have to hex him, next I see him."); to simply adding, "sexy stuff" when Brightling's attempt at a new transportation array took him not to the college gates but rather chose to dump him in the river on a spring day, requiring him to strip down to whatever "shirtsleeves and smalls" were and soggily trek back to his rooms. (This had been a common occurrence as Brightling fine-tuned his transportation array. "Note to self," one slightly water-logged page read, "take pains to avoid landing near ducklings in future. (Maybe a waterfowl avoidance clause?) The mother does not appreciate my presence." The scene had amused Felix so greatly he'd doodled it: a soggy Brightling with a duckling on his head, captioned "Prof. Nat. Brightling collaborates with colleague (1824)".)

In this way, half of the commentary in Felix's notebook was of minimal academic relevance, but he enjoyed engaging fully with Brightling's words, and with the terms of his contract, he could afford to take his time. His…attachment to the long-gone magical scholar was by no means best academic protocol. But he needn't ever publish on Nathanial Brightling, whom Felix wasn't sure he could be impartial about for love nor money. He only needed to transcribe the journals and produce a report for his client, who was paying so extravagantly for the privilege that Felix figured some partiality was acceptable.

His musing was interrupted by the sounds of Risa and Dani leaving for the night. They called out goodbyes that Felix just about managed to return before he opened the journal to his last-read entry. The words that Felix had been carrying around and fussing at like a well-worn trinket glared up at him in duplicate. "My array continues to bedevil me. I have the pieces but their configuration eludes me. This lonesome work wearies my soul." Tired, cold, and overworked (the combined hit of marking season and the Barrington after-hours heating turning itself off in an act of well-timed malice), this entry had rung Felix like a bell. He'd scribbled a "stay strong" in his notebook, under the trace of Brightling's words, and then packed up and taken the next day off. The sentiment had not been new for Brightling, whose isolation seemed to grow as the years went on, but it hit hard when Felix knew how *few* pages he had left to read.

Today, settling down, Felix wrote the date and a note to himself in the space copied over that Brightling now left at the top of each page of his work: "Probably my last day of reading, ten pages to go." He paused and then, in a fit of sentimentality, wrote, "I'm going to miss reading your words, Nathanial Brightling." His chest clenched, a bodily reaction to the sadness that Felix had no intention of dwelling on, so he turned his attention to the last pages. The first page was an array, broken into components. Felix labelled each section, noting the attention that Brightling had paid to the focus of the array: summarising the new ideas, the continuing threads from previous field notes, before moving on.

The next two pages were dense, almost frantically written, with Brightling's hand tighter and messier than Felix had seen it since the first volume. Felix read through the equations, runes, and musings, cramming his thoughts and commentary around the copied traces of Brightling's words where he could fit them. After two pages of this, he couldn't resist writing at the bottom of the second page, "Please, Brightling, my kingdom for you to write normally again."

Thankfully, whatever had panicked Brightling had subsided by the next set of pages, and he was back to his later practice of ample space and careful legibility. Felix wrote an emphatic "thank you!" with a doodled heart on the first page of his copy of these more readable pages. The man may be long in the past, but Felix had been raised to show gratitude.

After his early difficulty, Felix worked through the rest of the pages with alarming speed, noting any mistakes in and limitations of Brightling's approach, only to be relieved with each turned page that Brightling had seemingly caught each mistake himself.

After an hour had passed, Felix had only two pages left: one a complicated, full-page array; the other a short paragraph on the opposite page that Felix couldn't quite bring himself to look at. He let his transcription spell work, tracing out both, eyes unfocussed, before looking carefully at the array.

It was beautiful, a sophisticated transportation array that was a culmination of everything Brightling had been working towards, making use of and combining his interest in temporality, strictly defined foci, and self-reinforcing stabilising layers in complicated spells.

It was also, tragically, unfinished.

"You must have known," Felix said, speaking aloud to a man long dead in the hush of an empty archive. "You were so brilliant, you must have known this wouldn't have worked without a way to hold the definition of the focus."

Heartsore at the idea that Brightling's last contribution was unfinished, Felix sketched out his best guesses for the missing sections in his notebook. When he looked down at his notes, he realised that his suggestions were telling on him. Sometime over the past month he had incorporated Brightling's style of notation into his usual array practice.

With reluctance, Felix turned his attention to the last, far-too-short page, and read the words: "I shall try tonight, nothing left for it. I worry I am being foolhardy, but I have to try. To believe is to trust." and nothing else. The admixture of devastation and hope that filled Felix was heady. In an act of baseless optimism, he let himself imagine that Brightling really had managed whatever he was trying, and found somewhere safe, rather than become lost in the arcane tangle of the magic that they still did not understand.

Felix was so focussed on his hopes for Nathanial that he *almost*, almost, didn't notice the way a gleaming array was drawing itself on the cheap institutional carpet of the archive. But then, it was a rather big array, and the pulsing arcane glow was impressively potent, to say nothing of the ear-popping pressure of powerful magic being done in such an enclosed space, nor the way that Felix's journal notes seemed to pulse with their own arcane light.

At this scale, it took Felix several long moments to recognise the complex layers of glyphs and runes as those he had added to Brightling's final array moments earlier. Before he could grapple with this, a figure was emerging through a rift, first as an indistinct silhouette, then as an increasingly discernible one, until they fully emerged and stumbled forward.

Felix pushed out of his chair and reached to grab the figure, barely making it to him before he crashed against one of the unoccupied desks. Reading rooms were not designed for practical array work, and space was tight. Felix's mind was stuck in the rut of his grief over reaching the end of Brightling's journals. He could vaguely understand that he was looking at, and now supporting, a man who had emerged from the array—a somewhat scruffy looking one at that, in a loose shirt and strangely fitting trousers and a deeply unfashionable pair of glasses.

The man straightened, glancing around the room, eyes darting and face a confusion of emotions, but he did not release his hold on Felix. Instead, when he had done his survey, he peered back at Felix and said, accent oddly unplaceable, "Is this 2025?"

"It is," Felix said, mind a whir shouting impossibilities at him, trying to make him believe in something unbelievable. He tightened his hold on the man's arm and looked at him. He was handsome, the more grounded part of Felix's brain told him: a few years younger than himself, paler, with striking blue-green eyes. Felix didn't know enough about hairstyles to say for sure, but there was something distinctly outdated about the man's hair.

"And are—" the man said, voice betraying him with a crack, "*please*, are you Elmswarren? Felix Elmswarren?"

"I am. Who—?" At Felix's confirmation, the man had slumped forward like his strings had been cut, obliging Felix to take more of his weight. The array was fading, its glow fizzling away, leaving only the lingering press of powerful magic and the man.

"I hoped it would work," the man said hoarsely. He was shaking against Felix now, a tremble that could be tears, laughter, or an adrenaline crash. Probably some mix of the three. It might only be the aftereffects of magic exhaustion, but feeling how the man was clinging to him, Felix suspected there was more to it. As it was, Felix found that he could only cling back and try to accept the impossible.

"I should thank you for your final help," the man said when his shivering had diminished. "I had the start of it, but only trusted my work when your additions matched my best suppositions."

"Nathanial?" Felix ventured, because really who else could it be. "Nathanial Brightling?"

"Have you been collaborating with many other men from across history?" Nathanial grumbled, even as Felix hauled him into something between a hug and a more propped-up slump. He was still speaking into Felix's neck, the words indistinct. What mattered was how he was holding on, grip tight.

"I didn't realise I was collaborating with you." Felix said, holding Nathanial just as tightly. The fabric under his fingers felt strange, and the smell of Nathanial under the ozone scorch of powerful magic was a bundle of scents he couldn't place. They did things differently in the nineteenth century, Felix thought inanely.

Nathanial was clearly content to slump for the moment, likely recuperating from the exertion. Quite frankly, with the amount of magic he would have had to sink into an array of that size to safely travel some two hundred years across time, Felix was amazed he could still string sentences together. As only a *witness* to such a tremendous feat of magic, Felix's brain was flinging questions at him like a tennis volley.

"My transcription spell!" was where his ferret-run of a brain lingered. "It was working both ways?"

"Quite." Nathanial agreed, "though familiarising myself with some of your language was no easy matter."

Felix would be amused by the idea of a man of the early nineteenth century deciphering his twenty-first century slang once he could dwell on it. "And now you are here."

"So I am. You should have refrained from engaging with a lonely man's work so deeply," Nathanial said, almost defensively, with a sniff. "One cannot help but get ideas."

"I'm not complaining," Felix insisted, almost giddy. He'd helped facilitate the only time travel in recorded history. "I'm just surprised. I didn't think anything like this was possible." He carefully did not dwell on the fact that a week ago at drinks with friends, when they reached the stage of asking random questions, Usha had asked who they would most want to meet from history. Felix had said Nathanial Brightling without thinking, and then blushed damningly in a way that told his friends he had not been thinking only of the intellectual value of such a meeting.

It was beyond belief, and Felix pulled back to really look at Nathanial. He looked exactly as Felix had pictured him while reading his journals, but human and real. Waspishly handsome, eyes brightly intelligent, with the charming rumple of a scholar in the grips of research. Felix's eyes kept catching on little human imperfections: a smudge of ink on his jaw, a stubborn lock of hair, the lined furrows on his brow as if he spent hours scrunching up his face in thought.

"I am brilliant," Nathanial said loftily. "And I had help." This latter was gentler, and Felix squeezed his forearms in acknowledgement, even as he felt overwhelmed and stupid.

Nathanial gave Felix a moment to collect his dropped thoughts from across the floor, glancing around the room once more. His eyes snagged on the corner where Felix had left his slip of paper with his sigil-name, and he smiled. Pointing, Nathanial said, "Admittedly, this was one of my sneakier efforts."

It took a second, but Felix barked a laugh. "Clever! You wanted my name."

Blinking innocently, Nathanial said, "You had the advantage of me, I merely wished to know who I was communicating with."

"I can't say I blame you," Felix allowed. "I would have been mad with curiosity. And yet you didn't write anything directly to me?"

"All of it was for you, in a way," Nathanial said, like it was easy to admit something like that. "But I wasn't sure how…safe it would be. Who else would be reading."

"Probably sensible," Felix agreed, thinking *nineteenth century* and *queerness* like watch words. He rued not having the heads-up, but he couldn't blame Nathanial for the caution. And while he may have been more circumspect in his annotations if he'd known, Felix could admit he may have been worse, too.

"Then that last array was specifically to reach me?" Felix knew, but he needed the confirmation. "You must have used the ink as the tether."

"I merely wanted to see whether the promised wonders of your age lived up to your words," Nathanial said evasively. And Felix's heart gave a twinge.

"It really is you." Felix said. "You sound just how you write. I have spent the last month reading your journals; I can hardly believe it." He couldn't help the way his voice caught. "I'm so *glad* you are okay. You vanished in the historical record; I thought something terrible happened to you."

"It could have," Nathanial allowed. "I believed it was worth the risk." Taking another measured look around at his surroundings, Nathanial's demeanour was cautious, like he didn't want to get greedy and gorge himself. His eyes were bright and curious, but as though to not overwhelm himself, he was choosing something on each pass to focus on. He poked a foot at the stubby carpet with a moue of distaste that Felix found himself charmed by.

"Because of some small comments about the future?" Felix asked gently. He had an inkling, but some things were better named.

"In part. But— You said it has been a month for you," Nathanial said, eyes now resting on the pair of their journals, still open on the desk. He reached and ran a reverent finger over Felix's journal where their words met and mingled. "Whereas I had the pleasure of reading your marginalia for *years*." Nathanial was now making direct, almost painful, eye contact. "I would try and hasten it, writing pages of notes, trying to hear back sooner, but your words wouldn't come any faster. Whatever magic connected us would make me wait. I worried, when I read that you were nearing the end of your project. I feared I would lose my tether to you. I had to act promptly."

"*Oh*," Felix said, overwhelmed. And then, because he was an idiot with more degrees than braincells, "Wait, that is actually fascinating. My transcription array must have been interacting with whatever protections your journals had—"

"I favour a modified Grigsby protection array." Nathanial said, a small smile at the corner of his lips.

"Of course," Felix said, his brain whirring. "The mirror clause in Grigsby and my Inga stabilisation would have tangled and refracted. I didn't realise you had any external arrays, but I bet they were on the covers of your journals, and because it was archival practice here to overbind all books for their preservation in the 1890s, they were hidden."

Felix then winced, the sentiment behind Nathanial's words finally registering under the lure of arcane technical details. Inadequately, he said, "That must have been difficult, having to wait."

Nathanial was still looking at him, listening with alive eyes, but there was fear lurking there, too, like he was braced for some disappointment. "It was difficult, to have such sparse connection."

Felix paused, wanting to offer something of commensurate vulnerability. "I could have read faster, been finished in a fortnight, but I didn't want to run out. I had grown attached." That got him a fragile smile. Felix appreciated then what a very brave thing Nathanial Brightling had done, leaving his time and world behind on the promise of a handful of kind words and a better future scrawled in a journal. "I am glad you had patience. It is so very good to meet you."

"Likewise," Nathanial said, low and heartfelt.

And then, because Nathanial had done a brave, dangerous thing, and was looking at Felix with beautiful, intent eyes, Felix stepped closer and leaned in.

He knew it was the correct choice when Nathanial swayed into him. Felix meant it to be a brief kiss, a press of lips more than anything else, but when Nathanial melted into him, all liquid pleasure and trust, Felix couldn't help but drag it out into something lingering, catching, and sweet. His hands found purchase on Nathanial's hips under that strange clothing and held him close, real and here.

It was a kiss heavy with the promise of something more.

"We probably shouldn't do this here," Felix said, dazed, after a few moments, when he remembered they were still in the archive.

"Already the promised shine of the future wears off," Nathanial grumbled, and Felix looked at him, stricken, before it registered that he was being teased. Nathanial was no idiot, he hadn't come here because it was a perfect promise, but because he had looked at what he had, and what he could see, and made a reckless choice to go after something that could be better.

Felix laughed. "You are going to crash from all that arcane exertion soon, and I would rather it happen somewhere more comfortable."

"I suppose I can accept the wisdom of that," Nathanial said stepping away, before he froze. "I realise I am being rather presumptuous, and I did leave instructions with my bank, but it may take some time to—"

"Nathanial," Felix said, smiling, reeling him back in and, in an act of fondness he could barely account for in the privacy of his own mind, dropping a kiss on his forehead. "Calm. You can stay with me. I have space in my bed and on my sofa, whichever suits you best."

"Are you certain? I do not wish to make myself an inconvenience, I can—"

"I insist," Felix said, injecting warmth into his voice. "Help me put this all away, then we can go home, I'll show you around town on the way." He glanced at how Nathanial was dressed; he shrugged off his coat (he hadn't trusted the heating enough to actually take the thing off before now) and tucked it around Nathanial, then grabbed the blanket and draped it around himself like a wrap. Risa would likely forgive him the loan given the circumstances, and better both of them look strange for their cold walk home.

"You can tell me how different everything looks, and I can pretend I remember any history since the 1820s," Felix continued, placing the journal back into the lockable cabinet to be returned to storage. "Then we will come back later, and you can help me write this report on your own disappearance."

Nathanial laughed: a warm, unpractised sound. "I suppose it is the least I can do for making it a more complicated conclusion than you expected."

Felix beamed at him. "But a far better one than I could have hoped for."

THE CASE OF
THE LOST GRIMOIRE

ROBIN S. BLACKWOOD

Tags: agender, aroace, asexual, be gay solve crimes, college/university, fantasy, m/m (past), magic use, mystery, non-binary, past tense, professor, third person limited (multiple) point of view

Hidden in the Irish Sea, shrouded by mist, lies the Isle of Avalon, a land of magic. Not just the ordinary magic that happens everywhere—small spells to wash the dishes or stop the tea from going cold, or the haunted house you'll find in any town old enough—but ancient, powerful magic. People live longer here, the air is sweeter and the trees a brighter green, the stars clearer in the night sky, and the boundaries between worlds are thin.

The towers and spires of Quickquill Castle, the world-renowned thousand-year-old university of magic, rise high above Avalon's cliffs, defying physics in the way only a building created by wizards can. Students come here from around the world to become wizards. A few, through natural talent, hard work, or (most often) both, are brilliant enough to become Mages of the Quill, spending their lives researching and teaching at Quickquill Castle.

Just before sunrise one September morning, Dr Renwick Griffin—a Mage of the Quill—sat in his study, drinking tea at his heavy oak desk, enjoying his last weeks of freedom before students returned to the island.

Opposite him, his old friend Locke sprawled sideways in their chair, their back against one arm and their boots over the other, their tattered black coat slung over the back. As usual, they were drinking black coffee from a mug that read "You've got this, ghoul" which a student had given them years ago. (The student hadn't dared hand it to Locke, presumably thinking Locke might literally bite their head off for it, instead leaving it on Locke's desk. Locke had loved it, and stalked the library the next day with their usual menace while carrying the mug, watching students stifle laughter.)

Locke narrowed their yellow eyes at the chessboard, contemplating before making their move. "What should I get if I win this game?" Their claws tapped the table as they considered. "I know. That murder-mystery book you bought the other day? If I win, I get to read it first. You're reading three books at once already."

"Very well. *If* you win." Griffin examined the board. He usually won these games, but not often enough to get overconfident. After making his move, he glanced at Locke. "You know, this tea might be to your taste, if you ever wanted to try something other than coffee."

Locke raised an eyebrow, suggesting they considered this prospect highly unlikely.

"Most people who drink coffee the way you do are seriously dependent on caffeine. It doesn't even affect ghouls, so why not branch out?"

Locke stared at him, unblinking as always. Moved another piece on the chessboard—not the one Griffin had expected. (Using psychic abilities to sense each other's thoughts was off-limits during their daily chess game, making it one of the only times they could surprise each other.) "I like the taste. It's bitter."

Griffin laughed. "Of course you do." He moved again, and the game continued in companionable silence until Griffin finally won.

Locke half-smiled. "All right, you can read it first. Hand it over when you're done."

"Speaking of…do you want to join me in translating *The Grimoire of Ranulf Faulcon* this morning? I've noticed some references to demonic lore I thought you might recognize."

The *Grimoire* was a fascinating book, assumed lost for centuries. *Faulcon's Tome of Magical Lore* was well-known to every student, but the *Grimoire*, written fifty years later and shortly before his disappearance, was said to be where he'd collected the *real* arcane secrets, magic that had always fascinated Griffin. Within a year of its publication, the government had ordered every copy of it burned.

Locke grimaced. "It's nearly sunrise. I was about to head back to the crypt."

"It won't take long—though we can wait until evening if you prefer."

Locke considered for a moment, then shrugged. "Might as well go now."

Together they navigated the winding, runestone-lit corridors of the castle into the vast library. Dr Dana Faulkner, the librarian, was already working at her desk. Griffin greeted them—"Morning, Dana!"—and they looked up absent-mindedly to smile at him. Soon, Griffin and Locke reached the magically secured archive where the most powerful tomes were kept, off-limits to students except with permission from a Mage of the Quill. Not that there were any students at present; term didn't start until October.

Griffin took a large, ornate key from his pocket, turned it in the lock, and recited the phrase—"Libros non ob potentiam sed verum causa sapientiae peto"—that, with the key, granted access to the archive. (Anyone who used the key but didn't know the right words, or who said the passphrase insincerely, would be magically restrained until Dr Faulkner released them.)

"Enter!" the deep voice of Caedmon Fell—first High Archmage of the University—rang out, and the door swung open with a familiar creak. The smell of old books greeted Griffin as he stepped into the small, warmly lit room crammed with towering bookshelves.

In the centre of the room stood a wooden lectern.

It was empty.

Griffin stared for a moment. When he spoke, he could only whisper the obvious: "It's gone."

Locke, eyebrows lowered in a frown, stalked over to the lectern and slammed their hand down where the book should have been, hitting the wood of the lectern with a *thud* and a click of claws.

Griffin raised a questioning eyebrow.

"Thought it might have turned itself invisible. Stranger things *have* happened in this place."

Griffin took a deep breath. "We have to tell the High Archmage." The pages he'd already translated contained dangerous magic. If someone had stolen it... Griffin tried not to picture it, but he knew from experience that some people's interest in this kind of magic wasn't purely academic.

Griffin touched the silver, quill-shaped ring on his right hand. He closed his eyes, focusing magic into the ring; when he opened them, the ring glowed with blue light. The High Archmage's would be doing the same.

Through the ring, High Archmage Diana Okojie's voice rang out. "Doctor Griffin. What is the matter?"

"*The Grimoire of Ranulf Faulcon* has vanished. I entered the archive to find it missing from the lectern where I left it last night."

The High Archmage inhaled sharply. Then there was silence. Griffin glanced around for any clues, half expecting the book to reappear— books of powerful magic could behave strangely—but it was nowhere to be seen.

The rest of the room appeared undisturbed, not a book out of place on the shelves, not a smudge of dirt on the rug. Griffin sensed the magic of the spellbooks lining the shelves—could even see it if he looked closely, colourful sparks jumping between books—but couldn't sense any unusual magical presence. If not for the absent grimoire, he'd never have thought anything was wrong.

The High Archmage's voice echoed from his ring again. "Come to the Council Room, at once."

Griffin glanced back at Locke—without a Mage's ring, they wouldn't be able to teleport that far. It seemed a little rude to just leave them, but Locke gave a brief nod. "Go on. I'll join you."

Griffin touched the ring once again and recited the familiar words of his teleportation spell. He held the image of the Council Room—round table, tapestries, portraits, and all—in his mind. Silver-blue mist gathered around him, a swirling vortex that soon obscured his surroundings.

When it cleared, he was in the Council Room. High Archmage Okojie watched him from her intricately carved high-backed chair. The other Mages and Archmages of the Quill were teleporting in, each spell unique, spoken in the language most meaningful to the caster: Dr

...

...

...

Faulkner surrounded by white mist rustling like the pages of a book; Archmage Misra in a flicker of green and blue flames that licked their yellow robes without burning them; and Archmage Hardwick, a man Griffin rarely enjoyed seeing, his black-and-white vortex managing to look perfunctory as it vanished while he glowered around the room.

The High Archmage folded her hands in front of her with a rattle of beaded jewellery and gazed at the assembled group. "Is that everyone?"

Archmage Misra nodded. "The two other Archmages and the remaining Mages of the Quill are away from the Isle."

"Very well." She gestured to everyone present. "Take your seats. We have a serious matter to discuss."

They seated themselves around the table—Archmage Misra by the High Archmage's side, Hardwick a few seats away, and Dr Faulkner next to Griffin, the other seats empty until their occupants returned from their travels. Griffin's gaze flicked from face to face; most looked understandably nervous. Hardwick, meanwhile, looked as irritated as always. In all his years at Quickquill, Griffin had only seen Hardwick looking like he *wanted* to be anywhere during the occasional glimpse of him alone in his office.

The High Archmage announced, "*The Grimoire of Ranulf Faulcon* is missing."

Archmage Misra gasped.

Dr Faulkner fumbled with their glasses—which they'd been cleaning on the sleeve of their robe—nearly dropping them.

Hardwick turned to Griffin with a suspicious stare. "That's the book you were studying, isn't it...*Doctor* Griffin?" Hardwick had a gift for saying the word "Doctor" in a way that implied he doubted you deserved the distinction.

Before Griffin could answer, Locke emerged from the shadows, striding across the room to stand behind him. They eyed Hardwick with seething distaste. "It's the book *we* were studying. We went to the library, *together*, and found the book missing." They crossed their arms, leaving their claws very visible.

The High Archmage frowned. "You were not summoned."

Locke turned to her. "I'm a witness." They held out their clawed hands, palms up. "Thought that might be relevant."

"Very well. Can you describe everything you witnessed?"

Locke seated themself on the arm of Griffin's chair. Slowly, while the assembled Mages and Archmages watched, they reached into their coat pocket, took out a pomegranate—when had they had time to visit the buttery?—and cut it open with their claws. They set the pomegranate on the table and began unhurriedly scraping out the seeds.

The atmosphere grew increasingly tense. Locke—keeping them in suspense in retaliation for the less-than-welcoming greeting—ate a mouthful of pomegranate seeds. Eventually, they glanced back at the High Archmage. "This morning, starting when the clock struck midnight?"

Hardwick shot a glare at Locke, then announced: "The ghoul is *mocking* us. I don't know about anyone else, but I didn't become an Archmage to suffer this kind of disrespect."

Griffin felt Locke's presence reaching out to his mind, like claws gently scratching at a door. He let them in, and felt them think: *Should I tell him I always thought he was born for it?*

Absolutely not. They're already suspicious. The last thing you need is to antagonise them. Even in this serious situation, he couldn't help being amused by Locke's disappointment, reminiscent less of a feared supernatural being than of a child being told they couldn't have a pony.

The High Archmage sighed. "Unless anything earlier happened you think is relevant, starting when you entered the library should suffice."

With the air of someone who was showing infinite patience and deserved a medal for it, Locke recounted their chess game, followed by heading to the archive and finding the empty lectern. "Doctor Faulkner can vouch for us." They returned to eating pomegranate seeds.

Everyone glanced to Dr Faulkner, who said, "It's true, neither of them was behaving suspiciously…I don't think they could have stolen the book, they were within my sight the whole time." Her voice shook. "I can't believe this—I'm Faulcon's last living descendant, I heard about him throughout my childhood—and now the only surviving copy of his lost manuscript has disappeared under my watch?"

"This is not your fault," Archmage Misra said. "Everyone present knows the words to get into that room, which hardly narrows it down, but…am I correct in thinking only you and the Mages currently using the archive have copies of the key?" She looked at Dr Faulkner, who nodded.

Archmage Misra turned to Griffin. "Could someone have taken your key?"

Griffin frowned. "Highly unlikely. I keep it on me at all times."

"And at night?"

"I keep it in my bedroom, and I lock the door."

Hardwick raised an eyebrow. "And could anyone have entered your bedroom to take the key? Perhaps someone who is awake at night?" He cast a pointed glance at Locke.

Locke must have known Hardwick meant them, but blinked in a way that, with their yellow eyes and sharp-toothed smile, didn't look at all innocent. "I don't know why you're looking at me. I didn't see anyone prowling about at night. I'd have told you if I had."

Hardwick scowled. "Don't make fun of me, Locke. Did you take the key from Griffin's bedroom last night?"

This time, Locke stared at Hardwick in genuine bafflement. "How would I have got into his bedroom? I can't walk through locked doors."

In fact, Griffin would put money on Locke being able to get into any room in the castle, but admitting it wouldn't help their case. At any rate, they certainly hadn't been in his bedroom last night.

"Well, you two are known to be…" Hardwick paused, then smirked. "Close."

Griffin sighed. He'd hoped Hardwick would be above making insinuations about his colleagues' relationships at a time like this. Apparently, Hardwick considered fewer things beneath himself than Griffin had thought.

Locke, meanwhile, looked like the idea was barely comprehensible. They continued staring at Hardwick, maybe expecting him to reveal it was a joke. "…is *that* what you think about us? What do you take me for, a human?"

Griffin didn't take Locke's horror personally. He'd never seen Locke that way, and Locke didn't see anyone that way, finding the whole concept an off-putting one. Surely rumours hadn't been going around? How many people had been speculating about his and Locke's relationship behind their backs?

Hardwick looked furious. "Oh, you could never be mistaken for human. But Griffin always has kept strange company. I'm starting to think the two of you are so close, you might have worked together on this little plot."

Griffin rarely tried to look intimidating. He was a teacher, after all, and spent most of his time trying to encourage young people, not scare them away. Now, though, he stood, looming with his full height over Hardwick and letting the silver stars in his pupils glow with uncanny light. He took a deep breath, and when he spoke his voice was low. "Well, between my *friendship* with Locke and my own past…I could almost think you were seeking a prize for bringing up as many personal grievances as possible, Hardwick."

For a moment, Griffin worried this would turn into him and Locke against the rest of the Council, but the High Archmage fixed Hardwick with a glare. "Archmage Hardwick. May I remind you that every employee of this University—and this goes double for anyone honoured with the title of Mage of the Quill—is someone I or the previous High Archmage personally considered worthy of their position? In a situation like this, we are unfortunately all suspects, but that is no excuse to forgo basic respect for each other."

Hardwick glanced from Griffin, to High Archmage Okojie, and back. "My apologies, High Archmage," he eventually mumbled.

The High Archmage continued, "Now, remembering Quickquill's strict rules against species discrimination, and the even stricter rules against hexing your colleagues"—she gave pointed glances to Hardwick and Griffin in turn—"we need to establish, as best we can, everyone's locations at the time of the theft. Myself and Jyoti can vouch for each other, although that doesn't rule out the possibility that we conspired together." With this, she smiled in Archmage Misra's direction.

Archmage Misra nodded and confirmed the pair had been in their bedroom in the North Tower—some distance from the library—from eleven the previous night. It wouldn't have been easy for the two of them to reach the archive unnoticed—still, everyone was a suspect.

"Moving widdershins around the table…Doctor Faulkner?"

Dr Faulkner ran her hands through short blue hair, the picture of nervous energy. "I left the library around midnight last night, locked up as usual, went back to my rooms, and…ah, ended up falling asleep while reading at the desk in my study." She laughed, looking down at the table in obvious embarrassment.

The High Archmage smiled. "Well, you're certainly dedicated to your work—though there are more comfortable ways to sleep. Now, Doctor Griffin?"

Griffin had nothing to hide but still felt nervous as everyone turned to him—partly because he knew Hardwick wouldn't believe him. "Locke and I watched a film together. Locke set it up to project on the wall in the crypt. Not as hardworking as Doctor Faulkner, but we might as well make the most of our time before term begins."

"Quite understandable. And after that?"

"Afterward I returned to my rooms. I'm fairly sure everyone here except Locke generally sleeps at night."

Hardwick spoke up. "Did anyone see you heading back to your rooms?"

Griffin couldn't help but grimace; he'd seen no one. "Not to my knowledge."

Hardwick frowned. "So, we only have your word for it."

The High Archmage raised a hand in warning. "I'll ask the questions, Archmage Hardwick. Locke, you told us how you and Doctor Griffin discovered the theft—what were you doing at night? As the only one of us awake all night, your testimony is invaluable."

Locke finished the pomegranate, then gazed back at the High Archmage, unblinking. "I was doing my *job*. Preparing for the start of term, mostly—checking all the alchemical equipment was in good condition, making sure we had the right materials. Had a broken homunculus to repair, too. Only Hardwick doesn't have an alibi."

"Well, Archmage Hardwick?"

Hardwick scowled at Locke again. "Asleep, like any normal human being." Not, Griffin noted, an alibi anyone could confirm.

The High Archmage stood. "It appears there is still no evidence concerning who may have committed this theft. For now, we'll place extra wards on the archive to prevent further crimes while we investigate. And I sincerely hope we can all avoid making accusations without evidence."

The meeting ended with the Mages teleporting out of the Council Room to resume their duties—or, in Griffin's case, to pace around his study, glaring at the floorboards until they started to singe. No matter how many decades he'd spent earning every other Mage's respect, it seemed Hardwick would never view Griffin as anything other than a time bomb, a dangerous practitioner of dark magic who might betray everyone at any moment. Griffin could live with dislike, but when it turned into public accusations…well, he and Locke could both lose their positions.

Worse, whoever had stolen the book could use it malevolently. Just the first few chapters contained information on everything from curses to summoning demons, and Griffin suspected more was present in the yet-untranslated pages. Griffin had been trusted to study a book of dangerous magic. He would never forgive himself if the thief used it for ill. There was only one thing he could do…

"So. When do we start?"

Griffin jumped at the voice and spun around to see Locke leaning against his desk. "…what?"

Locke grinned. "I assume you're set on catching the thief yourself. I'm ready to begin whenever you are."

Despite their grave situation, Griffin smiled. Locke knew him well, and was more loyal than Griffin deserved. "I thought you'd be asleep. It *is* mid-morning—we can discuss this in the evening. I'm sure there's plenty of work I should be doing today…" Though he wasn't sure how he could focus on the mundane preparations for the start of the academic year with so much at stake.

"*Doctor Griffin*, if you think I'm about to leave you unsupervised…" Locke gestured towards the scorch marks on the floor. "You look about to set fire to the whole room."

They had a point. "Don't tell me you, of all people, are offering to work through the day?"

"I expect overtime pay."

Of course, they both suspected Hardwick. Griffin felt Locke's suspicion blending with his own. It was tempting to imagine someone so intent on making accusations, who always said the kind of magic Griffin studied should be banned, must have something to hide. Griffin pictured Hardwick being kicked out of the university and didn't like how satisfying he found it.

Locke's gaze met his, and he knew they had no such qualms.

Still, everyone was a suspect, and they had to start somewhere.

Hardwick was, as usual, in his office, the door shut. Griffin knew he wouldn't get anywhere by barging in. He also knew that, though

Hardwick didn't place much importance on such unintellectual pursuits as food, he did drink coffee.

Griffin headed to the buttery—empty without students, just a few homunculi awaiting orders. The homunculi clicked and whirred excitedly when he asked for a cup of tea. When it was ready, he handed them a shiny button from an old coat (homunculi liked to be rewarded, especially with anything they could use to decorate their nests) and sat waiting for Hardwick.

He showed up not long after, with his usual terse order of "coffee, black," and didn't give the homunculi anything.

Griffin called out to him as he was turning to leave. "Archmage Hardwick, just the man I wanted to see!"

Hardwick turned back, looking highly sceptical.

Griffin pressed on. "I was wondering—what time *did* you return to your rooms last night? Considering we both live in the East Tower, I'm surprised I didn't pass you on the stairs."

"Around 10:30. Why? If you're accusing me of anything…"

Earlier than Griffin. Perhaps that was why Griffin hadn't seen him—or perhaps he was lying. "Oh, no, *I'm* not one to make unfounded accusations. I was just wondering if you'd noticed anyone acting strangely."

"I spend my time working, not spying on people. There's no point questioning me, Griffin." Hardwick gave a cold smile. "There's someone *closer to home* you should be wary of."

Griffin stood and fixed Hardwick with an unblinking stare. "If you mean Locke, they are my friend. I've trusted them with my life many times."

"And of course, you're a man of flawless judgement. Your complete lack of regrettable past decisions is why there was no controversy about letting you teach here."

It was a petty insult, like so many others Griffin had endured from Hardwick over the years, but it crossed a line. Griffin had always tried to give a chance to people others judged harshly—if only because they had that in common—and was also fascinated by the kind of magic some people studied with evil intentions. He'd loved someone with such intentions once, had given him too many chances.

Griffin reminded himself that starting a duel with an Archmage would do the opposite of proving he was trustworthy. He spoke quietly. "If you sink any lower, Hardwick, you'll find yourself in the crypt."

Without another word, Hardwick turned and stalked back to his office. Griffin scowled after him, then sat down to finish his tea. No point letting the homunculi's hard work go to waste.

Soon after, Locke walked in and sat down opposite Griffin. "I searched his office. Couldn't find the book—if he's the thief, it's either in his rooms or hidden somewhere else entirely." Locke yawned and stretched out in their chair. "Should we search his rooms?"

Griffin shook his head. "I doubt we'd keep our jobs if we got caught, even if he was the thief. Let's not resort to that unless we must." Griffin hesitated, Hardwick's comments lingering in his mind. He switched to speaking mentally. *Locke...may I ask you something?*

What is it? You've been looking at me oddly since I came in.

Hardwick, just now, he... It felt wrong to even think it, but he couldn't ignore it either. *He made me question my own judgement. I trust you, but the last person I trusted...*

He'd thought Locke might be offended at his implication, but they just smiled. *You want to see my memories of last night, don't you?*

We don't have to. I know there's plenty of reasons you wouldn't want me looking. It was part of why he hadn't suggested letting Locke study everyone's memories earlier, in the Council Room: even an innocent person could rightfully object to someone entering their mind.

Locke shrugged. *Not like it's the first time.* They reached out with clawed hands to gently touch either side of Griffin's forehead.

Griffin was in front of a shadowy door, a half-real version of the door to the crypt. He stepped through the flickering doorway, watching the events of last night from Locke's perspective. It was strange, being about a foot shorter, seeing in the darkness of the crypt as easily as if it were day, having clawed fingers and sharp teeth. He was Locke as the night played out exactly as they'd described: hunched over a desk, mostly, claws carrying out maintenance on a clockwork homunculus with a care and precision they hardly looked capable of; prowling through the store-rooms to check that every alchemical ingredient was correctly labelled and organized.

"I'm sorry I doubted you." Griffin was once again in the broad daylight of the buttery, sitting across the table from Locke. "I...would not blame you for being offended."

"I'm not." Locke bared their teeth in a grin. "You'd know if I was." They walked over to the nearby drink fridge and glanced inside before sighing in disappointment and flopping back into their seat. "Thought they'd finally started doing blood for a moment there, but *no*, it's some blood-orange thing. Anyway, what's our next move?"

"I'll speak to Dana about the library's wards, try to figure out how the thief could have circumvented them. She'll be adding new ones today, in case whoever it is attempts another theft." He paused. "Would you be able to get past them?"

Locke grinned more widely than ever. "My days as a thief were a century ago, but I can get into any room in this castle—and most rooms anywhere else, for that matter."

"Try it tonight. Examine the wards, see if you can spot any flaws, and search the room for any clues I might have missed. If possible, keep watch in case the thief does return." Griffin paused. "But get some sleep first—it's almost midday, it must feel like two in the morning for you. I'll see you later."

That evening, Locke left the crypt to meet Griffin, who filled them in on the library's new wards. As usual, it was impossible to teleport inside, the statues guarding the main library door would bar entry to strangers, and entering the archive required both the key—which Griffin handed Locke—and the passphrase. It was now also impossible to teleport *out*, and the statues would stop anyone from removing a book without Dr Faulkner's permission. The most dangerous books had been enchanted so no one besides Dr Faulkner could pick them up without being frozen in place. Finally, Dr Faulkner had cast a listening spell so they could hear everything that happened in the library.

Honestly, Locke had expected more. Getting inside would be easy with the key, they weren't taking any books, and the statues should recognise them after decades of working here.

They climbed the walls of the castle to avoid the creaking stairs, slipping in through the window of the second-floor corridor outside the library. Climbing through any of the windows *in* the library would risk detection by Dr Faulkner's listening spell.

They crept past empty lecture rooms, holding their breath as they passed Dr Faulkner's bedroom and study. At last, they neared the double doors flanked by two huge eagle-owl statues. They stepped through, then remembered the creaking floorboards and Dr Faulkner's listening spell. Would teleportation still work *inside* the library? Locke focussed their mind on the shadows, watched the darkness draw in around them—then emerged beside the locked door.

They whispered, "Libros non ob potentiam sed verum causa sapientiae peto," as they turned the key.

"Your pronunciation is terrible," declared the door in the deep voice of Caedmon Fell. Because apparently he'd enchanted it not just to respond to a simple passphrase, but to correct people.

"Keep the bloody noise down, will you? The whole castle's going to hear." Locke kept their own voice low. "Anyway, are you going to let me in or just correct my Latin?"

After a long enough pause to sound reluctant, the door spoke again in its booming voice. "You may enter."

Locke rolled their eyes and crept into the archive. Even without the listening spell Dr Faulkner would have heard that door—it proclaimed everything loudly enough to wake anyone nearby—but at least she wouldn't hear Locke.

The carpet inside made it easier to move quietly, and Locke circled the room, examining every magical ward. All were flawless, not a weakness to be found.

Footsteps approached from the corridor. Locke couldn't risk staying much longer. Dr Faulkner would be here soon, and the thief hadn't returned. Either they didn't dare, or the *Grimoire* really had been all they wanted.

As Locke scurried down the castle walls on their way back to the crypt, it hit them. "Wait a second…" they muttered—then changed course, heading for the window of Dr Griffin's office.

"Have a seat, Dana."

Dr Faulkner peered nervously around Griffin's study before sitting opposite him, staring down at the desk between them.

"That archive door can be an annoyance, can't it?" Griffin steepled his hands on the desk, watching Dr Faulkner, who blinked in confusion. He continued, "I know it's an ancient magical artefact created by our first High Archmage, but libraries *are* supposed to be quiet."

"Oh—yes, it can be…disruptive."

"I'm concerned for your sleep with that in the next room. It's a good thing people don't often search for books of dark magic in the middle of the night, or you'd never get any rest."

"Thankfully, that doesn't happen often." She hesitated a moment. "I'm sorry—is there something you wanted help with? You sounded very serious when you called for me. I do have quite a bit of work—little time to sit and chat, much as I'd like to."

There wasn't a good way to break something like this. The two Mages made uncomfortable eye contact across the desk until Griffin finally spoke—quietly, because the last thing he wanted was for anyone to overhear this conversation. "I'd like to know what you've done with *The Grimoire of Ranulf Faulcon*."

"What—?" Dr Faulkner stared at him with wide eyes. "Renwick, you can't possibly think…" She glanced to the door, apparently remembered Locke was standing on the other side to keep anyone from intruding, and turned back to Griffin. "We're friends, aren't we?"

It was true that if there was any other Mage of the Quill he'd call a friend, it would be Dana Faulkner. They weren't close, not like he and Locke were close, but that was expected for a friendship of a few years rather than one nearly a century old.

Griffin sighed. "I hope we are."

"But you suspect me?"

"I think—and Locke thinks—that unless you've enchanted your desk to be more comfortable, it's unlikely you were too deeply asleep to hear Caedmon Fell's grand proclamations. And you had more opportunity to steal the book than anyone else. I just don't know *why*."

Faulkner leaned closer with a grave expression. "Because I read it. We know so little about Ranulf Faulcon's life, so when the book came into the University's possession, I started working on my own translation. I didn't care about the spells, only what clues I could find about *him*." She sighed. "Turns out he was a cruel, power-hungry man who claimed other people's discoveries as his own. I couldn't face anyone finding out.

So I transported it into a pocket dimension only I could access."

"Dana...no-one would have judged you. If you think I care more about your family history than whether you're a decent person, I'm honestly offended. As for the University, they only care whether you're good at your job."

"And the University's reputation? We've been teaching our students that Ranulf Faulcon was a great wizard for centuries."

"People used to be taught that the sun orbited the earth. Our teachings change with the times—if anything, you'd be thanked for discovering the truth."

Dr Faulkner was silent for a long time. They ran their hands through their hair and finally spoke. "I suppose I've thrown away any chance of being considered a decent person. Or good at my job."

She sounded so regretful that Griffin wished they'd been better friends sooner: maybe she'd have talked to him, maybe he could have convinced her not to do it. They didn't deserve to lose everything. He gave them the most reassuring smile he could. "I wouldn't go that far. I've made worse mistakes."

"Mistakes?" A bitter laugh. "I'm a thief now."

"And the University hired me even after I accidentally helped a loved one do something terrible. We're hardly going to condemn one of our own. If you give me the book, I could return it anonymously, find some explanation... You could keep your job."

She shook her head. "Thank you, but...no matter what story you came up with, I'd know what I did. I'll pack my bags." They turned to the door.

"Stay in touch."

She glanced back in surprise.

"You don't have to. I'd understand if you wanted a fresh start. But if you ever want to talk—or need help with anything—I'll be glad to hear from you."

Dr Faulkner smiled. "I'll remember that."

A few days later, Griffin and Locke were back in the library, poring over the returned *Grimoire* to uncover who'd really discovered all the magical secrets it contained. In Dr Faulkner's absence, Griffin and Locke had assumed many of her duties. It was strange to see her usual spot sitting empty (she'd returned to her hometown and was doing well in her new job), but Locke had taken the opportunity to talk the High Archmage into giving them a generous pay raise.

Locke turned to Griffin, frowning. "Has Hardwick spoken to you yet?"

Griffin shook his head. He'd returned the book anonymously, and while some people suspected the truth, the official story was that a spell had accidentally activated, causing the book to transport itself into a pocket dimension.

Whatever you believed, it was clear that Griffin had not, in fact, stolen the book as part of an evil plot to unleash dark magic on the world: something for which everyone should have been very thankful. Hardwick had seemed almost disappointed by the news.

Locke's lip curled in annoyance. "He owes you an apology."

"He owes you one, too—and I'm sure he knows it."

Hardwick had recently taken to silently avoiding Griffin, with the air of someone aware he was in the wrong but not ready to admit to it.

Locke laughed. "Well, at least I get to see the look on his face every time he walks in to see me behind the desk." They paused to cross-reference a spell in the Grimoire and scrawl something near-illegible in their notebook, then turned back to Griffin. "Now, how many of these spells do you think were invented by a ghoul? Bet you it's at least these five." They pointed to their notes. "When you type up my brilliant discoveries, you'd better give me proper credit."

Griffin raised an eyebrow. "I'd never dream of doing otherwise, but why am I typing up your notes for you? I'm not your secretary."

"You lost our chess game this morning, Doctor, and keyboards are hardly designed for claws." Locke grinned. "If I win this bet, you'll be bringing me coffee, too."

Griffin shook his head, smiling. "You *are* aware you officially work for me?"

"Of course I do, and you would do just *fine* without me, I am sure."

Latin translations by A. L. Heard

What We Call Ourselves

Lyonel Loy

Tags: arranged marriage, bipoc, character injury (graphic descriptions), character injury (permanent), fantasy, flirting, food (graphic descriptions), friends, genderless, ghost, human sacrifice, m/m, m/no gender (platonic), magic use, necromancy, pre-relationship, present tense, royalty, siblings, starvation, third person limited point of view, veteran, war, wedding

"I felt it," his sister says in a low voice. "The untethering. Henri called out to me this morning, and my name didn't feel like my own." She scrubs at her face. "But the coronation's not for a week. You're still king."

"Only in law," Cold Ash replies. "Intent matters, and in magic most of all. We two have agreed that you're now queen; everything else is pageantry."

He'd made himself a king too young. The crown's ancient magics—bound fifteen years ago by the power of the name he'd forsaken—have grown their roots too deeply into his soul. Cold Ash did not have to hear his sister's name spoken to feel its unwinding, ready to be woven in beside all the names given up to bind kings and queens to power.

"And it's still not right that I am," his sister says. She has said this many times. "You led us through the war, Ash. You faced down the dead. How can I take the fruits of peace from you? The—the price of your oath. Let me pay it instead. Haven't you given enough? I'll wed the Citadel in your place."

"What," Cold Ash laughs, "and break poor Henri's heart?"

Little sisters are always little sisters, even when they are queens-to-be; she goes red and swats at him. Cold Ash catches her hand and squeezes it.

"Our oaths are our own to keep," he reminds her—it was their mother's saying. "That bargain sculpted me a king for war. I was never meant for peace. But you: you'll be a good queen. This is a renewal, not a loss. Weave your old name into power and embrace the strength it will bring you. Have you chosen the name you will be queen by?"

"I will. I have." His sister clings to him with a queen's strength. "But you—will you take your old name back? *Can* you?"

"I don't know," Cold Ash confesses. It's a strange thought; there isn't much he doesn't know. "I felt it unweave from the crown's magic. It trails about me like a loose end now, waiting to be reclaimed. But I've been Cold Ash so long that it'd be strange, I think. Try it?"

"Zh—" his sister begins, but she stops and pulls a face.

"It's odd," Cold Ash agrees.

"For the best, maybe," his sister says, biting at her lip—but then she straightens and squares her shoulders like a queen. "I have chosen my name in your honor, King of Cold Ashes. All these long years you kept the last embers of our kingdom safe. I will be Kindling."

"Kindling," he echoes. It is a good name, one that settles over her shoulders like strength. "Queen of Kindling. May our realm burn bright again in your reign."

The Citadel's mages are huddled like motherless ducklings, staring wide-eyed at the crumbling sacrifice pit and picking at their sleeves. An academic lot, and anxiety-prone—Cold Ash appreciates the former trait and would fault no one the latter.

Fifteen years at war with a necromancer's horde has left half the realm anxiety-prone.

"You can sit by me and make more room," Cold Ash says, settling himself down by the pit's longest surviving side. "This is the oldest part of the Citadel, y'know. Predates the written record. Everything else was built up around it."

The mages brighten at the prospect of fresh knowledge, but only their docent—a wall-eyed, muddled-looking woman in her middle years—steps forward.

"Are you sure you don't want a ceremony, my king—I mean, my prince?" she asks, wringing her hands. Docent Soh has been wringing her hands since Cold Ash set foot in the Citadel. "Your letter did say—But we could rustle something up, if you've changed your mind...?" She trails off, plaintively baffled, before adding, "The cooks have baked a cake, a proper one for a wedding. They wouldn't hear otherwise."

"Cake sounds lovely," Cold Ash says.

"We tried to do up rooms for you, too, proper royal ones," a tiny apprentice pips, creeping forward. "But the Citadel didn't let us. It was the ghosts. They kept moving the furniture and shutting the doors."

"You can't tell the prince our dumb ghost stories," an even tinier apprentice hisses. " 'E's the king. 'E's fought *real* ghosts."

"I don't mind ghost stories," Cold Ash says, "and don't worry about the rooms, or the ceremony. I'm sure the Citadel's got it all figured out." Nothing about this is traditional enough for a ceremony anyway, in Cold Ash's view; bloodshed is far more customary a sacrifice than matrimony. But Cold Ash had been a boy when this bargain was struck, and a wedding had been a boy's idea of a sacrifice.

And in his defense, the Citadel accepted.

"Well, then," Cold Ash says, more loudly, to the pit or the walls or the huddled and listening mages. "As I swore fifteen years ago: royal matrimony for the knowledge to win a war. You've held up your end. I'm here to hold up mine."

Poor words, as ceremonies go.

But intent matters, and in magic most of all.

There is no chiming of unseen bells. No sudden chill, no shift in the air. The Citadel dumps knowledge into Cold Ash the same way it has for the past fifteen years—an essay on historical rites of welcome, written on ancient papyrus that Cold Ash briefly feels crackling at his fingertips.

He's always liked the smell of papyrus.

"Thank you," he says to his new building-spouse, with a sudden warm rush of fondness. And to the gathered mages: "The Citadel's got rooms ready in the old east wing. Let's go have a gander, then we can all have cake."

Cold Ash wakes in a bedroom full of ghosts and pillows.

"He *does* need them all," argues a skeletally waifish shade. They carefully position another overstuffed pillow on the treacherously teetering pile by Cold Ash's head. "Kings are used to lots of pillows. He's got to be *comfortable* here."

"Aye, but not so many 'e smothers," the shade of an old fish-wife grouses, as she energetically plumps the pillow pile by Cold Ash's feet.

"He won't! We'll keep watch—" the waifish shade begins.

"I really don't need so many pillows, but thank you," Cold Ash says in a hurry.

The waif shrieks, fades out entirely, and pops back into view. "You can see us!" they gasp, thin fingers clasped over sunken cheeks. "You can hear us— Oh gracious, he can— We didn't mean to startle you— I do hope we're not disturbing?"

"You're the one startled," huffs an old dead herdsman, and the fish-wife clucks agreement.

"Not a bother at all," Cold Ash says. It would take far more than a simple shade to disturb him. "I'm Cold Ash, pleasure to meet you."

"Oh," the waif gasps again, now looking quite distraught, "oh, but you're the King of Cold Ashes. And I don't remember my name, and that's so horribly rude of me! But she's Maryan, and he's Yonglun, and that's Eothain by the door—oh, he's gone. He's very shy."

"Lovely to meet everyone," Cold Ash says again, eyeing the wall poor Eothain had fled through. "And how did you...end up here, if I may ask?"

Shades are born of death, and tend not to mind the topic.

Sure enough: "Bonked right over the head!" the fish-wife Maryan declares, her hands swiping with ethereal excitement through wall-hangings and pillows. "And m'bones ground up to bless the mortar! Did ye ever hear of such a thing?"

The Citadel supplies pages of archaeological studies on human sacrifices when wall-raising and a single half-snippet of a poorly preserved contemporaneous account. "Only bits and pieces," Cold Ash says, untruthfully.

Yonglun cackles. "Mortar!" His craggy face is creased with mirth. "None of that in me day, me old carcass got slung right under the stones to keep the walls up." On this, the Citadel has only a single carved turtle-shell tablet to offer. "All fallen now. They grow tomatoes there, biggest and sweetest you'll ever see."

"I'll try some," Cold Ash promises.

"I don't remember that either," the poor nameless waif wails, and the Citadel has nothing to add. Odd.

"I can make inquiries if you'd like?" Cold Ash offers, and he immediately finds himself with an armful of overexcited shade as the waif launches themself forward to hug him. They wash halfway into his chest; ghost-cold wraps icy fingers around his lungs.

Cold Ash pushes down a reflexive banishment and tries to pat the waif on the back.

"Oh, *would* you!" The waif's skeletal face is all sunshine when they smile. "Oh, please do. I've always wanted a name. More than anything."

"Don't get your hopes too far up, sweetheart. It does need to be written *somewhere*."

Maybe the waif hadn't been a sacrifice like Yonglun and Maryan. Thousands of servants and minor mages must have died forgotten within these walls. Cold Ash knows everything ever written in the Citadel, but most of history goes unrecorded.

"I—I know," the waif says, small and sad. Their pale eyes are liquid with longing. "It's just nice to have someone try. It's been so long." They try to smile again; ghost-chill eases from Cold Ash as the waif pulls away, and Cold Ash almost misses it. "But—*oh!*—I'm being a bother. You just got here! Are you hungry? I get so hungry sometimes; I do wish I could still eat. Can we fetch you anything?"

"Ye can't hold a plate up proper and ye knows it." Maryan laughs like a creak of a straining net. "Bevy of eager living 'uns at the door, waiting to fetch their king anything at all 'e fancies. Go lets 'em in."

"*Please* don't," Cold Ash says in a hurry. He does feel like a cup of tea, but, "Y'know, I've drunk enough tea to fill a fish pond but never brewed a single pot."

What tea does he usually drink? A fresh cup was always at hand; he never had to ask.

You worry enough about the dead, our king, he was always told. *Let us deal with the rest.*

The rest of his morning—the rest of his life—is bright and wide-open and free. Cold Ash has no necromancer to fight; the necromancer is *dead.*

"Let's go find ourselves a kitchen."

The Citadel offers a small burst of knowledge like a tap on the shoulder, and Cold Ash adds, "There's one ready just down the hall."

The war is won. The war is done. Cold Ash has time to brew his own tea.

He has time for everything.

"Our prince!" Docent Soh gasps, winded and wheezing—she'd rushed in right through the shades and not even noticed the chill. "But the 'prentices made up a roster—surely you aren't making your *own* tea?"

"The apprentices were here," Cold Ash says cheerfully. The roster was not; every apprentice in the Citadel must have been clustered outside his door. "Eager bunch. I sent them back to their books."

"The main kitchens can brew your tea too," Docent Soh says, hands wringing, wall-eyes pleading, "or I could. Please, our king—you saved the entire realm, and we—we're just—we did nothing."

The Citadel of Mages had been the pride of the kingdom…fifteen long years ago. Home now to only those too weak, physically or magically, to have fought in the war—even wounded war-mages prefer the comforts of the capital these days.

"Utter rot," Cold Ash says as gently as he can manage. "Ten years ago, was it? I requested a field guide on identifying dragons with half their bits rotted off. You wrote it." He smiles, the crooked and rueful one he used when he needed his army to charge at skeletal hordes; he's never understood how it worked, only that it did. "They take all names off those reports, I know. But you poured your heart into that work, didn't you, Soh Minyoong? I knew you the moment I saw you."

Cold Ash has waited a decade to see her face, wall-eyes and all; no beauty could be more wonderful.

"Three days after you wrote the last word, the necromancer reanimated a swamp dragon." The memory still chills, but this kitchen—Cold Ash's kitchen now, reopened for him by the Citadel, with cheerfully bubbling pots and his shades listening eagerly—fills him with warmth. "Barely had a head left, never mind that *distinctive crest* all the proper books yap about. If you hadn't added that heuristic with the torso-to-limb ratio…"

Child Ash shakes his head to jar the old horror away.

"I can freeze dragonfire. A poison cloud? Would've been a hailstorm of toxic shards down on our heads. Your guide saved a thousand lives that day. How many do you think can say that?"

"You remember it?" Docent Soh has her hands clasped over her mouth; it makes her look endearingly like the waif. "It—it became my maestro's piece. I should never have made maestro—I'm not good with new spells or theories. But you wrote such a nice commendation, the circle let me challenge with it. It was only a review!"

"We can't all be working on new things and tossing that knowledge willy-nilly in a heap." Cold Ash laughs. "I know everything ever written in the Citadel, so trust me: it's no less important to make sure it can all be found."

"It looks delicious," the waif gushes. "Oh, this makes me hungry, I do wish I could try some."

"It looks like swamp water." Cold Ash has had far too much experience with swamp water, and bog water, and all other variations of fetid liquid. All that this sorry attempt lacks are drowned mosquito corpses. "Maryan! What manner of tea do you call this?"

"M'recipe, this?" Maryan, always fond of dramatic entrances, swoops cackling down through the ceiling. "Wrong sort o' berries! It's bearberries you need for sweetness, no' these—"

"These *are* bearberries—" Cold Ash begins.

"Bearberries for sweetness?" Yonglun surges in like an icy wind, first through the open door and then through Cold Ash. "A tarter fruit I'd never tasted! Well, that amn't bearberries neither, laddie, but you don't want bearberries."

"I've never had bearberries," the waif chirps, bouncing eagerly on translucent feet.

"I'll get you some to look at," Cold Ash promises, "just as soon as we've agreed on what a bearberry is. The Citadel just gave me a half-dozen descriptions, some with old leaf-pressings—and *none of them match up.*"

"It's those what bears like," Maryan and Yonglun say as one.

"Has there ever been a berry that bears don't like?" Cold Ash demands. Both scowl. "Soddit, I'm well-enough provided for." Kindling had arrangements made. Excessive arrangements. "Let's send down to the market for anything that looks likely, and we'll try them all."

"Hullo, Eothain."

Two months into his marriage, and Cold Ash has developed quite the ghost-sense for his shades: the waif is always heralded by a twinge in the belly, Maryan and Yonglun by the distant scent of ocean-salt or wool.

Around poor, timid Eothain, even the dishes seem to curl in on themselves.

"I'm making elephant-ear biscuits," Cold Ash explains. He doesn't look up; being looked at terrifies Eothain. "Last had them when I was eight. My older brother Haku brought Kindling and me to a little bakery by the palace; it's long gone now."

Just like Haku. He would have been the King of Bright Flames if he'd lived.

Behind Cold Ash, Eothain makes a little noise like a question.

"Citadel's got plenty of recipes," Cold Ash continues, greatly heart-ened—the spoons have stopped trying to hide behind the measuring cups. "All of them *vastly* different. The oldest use *fistfuls of flour* as a measure—did you ever hear of such a thing?"

"You were a king," Eothain whispers, paper-thin and halting.

Cold Ash would much rather keep talking about biscuits, but: *Eothain.* Words. At last. Cold Ash will chop his own hand off before discouraging him.

"That I was," he confirms.

"But you sacrificed yourself?"

"That I did." Cold Ash sprinkles anise powder over his dough. "Our oaths are our own to keep, Mother used to say. She picked flowers for Father every day of their wedded life, even when she was Queen, because she swore she would when she courted him."

He chances a look back. The subject is disturbing Eothain—his throat is sliced open ear to ear, and ethereal blood dribbles away into nothingness.

Eothain chokes on a gurgling gasp, hands flying up to clasp over his cut throat. "I'm sorry," he whispers, blood-wet, already fading from view. "I didn't mean to show you, I'll just go—"

"Seen far worse," Cold Ash says with frank honesty, "and I'd rather you didn't go. Biscuits want company in their making, or so Maryan tells me, and I fear she may be right."

"…I'm not good company." But Eothain stays, and the flow of long-ago blood slows, and fifteen years of war taught Cold Ash to take any small victory he gets.

"I must disagree there." Powdered clove next, but the recipes in his head are arguing on the amount; Cold Ash throws in as much as his nose can bear. "My first squire and the woman who killed her"—the necromancer had *some* living troops in the earliest days of the war—"hung about me bickering the entire year it took them to move on, Xinhui with a dagger still lodged in her left eye the whole time, that horrible little shit."

That is half a lie: Xinhui stayed as long as she could to help Cold Ash, still always smiling like a cat with mischief on the mind.

Fancy hilt, eh, m'king? Looks all dashing in m'eyeball I reckon.

I'm a soldier like the rest, highness, ye can't save us all. And took this lout here out w' me, aye? Ye there, what were yer name again?

Remember me w' joy, alright?

"I…" Eothain must be drifting closer—the mixing bowls are shivering. Cold Ash hides a smile. "I can stay. If it helps?"

"It very much would."

Eothain takes to his new role of biscuit-companion with a god-speaker's zeal.

"I found five-spice powder," he whispers, little sack clasped carefully in both hands, brow knitted in charming concentration. "Heard the cooks say it's easier than mixing your own blend for the biscuits? I brought you some."

Cold Ash has been plying the cooks with sweetmeats and wine, enough that they gladly ignore their ingredients going walkabout.

"Sweet of you," Cold Ash says with his best and brightest smile, just for the joy of seeing Eothain go pink. "Want to help measure it out? Let's try half of that big wooden spoon."

"I—I'll try. I'm not good at this like the waif." Eothain grips the spoon with trembling hands. "They always practiced a lot, so much that the mages got used to them moving things about."

"It's not a competition, love."

Eothain goes an unhealthy shade of red, and perhaps it's time to change the subject. Cold Ash clears his throat. "There was an effort to standardize measuring spoons a dynasty or three ago. Would've been useful. But they never got to agreeing on the sizes before…plague, or some such."

"I heard," Eothain says. "My parents had some of the prototypes in their collection. But they must have been all burnt, I think. There was a war, and we were losing so badly that my family brought me here to bargain for—"

The measuring spoon hits the counter with a clatter like a fallen knife; the sticky biscuit dough curls around Cold Ash's hands in a desperate embrace.

"You sacrificed yourself," Eothain says. Again.

"I did." Cold Ash squeezes the clinging dough, gently, and tries to pretend that it's Eothain's untouchable hands that he's holding—Cold Ash does not dare to try. The necromancer's shades had shattered in the power of his grasp. "But my sacrifice was only a marriage, Eothain. I didn't give up my life."

"You were a *king*," Eothain insists, raw and bewildered and hurt. "They said to be brave for the family. I tried, I really did. I couldn't."

"If it helps," Cold Ash says, "not much of an example your folks set, sacrificing somebody else."

"I've never been brave. I'm always scared. The waif was so excited when we heard the mages say that you were coming here, but I was scared of that too." The mixing bowl nudges at Cold Ash, almost like a caress. "But the waif was right; I'm glad you're here now. I wish I could hold your hand, but—I like this. I like baking with you."

"I'm glad to be here," Magic that Cold Ash does not dare to release swirls just under his fingertips, reaching. Seeking. "I like this too."

Cold Ash's scones have the consistency of under-fired bricks.

"That looks delicious," the waif gushes, as they always do; Cold Ash's belly twinges with something like sympathy pains. "It must smell delicious too! I do wish we could smell it."

"Nothing that says you can't." Cold Ash points out. More than enough has been written about shades, but nothing about *being* a shade; Cold Ash had switched up his line of questioning after months of fruitless prying on the name and fate of the poor waif. "You can see it, and touch it, too, if you focus. Hear it, if I do this—"

Cold Ash *thonks* a scone against the countertop.

Disturbingly, it both squishes and thuds.

"Here," he urges, "take one each and think very hard about smelling it. We could do a paper on the results, and I'll list you both as co-authors."

Eothain picks a scone up first, brow knitted adorably in his usual determination; the waif follows. Cold Ash slouches back against the counter and grins and watches.

"Oh," Eothain says. "Oh, it smells...very burnt."

"It smells delicious," gasps the waif. "Oh! If we can smell it, do you think we could taste it too? I'd love a taste."

"No harm trying," says Cold Ash, "but not that one, sweetheart. It's a lump of floury coal, not a scone. Dump it out to the midden-heap, please, and I'll get a fresh lot started."

"This is *delicious*," gasps the waif, muffled around a mouthful of scone.

"It's not too bad, if I may say so myself," Cold Ash agrees. His scones are finally recognizable as scones. "But you don't have to eat so fast, sweetheart. You can have them all, and I'll make more if you want. Eothain, what do you think?"

Eothain, chewing with the ginger air of a shade with a not-quite-woken sense of taste, makes a noise of uncertain agreement.

"They're wonderful." The waif crams half a scone at once into their mouth.

"Sweetheart," says Cold Ash, watching with amusement; the waif puts the next half away even faster.

The third scone is swallowed whole.

"Waif," says Cold Ash, with rising alarm.

"Did…did their mouth always open that wide?" Eothain asks, setting his picked-at scone down. "Waif? Is everything all right?"

"It's so good." The waif swallows a fourth scone. And then a fifth, and then they snatch up Eothain's half-eaten scone and gulp it down too. "Please, I'm hungry. I'm *hungry*."

"*Sweetheart.*"

"I'm so hungry," the waif whispers, small and soft and hurt. All the scones are gone. And the waif's eyes…

Their eyes should be pale. Their eyes should not be pitch-black.

They turn, and bite into the baking tray.

Metal crumples in their maw; the waif crunches and growls and swallows, and then the baking tray is gone.

Magic rises in Cold Ash without thought, ancient and familiar; he barely has to reach for it, and there is nothing at all the Citadel needs to add. He is the King of Cold Ashes, the necromancer's bane. He has fought and destroyed the dead for years…

But this is the waif.

This is Cold Ash's little waif.

"*I'm hungry,*" wails the waif, two-tone and ringing. Their pitch-black eyes are dead. Slivers of metal glint like broken arrowheads at their feet—the shredded remnants of the baking tray—and there is no other food here but Cold Ash.

"Sweetheart," Cold Ash says, but *Sweetheart* is not the waif's name. They have no name by which Cold Ash can call them back; all that is left is the banishment magic that swirls fire-hot in his throat, waiting to be sung.

But this is the waif.

Their dead black eyes are fixed on Cold Ash; their mouth is a yawning, gaping gulf. Soon they will strike; Cold Ash has fought the dead long enough to know. He does not want to make this choice—

But Eothain chooses first.

Eothain plants himself between Cold Ash and the waif, his face calm with a sacrifice's resignation even as the waif lunges, and Cold Ash thinks: *No.*

Cold Ash too knows sacrifice.

He will not choose between Eothain and the waif; he thrusts his sword-arm forward with the speed of war, right through Eothain, into the waif's gaping maw—and then he no longer has a hand.

Blood spurts from the ragged stump; blood coats the waif's sunken, starved face. Eothain screams and screams and screams—

—and a memory, forgotten even by its bearer, sinks into Cold Ash like the teeth of a starving shade:

A pit with walls of hewn earth, unclimbably high. A pit that Cold Ash knows. He has sworn himself there to the Citadel, twice over—but the pit he knows had forgotten its own ancient horrors; the height of its walls had been worn away by time.

A fresh-dug pit and open skies. Long before the first stones of the Citadel were laid, there was a sacrifice pit.

Offerings were made within it to long-forgotten gods, in the long-forgotten days before words were written.

The waif was thrown in and left to starve. The waif *starved.* How can even the King of Cold Ashes hope to sate such a horrific hunger? What food could be enough?

What does the waif hunger for?

I've always wanted a name. Perhaps it is the Citadel that whispers this memory; the words were spoken within its walls. *More than anything.* And Cold Ash has a name to spare. A name he can give.

A name with power.

"*Zhengyi.*"

Cold Ash wraps the name he once gave up with all his strength and his sorrow and his hope, and flings it from his tongue like a spell.

"I name you Zhengyi!"

His mother and father spoke this name over him at his birth; it was the only name of his they lived long enough to know. For fifteen years its power bound Cold Ash to the crown.

It was the last name Haku spoke.

Take Soraya and run. Zhengyi, run!

This name is desperation and love and loss; this name has power. "*Zhengyi!*"

"Oh," Zhengyi says, very softly. Their eyes are wide and sunken and pale. "Oh no."

"Oh gracious," squeaks Docent Soh. "Oh gosh. My king—I mean, my prince!—your hand! Oh goodness—"

"It's quite all right," Cold Ash says, for the umpteenth time, as he attempts to usher the docent out the door. "I'm doing quite well, if I dare say so myself. Look, I'm up already! The healers say the bleeding's stopped, and I never get infections either way."

"That'll be the magic in you," Docent Soh says, stopping mid-step *again*, caught between theory and concern. "You've got rather more than most, my prince. I wrote a report as a 'prentice on the effect on innate magic on…but oh! I'm rambling again, I do tend to, when what I meant to say was—your hand! My prince! The healers say it was bitten clean off!"

"Eh, something of the sort," Cold Ash says. He takes a step forward; Docent Soh follows like a duckling. "Nowhere near as dramatic as it looks or sounds, I assure you. Just a little accident. Nothing to worry about."

In the corner of the room, unseen by poor flustered Docent Soh, Zhengyi sobs in Eothain's arms; Yonglun hovers over them both in concern.

"Oh, yes," Docent Soh says with the air of the utterly unconvinced. "Of course, my prince—but are you sure you don't want anyone sitting with you? Your hand! If there's anything you need—"

"Very sure, and I'll be having a little lie-down. Be in the hall for breakfast, you just watch," Cold Ash says, and very firmly shuts the door.

"…and she's off," says Maryan, drifting in through the aged wood. "Safely out o' hearing, muttering about having healing soups prepared. That poor sweet dear."

"I'll drink them all tomorrow to make it up to her," Cold Ash says. He stumbles wearily to the bed—soothing healers and docent alike took more out of him than losing a hand—and sits down hard. "Zhengyi. Sweetheart. It's really all right."

And Cold Ash really does feel quite all right, if in need of a very long nap—Docent Soh was right about the magic in him.

But Zhengyi. Poor Zhengyi.

"I'm sorry," they sob, small and shivering and wretched. "I'm so sorry. It's all my fault."

"It really isn't," Cold Ash says. "Come sit by me, sweetheart."

Zhengyi only shrinks away. "I *can't*," they wail, and Cold Ash's heart twists. "I'll hurt you— I mustn't— I'll go to sleep in the walls and never bother you again—"

"You'll do nothing of the sort!" Cold Ash yelps, utterly aghast. "Absolutely not. I'll drag you out myself if you do; who's going to gush over my terrible baking if you're gone? Eothain, bring them here."

"I'll never eat again," Zhengyi's frail, thin shoulders heave with the force of their tears, even as Eothain chevvies them to perch on the bed by Cold Ash's side. "*Ever. I swear—I ate your hand.*"

"And it was only a hand," Cold Ash says firmly. "Sweetheart— Zhengyi. You are so much more than just a hand to me."

Zhengyi hiccoughs, thin and wavering, scrubbing at their eyes. "But—" they begin, then they fling themself over Cold Ash's chest— washing halfway through in their distress—and start crying afresh.

Ice floods Cold Ash where Zhengyi is embedded inside him; all the rest of him is warm with tenderness.

"You'll eat again," he murmurs, as fierce as a promise. "I'll cook for all of you. There are so many recipes just in the Citadel that we haven't tried, Zhengyi. We've got lifetimes to make up for between the lot of us."

"But if—if I get hungry—I might eat you again," Zhengyi whispers into Cold Ash's chest—their mouth might be around Cold Ash's left lung.

"You won't." Cold Ash wants to stroke Zhengyi's back. He wants to take Eothain's hand and hug Maryan and Yonglun—all of them look so worried. "Zhengyi. Look at me. I'm the King of Cold Ashes, aren't I? Everything takes practice, even eating. We'll figure something out. You have a name now. I can call you back."

Zhengyi looks up.

Their pale eyes are so frightened and so full of hope.

"Can I really have it?" they ask, but their longing is so great that the force of it washes even through Cold Ash. "It's your name. I already took your hand."

"It was my name," Cold Ash agrees. "And that means it's mine to give, and there's no one better I can think to give it to."

It is the greatest truth in the world.

"Still full o' lumps, laddie," Yonglun cackles, prodding at the dough with a spectral finger. "You gots to thwack it more."

"Right," Cold Ash mutters, shaking stiffness out of his protesting off-hand. He relied on his lost hand far more than he'd realized; with the help of his shades, adapting has been more an adventure than a chore. "Right then, Zhengyi: let's give this another go."

Zhengyi adjusts their grip on the mixing bowl, tongue peeking out in fierce concentration; Eothain can now confidently hold the dirty spoons whenever Cold Ash needs a break.

"Still a tad too wet," Cold Ash decides; he doesn't like how the dough wobbles. "I've got the flour, let's add—ah, sod, what is *that*?"

He's reached out, by habit, with his missing hand—he *doesn't* have the flour, but when he swipes right through the flour-sack with the empty air where his hand used to be, a shock of *something* washes like cold water over the linen-swaddled stump of his arm.

"What be *that* there?" Maryan demands.

"Oh, goodness," Eothain says.

Zhengyi clutches the mixing bowl to their chest and squeaks.

"That be mighty queer," Yonglun muses, "but no queerer than all the rest 'bout you, reckon."

At the end of what remains of Cold Ash's arm, the faint impression of a ghostly hand shimmers.

"Well," Cold Ash says, bewildered. When he flexes the torn muscles of his arm, the ghost-fingers twitch; shredded nerves shiver, lightning-sharp. "I *am* married to a building full of ghosts."

And even the Citadel has nothing to add to that.

"We sent you off to a peaceful matrimonial retirement," Kindling wails. Beside her, Henri nods in worried agreement. "How did you lose a hand? You came out of a *war* with all your bits in place!"

"Silly things happen when they're least expected." Cold Ash flashes his best ruefully crooked smile, stump hidden safely in the bellowing recesses of his cloak. Former kings, according to Kindling, must have magnificent cloaks. "You know how it is."

His new ghost-hand looks almost whole now in his practiced sight; almost like a strong shade's. Cold Ash wouldn't mind Kindling seeing it, or Henri, but too many of Kindling's new courtiers built up ghost-sight in the war, and Cold Ash isn't ready for that excitement.

"I've been relearning to write with my off-hand, and teaching some...waifs and strays their letters while I'm at it." Zhengyi in particular has been proving a quick study, and Eothain delights in helping. "Going well. Did a whole scholarly report for the Citadel, and I've started writing a book."

"Oh!" Henri gasps in delight. Henri is easily delighted, which delights Cold Ash. "That's wonderful. About the war?"

"No, no," Cold Ash laughs. "There'll be enough written about the war without my help. It's a very sappy romance about Mother and Father. You'll love it, Henri." And to Kindling, "Speaking of which: have you asked him to marry you yet? Sweet young man like this, someone else will snatch him up if you don't."

Cold Ash was a king and a warrior for fifteen long years. He's been Kindling's older brother since the hour of her birth, and will be to the end of their days.

And little sisters will be little sisters, even when they are queens.

"You're *awful*." Kindling's face goes redder than Yonglun's delicious tomatoes. "You're the absolute *worst*. And *yes*, I have, we were going to tell you after we asked about your hand. Your *hand*, Ash!"

"It's just a hand. I've gained far more." So much more than he'd dared to hope. "Let's get out of this throng—I've got something to show you."

The crowd parts for them like a laughing, joyous sea—queen, prince, and future consort.

The war is truly done. All the world is bright.

BEAUTIFUL AND TRUE

Mare Griffen

Tags: creature shifter, established relationship, f/f, modern with magic, mythology inspired, past tense, secret identity, third person limited point of view, unicorn

Would you still want to know the truth, even if you couldn't share it?

W	Heart pounding, Vee stared down at the message written on the first page of her library book. The letters, inscribed in a familiar, elegant hand, were dwarfed by the book's frontispiece, a solemn unicorn in profile. The tip of the creature's long horn landed right on *it?*, like punctuation.

Vee ran her fingertips over the message, and the question mark smeared, ink still wet. It was minutes old. *Seconds.* Looking up and around, she stumbled to her feet and out to the main corridor of the isolated library floor—but there was no one there. Somehow, in mere moments, she'd missed them.

She returned to her desk at the back of the stacks, where she stored her research materials, and studied the question. Nerves made her hands clammy. It shouldn't have felt so *charged*. She'd been receiving notes on her research materials for months—always in this sweeping cursive, written using one of Vee's own pens, left in the fleeting moments when she had stepped away.

At first, it was an annoyance—who *wrote* in library books? Who took notes on *someone else's research*? But the citations given turned out to be valuable, the questions and criticism insightful, the details offered, rare and strange though they were, ultimately *verifiable*. Fascinated and starved for attention, Vee forgot to worry about how unhinged her correspondent must be, and started writing back.

Normally, the notes touched on specific aspects of her research: suggesting new texts to dig into, offering counterpoints to Vee's interpretations of sources, always encouraging her to keep looking. The notes didn't normally suggest *an answer*. They didn't normally imply that her correspondent knew some deep truth that they had been leading Vee toward all this time.

This one felt different.

Would you want to know the truth?

What kind of question was *that*? Of course she did! Of course she wanted to know the truth about unicorns—whether, if she looked into the past, something would look back. She'd only spent her whole *life* trying to find proof. Of course, if someone could miraculously tell her whether unicorns had ever been real, then Vee wanted to know.

But what would be the point of knowing and not *sharing* it?

Vee wasn't putting years into a PhD program and writing an entire dissertation just to shove all her work in a drawer when she was done. The whole point of discovery was to *share*. To add knowledge to the world. She wanted to *prove* that unicorns were once real, not find out and keep it to herself.

Was "knowing the truth" even a serious offer, or was it an intellectual exercise in prioritization? *How pure is your search for answers?* She'd loved that sort of hypothetical in undergrad, loved staying up late in the library with classmates posing strange questions and then dissecting them with far more vigor than they deserved. But surely, the person who had left her notes for *months* knew by now that this was not a game to her.

Her letter writer had never mocked her before. Teased her, challenged her, occasionally flirted with her—or so it felt, though it could be hard to tell in text. Vee wouldn't have kept responding if she'd been mocked. She almost stopped responding over the flirting. She had a girlfriend, after all, though she thought Aly would find the whole thing more amusing than anything.

She wished she at least knew who her messenger *was*. Now more than ever, with this offer of potential *truth*.

Looking back down at the book, the elegant taper of the unicorn's horn pointing to the question, she penned a return message—on a sticky note, as, unlike her odd pen pal, she didn't like to *deface* library books:

Of course I want to know the truth. But the point of knowledge is to share it, not hoard it.

Then she closed the book, leaving the sticky note to mark the page. It was not without reluctance, though, that she pushed it aside to return to her reading.

All afternoon, as she tried to focus on her work, the book and its message hovered in her peripheral vision. She couldn't help wondering if she should seize the offer, despite her convictions.

"Do you want to go for a walk in the woods this weekend?" Aly asked.

Vee was still thinking about that note, and didn't immediately parse the question. She had to pay better attention, or she would miss Aly's whispery voice. She leaned in to hear her better. "What?"

"The woods. This weekend." Aly took a sip of her latte—oat milk and extra sugar, Vee had memorized her order—and licked the milk foam from her upper lip.

That was another distraction altogether, but Vee tried to rein in her focus. "The woods, again?" Sometimes it seemed like they were *always* out there when they were together. Vee didn't necessarily mind, but she wasn't a natural in the outdoors the way Aly was.

"Yes, the snowdrops are blooming," said Aly. "I want to pick some, to dry them."

To Vee's fascination, Aly had focused her ecology degree on the local environment. Most ecology students she had met researched faraway places—rainforests where the density of plant and animal life offered endless opportunities for study. But what Aly wanted to know about most were the ordinary flowers they stepped on while walking to class.

Then again, Vee's dissertation was focused locally, too. Only on local stories and myths. Fairy tales.

"All right," she agreed. "I guess you can drag me away from work for a little while."

It wasn't a hardship to be dragged anywhere by Aly. Vee had been following her since the first time their fingers caught.

And perhaps it was for the best. It would let her put that message, and its writer, out of her mind. She wanted to focus on the person who was actually in front of her.

Aly's sweet lips curled in a smile. She had milk foam on them again. Vee leaned in to dab it away with her napkin.

"How is the work going?" Aly asked. Her tone was strangely tentative. Normally, Aly was eager to ask about Vee's work. The only person who was. "Any recent breakthroughs?"

"Sometimes I think only going back in time would give me a breakthrough," Vee admitted, and Aly chuckled, though there was a pinched quality to her expression, like she wasn't satisfied with the answer. "Go back to when England was all old growth forests—it used to be practically a rainforest, you know? Right, of course, you know that—and find them, if they're there. Ask those people in their villages and castles, have you *actually* seen a unicorn? Or are they all just stories?"

"Best go back *really* far, or else you'll only find those scientists mashing bones together and *calling* it a unicorn."

"Oh *God*." They'd gone to Germany to see the Magdeburg "unicorn," a fossil that naturalists in the 1700s had put together, thinking it an accurate example of the creature. Really, the thing was a wretched composite of a rhinoceros skull, mammoth femurs, a narwhal's tusk, and God only knew what else—coming together as a bipedal monstrosity shaped more like a sentient triangle than an equine.

Aly, supposedly the naturalist between them, had found it hilarious. "At least they were earnest!" she had said.

Vee had groaned, saying, "The fact that Leibniz tried to legitimize this thing makes me think we should write off calculus entirely. What was he *on*?"

"We can't always be right about everything," Aly had said cheerfully. "I think it's delightful. Can you imagine meeting one in the woods?"

"I'd have to run in terror. Fortunately, it's so top-heavy I think it would fall on its face before it could catch me."

Vee tried not to think about the Magdeburg unicorn, or other failures of scholarship, too often. She did like to remember Aly's laughter as they imagined the thing trying to walk, though.

"I still think they were onto something," Aly said now, a smile tugging at her lips. "It looked realistic to me. Maybe we'll find one on our walk."

"If I found out unicorns were real, and they looked like that, I think it would actually break me emotionally."

"That would be a shame after all this work." Aly looked at her knowingly. Thankfully, there was a sparkle in her eyes again. And a bit of teasing. "You would want to meet it anyway."

"God, I *would*," Vee groaned, planting her face in her hands in despair. No matter how strange and messed up the unicorn turned out to be, she would still want to see it.

Aly laughed, patting Vee's arm. "Don't worry, I'm sure it would be more magical than that."

She was still teasing, at least a little, but Vee liked the way Aly teased her. She had been so shy when they first met, but now Vee had earned her humor and it was delightful. Even if it was sometimes at Vee's expense.

"Hopefully we'll meet one, then, and it will actually have *four* legs," Vee said.

Aly nodded enthusiastically.

And that topic lapsed as they went back to their drinks.

Vee had met Aly on one of the rare nights some acquaintances from her PhD cohort had managed to drag her out of the library to go get drinks. Of course, she'd been rapidly ditched by said acquaintances for more fun companions elsewhere, so she was sitting alone.

Sipping on her boring drink, half hidden in the grimy shadows at the corner of the room, she was feeling increasingly tempted to flee the dingy graduate student pub and go back to the library. Then a beam of light hit her squarely in the face.

Not literally. But that's how it *felt*. An explosion of brightness in the dark room as suddenly the crowd parted and Vee saw *her*.

Aly was waiting by the bar, anxiously twisting her hands together. Her white-blond hair glowed under the bar lights, her short dress pale and stark against the surrounding darkness. Vee got to her feet automatically, mesmerized.

She didn't normally *approach* people. But this time, she found herself walking over to the bar as if drawn by a beacon. Maybe it was the strength of the drink going to her head, maybe graduate school was just generally unraveling her, but either way, she went over, feeling...*hypnotized*. Aly was pretty, gorgeous even, but that wasn't why. Vee felt like she was browsing a new shelf in the library, and her fingers had serendipitously landed on just the right book.

As Vee reached her, Aly was turning away to pick up her pint of beer from the bartender. Vee wasn't great at talking to strangers and asked awkwardly, "Is that any good here?"

Aly startled, sloshing liquid over the rim of her glass. *Whoops.* Vee hadn't been trying to sneak up on her. But Aly gathered herself and turned to her. "I wouldn't know," she said, peering at Vee over her glass, which she held close to her face like a shield. "It's my first time here."

"I haven't been much either," Vee admitted. "I'm usually in the library all day, doing research."

"Me too," said Aly, seeming relieved to have that in common. "Although, for me, research is out in the woods."

"In the woods?"

"I study flowers. Little wildflowers and ferns and things. I'm doing ecology. Field work."

"Oh. Cool!" She must be so much more tuned in to the natural world than Vee was. Vee couldn't remember the last time she'd touched a wildflower.

Belatedly, she held out her hand, grimacing at her lack of manners. "I'm Vee. Sorry."

Aly took her hand with delicate fingers. For a half second, Vee thought she was about to kiss it, like a knight out of a story, but she just shook it lightly. "Aly. What are you studying all day in the library?"

It was always embarrassing to admit, though Vee tried not to let that show. "I'm studying unicorns. Medieval stories and myths, really. And old naturalist texts, you know—I want to know if they were ever real."

"Oh. Fascinating!" She seemed a bit startled, but then, after a steadying sip of her beer, she leaned in. "Do you *think* they were real?"

"Well, I try to take a scientific view. Got to follow the evidence," Vee said. She bit her lower lip, considering. "I want to, though?"

"I like to believe in those sorts of things, too," said Aly, sounding genuine. "They're nice stories."

Her earnestness almost made Vee want to say, *or more than stories*. To, for once, not minimize how much she wanted it to be true.

"It makes the world feel a little more magical," she said, and Aly smiled. "When you finish that one, can I buy you another?"

"Sure," said Aly, and followed her back to her seat in the corner, sitting down with Vee in the shadows. Though, at least to Vee's eyes, the shadows couldn't hide her at all. And, despite her best intentions, Vee did not make it back to the library that night.

Vee didn't talk about her unicorn obsession with most people. She'd learned over the years that people thought her willingness to believe in unicorns was silly and childish. She was tired of being told she was ridiculous, that her dreams were impossible.

But with Aly, what was supposed to be impossible started to feel possible again. She may not have had the same passion for the subject that Vee did, but when Vee brought up her research, she always listened seriously and let the possibility of unicorns *really* existing, in some place and time, linger between them in the air. Let *Vee* believe it, without mockery or minimizing.

Once when they'd been out for coffee, and Vee had been off on an impassioned rant about how close-minded it was to simply *dismiss* the existence of a creature that showed up in so many stories and myths just because there was no concrete evidence—as if people didn't believe all sorts of things without concrete evidence—and how you would never get anywhere without at least being able to consider that the world was larger than you imagined—

She had caught Aly smiling at her and had cut off mid-rant, suddenly embarrassed. All that earnestness felt like too much all at once.

But Aly had only taken her hand and, like Vee had once imagined, kissed it. "Why'd you stop?"

Vee had felt herself flush. Aly...she made Vee feel like, just maybe, she didn't have to hide her true feelings about her work. Aly's openness made her feel *bold*. Sometimes just talking to Aly, having her listen, felt more rewarding to Vee than making progress on her dissertation.

She had almost given up on trying to connect with other people. But Aly changed that. Something about her tugged on Vee's soul. It was like her tangled insides had finally found the pin that would work them free.

It wasn't until after their fifth date or so, however, that Vee started to realize she might have to do the same for Aly. She'd been so caught up in the ease of their conversations that she hadn't realized how infrequently Aly let slip her own deeper feelings.

They were lying side by side in bed, having gone back to Vee's flat after getting drinks. Vee pushed a wild strand of Aly's long, pale hair behind her ear, and Aly studied her with big eyes and asked, "How *did* you get interested in unicorns, anyway? I never asked."

"I don't know." Presumably, at one point, she must have heard the *first* story. Read the first book, or seen the first film that made her wonder. But passions so old became part of one's very being. "I guess every child must read some fantasy book with unicorns in it at some point? They have them in kids' movies."

"My Little Pony?" Aly asked with a quirk of a smile. "Barbie?"

"God, no." The unicorn stories Vee liked had been more...*eerie*. More about going into the deep woods and finding something strange and redefining one's purpose around it. "No," she continued, thinking it through, "I think I liked the idea that they could be dangerous. Mysterious and untameable."

Aly studied her but didn't offer her own opinion. She was doing it again, getting Vee to talk about herself without revealing anything of her own in return. Normally Vee didn't catch it fast enough to change the direction of the conversation, but this time, maybe she could get Aly to share, if she created an opening?

"Feel like I should have gone out in the woods looking for them," Vee added. "Haven't seen one out there, have you?"

"Unfortunately not," Aly said, then bit her lip, looking away as if debating whether to add something. But ultimately, she didn't.

Swallowing her disappointment, Vee went on, "Maybe I should try again. Could still be out there."

"Perhaps it needs to be the right moment," Aly said, seeming wistful.

No matter that she hadn't quite succeeded in getting Aly to open up the way she'd hoped for, Vee pulled her in close and wrapped her arms around her. Aly sometimes had these moments of unaccountable sadness, and Vee didn't want her to fall into that. As she often did, Vee wished she knew what Aly was thinking.

Aly stayed overnight, and morning found her cheery again, making tea in Vee's kitchen and chatting about her upcoming classes. They didn't talk about unicorns or going out into the woods again that morning, though Vee found the thought turning over and over in her mind. She'd always believed that unicorns had *once* existed, that the myths might be more than just stories, but now she wondered about the present. If the countryside's buried past might be more alive today than she realized.

It made her feel young, to think of it that way, to consider that magical creatures might still be wandering the nearby woods. And it put extra energy into her work that week—though the hint of sadness in Aly's expression hovered in the back of her mind.

Whenever she turned to her work, she turned back to Aly. The two had become intertwined.

When she was with Aly, Vee started to understand the appeal of the outdoors. Aly shared her knowledge of the local plant life with as much enthusiasm as Vee talked about her own research, and Vee always learned something when they were in the forest together—how to identify different flowers, how the ecosystem functioned, what had changed as a result of human development. More than anything, Vee liked watching her, liked observing the care with which she stepped between the plants, always aware of what was underfoot. Aly was so serene and beautiful against the backdrop of the trees.

Well, *normally* Vee liked watching her. Today she was preoccupied.

"You're treading on the snowdrops," Aly called, and Vee stopped, moving around a patch she'd been about to step on—even though it was kind of pointless trying to avoid the flowers. They were *everywhere*.

"You're barely looking at them," she complained. Wasn't the point of coming out here to study the snowdrop blooms? Aly had said she wanted to pick some.

"I'll get some before we go back," Aly said quietly. She seemed even more in her head than usual. Maybe they both were.

Vee had gone back to the library a few times since receiving that message, but hadn't found any other notes since. She didn't know what that meant, whether to start mourning the correspondence entirely, or push harder, or concede that she'd keep the secret even if she really would rather share it as proof, especially if said secret was, in fact, about unicorns being *real*—

"What would you do if you never got an answer from your research?" Aly asked. She wasn't looking at Vee, instead studying some bark on a tree. "Would you still care?"

"You don't think there's an answer?"

"I'm just asking."

Vee had always known it was possible she'd search forever, especially if unicorns *didn't* exist. It was hard to prove a negative, hard to ever say, with utter certainty, that the answer was *no*.

And so she kept trying.

"Fail out of my PhD?" she said, in answer to the first question. "I don't know. I guess it's depressing to think about never really knowing."

"So...you only want to know?" Aly said. "Not prove it to anyone else? Not share it?"

Vee stopped walking.

"What did you say?" The way she phrased it...maybe it was only a coincidence. After all, Aly rarely cared what anyone else thought of her work. Unlike Vee, who was feeling increasingly desperate for people to understand that her research wasn't ridiculous, Aly approached her own project solely from a place of interest. She wanted to understand how their local environment came together, the growth cycles of the different plants, the weather patterns, the impacts of human intervention on the forest. She never seemed concerned with what others thought.

Aly had also stopped walking and turned halfway toward her, speaking without quite looking at her. "Would you want to know anyway?" she asked, and now her voice wavered. "I don't think all knowledge is ready to be shared with the world, is all."

"Aly," Vee demanded, *"what are you talking about?"*

Was *Aly* the one leaving mysterious letters in her notes? If so, then *why*? They talked about Vee's research all the time, and Aly had never let on that she had anything more than a cursory knowledge of the subject. If she was interested, if she had sources Vee didn't, why hide it, why *play around* with Vee's entire life's work? She had never gotten the sense that Aly wanted to make fun of her, nor did her pen pal, but then if she knew something, why not *say it plainly*?

Aly *knew* how important unicorns were to Vee.

"Knowledge can be dangerous," Aly said stiffly. "All those stories...they hardly end well for the unicorns, do they?"

The unicorns...from the Middle Ages? "I don't think those unicorns from the past are at much risk *now*."

Aly steeled herself. "They *won't* be," she said. And, expression shuttering, she turned and walked up the path.

Vee stumbled after her, bewildered and hurt. "*Aly*."

Aly kept walking.

What had Vee done *wrong*? What was so terrible about wanting to share the truth?

Except, maybe, if it wasn't solely *her* truth.

She stood in the chill forest, among the half-crushed snowdrops, as Aly disappeared down the trail.

Vee's worry and frustration grew as she returned to her study nook in the library stacks.

She looked at the closed book that held Aly's messages—for it *must* be Aly who had written them, her reaction had been too charged for it to have not been. Why Aly had obscured it, though...well, clearly she cared more about unicorns, and about Vee's *belief* in unicorns, than she had ever let on.

Apparently, however much Vee had shared her true feelings with Aly, she had not been receiving the same trust and honesty in return. But why?

Vee opened the book, tracing over the notes with her fingertip. With the benefit of a new perspective, she could see Aly in them. The delicate handwriting. The detailed questioning of Vee's assertions. Aly's critique of her research had always been empathetic but incisive, and she saw the same in these notes, if with more fervor around the subject than she displayed in person.

She opened her notebook to a fresh page and started compiling every note Aly had left. A few messages stood out, like brighter stars in the constellation.

- *It's hard to parse which parts of a story could be true or just a myth. I think this idea that unicorn horns can cure illness is probably a myth—though I'd imagine it would make people want to go hunting for them.*
- *In response to your question, no, I don't think Pegasi were ever real. The biomechanics of their flight don't make sense. Their wings would have to be almost impossibly large to support their weight, and there are no extant large mammals with wings to refute that. Meanwhile there are plenty of large mammals with horns or antlers of some kind.*

And then, her response to Vee writing, *If we haven't found any unicorns with modern technology then I think they must be extinct.*

- *Or just very good at hiding.*

Now Vee heard Aly's voice in the messages. And the level of interest and care shown here sparked new longing in Vee. She wanted that *from Aly*. Wanted what was truly in her heart, unobscured by academic distance.

Perhaps Aly had wanted her to try harder to find out who was leaving the messages, and the notes were their own request: *Come closer and learn more.*

Now she regretted not following Aly in the woods. It could be hard to tell with her, when to chase and when to let her be. Maybe Vee hadn't been chasing enough.

She turned back to Aly's most recent note.

Would you still want to know the truth?

"I want to know *your* truth," Vee said softly.

Whether that was the culmination of her research or something else entirely, if it was important to Aly, then she wanted to know.

I want to know, she wrote. *I'm coming to find you.*

She left the book open on the desk to let Aly respond, though Vee doubted she would have a chance. Vee was going to find her first.

By the time she left the library, her notebook in hand, dusk had fallen. She returned to the woods, following the now-familiar trail.

Even though she knew the way, the woods were unsettling in the dark, especially when she was alone. Still, her intuition told her that if she were to find Aly anywhere, it would be here. Much like Vee tended to retreat to the library when upset, Aly often wandered into the woods to calm herself, wanting to be alone.

Vee walked slowly along the path. It was chilly, and she wrapped her jacket tighter around herself. She couldn't see Aly's wildflowers very well, now, but she tried to avoid treading on them anyway; Aly would be upset if they were flattened come morning.

When she got to about the midpoint of the trail, which eventually looped back around toward campus, she stopped. *Something* had caught her attention, made the hair on the back of her neck stand up.

A *crack*, off to her left in the trees. Something stepping on a branch, and then another, soft steps leading off into the forest.

Heart pounding, half certain she was following a deer, afraid it was something more dangerous, Vee followed.

Tracking the familiar paths of her favorite stories as much as the sound itself, she traipsed downhill through the trees. When it was so dark she was navigating by sound and gut feeling alone, the steps before her stopped.

So did Vee. She waited, heart pounding, clutching the strap of her bookbag for support.

A soft, equine nose touched her cheek.

Vee froze, breathless. The creature nudged her temple, then her hair, inspecting. It blew out a loud breath, warm over her skin. The darkness was so dense that Vee could barely see it beyond the vague outline in her peripheral vision—though maybe it was really fear blinding her.

The creature—horse—*unicorn?*—nickered, a low rumbling sound that she felt through her body. Trembling, Vee reached up to touch its cheek. Felt the sleek fur, the strong cheekbone. It didn't move away, and finally she gathered the courage to step back and let it come into view.

The unicorn—for of course that was what it was—was so much stranger than she had anticipated. Leggy and angular, bony and sharp at the points where a horse's body would have softened, with translucent, silvery fur, a long unkempt mane, and dark, tragic eyes. Vee touched its nose, hand shaking, and it huffed another hot breath over her skin.

Vee's voice trembled, but she tried to stand tall. "You know, you could have said something. But…I'm sorry that you felt you couldn't."

The unicorn snorted, shook itself, mane flying, and then in a shimmer of light, standing before her was Aly. She looked tired, hair messy like she'd been running her hands through it, eyes big and shadowed.

Vee reached out, even more cautious this time, and touched her cheek. "Did…you think I wouldn't believe you?" She wasn't sure she fully believed this was happening *now*, to be honest. And yet, looking at Aly, touching her skin, her hair…it felt *right*. True.

"I knew you would," Aly said. "You always have. But what would you do with the knowledge?"

That struck deep, and just as true as the realization of Aly's nature. And looking at her, the fall of her hair, the echoes of that otherworldly shape hiding within her, the impulse rose again, to share it, to scream to the world, *I was right!*

But at what cost?

"Is that how I scared you off?" she asked.

"You've read all the old stories," Aly said. "And…"

"…they don't often end well for the unicorns," Vee finished. Yes, the stories often brought comeuppance to anyone who wronged the unicorn—but not without the creature being hurt, pursued and taken advantage of for its magic.

Aly nodded.

Could Vee really give up her research? She would have to abandon her line of inquiry to keep Aly's secret. Could she forfeit her chance to be the one who found the answer?

In the moment, looking into Aly's eyes…there really was no contest. A *real* unicorn was standing in front of her, trusting her with its safety.

Vee swung her pack off her shoulder, took out her cherished notebook, and chucked it off into the trees. She heard a *splash* as it landed in a puddle, and winced.

Aly smiled. "I never wanted you to give up *all* your research, or forget everything you know," she said, taking Vee's hands. "Not at all."

Vee squeezed her hands. "You know, once, I didn't care about turning it into work. All I wanted was to *know*. That you were out there. That you were *real*. Even if only in the past."

And now, to be trusted, loved enough that a *real* unicorn wanted to show itself to her… How could Vee have wanted anything more?

"I wanted you to know for a long time," Aly said. "I was hoping you'd figure it out."

"I'm glad I know now," Vee said. "Can I…can I see it again? Your magic?" It still felt like a show of trust, even though Aly had shown her once already.

Aly nodded, and then, with another incomprehensible gust, stood before her again as a unicorn. Feeling bolder now, less afraid, Vee pet her cheek and the long slope of her nose. Carefully touched the glimmering horn. It was made of fine bone that was deadly sharp at the point. How wonderful, to be so close to such strangeness.

Aly leaned in and pressed her long face to Vee's chest, careful of the placement of her horn. Vee wrapped her arms around her head. Poor thing, to have had to carry this secret so long, to tread so carefully. The history was vague, but the weight of the stories was heavy. The danger foretold for any magical creatures that dared to step out of the woods.

"You were right," Vee said quietly.

Aly's ears flicked in inquiry.

Vee smiled to herself. "*Much* more magical than any of the fossils."

Aly huffed out a breath and nipped at her shirt in admonishment.

Vee laughed.

"Just as magical as the stories," she said, tangling her hands in Aly's mane, leaning in to kiss the base of her ear, Aly's forelock tickling her nose. "I won't tell."

With another swirl of magic, Aly shifted back into her human shape. Vee stood on her tiptoes to kiss her forehead, just as she'd done with Aly's unicorn shape, and Aly smiled, gentle and real. This was a rare thing for her too, Vee thought. This trust.

She took Aly's hand. And as they walked back through the dark, misty woods toward campus, Vee felt like she might have stepped right into one of her favorite childhood stories. Like she'd followed a unicorn into the painted forest of a picture book, onto the winding path between watercolor trees, into the inky darkness.

But the truth, it turned out, was even more beautiful than the stories.

LIVING LEGENDS

NICOLA KAPRON

Tags: bilingual, bipoc, college/university, depression, dysphoria, first kiss, friends to lovers, immortal, library, love declaration, m/nb, modern with magic, non-binary, past tense, pining, professor, reunion, third person limited point of view, veteran

"The long-term research wing is this way," Sam said, opening the door with a flourish. It was a heavy wooden thing, thick and designed to muffle as much sound as possible. "You should be good to use it for two weeks."

Kotaro let them enter first, waiting until the floor-length sweep of their black hair was safely inside before he followed them. He was about a foot shorter than them still, but then, immortals didn't grow. Both of them had been lucky enough to have their forms fixed by an early death at the prime of life. Sam was of European stock and tall besides, while Kotaro was Japanese all the way through and stood about five foot three. Each had an air of being detached from time, but that couldn't be helped. They were both closing in on their five hundredth birthdays, after all.

Kotaro's dark eyes flickered from shelf to shelf, cataloguing the layout of the research wing with all the wariness of a career soldier. With his subdued, grey-toned clothes, he looked like he was trying to blend into the walls. It didn't surprise Sam. Their oldest friend—for two definitions of the word—had indeed been a soldier, after all, and academia was a foreign battlefield to him. How fortunate that he had them in his corner as he ventured out of his comfort zone. After all, they hadn't hesitated to embrace the quirky librarian lifestyle, bright fashion, chained spectacles, and all.

"And I can simply…stay here?"

"If you're dedicated to learning, and you promise not to eat near the books, you can get permission from me to stay overnight. That's how our long-term study works," Sam confirmed. "I set it up on the ground floor when the university hired me. I'll supervise, of course, and I kick out anyone who breaks the rules. But that shouldn't be a problem for you, right?" They shot him a bright grin.

Kotaro's shoulders relaxed slightly. Good. Not all immortals responded well to becoming frozen in time. Sam had seized the opportunity to travel, meet new people, and study, but Kotaro had been retreating from society from the moment he'd woken up on his last battlefield.

Looking at him now, Sam couldn't help comparing him to how exhausted he'd been the last time they'd met in person: tired, empty-eyed, bordering on non-verbal. In hindsight, it had probably been severe depression. At the time, all Sam had known was that Kotaro was slipping through their fingers. It had taken Sam centuries to coax him out of hermitage again. They weren't going to miss the opportunity to reconnect with him now that he was here.

"Understood. I won't eat," he said.

"What? No, you do need to eat."

"But the books—"

"I have a kitchenette near my room. When it's time, I'll drag you over there, but you can't just skip meals. It has a measurable impact on our mental health, if not our physical health."

Kotaro tilted his head slightly. "I didn't know that."

"Well, this is the kind of thing you came here to learn, right?" Sam chuckled and led the way to the recent history section, beginning about two centuries back, when Kotaro had decided to live in the woods rather than face the oncoming Opium Wars. "Come on. Let's start here."

They plucked several reliable history texts and some cultural primers from a pile they'd gathered in advance and guided him to a reading corner. Then, they doubled back to their computer to check the list of titles they'd written up while he settled in. It had been so difficult to lure Kotaro out of seclusion. This was a rare opportunity, and they were not going to let it go to waste.

Let's see, they thought. A nice balance of harsh realities, bittersweet discoveries, and some of the genuinely wonderful things that had happened over the last two centuries. Kotaro wouldn't appreciate it if he felt they were trying to soften the blow or sugarcoat things. He also wouldn't appreciate it if he found nothing but negatives in this era. He'd already retreated from the world once. They'd rather he didn't find a reason to do so again.

"How's your grounding on recent Japanese history?" they asked when he came up for air a few hours later.

Kotaro laced his hands together above his head and stretched, then settled back into his usual upright posture. "Better than my understanding of recent North American history."

That didn't necessarily say much. "Do you want me to flag some topics in that area as well? Japan's quite the soft power these days. It might help attract interest to your seminar if you can make comparisons."

"I'll think about it," he demurred.

That was probably a "no." Fair enough.

The seminar in question was the reason Kotaro had left his small, traditional Japanese-style house in the woods and crossed the ocean to find Sam again—or, at least, that was his excuse. Privately, Sam suspected that Kotaro had simply gotten restless. Two hundred years of seclusion was a long time, especially when you had precious few people to correspond with. Like Sam, all of Kotaro's friends had aged and died, not lucky enough to rise again after death. Unlike Sam, he hadn't gone out of his way to make new friends. He must have spent those two centuries feeling terribly alone.

There was something a bit ironic about a hermit immortal leaving seclusion to give an online seminar about the war he'd died in all those years ago. It was a worthy piece of academia, of course, just…a bit ironic. Though, as Kotaro had said in his letters as they set this trip up, a lot of people had died in the Sengoku period. He hadn't been special. He'd just gotten back up.

Sam straightened the stack they'd assembled, delivered it to his table, and left him to it. They did still have other responsibilities on their plate. The duties of an academic librarian were a far cry from the duties of a soldier, a traveling merchant, a local politician, or any of the other roles they'd taken on over the years, but Sam found they fit better than any of the others had, even when the new crop of students came in and invariably had to be walked through every step of using the online databases. Some of them had been older than Sam. Immortals were rare, but they tended to run in the same circles eventually as everyone else died on them. Sam had had the chance to speak to several elder immortals over the years at their new career: men, women, and others who'd died and been suspended in time in the European dark ages, the Qin dynasty of China, and other places where history had, however briefly, come to a halt. They'd also had the chance to help those older immortals navigate the library databases. Better that people had trouble accessing information than for there to be no information to find.

Kotaro made his way through the stack of books laid out for him with the grim determination Sam remembered: a solemn and unrelenting pace that chipped steadily away at his goal until it was gone. It was good to see that his study habits hadn't changed. He read quickly, of course—keeping in contact with them had helped him adjust to the changing rules of the English language, as did the dictionary by his side. Sam had been prepared to assist with any translation difficulties, but they were glad to be unneeded. It gave them more time to plan the next day's selection as they filed returns behind their desk.

It was a slow day. None of the students headed into the long-term research section by accident, and the one teacher who'd booked a room was shut away, typing frantically. She was working on a PhD on Indigenous textiles using examples from her family's heritage, and Sam had served as her rubber duck more than once as she tried to get things in order. Not Sam's area of expertise, but they wished her and her advisor luck.

Finally, Kotaro set down a book and glanced out the window to find the setting sun. "That's enough for today. If I keep going, I won't be able to process."

"That works," Sam said. "I'm working for another hour. You can either hang out by the desk with me or head back alone."

Wordlessly, he rose and joined them by their desk. Sam's grin brightened at his approach. It really had been too long since they'd been able to see each other. Letters were well and good, but they just weren't the same.

"Let me pull you up a seat."

Sam had a rolling chair, so it was easy enough to scoot aside and make room for one of the steadier chairs that went with the tables. There was another rolling chair nearby, but it was by a computer station. Best not to separate those; the students had enough back problems already.

"So, what do you think?" they asked, gesturing to the library. Fields of bookshelves, neatly delineated pathways, and a quiet atmosphere that was perfect for reading. Simple decorations hung on the walls: old photographs, heritage paintings, a blanket donated by a teacher's family after the university had helped them reclaim artifacts stolen from an ancestor's grave and placed in a museum. "It came together nicely, didn't it?"

"It did." He dipped his head in acknowledgement. "Forgive me for doubting you. I should have known you'd be able to design, construct, and persuade the university to pay for your ideal library."

"Hey, what's the point of living forever if you're not going to pick up on a few things? But it really did come out well. You were right; keeping the tones warm and the decorations restrained made for a welcoming but professional atmosphere. Though, I still think a few more pillows wouldn't be amiss."

"You think every room could use more pillows."

"And I'm always right." They laughed, then lowered their voice again. "In all seriousness, thanks for advising me. Interior design is a complex subject. More of a minefield, really."

Kotaro hummed in agreement. "You seem to have done well for yourself regardless."

"I've definitely tried. Had to keep myself busy somehow."

Time didn't stop moving just because Sam had stopped being affected by it. They wondered how long they'd be spending in one place this time. A good while, hopefully. The library had been finished about forty years ago, and Sam had been there ever since. Some universities were centuries old. If the one Sam worked for could last that long—so long that the buildings were older than most people ever lived to be, and the institution became a cultural touchstone—that would be nice.

"What are you doing?" Kotaro asked after a moment.

"This is our database software," they explained. "I'm checking returned books back into the system. Then I'll put them in the re-shelving cart and let one of the others return them to their homes. After that, I'll double check to make sure Professor Davis doesn't need any assistance, do one last round to make sure there aren't any stragglers, and head to my room."

"Am I not a straggler?"

"Of course not. You're coming home with me, so that makes you a loan."

Sam's room was in the back of the library near the storage rooms, well away from the public areas. It, along with the other rooms set aside for long-term research stays, was relatively simple. Sam had been staying there for decades, though, so they'd had more than enough time to set up shop and make it feel like a home. One full-sized bed and one futon they'd laid out for Kotaro, a kitchenette that could handle most forms of cooking—so long as it didn't require an air fryer or anything ridiculous—a couch covered with extra cushions, a table, and space for both personal and work computers filled the room. And bookshelves, of course. Lots and lots of bookshelves. And yet Sam's books still ended up spilling out over every surface. It was almost like getting more bookshelves only guaranteed they'd get too many books to fit into them. Funny how that worked.

Most of Sam's collection was personal, but there were a few on loan from the library. The nice thing about living where they worked was that it was very easy for them to borrow a book one evening and give it back the next day. They didn't even need to sleep if they got sucked into a particularly compelling tome—though they really should. Like eating, sleeping had a measurable psychological benefit on immortals.

"Here we are!" Sam said brightly. Now that they were in the residential area, the need to keep their voice down was gone. "Home sweet home."

Kotaro looked around, his dark eyes tranquil, and nodded. "It looks very you."

"What's that supposed to mean?"

"It's comfortable and clearly intended as book storage first, home second."

"Hey! Well, I guess that's true." Sam shrugged and headed into the kitchenette. "I'll make tea. Green or black?"

"Green."

An old favourite. Sam set the kettle on and returned to find Kotaro perched primly on the couch, having moved the extra pillows out of the way. Typical.

"How far did you get?" they asked, sitting down on the other side. They pointedly did not move the cushions out of the way. One was supposed to sit on them. That was what the pillows were there for.

"Not as far as I could have." He gazed into the middle distance. Kotaro hadn't been brought up in a samurai family, but during the Sengoku period, ashigaru were only a step below. He'd been taught stoicism and refinement at an early age.

It would be asking too much to demand he make himself easier to read. Sam drew on the wells of patience every immortal developed sooner or later and waited for him to get his thoughts in order.

"They instituted factory safety precautions," he said finally.

"Yeah."

"It came too late for many."

"Yeah."

"But it did come eventually," he concluded. "And now there's an entire organization dedicated to making sure that safety standards are never so lax that workers die for nothing again."

"Multiple organizations," Sam put in. "OSHA, CCOHS, ArbSchG...all around the world, people gathered together and demanded their governments protect them. Even in Japan, there's the Japanese Industrial Safety and Health Act. Things are getting better."

Kotaro's eyes softened. "You did tell me they would. Lord Oda would have been pleased."

"Because the guy who made the skulls of his enemies into drinking cups was all over worker's rights. Now there's an interesting angle you could take during your seminar."

"My seminar focuses specifically on the 1582 battle at Nijo Castle, but I suppose I can bring some of that in. One cannot understand the enormity of Lord Oda's loss until they understand what kind of man he was, after all."

"Larger than life?" Sam guessed. "A bold military strategist who could give a speech with the best of them? A quirky, quirky man?"

"All of that and more. Tokugawa and Toyotomi would have been nothing without him. If anyone deserved to unify Japan after a century of civil war, it was Lord Oda."

Sam had heard this speech before, written and ranted, but they settled down to listen to it again. Kotaro's deceased lord was still near and dear to his heart over four hundred and fifty years after both he and Nobunaga had died. Sam wondered what it was like to care that much about a ruler. They'd always been a drifter at heart before settling down at their library.

"It's a shame I never got to meet him," they mused. "I was looking forward to it, but…"

"That bastard Akechi backstabbed him before the arms deal could go through," Kotaro finished. "And then both he and Nobutada committed seppuku, leaving the Oda clan neatly decapitated for Toyotomi to take power." The softness in his eyes faded to dull grief, as it always did when he spoke of Nobunaga's death. Even Nobunaga's son, Nobutada, who Kotaro had died defending at Nijo Castle, didn't merit that kind of sorrow.

This was what they called preferential treatment. Though Sam probably shouldn't talk.

"Do you wish you'd stayed?"

He shook his head, still morose. "I was a soldier my whole life. I had no wish to be treated as an ancestor spirit or enshrined as a…" He visibly searched for an English word, then gave up. "Kami. If I could no longer fight for my lord, then I had no place in my homeland. And when you were the one who picked me up off the battlefield, it felt like fate."

That sounded about right. Everything Kotaro had worked for—his reputation, his duties, his lord—was now considered to be beneath him. His home was no longer his own, so he'd set out to find somewhere else to belong.

That he hadn't found it was one of Sam's greatest failures.

"What else would Lord Oda have approved of?" they asked. "What would he have thought of the LGBT rights movement?"

Kotaro laughed, a burst of sudden birdsong that made the whole room brighter. "Oh, he would have been thrilled. He'd be threatening the Diet if they didn't start catching up to the West right this instant—no, he'd be demanding they surpass every protection the West has laid out under pain of death."

Sam found themself cackling as well. "A samurai from 450 years ago demanding to know why the country hasn't progressed enough…you just know that would be justifying someone's deeply held fears."

"It would. But imagine the looks on their faces!"

Sam had arranged for an early shift the next day, so they ate quickly and hit the stacks around 8 a.m. They'd been woken up earlier by Kotaro stumbling around at dawn, because the rhythms one grew up with weren't that easy to shake. Jet lag must have been hitting him in earnest. He'd spent the first hour or so staring blankly at the wall, pretending to meditate, while Sam bustled around him, preparing for the day. He seemed to finish waking up when Sam was leading him through the stacks.

"This isn't where we went yesterday," he noted.

"New day, new topics!" Sam said cheerily. "No, seriously, 'cause you've picked the angle of comparing the values of the past with the present, I thought we might want to take a step away from raw history and take a look into which values you'd prefer to work into the lecture. So I booked us a few hours in the office to talk about what, precisely, you want to discuss. I saw your overview, of course, but we can do more."

Kotaro nodded. And then, as they ushered him into the small, cozy office by the research library's main desk, he said, "This is your office."

"Sure is. That's why it was easy to book on such short notice." Sam sat down in the swivel chair and turned it around so they could rest their arms on the back. They'd love to be able to prop their chin up on it like a bratty delinquent, but there was only so low you could slouch when you were six foot three. "Let's start with the Sengoku period. What values made a man stand out back then? A woman? The rest of us distinguished guests?"

"That's always a difficult question," he murmured, settling into his own seat. He made a complicated face as the wheels slid across the floor. "How do I make it stay still?"

"Don't push off the floor, and don't shift your weight too fast."

"Understood."

They discussed the forms of genderfluidity from Kotaro's youth—the carefully regimented third gender of the wakashu, the freedoms that some of the lower class had to reimagine themselves completely, the stories of daughters and sons whose bodies and minds were at odds. Of course, the difficulty was that the past was a foreign country, and the past of someone else's country was doubly foreign. Kotaro frequently ran into difficulty picking a word in modern English, and occasionally gave up even trying and told an anecdote with as simple a vocabulary as possible.

"The problem is that the words people will expect of me did not exist when I first died," he grumbled. "They aren't even from the same cultural background. Of course they do not fit."

"Different traditions, different mindsets," Sam agreed. "Not to mention different time periods."

"Learning to speak about the past in the language of the future…you could spend forever trying and still fall short."

"You could. But it's worth making the effort."

"One should always make an effort." Kotaro looked away. Sam followed his gaze past the bookshelves and toward the window. Noon had come and gone while the two of them had been chatting. "But only time…what is the word…chooses what the outcome will be."

"Time, and people. You can't go making other people's decisions for them—at least, not in my position." They chuckled. "The duty of a librarian: to help people find the information they need to make their own choices."

"Is that the duty of an immortal as well?" he asked.

"It could be," they allowed. "Personally, though, I think an immortal's duty, first and foremost, is to live. Just like a first responder must keep themselves safe before trying to save anyone else."

After all, living forever wasn't synonymous with living well.

"It's not meant to be an end," they continued. "It's just something to build on, that's all. I do better with a foundation to build on."

He nodded, eyes still fixed on the glass. On the other side, a bird fluttered past, its grey feathers shining like steel under the sun. "You do, don't you?"

"Step one is always the hardest for me." Sam busied themself with shuffling through some papers on their desk. "You seem to do a better job of getting things started."

"Perhaps. But I have some difficulty ending them."

"We're immortals. We all have trouble with endings. Can't understand what you haven't experienced, after all!"

The corner of Kotaro's lips curled up slightly. "I'm still not sure I understand what I have."

Sam slowed their hands, setting down the research materials they'd gathered for the next phase of library research. It sounded like there might be an invitation of sorts in those words. They waited, but Kotaro didn't follow up on it.

Fair enough. The two of them had all the time in the world to find the right words.

At the end of the first week, Kotaro had caught up on most modern advancements; made his first careful attempts to incorporate that information into his seminar's proposed examples, anecdotes, and exercises; and understood the basic logic of how the library's online catalogue functioned. That was already more than many people ever cared to learn, mortal or otherwise. Sam took great pleasure in watching him pick new topics and technologies apart. Even the areas they had little to no expertise in, such as military tactics, were fascinating to watch through Kotaro's eyes.

"Apologies if I've bored you," he said, following Sam into their office after a day spent in the military history section. "I assure you, it is important."

"You could never bore me," they said honestly.

"I need to draw parallels to more recent conflicts so my audience will understand exactly how terrifying Lord Oda was to his contemporaries. The Siege of Mount Hiei alone would have burned his name into history, and he did so much more. This was a man who called himself a demon king ironically and had many, many people take him at his word. That he died due to the betrayal of a trusted vassal was…" Kotaro lowered his eyes. "It broke Nobutada's spirit."

"And so Nobutada committed seppuku rather than fight his father's enemies."

"He was so young. We were all so young."

"It was a difficult time to be alive."

"And yet somehow, this peaceful age seems more daunting. At least back then, I understood what was expected of me." He clasped his hands loosely in his lap. "The world changes too quickly. The shrines of my youth were torn down for skyscrapers and the castle I died defending has become a tourist attraction. I feel… hopelessly out of place."

Sam paused for a moment. Should they risk pressing him?

They hadn't when he'd left their side all those years ago. He had been barely speaking at that point, and the idea of interrogating him over his pain seemed cruel. But he seemed willing to talk now, and Sam would surely regret it if they parted ways again and they hadn't asked.

"Is that really a new thing?" They glanced down at their hands as well, tightening their grip on a mug. It had many colourful cats chasing a ball of yarn around the outside. The brightness of it was grounding. "I feel I should apologize, Kotaro. You seemed like you were looking for something the entire century and a half we traveled together, and I don't think you ever found it." No. "I wasn't able to help you find it."

For a moment, neither did anything. Silence settled over them like an old blanket, threadbare and worn, not enough to contain a scrap of warmth. Then Kotaro spoke.

"You take too much responsibility onto your shoulders, as always. You've been so carefree this visit that I nearly forgot what regret looked like on you." Slowly, deliberately, he leaned forward. His expression was solemn, but his eyes were terribly kind. "I wasn't the only one searching for something during our travels. You seem happier now, Sam. More settled. Did changing your pronouns help that much?"

Sam was startled into laughter. "Yeah!" they managed after a few seconds. "It really did."

"I'm glad," he said simply. "I had feared…"

"What?"

"That you were on your way out. You became so flighty, desperate, throwing yourself into every danger that passed by to keep yourself from thinking. I saw something similar during the war. A young man throwing himself into battle with no intentions of coming out again, not for honour or to defend his lord, but simply to escape what his life had become…" Kotaro shook his head. "It…raised? stoked?…bad memories in me. And I was already spiraling. I could not stay and watch you fall apart. Though of course, you are not a man now," he finished, with the vague confusion of a man who predated modern gender discussion and was not entirely clear on the terms.

"I never was a man," Sam explained. They'd said it before in writing, but there was something different about putting it into words. Firsthand sources were always the richest. "I just didn't have the words for it. Or the context to understand what was happening to me." They set their mug on the desk and rubbed their wrists. Even now, the ghost of that old, bone-deep discomfort lingered.

It wasn't as simple as being born in the wrong body. Sam liked their body—even loved it on a good day, now that they wore their hair long and had given themself permission to wear lipstick and skirts. But there was a creeping sense of wrongness in the firm lines of their chest, their chiseled cheekbones, their large hands. It was a distant kind of hurt now, no different from any other lingering pain—an old injury, a birth defect that had never quite healed and likely never would. After all, to be entirely sexless was not humanly possible, even for immortals. But a non-binary gender presentation was, and that was all the medication they needed to make the pain manageable.

To think that Kotaro had been able to tell something was wrong, and they had blown him off, chasing their own self-destruction just to avoid dwelling on a problem they had no words to describe…

No wonder he'd left.

Kotaro's lips twitched upward. "Is that why you became a librarian? So you would never lack for words again?"

Sam laughed. "You know, it just might be!"

A few more seconds and their laughter petered out. They found themself just looking at their old friend, seeing him anew. He still looked as young as he had the day they'd met, but he no longer felt youthful at all. His raw edges had been tempered, his gaping wounds sutured. Sam flattered themself to hope they'd had something to do with that. They appreciated the quiet and thoughtful man he'd become, so different from the ghost who had walked away when both were at their worst.

"Do you have the right words now?" Kotaro asked softly, cautiously.

"I hope so," Sam told him. "What words do you need?"

"I feel…" He paused, thinking. "Unmoored. The passage of time no longer hurts as it once did, but I cannot say I am making the best of things. I did not change as you did, and I'm beginning to wonder if I ever will. I don't wish to become a relic of the past," he said with a sudden intensity. "I may not be able to die, but I refuse to stagnate."

"Then don't." Sam grinned and clapped him on the shoulder. "You've already taken the hardest step and gone outside your comfort zone."

"To be at your side is hardly uncomfortable."

"You know what I mean! You left the house, got a job, moved to a different country for research purposes, and—most importantly—went to the library. Have you encountered the phrase 'life-long learner' yet?"

He shook his head.

"Really? Well, it's a good phrase." Sam took a moment to arrange their thoughts. "It describes the kind of mindset I want to keep going forward. The idea is that you should keep yourself open to growth and nurture a sense of curiosity inside you, so whenever you encounter something you don't understand, you try to learn about it rather than reject it. It's meant to help you remain open to new ideas no matter how much time passes. You push yourself rather than stay in one place, and you encounter new challenges, obstacles, and experiences. It helps you avoid getting set in your ways."

"I see…"

"So," they concluded, "you've already taken the first step by resolving to learn instead of stagnate. As long as you keep your mind open to new things, you'll never become a fossil, no matter how old you are."

"You're older than I am," he grumbled, but he seemed lighter, as if a weight had been lifted from his shoulders. "Keeping an open mind and reserving judgement…is more difficult than it sounds. I failed before when I left you."

"Don't tell me that you learned nothing from going back to Japan two hundred years after you died," Sam said. "I won't believe you."

"I don't regret going back," Kotaro said, his eyes bottomless. "I regret not going there with you. Maybe, if I'd had your eyes on it, I wouldn't have felt so alienated from the land of my birth." He smiled. "All these centuries, and the world has never been more beautiful than when we're together."

If Sam had still been holding their mug, they would have dropped it. "You can't just say that. Think of my poor heart!"

"When was I meant to say it?" he asked. "200 years ago? 400?" He shook his head. "I hadn't the words back then to say why I followed you for so long, even as we both began to crumble under the weight of time and loneliness, and neither of us had the…ears to hear them. But perhaps now…now we can finally speak of it."

"Are you sure?" Sam asked weakly. "You wouldn't rather talk about your seminar some more?"

"If you don't want to define whatever lies between us…"

"No. No, I want to. Just…give me a minute." They fumbled for their mug, thought twice, and dug out a can of cold coffee from the office minifridge. Then they chugged the whole thing in one go.

"Okay, I'm ready. But really, it's been centuries since we saw each other. I might not be the person you…fell in love with." The words tasted strange. Bittersweet.

"You haven't changed that much, Sam."

"You haven't either. Kotaro, what do you want from me?"

"I want to be part of your life." Kotaro's gaze was magnetic. They couldn't have looked away from him if they tried. "For as long as you'll have me. And…in whatever way you'll have me."

"You sure?" they asked with a lopsided grin. "I might not let you go again. Forever is a long time to spend with one person."

Kotaro smiled. In all the years they'd traveled together, Sam had never seen his eyes so soft. "Are you going to let me isolate myself again?"

"No."

"Then we'll be fine." Again, he leaned into Sam's space, only pausing a few inches away from their face. One hand brushed their cheek, an invitation to angle their head downward. "May I?"

"No regrets," Sam murmured, and closed the distance between them.

Kotaro's lips were softer than they'd imagined. He'd been so worn when they met him, and more so when they said goodbye: a freshly killed soldier, a living ghost, an echo of a man already dead. Now he fit neatly into Sam's lap, solid, warm, and thrumming with life. The sound of two racing heartbeats filled Sam's ears as they worked out the best angle for a kiss given their height difference.

Clearly Kotaro's fears of stagnation were utterly unfounded—he figured it out first.

After two weeks, Kotaro had finished updating most of his seminar-related documents with plans for the rest, opened about forty different tabs on various academic websites, gone on his first multi-hour wiki walk, and officially moved in with Sam. He had not, however, figured out how to operate the online learning platform his seminar was going to be hosted on.

Sam had assumed this would be easily remedied.

It was not.

"How did you even do this?" they asked with genuine amazement, looking at the warped image displayed on one of the library computer screens with awe. Every single link was broken. Half the images were refusing to load, and the other half were showing in the wrong places. It was a truly spectacular disaster. "I didn't even know you could break the site this way."

Kotaro squeezed his eyes shut and rubbed the bridge of his nose. "Can you fix it?"

"No idea! Let's find out."

Sam did manage to get everything working properly again in a few hours of work. However, Kotaro no longer trusted the site. He approached it cautiously, like he was venturing into enemy territory every time he entered the URL. It was not a surprise when he formally asked Sam to help him get the seminar filmed and uploaded.

"You could do it yourself," they told him. "I believe in you. It's not that much more complicated than the online catalogue."

"Sam, please. Do not leave me to fight this battle alone."

"Okay, okay." They chuckled and wrapped their arms around him, pulling him close. "I'll help you if you need tech support."

"Thank you," he exhaled, and buried his face in their chest. "I have not been a life-long learner long enough to deal with this."

"No worries," they soothed, tucking his head under their chin. His heartbeat fluttered against their skin like butterfly wings. "We have time."

WRIT OF EVOCATION

D. E. TOWRY

Tags: deity, fantasy with technology, immortal, imprisonment, library, m/nb, magic use, magical mishaps, non-binary, panromantic, past tense, pre-relationship, student (graduate), third person limited point of view, trans man

I ovene reviewed his mental script as he made his way to his advisor's office. While generally fair to her students, her...*inflexibility* regarding certain requests was infamous. The Academia Magicae Antiquae was one of the oldest academies in the imperial provinces, with the largest library this side of the interior sea. No one would argue that access to the grimoires and other rare or ancient texts should be restricted, but even the most dedicated of her students might never see the stacks of Special Collections before achieving their Writ of Mastery.

Iovene paused outside Magister Clostra's door to tame his rebellious curls into a small, neat queue and straighten his waistcoat and jacket. Hoping he looked confident, if not tall, he knocked. At the curt invitation to enter, he turned the latch and stepped inside.

Forys Clostra, Magister Superius Historiae Grimoiris, sat at her desk, facing the courtyard window with an open book surrounded by scribbled notes and diagrams. A feather pen tilted at an exhausted angle on its rest. Her small office was tidy, with well-organized bookshelves and papers stacked at the corners of the small side table.

"Magister, good morning," Iovene began with a smile. "I—"

"No." She didn't look up from her reading.

Iovene's smile faltered. "I beg pardon?"

"I am denying your request to access Special Collections, Novice. Again." Magister Clostra closed the tome and folded her hands on her desk before lifting her hazel eyes to Iovene, waiting frankly for his response or departure. For a petite septuagenarian, the magister had a presence five times as large as her office.

"With respect, Magister," Iovene said, scrapping the first part of his mental script, "your fellow magisters allow anyone who has completed the preliminaries access to Special Collections. I've begun my third year, passed the preliminary exams, submitted all the required forms, *and* I have signatures from each member of my committee." He plowed on before the magister could deny him again. "*Also*, I'm six months ahead of the average student in progress toward my thesis defense, *and* I've gone as far as I can with secondary sources." He flipped open his satchel to pull out a half-inch stack of papers tucked into a green folder. "Here's a complete annotated bibliography."

Magister Clostra's expression darkened as Iovene spoke, her lips set in a thin line. She glanced at the folder but did not reach to take it.

"My colleagues are too quick to allow students access to our dearest and rarest volumes." She sighed and opened a drawer. "But I suppose, as you've put in the work with the preliminaries and the texts…"

Iovene locked the whoop of triumph bubbling in his chest behind a placid smile. "Thank you, Magister."

Magister Clostra made a *hmph* as she retrieved a form and began filling it out. "I trust you don't need a lecture on best practices for handling grimoires and old tomes, do you? Good." She signed the page and held it out to Iovene. "Don't give me reason to regret this."

Iovene raced across campus to submit his paperwork to the library staff. Finally facing the massive ironwood doors of the Special Collections wing, Iovene signed his name on the empty sign-in sheet, then put his hand on the stone disc to the left of the form. The sigils and runes carved into its surface activated in a complex geometric pattern, and the edges of the door glowed green as the lock disengaged with a low *ker-thunk* before swinging open with a breath of parchment and old leather.

Unlike the more modern main library, the Special Collections were maintained in the old monastic style. Bookshelves lined the walls—imposingly tall affairs that required stools and ladders to reach their top shelves—with occasional pigeon-hole shelves where scrolls were stored. Low glass cases housed those tomes that needed special care, and small desks and podia dotted the rooms for students' use. Tall windows illuminated the room, and candelabra with hovering mage lights brightened as the day wore on.

As the doors swung shut behind him, Iovene inhaled deeply, filling his lungs with air scented by the countless mages and natural scientists that had come before him. Words couldn't encompass the ecstatic frisson that hummed through him.

Knowing he was alone, Iovene laughed and stretched out his arms as if offering a hug to an old—or new—friend. He kicked into a traditional dance, humming an old melody to keep time. He was here, at last!

The dance took him to the center of the room. He stopped mid-step—arms raised, balanced precariously with one foot off the ground—as a faint gleam on the floor caught his attention. A trick of the light, maybe, giving the woodgrain that faint, red-violet glow? He lowered his foot and bent to look.

It was writing. *Esoteric* writing: old, manuscript-style script with sigils, written in what looked like one of the ancient linear syllabaries. He stepped back and scanned the floor. Had someone been practicing a summoning? In here? That seemed *particularly* unsafe.

On further examination, there was no doubt about it: this was a spell circle with a summoning triangle at its apex, though the faint shimmer made it difficult to read the writing on the dark hardwood. It was a complicated operation, particularly considering that the circle itself had been burned into the floor. Why hadn't anyone noticed it before? Iovene was sure he would have heard stories if anyone *had* noticed…

Iovene crouched in the center of the circle. It was from one of the older grimoiric traditions, though not one of the well-known ones. The summoner had copied the spell and substituted words where needed. It was admirably formulaic, though "here I bind until my pleasure dictates its release" set alarms off in his head. Iovene lifted his gaze to the name inscribed in the summoning triangle, worried what he might read there.

Suddenly the air crackled with electricity, making the hair on the back of his neck stand up. He staggered to his feet. Just *looking* at the words shouldn't have done anything—

Storm clouds gathered in the room, billowing out from somewhere near the ceiling. Flashes of levinfire sparked in the roiling mist, giving the impression of gnashing teeth. A gust of wind jostled the shelves and tomes, catching Iovene's jacket and pulling his hair free of its queue. He covered his face as the clouds and electricity swirled into a central point above the summoning triangle. Gale and flame coalesced into a corporeal form.

Human-like and nearly seven feet tall, the being's skin was dark violet with a metallic glimmer. Curving horns crowned their head above a fall of dark hair that snaked down their back in languid, oiled curls. Leathery, dragon-like wings folded over the figure's broad shoulders, the wings' finger-claws hooked together at the collarbone like a taloned brooch. A layered skirt of blue and black cloth, slit to the hip, was belted at the waist by a thin chain. Peeking out from under the skirt was a long, flexible tail that swayed just above the floor. They wore more wealth in gold and silver jewelry than Iovene had ever seen on one person.

High cheekbones and a proud, falcon-like nose framed eyes that glowed an intense, almost electric blue. At the center of the figure's brow was a dark, slightly raised line that Iovene realized must be a third eye, closed to the outside world.

"Gods in the temples!" Iovene staggered back a step. Instinct shouted *run!*, but he stood his ground.

The arcane being's gaze bored into Iovene, then swept the room, perplexed, as if they'd been expecting something that wasn't what—or who—they found before them.

"I, uh—hello." The being's gaze snapped back to Iovene. He felt a little unsteady but straightened his waistcoat and jacket. "My name is Iovene. Iovene Maris Pontariae, Novice of the Academia. I, uh…" *Amateur mistake!* Why had he given his full name to an arcane being? That was near the very top of things *not to do.*

The arcane being's lips curved up slightly, amused to note the same mistake.

"Greetings, Iovene Maris Pontariae." Low and resonant, their voice carried a whisper of other voices and languages just beyond understanding. "What manner of 'novice' are you, who can summon me from another's circle? And without uttering a word?"

Iovene wished he felt a fraction as composed as he wanted to be. "Uh, that's a good question." He glanced down at the names written in the triangle. He hadn't had time to interpret them before the being had appeared. "Are those your names?"

The being lifted their chin, imperious. "Dzemnayth, Prince of Zashanath, Sixth Arcane Lord, Lord of the Deep and Master of the Void." The shelves trembled as the layered resonance of their voice intensified. "I was *summoned* here, half a century gone. My summoner—" They let out an abrupt growl before continuing. "My summoner left me bound to this plane and place, trapped without form. Until I resolved again at *your* silent summoning, Iovene Maris Pontariae."

"I beg your pardon, Your Grace," Iovene replied, the words coming in a rush. "I didn't recognize you. Most books describe you, uh…" He supposed the lightning-strewn fog *might* have been a clue, given the depictions of *a cloud of void, dotted with stars*, or *a mass of marine creatures knotted into a vortex of darkness*. "Rather differently."

The arcane lord's lips curved up. "Shall I take a more poetic form?"

"No! No, this form is great!" Iovene felt himself flush.

"As liquid water fits a vessel, so the form fits the summoning." Dzemnayth's amused expression suddenly disappeared. Tail twitching like an agitated cat's, they surveyed the room again. "How is it possible that you see and speak to me? You are not the one who summoned me. Nor, I think, are you related." The lid of their third eye fluttered as if it might open.

"I'm not sure, Your Grace. My studies say it's impossible, especially without a full operation—performance, materials, and the like. I have read about sorcerers usurping conjurations by giving a better deal…" Iovene stopped, cheeks warming even more. An arcane being might not appreciate his lecturing tone. "But unless I'm mistaken, we've not made a contract, Your Grace."

Dzemnayth's tail gave a thoughtful flick.

Iovene shifted his weight and cleared his throat under their pointed gaze, hoping they didn't notice his heart rattling in his ribcage. "Uhm,

Your Grace, you said you were summoned here fifty years ago? The summoner never returned?" That was bad form in *so* many ways, not least of which was leaving the summoned being trapped in the location of the summoning.

"The summoner went ashen and fled the room, never to return," Dzemnayth replied. "I watch carefully all those who enter these chambers, but the summoner is never among them. The summoner is gone. I remained, unable to affect my prison or engage with its visitors." Their glance slipped back to Iovene as if to say, *until you*.

"If I may," Iovene said cautiously, "I'm studying grimoires and evocation. I'm not sure how I was able to use someone else's circle, but since I *can* speak to you, perhaps I can figure out how to break the summoning and set you free."

"Not possible." Dzemnayth's tail lashed. "The summoner must do it."

Iovene was unsettled, but he didn't find Dzemnayth nearly as intimidating as Magister Clostra. "You aren't able to describe the summoner, correct?" The arcane lord hesitated, then inclined their head, which Iovene took as confirmation. "That says something about the ritual the summoner used. And I can see the circle." *How* was beside the point. "That summoner was wrong to summon you and bugger off. You shouldn't be stuck here. Please, let me help."

Dzemnayth stared hard at Iovene, eyes alight. They lifted a hand in acquiescence. "As you wish. The conversation will, at least, be welcome."

Dzemnayth was able to point Iovene in the right general direction, so it didn't take long to find the grimoire the summoner had used. The author had penned the text a thousand years ago, at a time when the ability to bind spirits to crystals, shells, locations or (dangerously) people was a sign of an accomplished magus. The author's conjurations were specifically created to summon an entity and keep them from departing without the summoner's leave, preventing the entity from breaking free or being freed by someone else. It was all right there, plain as daylight and horrifyingly unethical, even by the standards of when it was written. Iovene chased down some references to breaking bindings and reversing summonings, but didn't find much that would be helpful.

Even contemporaries of the anonymous author didn't have much to say beyond *do not do any of this under any circumstances.*

Having made little headway with the grimoires, Iovene realized he could search for the summoner directly. He was halfway down the stairs when it dawned on him that he should have said something to Dzemnayth before running out, but it didn't take him more than a quarter hour to return with his prize. He crossed the threshold with a breathless "thank the gods!" that no one else had come into Special Collections yet.

Dzemnayth re-coalesced in a shimmer of levinfire and shadow. Their tail gave a curious flip. "What are those?" They motioned to the stack of oversized books Iovene had hauled up the four flights of stairs.

"Admissions photos!" Iovene grinned, dropping his haul on the closest table. "Every group of first years have a silverprint taken when we're admitted. I wasn't sure how long it's gone on, but it looks like the tradition started sixty years ago!"

He gestured to the books, each about two inches thick, leather bound and sewn in the old style. "The library keeps copies in the reference section." He flipped open the newest and turned to the back. The silverprint had been taken with the first years standing in front of the fountain in the courtyard. There were a dozen people in the picture— winter admissions were typically fewer than in spring or fall—most in their twenties though a few were older. Iovene pointed to a face in the second row.

"See? There's me." He laughed. "I look ridiculous." He'd had to stand on the edge of the fountain to be visible and had stupidly left his hair loose. It was a blurry cloud around him, but he was wearing the biggest smile of the group.

Dzemnayth leaned over Iovene's shoulder, peering down at the silverprint with a slight smile as they reached to touch the image delicately with clawed fingers. "A marvelous invention." Their expression had become wistful, though their eyes were bright with interest. "A moment of time, frozen. You are the only one who looks happy."

"You have to wait a while for the image to take, so most people don't smile. I just couldn't help it." Iovene waved a hand impatiently. "That's not the point! This is the last *sixty years*. The person who summoned you *must* be in here."

Dzemnayth went still, gaze lingering on the picture, their wing claws half unhooked in a way that implied surprise. The moment lasted a few heartbeats before Dzemnayth's tail whipped sharply to the right, nearly slapping Iovene's leg. They closed the book, set it aside, and moved each tome until they reached the oldest volume.

The two of them stood silently, shoulder to shoulder, as Dzemnayth scanned each silverprint carefully then turned the page. There was the *slightest* chance the summoner had come to the Academia before the silverprint tradition began, but Iovene thought odds were better they'd be in one of the earlier images.

Dzemnayth took only a couple minutes to glance over each picture, but with twelve or more silverprints a year of groups anywhere between ten and fifty students, it was slow going. Iovene's focus wavered after fifty-some pages, and he thought he detected a waning resolve in the arcane being's expression. Their tail had gone still but for the slightest movement at the tip.

Dzemnayth shook their head, turning another page. "I do not think—"

Iovene glanced up at Dzemnayth when they didn't finish their sentence. The arcane lord's eyes were afire with inner light, eyebrows drawn together, lips drawn back in pain. Their third eye fluttered, then opened, revealing a pool of deep crimson slashed with a single, long pupil.

Iovene averted his eyes. Whatever power lay locked behind that third eyelid was certainly *not* to be gazed upon directly. He looked at the page and read the date: forty-nine years, ten months ago. A group of ten first-year students stood shoulder to shoulder in front of the courtyard fountain, expressions flat in the style of the time, when silverprint exposures needed ten times longer than today. Iovene scanned the faces. One seemed vaguely familiar.

Smoke rose in wisps around that face, and a dark ring burned into the silverprint. Iovene looked at the names written below the image. The name for that face hit his retinas with such force it felt like he'd taken a blow to the head.

"Oh, gods." Iovene took a half step back. "Magister Clostra." *Novice* Clostra then.

"You know this woman?" Dzemnayth snarled.

Magister Clostra. She'd been here the whole time, and somehow never once returned to Special Collections? Never tried to unbind the arcane lord from this place? Was *this* why she generally refused to allow her students access? So they wouldn't repeat what she'd done? Or find out?

"I'll go to her office and…make her come up here and set you free. And if she *won't*…" He was less sure about that possibility, but maybe Dzemnayth could show themself to others, argue their case…

Dzemnayth's third eye blazed as their wings opened and stretched wide, and their tail snapped side to side, whiplike. Though no longer a look of snarling pain, their expression was still deathly grim.

"Who is the summoner?" Dzemnayth demanded.

"My advisor. She gave me permission to enter here just this morning," Iovene was already on his way toward the exit. "I'm going down—maybe she hasn't left yet!" He didn't wait for a reply. Sprinting out the heavy doors, he hit the stairs at a dangerous run. A couple of students heading up jumped out of the way with shouts of indignation.

The magister hadn't left yet. After a perfunctory knock, Iovene opened the door, shoving it closed behind him. Magister Clostra looked up from packing her satchel with a glare.

"Novice," she said, tone dangerous.

Iovene stood as tall as he could, hands clenched at his sides. He'd already barreled past the point of no return, but a kind of quaking fear had come over him. The sort of fear he *should* have felt facing Dzemnayth.

"How could you??" he demanded, hating how tremulous his voice sounded. In retrospect, he should have planned what to say on the way across campus.

"I beg your pardon?"

"You summoned an arcane lord and just *left them trapped* there all this time?"

The magister went ashen, and her aura of uncompromising stoicism vaporized. As confusion and fear played across her features, she looked suddenly smaller and older, thinner and worn.

"What did you say?" Her voice rasped over the words.

"I met Dzemnayth. You need to go up there and set them free." Iovene didn't so much jump into the opening her confusion created as stumble into it. He'd expected resistance, maybe immediate denial. He hadn't expected her to look so *afraid*.

"That's not possible." Confusion took prominence in the magister's expression. She clutched the satchel still balanced on her desk. "You— *How?*"

Iovene hesitated, then gave a quick summary of events. How he'd come into Special Collections and saw the faint glow of the spell circle; how Dzemnayth had appeared and told him what little they could of how they'd come to be there; how he'd borrowed the silverprints to identify the summoner and how the arcane lord had recognized her.

Magister Clostra shook her head. "No...no, that's not *possible*. You didn't even perform a ritual. That thing shouldn't be able to show itself to you. And you shouldn't have seen the circle, it's long gone."

Iovene balked. "That *thing?*"

"I knew you would make me regret granting you access." The magister laughed bitterly. "But this is...impossible. Intolerable." The confusion and fear dissipated in moments, replaced by cold anger. Her gaze was sharp as it landed on Iovene again. "Impossible."

Iovene held his ground. "Impossible or not, I saw the circle and I've spoken with Dzemnayth and—"

"Such beings cannot be trusted, and their retribution is swift and cruel. You know that."

"Do you deny that fifty years ago, you used a binding ritual to summon Dzemnayth, bound them in the Special Collections wing, and never went back to free them?"

The magister did not deny it. She didn't say anything at all. When she finally spoke, her voice and expression were icy. "I suggest," she said, "if you wish to retain your position at the Academia, you forget about this and continue with your studies."

The words hit Iovene like a slap to the face. He wanted to speak, but the words shriveled up like burned paper, blowing away like ash.

"I don't know how it's possible you could have seen something that isn't there, nor spoken with an entity you did not summon, but I am willing to overlook these wild accusations. Now, if you'll excuse me, I'm late for a dinner appointment." As she spoke, the magister's customary steely aura coalesced around her again.

Iovene said nothing. He didn't know what *to* say. Continuing to push would have consequences, and he'd rather fight when there was some hope of progress. Maybe there was no shame in making a tactical retreat to regroup.

Iovene took his leave.

Iovene didn't return to Special Collections. It was cowardly to avoid Dzemnayth, still trapped but now with the knowledge their summoner had remained on the Academia grounds this entire time, but he needed some space to think. And he wanted to consult his friends.

The group met after classes at a table and benches sheltered under a bower made by the lower branches of a venerable ash tree. Iovene was usually last to arrive, and he didn't break that streak today.

"There he is," Lian said, her lips curving up in a sly smile.

"I would learn by now, you would think." Urrah sighed, setting two pennies on the table. He shook his head, the bells in the tassels of his traditional scarf adding a gentle chime to Lian's laughter.

"At least you don't bet so much anymore." Verix chuckled and took a pull from her pipe, letting out an elegant stream of smoke.

"You look *terrible*," Lian said as Iovene sat by Urrah.

Everyone turned to examine him more closely. Iovene's heart clenched at the concern he saw on his friends' faces. He'd been debating how to explain everything to them, but maybe he didn't need to have a perfectly wrought essay.

"This is going to sound completely mad, but…hear me out?"

All three watched him intently as he recounted his day. They began to congratulate him on *finally* gaining access to Special Collections, but hearing that an arcane lord had been summoned, abandoned, and imprisoned there killed the festive mood.

"A five-decades-old spell circle? In the middle of Special Collections?" Urrah asked, steepling his fingers in front of his lips.

"Search me. It—or what remained of it—was still there," Iovene said. "I've been wracking my brains as to why, but even Clostra didn't seem to know. None of you ever noticed it?" Judging by their incredulous expressions, none of them had seen the glimmering spell circle in their own visits.

"We would have said something if we had," Verix said, lifting her pipe like a shrug.

"Maybe you have to be special to see it?" Lian asked. "Maybe you've got some fae in you, like Verix?"

Verix rolled her eyes but couldn't quite hide the smile peeking at the corner of her lips. "I don't think it works that way."

Urrah closed his eyes, his expression meditative. "You've read about writ theory, yes?"

"The different layers of agreements between magi and magical entities? Sure, but I thought that had to do with entities being used against other magi they work with," Iovene said.

"Of course, yes, but..." Urrah opened his eyes. "It will be in my notes; I do not remember the book exactly. There are tales of spirits being...scooped?"—he looked to Lian; she nodded in confirmation—"from their summoners by other sorcerers because the relationship is somehow better."

"But I've never summoned *anything*, let alone *Dzemnayth, Lord of the Depths*," Iovene said, dropping his voice to a whisper on the last words.

Urrah shrugged. "It is the only way I can think for you to see the circle."

Ivoene raked his hair back into its queue. "But I can't release the binding or convince Magister Clostra..."

"Just ask for our help so we can say, 'Yes, of course,' " Verix said, tapping out her pipe. "Make us witnesses and we can confront Clostra together."

"Or go to the headmistress?" Lian suggested.

"The headmistress should be our last resort," Urrah said thoughtfully. "If we cannot on our own convince the magister, we can speak to our own advisors."

They trekked up to Special Collections to (hopefully) see Dzemnayth. It was possible Lian, Urrah, and Verix wouldn't be able to see the arcane lord, or that Dzemnayth wouldn't reveal themself, but it was worth a try, if only to demonstrate more support for the arcane lord's freedom.

Iovene entered first, leaving the others to wait in the hall. Special Collections was still (or again) empty, and Dzemnayth materialized much like before, though this time Iovene could hear the throaty roar of the sea beneath the thunder and lightning. The arcane lord's expression was stony, the third eye closed again.

"You have not succeeded," Dzemnayth observed dryly, and their tail drooped toward the floor.

"Not yet," Iovene said. He filled Dzemnayth in on the meeting with Clostra. "We're going to have to apply more pressure, so I met with some friends, and—"

Dzemnayth's wings snapped open with a sound that startled Iovene into taking two steps back. The being bared fangs. "*No.* You will bring no others here," Dzemnayth snapped. "No friends. No magisters. None."

Iovene blinked, glanced toward the door, then back to the arcane lord. "Are you embarrassed?" he blurted.

The roar of a tempestuous ocean rose around them, and Dzemnayth's eyes flashed with arcane levinfire. Even without their third eye open, these were all signs of danger not to be trifled with, but Iovene didn't feel the need to run.

"That's understandable. I'd feel embarrassed, too, maybe even a little scared." Iovene met Dzemnayth's gaze, feeling more annoyance than fear. "I'm trying to help you, you know?" he shouted, lifting his voice over the intensifying roar and lightning. "I could get expelled for this! And it'd be worth it, but I'd prefer *not* to, so a little cooperation on your part would be great!"

"Why is this *school* of such importance?" Dzemnayth asked. Their voice was the storm. "Why should I deign to show myself? Why should I not raze it to the earth when I am free?"

Iovene wasn't sure what happened next. The library was gone, and he was standing on the deck of his uncle's fishing boat. The sun was bright overhead, the breeze tugging at the rigging. Dzemnayth wasn't visible, but he knew they were there, *searching* for something.

Translocation? No, a memory: Dzemnayth had plucked it out of his mind. Iovene's annoyance added a coat of indignation. "You could have just asked—"

Iovene caught sight of himself at the railing near the bow. It had been his sixth birthday, and his uncle had asked him to stay out of the way of the nets and fishing gear at the stern.

But I want to help! Iovene had pouted, stomping a small foot.

His uncle had laughed while braiding Iovene's hair. *All right, all right,* he'd said. *Let me teach you a song my father taught me. It will help draw the fish to our nets.*

Iovene drifted to the railing to stand next to his younger self. He often thought back on this memory, how recklessly he'd hung over the railing, feet kicking idly just above the deck, skirts tugged by the breeze. He'd sung the song over and over. It had a jaunty, lilting melody and nonsense lyrics, at least as far as Iovene could tell.

Then it had happened—the shadows beneath the boat had moved. His song had faltered as a whale-like leviathan, entirely too large and with too many glowing eyes, peered up at him.

They had stared at each other, little Iovene and the leviathan, for what felt like hours. Then the leviathan had turned and disappeared down into the deep again. When Iovene's uncle had commanded his people to start bringing in the nets, they'd had triple the catch they'd expected that day.

With a blink, Iovene was back in Special Collections. The storm had died and Dzemnayth was staring at him with undisguised surprise, wings half furled, tail poised in a questioning curl.

"How many generations have your family been fisherfolk?" they demanded.

"My uncle always says twelve generations," Iovene replied slowly. That leviathan wouldn't have been the arcane lord themself, but perhaps one of their lieutenants, a familiar spirit?

"Would that mean your family has a writ?" Lian asked. Iovene jumped half out of his skin and turned to the door. Lian, Urrah, and Verix were standing there, the door shut behind them, looking shaken, awed, and bemused.

"We heard you shouting," Verix explained, "so we came in."

Urrah nodded slowly, tassels chiming. "Just so. And yes, I would expect that would be a family writ."

"That means we don't *need* Magister Clostra." Iovene whirled toward the shelves, pulling down the spellbook Clostra had used. He glanced at Dzemnayth, who had folded their wings again, and thought he saw a hopeful spark in their gaze. The silence between them felt like an ever-widening gulf. Dzemnayth would return to their realm and their duties, and Iovene would be back to studying, to his regular routine. Unless Magister Clostra managed to have him expelled.

Dzemnayth allowed Iovene's friends to stay, even spoke with them a little, while Iovene drew the spell's intricate design. When it was ready, everyone gathered within the circle, and Dzemnayth moved to the binding triangle. They stepped up into the air, hovering above the floor.

Iovene looked at Dzemnayth a beat longer than necessary. "If you're ever in the seas around Pontaria, stop by?" His cheeks warmed; he was glad his friends were standing behind him.

Dzemnayth's tail swished slowly behind them, curling up in a curious loop at the apex of the arc.

"I will remember," they said, lips curving up into a smile.

Urrah had added some changes to Iovene's words to make clear he was "scooping" Dzemnayth free of Clostra's original spell. Each word Iovene spoke brought more energy into the room until, at the ritual's end, a wave of green light crackled around the binding triangle. Dzemnayth's expression split into a fanged grin that went a little too wide for their face. Their form seemed less solid, more malleable, as they lifted their arms over their head, calling a bolt of blue levinfire that struck from nowhere—everywhere—blinding them all.

When the afterimage faded, Dzemnayth was gone.

With the help of his friends, Iovene cleaned the floor of both his chalk summoning circle and the red-violet gleam of Clostra's spell, now visible to all. By the time they finished, it was long past midnight, so they convened in Verix's room for drinks—Urrah had water while the rest shared a bottle of wine—and chatted until morning.

Iovene skipped classes the next day, slept in, and dreamed of the song of the sea crashing rhythmically against the sand and the low hum of a leviathan rippling up from the depths.

After he woke, Iovene went to see Clostra. While she undoubtedly knew the summoning had been broken, it would be courteous to tell her in person. And he'd have the opportunity to demand an explanation.

But her office was empty—*completely* empty. Papers and books gone, shelves bare. The only sign that she had ever been there was an envelope resting on the desk, addressed to Iovene in her steady hand. Inside were two letters of recommendation and one letter to Iovene himself.

> Novice Iovene,
>
> I concede that you are the better magus. I do not know how you were able to break the summoning, and so quickly, but I have concluded I do not care to know. That I am alive to write this means you had some control over the entity.

The letter continued into a hasty explanation. As a young student, Clostra had attempted to impress a talented classmate by summoning an arcane lord, choosing Dzemnayth at random. When the summoned lord proved a furious nightmare, she fled in panic and later sent a well-meaning dupe to clean the circle and check for damage. Nothing seemed amiss, and the entity never appeared to anyone else, but Clostra refused to return to Special Collections again, finding other ways to get the texts she needed for her studies.

After they received their Writs of Mastery, her classmates mostly left the Academia, but Clostra was unable to follow. If she was away from the Academia for more than a few days, she would become gravely ill. She knew the summoning bound her but couldn't find the courage to break it, convinced that Dzemnayth would kill her if freed. She contented herself with a position at the Academia.

I suppose I must thank you for my freedom, Clostra concluded. It seemed as if she had wanted to write something more, the pen hesitating, making a small dot after "freedom," but all that followed was *Sincerely, Magister F. Clostra.*

Iovene put the letters in his satchel and made his way to class.

Five Months Later

Winter break meant Iovene had arrived home just in time for the Midwinter festivals. He had a lot of studying to do before returning to the Academia, but it was good to be by the sea again. Sitting on the blanket he'd spread over the sand, Iovene hoped Dzemnayth was happy back in their own world.

"Yours is a pretty town."

Iovene's head whipped around to find Dzemnayth standing beside the blanket, one wing lifted like a parasol to shade their face from the sun. They looked as they had in the library, only *brighter*, possessed of radiant inner light.

Iovene scrambled to his feet. "You're here!"

"As are you." Dzemnayth's tail gave an amused flick. "I have missed Midwinter? There are tales of great celebrations."

"You what? Oh, no, you're early!" Iovene grinned, then paused. "Are you…just stopping by?"

Dzemnayth canted their head. "I intend to remain a time. Is this amenable?"

"Absolutely!" He started to reach for Dzemnayth but stopped himself before giving the Lord of the Depths a *hug*. Then Dzemnayth's fingers met and laced with his. Their skin was as cool as stone washed by the waves.

"Will you come for dinner?" Iovene asked.

"I will," Dzemnayth said. They shifted the position of their wing to shade them both. "Your family. What will you tell them?"

" 'Surprise'?" Iovene laughed and gave Dzemnayth's hand a gentle squeeze. "I'll say we met in the library."

BELONGING

SWEV

Tags: aromantic, college/university, f/f (background), fantasy, friends, lesbian, magic use, micro-aggressions (classist), present tense, student (college), third person limited point of view

The assembly hall is busy after the lecture. Students, clad in the university uniform, are congregating at the bottom of the stairs, queuing in a disorderly fashion to receive an amulet for the cross-class assignment. Pairs of students greet one another, the second-year magic students looking well at ease and the newly arrived scholars less so.

Sid clenches her own amulet. *Magic.* In the palm of her hand. The thought is enough to distract Sid from the chaos around her.

The amulet is formed from dark metal and shaped as a pair of towers, the sigil of the university; it's inlaid with blue streaks of magic. It feels odd. Alive, almost. Sid rubs a thumb over it. She'd thought it would feel wilder than it does, that the magic in the amulet would struggle against its bonds. Instead the magic flows through the metal, nearly imperceptible.

Sid keeps a tight grip on the amulet as she waits for her partner. More students vanish out the door. It should be a comfort that they're all dressed like her, that she doesn't look as out of place as she feels, but it just makes Sid feel small. She straightens the pleats of her skirt; even secondhand, it's more expensive than any piece of clothing she's owned before.

Suddenly, the amulet in Sid's hand starts humming. It doesn't move or make a sound, but Sid can *feel* the humming, a vibrating sensation radiating into her wrist. She stares at the amulet, her heart beating rapidly. Then, she realises with a jolt—her partner must be near.

Sid looks around. In the sea of university blues, she spots a woman with dark hair, her golden hairpins glinting in the sunlight. She weaves between the other students as she approaches, her stride confident. Sid wonders whether she's in the way, if the woman is heading towards someone behind her, but she's looking directly at Sid.

Something about her makes Sid's shoes feel far too big, her loose curls messy and dishevelled.

The woman—Sid's partner—comes to a stop before her. "Hi," she says, peering up at Sid with a curved eyebrow. There are freckles scattered across her nose—lighter than Sid is used to, not darkened by the sun as they would be back home. The woman offers her hand. "I'm Tiend'el. Call me Ti."

"Hi," Sid says shakily. Ti's hand is smooth and uncalloused. "Sid'i'va Fen. Or…Sid, I suppose."

"So, it's you and me for the next few months, huh," Ti says with a small smile. Sid nods, but before she can respond, Ti tosses her head towards a staircase. "Come on, let's get out of here."

Without waiting, Ti turns and Sid scrambles to keep up.

Ti leads them through the tall, unfamiliar corridors, deeper into the building housing classrooms and study rooms. Sid follows closely; she'd barely managed to find her way to the lecture hall. She clutches her bag closer as they ascend a staircase. It's nothing like home here. She doesn't *miss* the vast nothingness of her village, the expanse of fields around her, but she misses the sky, the way she knew where everything was.

She'd arrived in town yesterday, in a market square not far from the bridge connecting the city and the university, and she'd immediately lost her way. The memory is enough to make her walk faster to keep pace with Ti.

They start down another corridor, decorated as lavishly as the rest of the university, but Ti halts before a door and pats at her pockets. "Where'd I put that thing…" She fishes out the amulet and presses it to a circle of black stone beneath the door handle. There's no sound when the door unlocks, but a veil of magic parts, curling around their amulets for the briefest of moments and allowing them access to the room.

Sid fingers at her amulet, hoping to feel the magic again, but it's vanished without a trace. She peers into the room; trepidation has squeezed at her heart all morning, but the sensation dissipates as she steps through the doorway, replaced by a giddiness that wells into her throat. She's really *here*.

The room isn't large, but it's bright and pleasant, with light spilling through the tall windows. A large wooden table and a couple of chairs are placed in the centre of the room, the seats and backs covered with plush blue fabric. Sid's eye is drawn to the built-in bookshelves to the side. She steps closer and takes in the variety of books stacked there, titles she recognises from the reading list the professor mentioned in the lecture. She runs her fingers across the spines of a few of them; she'd borrowed older copies of these from the small library in her town, but these are the latest editions, pristine in their bindings.

"Why would they put us all the way up here," Ti mutters as she drops into a chair. "We're so far from the café."

Sid glances at the windows—they're a few stories up, that's true. Grazing her hand over the fine velvet of a chair, she enjoys the texture of the fabric before sitting down.

"So," Ti says. "House Fen, you said—we don't see many farmers here. You're awfully far from home."

Sid clears her throat. "I suppose I am. The journey was long, to be sure." She hesitates a beat before changing the subject. "We should look at the assignment."

"If you say so." Ti pulls out her writing utensils, fiddling with the inkwell without opening it. "What'd the professor say?"

"I…" Sid frowns. "You weren't there for the first lecture of the term?"

Ti shrugs, a crooked smile on her lips. "I was flirting with the new waitress in the café." She raises an eyebrow. "You know how it is, right? Do you have someone back home?"

"No," Sid says, shaking her head. "I was more interested in studying."

Ti chuckles. "And no one here has caught your eye yet?"

The topic makes Sid press her lips together. The *fascination* that other people have with romance has always been strange to her. "I've never really had any interest in that sort of thing," she says, hoping that Ti will drop it. "So, the assignment—"

"Ugh, yeah—"

"We have to do a series of magical experiments and analyse them."

Ti snaps open her quill case and an empty candy wrapper falls out. Crinkling it between her fingers, Ti eyes Sid. "You realise this is just a way for them to save on teaching costs—pairing us across years like this."

"I— All right?" Sid says. "I don't see how that matters?"

Ti slowly shreds the candy wrapper. "What's the hand-in format?"

"A report. I took notes." Sid rummages in her bag and removes a sheaf of paper. "Here," she says, handing the notes to Ti.

Cocking her head, Ti turns the pages too quickly to actually be reading them. She makes an odd chuckle as she reaches the end.

"What?"

Ti shoots her a lopsided grin. "Your handwriting is terrible. Professor Zenbrol won't be able to read the report."

Sid's cheeks warm at the words. Surely Ti didn't *mean* to be rude. She must have meant it to be a lighthearted jab.

It still stings.

"The lecture was all over the place," she mumbles, unsure whether that's truthful. She's had ample time to imagine how university lectures would be, but she'd not anticipated that her first-ever lecture would be such a jumbled mess.

"Sounds like him, yeah." Ti drops the notes on the table.

Sid's ears perk up. "You know him?"

"He taught a class in my second semester, magical theory," Ti says with a grimace. "He usually only does research. It shows in his teaching."

Curiosity gets the better of Sid and she leans forward. "Which was your favourite class?" she asks, expecting it to be an easy question.

"Ah…" Ti's nose scrunches up as she considers her answer. "Sociology, I think."

Sid frowns. "Not magic?"

Ti lets out a short, bitter laugh. "No. Not magic."

Sid wants to ask more questions, but the air between them feels less inviting than it did a moment ago. She reaches for the papers instead, scrutinising her notes. "I suppose you're right. I should rewrite this."

She dips her quill in ink and while the scritching of the nib against the paper fills the room, Ti quietly fiddles with another candy wrapper. Sid sinks into a pleasant headspace as she works, not entirely noticing the minutes passing.

"Right!" Ti says, a sudden exclamation that almost makes Sid drag the quill through the sentence she's writing. "While you do that"—Ti nods at the paper—"I'm going to head off." She dumps her things into her bag and gets to her feet.

"You're leaving?" Sid asks, her voice higher than intended.

Ti raises an eyebrow at her. "No sense in me sticking around while you're busy transcribing, right? Besides, if I leave now, I might be able to catch Amelia before her shift is over." Her eyes crinkle at the corners.

"I—guess?" Sid says.

"Great—see you tomorrow!" Ti calls out. She disappears out the door, dark hair billowing behind her.

The door closes with a soft *click*, and Sid stares at it for a beat before shaking her head and refocusing.

The tower bells chime, a pleasant carillon far more complicated than the single half-hourly gong that Sid has been getting used to. She looks up from her notes and finds the room bathed in the light from the sunset. Sighing, Sid gets to her feet and stretches her cramped limbs. She didn't mean to stay this long; the light will vanish soon and she'll risk getting turned around in the dark corridors.

Sid gazes out the tall windows. Beneath her lies the courtyard, the cobblestones set in a swirling pattern that she'd not noticed when walking through it earlier. The walls of the university obscure the bridge to the city, but she can see the buildings of the old town, can imagine how the vibrant markets are quieting for the day. She sighs as she takes in the city: it's a gleaming array, the rays of light catching the metal roofs and elaborate spires.

Her eyes are drawn to the horizon behind the city. Far beyond what the naked eye can perceive, Costrein is separated from the rest of the world by a mountain range. She imagines them: topped with snow, reaching into the sky—but all she can see is vast expanses of farmland and a shadow in the distance that might be her village.

It's so far away.

A sudden pang of homesickness makes Sid tremble. She's just a farm girl. What's she doing here?

She swallows hard, steadying herself on the windowsill before turning to pack her things. As she does, a crackle of magic illuminates the wall torches, casting the room in a light bright enough to read by. Sid stares, taken aback.

Magic had been a rarity in her town—something the cleric at the officiary's office possessed, mostly used for sending missives to the capital. Here, it's used for minor things: for lights and keys, available even to students. It ought to be a grander thing, Sid thinks, something guarded and used sparingly.

Before leaving, she casts a glance out the window. The café seems busy, bustling with movement, yellow light spilling out onto the cobblestones. Sid wonders if Ti's still there.

A braver person might pop into the café and check.

The mere thought makes Sid's throat feel tight, and she turns away from the window.

The next day, the room is empty when Sid arrives. She relishes the brief sensation of the magic parting for her and unpacks her things with a light, anticipatory feeling in her chest at the prospect of getting properly started with the report.

A full bell passes.

By then, her excitement has dwindled. Sid is watching the hourglass on the table when, finally, she feels the hum of the amulet in her pocket.

Ti enters, yawning her way through a greeting.

"Good morning," Sid answers as Ti sets her bag on the table. "I cleaned up the notes."

"Oh, nice," Ti replies. "But before we do that"—she gestures to the notes and books in front of Sid—"we should go to the café and get a coffee. Amelia is working till noon—"

Sid clears her throat. "Um. No thanks," she says, trepidation making her voice thin. "We have to work on the report, remember?"

"Right," Ti says. "Sure." She sounds disappointed.

Sid rolls her quill between her fingers. "So, I made a list of all the things we need to do." She slides a piece of paper across the table. Deadlines are neatly written in capital letters at the top. Ti skims it as Sid explains how they need to manifest magic and analyse it.

Halfway through Sid's outline of the schedule, Ti interrupts her. "There's no way we'll get through all of this."

"I— But we have to," Sid says with a frown.

Ti runs her finger down the paper. "These are all just categories. Subjects." Her eyes light up. "We should establish an angle and cover a spread of it! If we—"

Sid cocks her head. "An angle?"

Ti nods eagerly. "Yeah, putting our own spin on it, y'know. Surely they taught you that in...where did you go to school?"

Sid straightens her spine. "Back home," she says flatly. "And we need to do what the professor said and write the analysis—it doesn't need to be more complicated. We—"

"Come on," Ti snickers, "do you really think Zenbrol wants to read a hundred identical reports? He'd be over the moon if we did a bit of research on our own!" She lets the outline drop to the table, her smile wide. "He lives for that stuff."

"I don't think we should worry about that." Sid shakes her head. "We just have to get through the list."

Ti's smile fades. "I'm telling you, we can't." There's a hard note in her voice.

With a scoff, Sid picks up the list. "I'm sure the professor wouldn't give us an impossible task. Let's start at the top. All you need to do is manifest the magic into a ball, and then I'll describe its properties, all right?"

Ti stares at her for a long moment before bobbing her head in a strange half-nod. "Fine," she says, and Sid falters. Did she say something wrong? But Ti lifts her hand, and a swirl of magic appears in her palm, taking on a spherical shape. "You need me to hold this for what—half a bell?"

Sid nods and picks up her quill. "Hold it still, please." She turns over the small hourglass and the sand starts trickling through it.

The time passes in silence. Sid observes the conjured magic, noting the shimmering blues, the speckled light setting it aglow from the inside.

The orb swells and shrinks, the constant motion reminiscent of waves breaking on the shore, and Sid resists the urge to reach out and touch it.

Sand streams through the hourglass. When about half the time has passed, the magic twists, breaking slightly away from itself, and Sid looks at Ti. There's a sheen of sweat on her brow as she forces the magic back into a spherical shape. Is she struggling already?

By the time only a few grains of sand remain in the upper bulb, Ti's arm is trembling, and she clutches at the table with her free hand, her face flushed. The orb of magic remains intact, but it's more unstable now. The magic pushes at the constraints of the sphere, seeking a way out of the invisible boundary.

A small part of Sid is curious to see what would happen if Ti's strength ran out, if the vibrating matter inside of the orb were released.

Before Ti loses her grip on the magic, the last grain of sand drops to the bottom of the hourglass.

Sid taps it. "Time."

With a loud gasp, Ti releases the magic and it dissipates. "By the bedrock," she groans. She sags in her chair and inhales jaggedly. "Are you sure that was only half a bell?"

Sid nods, peering at Ti. "Only half a bell."

It's strange—such a simple task shouldn't affect Ti in this manner.

Sid hesitates before asking, "Can you describe how it feels? The magic, I mean. Warm? Cold?"

Ti shrugs without looking at Sid. "I don't really notice." She straightens and picks up her quill, scrawling some notes on a spare sheet of paper.

Disappointed in the answer, Sid follows suit, jotting down notes in the margins of her observations.

Once satisfied, Sid nods and looks up. "All right, for the next one you'll be—"

"You must be joking." Ti's lips are curved into a smile but there's no warmth to it. She gets to her feet. "I'm starving. I'm going to the café."

"But—" Sid starts.

"No," Ti says sharply, and pushes her notes towards Sid. "Read this while I'm gone. It's just some ideas," she says, heading for the door. "Might be useful."

Sid frowns as Ti leaves. She picks up the notes. " 'Abstractions from ordinary utilisations'—are these titles?" she mutters to herself. She skims the rest before dropping the paper.

The room feels stuffy. She rises from her chair and pulls open the windows, breathing in the late summer air. The breeze brings with it noise from the city, a distant buzz from people in the market, braying animals, and a cooing pigeon perched on a nearby ledge. Sid tries to ignore the noise.

Had she pushed too hard? Yesterday hadn't been *great*, but they'd still been friendly this morning, hadn't they? She'd not asked much, but the look on Ti's face when she left suggested otherwise, and Sid is suddenly uncertain.

Sid swallows and looks towards the blurry horizon. She shouldn't get distracted. Ti doesn't need to like her. They just need to get along until the assignment is done. Sid turns around and faces the empty room, steely resolve in her spine. She's spent years preparing for the path ahead. She can make this work.

The partnership doesn't improve over the next few weeks.

Ti pushes for more frequent breaks, often leaving their sessions prematurely, and her behavior grates on Sid. She can't work on the report without the manifestations, and they're progressing at a snail's pace. They should be doing *more*, not *less*.

Today, when Ti conjures an illusion of an apple, fuzzy at the edges and wholly unconvincing, Sid sighs. "It's not realistic," she says, perhaps too harshly. Her patience is wearing thin.

Ti drops the illusion with a groan. Bright specks of magic flicker before vanishing. "We've been at this for five bells." Ti rubs at the dark shadows under her eyes.

It's strange—Sid had expected Ti's exhaustion to lessen over time, for her magical skill to strengthen, akin to a muscle being exercised, but instead she never seems to build a tolerance.

It doesn't matter. They have work to do. "According to our schedule—"

"*Your* schedule," Ti bites back. Her hand is shaking as she clears her side of the table, shoving empty food wrappers into her bag alongside her notes. "I'm done for today. See you tomorrow." She gets to her feet.

Sid quells the urge to argue. "Yeah, see you," she replies instead, watching as Ti leaves.

Another afternoon by herself, it seems.

Sid stomps from the auditorium.

Even midway through the semester, Professor Zenbrol insists on spending his lectures rambling incoherently. Clusters of students have taken to chatting amongst themselves—a distraction on any given day and, today, an unwelcome reminder that Ti hadn't made an appearance yet again.

Sid weaves her way through idling students; a pair of them casually toss a ball of magic back and forth, and Sid grits her teeth at the display.

As she enters the study room, Sid's amulet hums. Ti sits at the table, a page full of doodles in front of her.

"Finally!" Ti exclaims. "Where have you been? I've been waiting for ages!"

"Where have *I* been?" Sid eyes the coffee cup on the table. "I suppose you went to see your girlfriend instead of *attending the lecture?*"

Ti frowns. "Lecture?"

Frustration bubbles in Sid's chest. "We talked about it yesterday!"

"I forgot." There's a hardness in Ti's eyes that Sid's growing used to. "We both know those lectures are a waste of time. What's your issue?"

"My *issue*," Sid snaps, "is that you're gambling with our—with *my* blasted future! If I don't do well here, I'll wind up with some tedious job in the city—"

Ti lets out a surprised sound, a glimmer of laughter in her voice. "That's what this is about? That's years away! You'll be fine!"

Sid shakes her head, taken aback. "You don't get it, do you?" She stares at the woman in front of her. Ti is rich enough to afford magic. Of course she doesn't need to worry about the future. "I'm just a farm girl," Sid bites out. "If I don't put in the work now, then it's too late." She runs her hand through her hair, clenching the loose curls in her fist. Her words are an echo of her mother's when she'd insisted that Sid help with the harvest instead of studying.

Ti frowns, her nose scrunching up. "Plenty of people start in one place and work their way up. Don't underestimate getting to know people—it's not all about school, you know. Besides, scribes are always in demand!"

Sid almost wants to laugh. A scribe. She came here to *do* something with her life. The thought of being limited to clerical tasks at the library *stings*.

Instead of laughing, she turns around and heads for the door.

"Wait," Ti says, confusion in her voice. "Are you leaving?"

"Yes," Sid says flatly and steps into the corridor without hesitation. She ought to stay and work on the assignment, but the thought makes her skin prickle with anger.

This isn't at all what she thought university would be like.

As dawn breaks, Sid sits on a cold bench at the edge of the courtyard, her back against a wall. In the far corner, the lights in the café are on, warm and inviting, and through the window, Sid sees a figure moving about. Amelia, perhaps. She looks away.

It's dead quiet in the courtyard, much as she'd hoped—most of the students won't come bustling from their dormitories for a while.

It's colder out here than she'd expected. A street lamp nearby radiates a touch of heat, and Sid stares at the speck of glowing magic inside of the glass dome before pushing her hands deeper into her pockets. A walk would warm her up. She could cross the bridge into town—it's not far, but even after several months, she's not yet stepped outside of the school grounds, dreading that she'll lose her way again. Her chest feels tight. How can she ever hope to explore faraway regions if she's afraid to go beyond the drawbridge of her school—her *home* for the next few years?

The university doesn't feel like home, though—not really. Not even the brick walls feel familiar, adorned as they are with elaborate swirling patterns, not wrought by any regular mason, but by magic.

She should be happy. Magic surrounds her these days. She made it here, with nothing but the house of a lower rank and a wealth of self-obtained knowledge.

But...a scribe. Is that all she'll amount to?

Her throat is closing up, burning and unpleasant, and there's a telltale prickling in her eyes.

The amulet in her pocket hums.

Sid scrubs at her cheeks in what she hopes is a subtle motion and pats at her pocket, quieting the vibration. Ti's familiar footsteps approach, and Sid swallows. She was never good at hard conversations.

"Hey," Ti says, two tall cups in her hands. Her hair is tied into a messy bun; she looks tired. Ti comes to a stop and wavers there, uncharacteristically unsure. "Can I sit?"

Sid hesitates before shifting to the side, nodding jaggedly.

Ti hisses as she settles on the cold bench. "Blasted season. Here," she mutters and hands Sid one of the cups. "I saw you from the window." She nods towards the study room.

Sid sniffs at the drink, catching a whiff of spice; cardamom, perhaps. She's not accustomed to the scent, and she cradles the tea closer, wrapping her stiff fingers around the cup. Steam rises from it, pale tendrils curling through the air, and Sid stares at it, uncertain where the conversation should begin.

"Listen," Ti starts, her voice slow and unsteady. "I—" But Sid suddenly knows what she wants to say.

"I know this assignment isn't important to you," Sid interrupts, her voice quivering despite herself. She wills away the thickness in her throat. "But it's important to me. And I can't do it without you."

"You don't—" Ti begins but breaks off before starting again. "You don't have to explain yourself to me. My mother tells me that I can be a bit...insensitive."

Sid stares at her cup and nods, acknowledging Ti's words.

Ti continues, "I know you're worried about what happens after graduation. I didn't mean to come off as...arrogant, regarding that. I know it's not easy for everyone. But I'm sure you'll do fine."

"And if not, I can always work as a scribe," Sid says bitterly.

With an odd little noise, Ti turns to Sid. "What do you have against scribes?"

"I—" Sid shakes her head. "Nothing, really. I just don't want to *be* one, you know?"

Ti opens her mouth but seems to think better of what she was going to say.

"What," Sid says flatly.

"Don't take this the wrong way," Ti says, "but why would you go into magical theory if you don't want to be a scribe?"

It's a fair question. Sid leans back against the brick wall. "No one at home understood it," she says.

Ti chuckles. "Try me?" She takes a sip of her drink, and after a beat Sid does the same. The warmth of the cardamom is sweetened with honey, the taste exploding on her tongue.

Sid sighs, gathering her thoughts. "It's about magic, I suppose. I went to the mines when I was a kid."

The memory comes back to her as easily as breathing: glimmering streaks of blue threaded through solid rock—veins of magic. She'd reached for it, *fascinated* by the mineral's shimmer and how it seemed to shift despite being solid, but her father had snatched her away before she could touch it.

"You went to the mines?" Ti raises an eyebrow. "I figured you'd never left your farm before."

She's not far off, but Sid still bristles at the assumption. "The harvest was bad, so my dad took a job there for the season. I went to visit him."

"Dangerous place for a kid," Ti comments, and Sid nods.

"I saw where they treat the magic." It had pulled at itself, a writhing chaos of pale blues, twisted and tamed into a stable orb the size of her father's fist. "It…left an impression." The words feel inadequate. The air had felt like lightning was about to strike; she'd dreamed about it for years afterward.

She'd *wanted* it, with every fibre of her being. But the sight of magic struggling against the bondage of the orb had also felt *wrong*. Unnatural.

Sid sips at her drink. "They say there's different magic in the mountains," she says. "Untreated magic."

"That might be a fairy tale," Ti says doubtfully.

Sid shrugs. "Or it might be true. And…I want to try." Sid bites her lip, then turns to Ti properly, suddenly desperate to make her understand. "Think of what it'll mean if it's real. The magic must be naturally filtered through the rock or originate from somewhere deep in the mountain, or—or, I don't know— But the magic we have here—" She gestures towards the speck of magic in the street lamp nearby. "It's magic that has to be *bent* into shape! Untreated magic might be easier to wield. There might be a whole new subset of—well, of everything! I could study that sort of magic and compare it to what we already know!"

Ti's expression turns serious. "And you might have a chance at getting your hands on it."

Sid swallows. "I mean…yeah."

"Why didn't you just go into magic?" Ti asks, and Sid wants to laugh.

"Like it's that easy?" Sid presses her fingers against the cup. The sweetened drink is getting colder. "Not everyone has that kind of money." She thinks of the orbs of magic getting shipped out of the mines—each of them costs a fortune.

Ti doesn't say anything, and Sid doesn't want to look up. There's pity on Ti's face, Sid's sure. She trembles—from the cold, she tells herself—and fidgets with the cup before swallowing the rest of the drink, hoping that the lukewarm tea will warm her bones.

"Can I try something?" Ti asks, her voice cutting through the quiet.

Sid's eyes dart to Ti's. "What?"

Ti looks serious, but her face is alight with something that Sid hasn't seen before—a determination, of sorts. "Trust me," Ti says, and Sid finds herself wanting to.

"Yeah, all right," she says, and Ti reaches out.

Ti's fingertips hover over the back of Sid's hand, and she stretches her fingers, summoning a ripple of magic from thin air and spreading it across Sid's skin.

"Oh," Sid murmurs, and there's a bubbling sensation in her chest.

Over the years, she's imagined how magic might feel, but in reality, it feels silky. It becomes a protective layer on her skin, keeping the chill at bay. Sid's heart beats faster.

Magic.

She barely breathes. The glow seems alive, writhing and twisting in arcs around her fingers.

It seems to last an eternity, but soon Ti's hand starts trembling. Sid closes her eyes, trying to etch the feeling into her memory before gently pulling away.

Sid focuses on Ti. "Thank you." She hopes that the depth of her gratitude is apparent.

"Yeah, no problem." Ti smiles wryly. It fades quickly; she exhales softly and turns her gaze to the cup in her hands. "Do you think I'm a burden?" Ti asks, the words coming out in a rush.

"A burden?" Sid ponders the question, glancing at the way Ti fidgets with her cup. "How do you mean?" she asks carefully.

Ti shrugs, loose strands of hair covering her face. "With a different partner you would've been halfway done with the assignment by now. Magic is…hard for me."

"I've noticed," Sid says. "It's unusual, isn't it? The fatigue."

Ti is silent, and when she finally speaks, her voice sounds small. "It is. Every kid dreams of magic, and I was *so* excited when I got the orb, but now…I wish I didn't have it."

The thought is ludicrous to Sid. She opens her mouth to object, but stops herself when she sees Ti's clenched jaw.

"I don't have a dream like you do," Ti says. "I don't know what I want to do after graduation, but I know I don't want to do anything related to magic. It's exhausting."

Silence hangs in the air. Sid tries to imagine it—the not knowing. Her yearning for magic, for a distant adventure, has been a part of her for almost as long as she can remember. If she'd not had that, she's not sure what would have driven her forward—or who she'd even be.

Finally, Sid slowly shakes her head. "I don't think you're a burden."

"I'm making your task harder," Ti says, her shoulders tense.

Sid lets out a chuckle. "Yes. But not on purpose, right?"

Ti glances at her, a slight frown drawing her eyebrows together. "Right. I suppose not."

"*It's not easy for everyone,*" Sid says, repeating Ti's words back to her. "We'll figure it out together." Slowly, Ti nods, and Sid is relieved to see the worried twist to her face fading. "I wish we'd talked about this earlier, though," Sid adds. "The bits about your magic, I mean."

With a grimace, Ti straightens her back. "I know. I don't really like talking about it."

Sid swallows hard. "It's…not just *your* fault, you know. I saw that you were struggling. I should have tried to understand." *Sorry* sits on her lips, but it has always been an uncomfortable word for Sid—it makes her feel vulnerable. Still…Ti confided in her. Sid squeezes her eyes closed for a moment before letting the words out. "I'm sorry. About pushing so hard."

"Don't worry about it," Ti mutters awkwardly, but she shoots Sid a soft smile, and Sid feels the tightness in her chest lessen. She breathes in deeply. They still have work ahead of them, but she finally feels like she understands the woman beside her a little better.

The carillon sounds, and Sid looks up. More time has passed than she thought—the street lamps have turned off, a slow, unnoticeable fade, and around them the courtyard is growing noisier as students come trailing out of their dorms.

"We ought to do some work today," Ti says, bumping her shoulder into Sid's.

"We should, yes." Sid nods. "If you feel up to it?"

Ti gets to her feet, stretching her arms above her head. "Yeah. But let's bring some breakfast to our room, otherwise I'll tap out after a quarter of a bell."

Sid chuckles. "Sure." After a moment's hesitation, she says, "We could get breakfast from the café… Is Amelia working? It'd be nice to put a face to the name."

Ti's expression brightens and she nods vigorously. "She is!"

"Let's go, then." Sid rises with a smile, her empty cup in hand. Her limbs are stiff from sitting in the chill, but warmth spreads through her as they make their way across the courtyard to the café.

Ti slides the almost-finished report across the desk towards Sid. "I like it," she says with a satisfied nod. "Zenbrol will be fawning over you once we submit this."

Sid chuckles. Even if the professor *doesn't* like it, Sid knows they've done good work.

She rereads the title: *The Cost of Magic and How to Manage It: Replenishing Energy.* After their talk, they'd changed their approach to focus on Ti's difficulties with magic, and everything had fallen into place.

"D'you reckon you can find your way back to the store where you got these?" Ti pops a candied orange slice into her mouth.

"Maybe," Sid says as she skims the report. Despite the heavy snow outside, she'd gone to the market by herself yesterday. It hadn't been nearly as overwhelming as she'd feared, and by the end, she'd actually enjoyed the solitary outing.

Ti gestures at the candy. "They're very energising. A few more of these and I could even go for another exercise, I think."

Sid hesitates. "I think we've done enough for today." She caps her inkwell. "You've sworn by Amelia's hot chocolates lately. Let's go see if they're *actually* that good, or if you're just biased."

With a brilliant smile, Ti jumps to her feet. "Oh, they're that good, believe me."

A huff of laughter escapes Sid. "I guess we'll see," she says, and carefully places the report in the bookcase for safekeeping. "Come on."

Sid leads them out of the study room, and the two of them make their way through the now-familiar hallways. Ti chatters about which subjects she can choose next semester, and Sid smiles, delighted to help her friend weigh the options. All the time she'd spent dreaming about university—this is exactly what she'd hoped for.

FIELD RESEARCH

DEI WALKER

Tags: bipoc, cultivation, doctor, drug use (accidental), fantasy with cultivation, friends, non-binary, past tense, scientist, slice of life, third person limited point of view

[Expedition Log: Danxi Mountain Ecosystem Survey]

The Danxi Mountains were far shorter than Yahui remembered from their last visit. It had been late autumn then, snow-capped peaks soaring impossibly high and stabbing the blue underbelly of the heavens. Now the peaks were cloaked in summer clouds, misty white tendrils reaching down to wind through the trees and bushes, shrouding the spirit beasts in protective cover.

Yahui pushed through another thicket of obnoxiously thorny brush. They glowered as vines reached for their robes and dug into the embroidery along the hems, snarling the threads. They dropped a hand to the machete at their hip—

—only for a pale hand to still the motion.

"Just a moment," came the soft voice of their senior, Ailin, "and I'll have you untangled."

"I can manage," Yahui said tightly. They half turned to glower at Ailin, but the pack on their back hid their senior. "It's—"

A hand seized their hem, making the argument irrelevant. Not that Yahui could argue overmuch with their senior, but it was the principle of the matter. They hadn't wanted a supervisor for this project, had hoped to spend their time alone in the mountains cataloguing the spirit beasts in blissful solitude.

But that hadn't met with the sect elders' approval.

"It's too dangerous," one had said, voice betraying no emotion. "The purpose of your visit is to see what remains there and how the city's growth has affected the ecosystem. Who knows what will have entered? Should you encounter some kind of danger, run into something larger than your skills allow you to manage…"

Her words had died away into quiet, the other elders nodding.

"Beyond that," a second had chimed in, cocking their head, "you would do well to spend time with others. We appreciate your intense focus on cultivation and your skills, but you are neglecting an important part of your development, Yahui: the community you are with. Otherwise, what is the purpose of being in a sect? You may as well cultivate alone."

Yahui hadn't been able to keep their nose from crinkling, shoulders pulling back before they corrected their posture and smoothed their face. They had brought their hands together inside the copious sleeves of their robes and inclined their head, ceding the point.

The threat was clear, subtle as any of the masters' teachings: if you want to stay, play by the rules.

"Ailin will accompany you," the first elder said, her mouth curving slightly in what might have been a glimpse of humor. "She has knowledge of the mountains, of medicinal plants, and of those plants used in cultivation pills. You will complement each other nicely."

There had been no point in arguing; Yahui had only conceded with a thin smile, bowed, and reminded themselves that they would pay any price to stay with the Five Dragons sect. It was everything they'd wanted from childhood, when they'd watched the adepts leap from roof to roof as graceful as butterflies, moving as swiftly as arrows, always with money to spend and the most luxurious clothes. Sweeping their parents' inn, they'd aspired to be like them—and far better mannered, given the way the adepts often ended up destroying furniture. The way they paid so carelessly, leaving more cash than was needed, coins cast with cheerful abandon and rarely any regret—

What would that life *be* like? Yahui had clutched their childish envy close to their chest, and over time it had grown into an adult's aching need to belong. Joining the sect took natural aptitude or virtually inhuman levels of determination. Ailin had the former, and Yahui had committed their life to the latter. They would succeed or die trying.

A tug on their hem brought Yahui back to reality—the unpleasantly hot, humid forest, their senior untangling them from a thicket, and the slowly lengthening shadows of the day urging them to find a campsite for their research base.

"There," Ailin said, hands retreating from Yahui's eyeline. "You should be free now."

Yahui grunted once in what they hoped was a solicitous manner. "We should keep moving," they said. "We don't want to be setting up in the dark."

Behind them, Ailin hummed in agreement. "It's a shame this is too dense to fly through, even branch to branch. Good for the area, for the beasts and plants, but poor luck for us."

"You're telling me," Yahui muttered, tugging their robes closer. "The only good sign is that there are so many plants, even if we've scared off most of the wildlife."

Ailin made another contemplative noise. "There ought to be a pond or a river, even a stream, somewhere ahead. Isn't this where some of the water that flows through the city comes from?"

Yahui sighed. They'd had to go and start a conversation, hadn't they? "Yes." Carefully, they pushed aside more of the shrubbery and continued picking out a path.

"Would you like me to see if I can find it?" Ailin asked helpfully.

No. I'd like to be the one to do something important, for once. "If you think that would be best, Senior," they said instead, hoping their voice was deferential enough.

The rustle of Ailin's footsteps on the leaf-strewn ground stopped. For a moment, only raucous birdsong and the varied chirps and buzzes of insects surrounded them. A breeze spiraled through the air, a brief and welcome reprieve from the stifling heat. Yahui turned, setting their feet more firmly on the ground as their senior sank onto one knee, spreading both her hands onto the forest floor. The breeze tugged at Ailin's hair, long strands reluctantly sliding away from the perfectly brushed river of ink-dark silk. The breeze grew stronger, carrying the faintest hint of cool moisture across the back of Yahui's neck.

Ailin's fingers dug into the soil, curling into it for a long moment. They unfurled, and she rose, dusting the dirt from her hands. The breeze died down, her hair falling back in place effortlessly. "Another li ahead," she said. "A few minutes' walk at best."

One day, Yahui would be that poised, collected, important. One day, what they did would *matter*.

It would be nice if that day came sooner rather than later.

The clearing was where Ailin had predicted, a fact that pleased and galled Yahui in turn. Perched uphill from the stream, the ground here was spongy with moisture, carpeted in hundredflower moss.

Yahui set their bag on the ground and counted their blessings. Because this project had been sanctioned by the sect, they'd been provisioned accordingly, including storage bags and rings. The bags still had a bit of weight to them, but nowhere near the heft they would have needed for true provisions for several weeks in the wild.

They reached into the bag, thinking of the tent they'd been given.

Their hand closed on the end of something and, carefully, they withdrew it, lifting it up hand over hand until the bag fell away from the bottom.

They squinted.

This seemed far too small. The provisions list had included a four-person tent, which would be enough for the two of them and their equipment in the event the weather turned.

Yahui wrinkled their nose, worry settling in their gut. They looked to Ailin. "Did you bring a tent, Senior?"

Ailin lifted her head, ink-brush eyebrows arched in confusion. "No. My equipment is medicinal—pills, poultices, and the like—in case of an emergency. Cataloguing equipment as well—ink and brushes, sample jars, boxes…" She trailed off. "Did they not send us a tent?"

"Oh, we have a tent." Yahui set the bundle of sticks and oilcloth on the ground. "But unless this is a particularly expansive pavilion…"

Ailin rose and crossed the clearing, each step scenting the air with something indefinably *green* as the moss squished beneath her feet, tiny white blossoms retracting with the pressure. Not unpleasant, but a dark and earthy scent, full of moisture.

She touched the fabric with a hand, jade bracelets around her wrists clicking together. "This hasn't been imbued with anything."

She sounded startled about it. Good.

"Can you set it up yourself?" Ailin asked.

Yahui drew back with a scowl. "I am not a complete incompetent."

The elegant senior's shoulders drooped. "That is not at all what I meant, and I do not doubt your competency. But I know full well how frustrating pavilions can be and did not wish you to think I felt I was better than you. Too much your senior to assist." Her lips thinned. "If you wish to do it on your own—"

"Apologies, Senior," Yahui said, eyes flicking down.

Why had the sect not let them do this *alone*? This would have been infinitely easier alone. One pack, one set of gear, only their thoughts to keep them company. They could have counted species and taken samples perfectly well all by themselves.

They should have been issued multiple tents, or at least one tent that wouldn't be quite this...intimate. Yahui crinkled their nose and scowled, pointedly ignoring the soaring birdsong in the air and the rich wet-green scent of moss and flowers that tickled the back of their throat. No place this pretty deserved to make them feel this miserable.

Yahui drew in a breath redolent with life, squared their shoulders, and began to set up the tent.

[Research base camp established with minimum difficulty. Observed provided equipment did not match with predicted issuing, though technically adhered to checklist; note to speak with supply department upon return.]

The small river was picturesque, as though one of the ink paintings in the halls had come to life. The water ran high, rippling where it touched the banks, the clouds parting and turning the water briefly silver.

Dark-green reeds sprang up along the banks, their serrated ranks broken rarely by the amber-gold of a honeyblossom tree. The whole scene was beautiful enough to make Yahui's heart ache.

They pushed the sentimental moment away. The purpose of this venture wasn't beauty or sentiment; it was cataloguing and analysis.

"It's lovely," Ailin murmured behind them. "And look—there at the edge. What is *that*?"

Yahui glanced behind, affronted by the interruption, then followed Ailin's eyeline.

Paddling through the reeds was—

If asked, they would have been hard-pressed to answer properly. It looked like an overlarge duck or perhaps a juvenile goose, long-necked and sharp-eyed.

It was also purple.

"It's new," Yahui murmured. "I haven't seen anything like that in the texts or heard about it from the masters. We need to get a sample of something—a feather, if nothing else—to bring back, or no one will ever believe us."

Their heart pounded with enthusiasm and the bright, desperate *need* to get their hands on this bird and find out what it was, measure its wingspan and trace its feet and see if it had a goose's tongue or something more sinister within. The sunlight flashed off feathers gleaming iridescent like the inside of an abalone shell.

"I'm going after it," Yahui told Ailin.

Their senior's eyes widened; she shook her head. "We should watch it first. Observe behavior and characteristics before we attempt to inspect it directly," she urged. "And you are quite fast, but I don't know if you're fast enough to catch it if it's in the water or can take wing. Best we wait."

Yahui's mouth firmed, shoulders drawing back with frustration, but they nodded. Fair points—and better for the report if they included notes about behavior, potential feeding activity, and population size. Their heart skipped a beat, then soared at the thought of a *multitude* of these spirit beasts, a flock of these purple-feathered, copper-beaked birds arrayed before them...

"Are you all right?" Ailin asked in a near-whisper. Her eyes had narrowed under a brow beetled with concern.

"I am fine," Yahui retorted more sharply than intended, focusing resolutely on the goose. It seemed normal: dabbling, hunting for food in the reeds, occasionally fanning out its wings. Each time it did, they glistened in a way that made Yahui's breath catch in their lungs. Beautiful, they decided; it really was beautiful.

It clambered inelegantly out of the water to explore the riverbank and the grassy sward that led toward the place Ailin and Yahui kept watch. Another glance at Ailin revealed her taking quick, precise notes on a slate.

"It's time," they whispered. "Quick, before it gets away. I'll go around and try to come up between it and the water."

Yahui gripped the fine mesh of the net and slunk away before Ailin could answer. It played out perfectly in their mind: sneak around, catch it unawares, throw out the net. The weighted edge would hit the ground, any flailing would entangle the beast, and they'd be able to take measurements and gain all the data they needed. They'd monitor the spirit beast for a few minutes before releasing it to make sure nothing predated upon it during a period of stress or exhaustion, and then return to their count.

Everything went according to plan until Yahui's hands met the spirit beast to measure it after extracting it from the net. Gently extending a wing to measure its wingspan was difficult but not impossible. It was easier, they were willing to grudgingly admit, with two to handle the beast.

Yahui's hands began to tingle as they turned to Ailin, ready to ask them to measure the outstretched wing—

—only for there to be *two* Ailins, both with equally furrowed brows, peach-blush lips pursed in concern. They spoke in harmony. "Are you well, Yahui?"

"I'm fine," they tried to say. Tried, for their tongue fumbled and twisted, nonsensical words spilling forth.

Oh, they thought as the world swam before them, Ailin turning triplicate. The sect could have simply sent one of her instead of three.

[Discovered: one new species of bird, resembling Anser cynoides with several notable variations. Feathers are purple, beak copper. Additionally, feathers appear poisonous and with hallucinogenic qualities. Specimen was released shortly after inspection. Further research and protective equipment

suggested.]

"Here." Ailin crouched in the brush at the base of a knobbly bloodsap tree. Sliding the ends of her capacious sleeves over her fingertips, she indicated a plant peering out from between the roots of the tree. "It's *shanmeia noc*—" Visibly catching herself, she switched from the scientific tones. "It's dreamflower."

Yahui raised a skeptical brow. "Are you sure, Senior?"

"Which one of us has been studying medicinal herbs with the healers of the sect for years?" Ailin's lips tipped up at one corner, taking the sting from her words. "We can take a small sample to be sure—or, if we find several of them, even bring one back to the sect and try to cultivate it. We'll need to mark it well on the map, see about having someone set protective wards around this place."

Yahui reached into the storage pocket in their sleeve to pull out collection equipment, scissors, and a small bag while Ailin continued to speak.

"Do you remember when Sishan fell? Broke his leg?" Ailin extracted herself carefully from the brush. "We had to give him some of the last pills in the entire sect, the agony was so great. Something like this is priceless. I will look for more while you record this."

Yahui opened their mouth and closed it again, nodding with as much good grace as they could muster. The plant didn't look like much, but if it was what Ailin suspected, then this stretch of land would need to be closely monitored. Dreamflower acted as both a painkiller and soporific and was a component in a number of higher-tier pill combinations. Its connection with the subconscious helped cultivators break through to higher levels of skill. The sect healers and alchemists would be beside themselves if this really was the herb and it was so close by—but it would need to be confirmed first, and protected meanwhile.

They clipped off a length with both leaves and several of the purplish flowers that gave the plant its name. They packed the sample away carefully in a jar and secreted it into the storage pocket. This was the kind of thing that couldn't be left to risk.

Carefully stepping away from the bloodsap tree, Yahui looked around the clearing for their senior.

A swirl of white and peach-colored robes drew their gaze. Walking toward Ailin, Yahui mentally catalogued the rest of the trees they passed by—more bloodsap trees, the sticky dark-red sap oozing out from the wrinkled bark; a simple, straightforward cedar, with two Leelan's thrushes singing in the branches; and Ailin, standing in front of a clump of berry bushes, cheeks pink and mouth open with obvious delight.

"There is an entire *patch*," Ailin said breathlessly. Her eyes gleamed. She grabbed one of Yahui's arms, tugging them past the bushes. "Come quickly. I want you to ward it."

Yahui blinked. "Ward it? Me?"

"You are one of the best in the sect at protective arrays and wards, and this is important. You ward it," Ailin ordered, clearly drawing on all her authority as senior in the sect, "and I will return to camp for a sample jar."

Yahui heaved a sigh but ceded the point. They watched for a moment as Ailin retreated toward the camp, and it was left to them to do the dirty work.

They'd had to get close to the tree, sap clinging to their robes and making them look as though they'd been accomplice to a murder, when something chimed once. Yahui frowned, turning to see where the sound had come from. Their foot slid, catching on a root. A slip, a stumble, another chime.

Something bit their ankle—or tried to, making a valiant lunge through the layers of their robes. It still hurt.

And the chiming didn't stop. It doubled, trebled, quadrupled, like a ceremony at a shrine where no one quite knew the rhythm. Something lunged again, coiling around their ankle.

Yahui tumbled to the ground.

They surged upright in time to see a number of serpents—no, not simply serpents, *winged* serpents—emerging from a tangle of roots. Each one was twice as long as their arm from fingertip to shoulder, scales dark on top with a paler, creamy underbelly, and each had a set of wings in one of various shades of brown.

Chime-snakes. Uncommon, alleged to have excellent magical properties when captured. Musical.

And highly territorial.

Yahui cursed and rolled onto their knees, shoes tangling in the hem of their robes. Their hands slammed into the dirt; a rock skidded across their palm. More curses spilled from their lips in a torrent of frustration, words that should by all rights singe the flora in the vicinity and scald what passed for ears on the snakes.

They had no such luck.

Yahui lurched to their feet and bolted away with little grace and less dignity. Head tucked down, their eyes on the ground before them lest some rocks or roots make them fall, they barely had time to slow and avoid crashing into Ailin.

All the while behind them, chimes rang, a dozen children somehow given access to cymbals and pots, the cacophony coming ever closer.

"Run," Yahui said, wrapping their hand around Ailin's bicep and tugging her along. "Before they catch us!"

Ailin's response fell away under the susurration of wings and perpetual ringing. They raced back to the camp, neither hesitating to push away rocks and the earth with some of their stored energy to make the run go more swiftly. Steps became long leaps to glide over the water-soaked trail, and then the camp was in sight, tent tempting them with safety.

Ailin dove inside, Yahui a breath behind her. Yahui fumbled with the tent flap, fastening the ties with frantic haste.

The chiming sounds hadn't stopped.

Ailin's eyes were wide, cheeks flushed from exertion. "They'll go away," she said confidently, "once we don't come out again."

Yahui crossed their arms and scowled. The cloth panels of the tent flexed as the serpents investigated, the chiming incessant. Wingbeats buffeted the air; what would have been nearly silent when one or two were in flight was a cacophony with more than a dozen of the spirit beasts to be kept at bay.

"Are you sure?"

"Even if it takes a while, eventually they'll tire." Ailin's chest rose and fell with heavy breaths. She touched her head and tried to arrange her hair back neatly in place. "We might as well finish recording the dream-flower sample and collating the data from the day."

"It's almost tempting to test it on ourselves," Yahui muttered. "I won't, I promise," they added quickly, flinging out a hand as Ailin's head jerked up, her gaze dark pools full of shock and horror. "I would not be so foolish, no matter how interesting it might be."

"Did you get the ward up? Before…?"

Yahui grimaced and shook their head. "As soon as they leave—or tomorrow morning, maybe. Ward one of the ones *not* surrounded by a nest of irritable chime-snakes."

They reached into the storage space in their sleeves and pulled out a clump of soft cotton wadding. It had been intended for sample jars or boxes with delicate contents, but they'd thought of a more pertinent use at the moment.

The chime-snakes pressed against the walls of the tent, shapes undulating across the fabric. Yahui tore four small sections off the wadding and rolled each between their fingers, forming small tubes. They proffered two to Ailin.

"What—?"

"Ear plugs," Yahui said. They took the other two and pressed the cotton against their ears, deep enough to keep it secure. The chiming dulled but didn't vanish. Rather than the clangor of bells outside her window, they sounded like they were outside the sect compound.

Ailin grabbed for them, sliding the wadding against her ears. Her eyes closed; the furrows in her brow easing. Her lips moved in what might have been words, but they were soft enough Yahui couldn't hear them through the padding.

"Say again?"

"Perhaps," Ailin half shouted, "we might—record the sounds? I believe we were given a recording stone in here, somewhere."

Yahui glowered at their senior. "Why? Why would you want to remember this? I'm never going to be able to sit in a tent without remembering this!" They made a wide gesture as though to encompass the entirety of the situation. "Never hear a chime or a bell without having nightmares."

"Perhaps it's communication," Ailin said earnestly. "Or we might be able to use it for musical purposes. There are some who do that, you know—take the sounds of nature and turn them into music."

"This is not music," Yahui grumbled. They raised their voice over the sounds of the chiming winged serpents. "This is *torture*. It's as bad as the transcription assignments the first-years get. Worse," they added glumly, "because you at least know when that will be over."

Ailin reached for a brush and slate. "We should take advantage of this. There is much to be learned from the opportunity."

Yahui pinched the bridge of their nose between their fingers. "Like what? How long chime-snakes can go without sleep?"

"Or," Ailin said, a smile tugging at her mouth, "how long we can."

[Encountered a nest of minghe, colloquially called chime-snakes. Previous reports state their sound is "delightful," "relaxing," and Wang et al. refers to it as "more relaxing than crushed haw-ice on a summer's day." Repeated and continued exposure suggests these reports only refer to when one minghe is found in isolation, and are not the result of exposure to a nest for in excess of six hours. Additional observation: minghe are capable of maintaining alert aggression and monitoring for at least six hours and are not daunted by darkness.]

"This is the third one today," Yahui murmured to Ailin, watching the movement of the shrubs below.

The past three days had been precisely the sort that Yahui had hoped for on this assignment: pleasant weather, even slightly cooler than expected. They had completed several significant stretches of surveying and sampling, and they had managed to ward the dreamflower patch against violent weather, beasts, and spirits.

The situation was verging on idyllic as water in the nearby stream raced past, no sweet burble but a full-throated rush of enthusiasm. Yahui and Ailin sat together, closer than might have otherwise been comfortable, perched in the crook of two branches of a massive tree, able to see both the water and the forest simultaneously. Their heads were pressed so close that Yahui smelled the lingering traces of Ailin's camellia hair oil. "This area should not be so densely populated with spirit beasts."

Ailin made a soft sound of agreement, the writing brush in her hand moving swiftly as she made notes. "Do you know what this one is?"

"Rare." Yahui caught their breath. "Boar-shape, red-and-white striped body...it may be a boar on the Path."

It was not unheard of for spirit beasts to gain greater degrees of sapience and pursue their own path of self-improvement, sometimes shifting appearance as they did. The earthy, rich smell of ink settled at the back of Yahui's nose and along her tongue as they watched Ailin sketch the beast walking below them.

It paused. In the watery afternoon light, its tusks shone the aged off-white of pale winter butter. One was chipped halfway down its length, while the other curved up and arced in a circle that would easily surround either of the researchers' wrists.

Yahui tried to keep their breathing regular, their heartbeat normal. It was virtually impossible, but they had learned from their eagerness with the purple goose and their literal misstep with the chime-snakes. They were not going to screw this up a third time. Couldn't risk it, because no matter how carefully Ailin had written the day's notes, the elders were likely to poke and prod and peel the nice words away to reveal how deeply flawed Yahui was—how unready they were for even something as simple as a survey.

Leaning against the trunk, Yahui slanted their gaze toward the forest canopy. It was midday, but light was already waning as storm clouds crept along the sky. The growing darkness made the hairs at the back of their neck prickle, but they pushed the discomfort aside. They needed to do this survey properly, and complaining to their senior that they felt *strange…*

Even Ailin would laugh, and there was no way to make it sound better in their writeup.

In the distance, thunder rumbled like a wildcat. Ailin's elegant phoenix eyes widened. "That does not sound promising."

"You can climb down if you want," Yahui murmured, "but I will remain. I have allowed too many mistakes, Senior."

"Ailin," she corrected, the thinnest thread of irritation heating her voice. "After everything we have been through—are we not friends?"

Yahui chose not to respond. The prospect of *friend* was an uncomfortable one; it implied companionship and shared interests rather than the obligation a senior had to their junior. Hadn't they done their best to ensure that Ailin had all due respect? Panic flared briefly in Yahui's chest.

A breeze picked up, dancing through the leaves and tugging strands of hair loose. Yahui gazed down at the beast, watching it root among the shrubs and dirt at the base of the tree, the dark-red tip of its tail swishing in the wind. The beast lifted its head, scenting at the air, and grunted once.

The feeling of wrongness swelled as they watched the beast trot back into the depths of the forest. Higher in the tree, branches danced in the rising winds; Yahui watched as ripples on the stream were lashed to greater force, the foam around protruding rocks turning to froth.

"We're descending," Ailin announced.

Yahui turned startled eyes on her. "We're—? It's perfectly reasonable to remain here. We've work to do. *I* have work to do. I cannot shirk—"

"Must it come to this? Your senior is ordering you, if so." Ailin disappeared the writing brush and her notes into her ample sleeves. "You have already had encounters with a hallucinogenic goose. We have been accosted by winged serpents and failed to get any sleep one night. I will *not* be responsible for head injuries—or worse—because you insisted on remaining in a tree during a storm in order to further the survey."

"I—"

"The appropriate response is 'Yes, Senior.' " Ailin smoothed her hair and robes, then slid off the branch, landing on the ground with enviable ease. She cocked her head, looking up at Yahui. "If you are not going to care for your own well-being, I will." She paused again. "I am waiting."

Still grumbling, Yahui settled their robes, sparing one last glance toward the water. A single fat raindrop splattered the branch where Ailin had been sitting.

This was positively *unfair*.

Yahui dropped with far less grace than Ailin.

"You," Ailin said firmly, "need to sneak out and spend more time drinking on rooftops."

"I— What!?"

Ailin ducked her head as another raindrop splattered on the water-soaked earth beside them. "You also clearly need to have more fun."

The cloudy afternoon sun's pale yellow shifted to an unpleasant dark hue in a matter of breaths, an ash-dark cast tinted with a sickly green.

"More *fun*?" They knew how to have fun. It was simply that there wasn't much time, focused as they were on their studies. "I don't have time for fun."

"That has been made abundantly clear." A smile tugged at the corner of Ailin's mouth as they hurried back toward their camp through the rain. Thunder rumbled much closer to them, and something piggish and startled squealed off to one side.

The two cultivators picked up their robes and ran.

They were making a habit of diving into the too-small tent; it was a habit Yahui did not like. Grumbling, both slipped off their muddied shoes, tucking them near the entry flap. Yahui secured the ties, scowling as the sound of the rain increased.

"I will start transcribing the notes," they offered, voice curter than they would have liked. They needed to do something. It itched at them, frustration and the futility of the situation calling back to days working at the family's inn. There was always something to do, but the inn stayed as it always was. This... There was nothing to do short of meditate, cultivate, or transcribe notes. The latter would at least be productive.

Ailin did not argue, surrendering the notes to Yahui with an uncomfortably knowing look. It allowed them to focus on something rather than permit their stomach to churn and their nerves to reflect on the situation.

A roar broke through the storm, the rumbling vibrating Yahui's bones and making the tent walls shiver under the onslaught of rain. They jerked their head up and met Ailin's startled gaze. It lasted an impossible several heartbeats before stopping as abruptly as it had begun.

"A landslide," Ailin said, lips pursing. "With all the moisture—you saw how high the river was running, how wet the ground has been."

"How do you know?"

"I was raised in the northern mountains. They were not uncommon."

Of course. It would be that simple.

"Why did you even get *assigned* to this?" Yahui's voice caught, pitchy and frustrated. They sucked in a ragged breath. "This was supposed to be a solitary assignment. Proving myself. And then the Sect Elders attached you to me!"

Ailin snorted softly, reaching out and poking Yahui lightly on the shoulder. "I was not assigned. I asked."

"Asked—?" Why would someone like Ailin, clever senior with a world of possibilities, wish to be included in something like this? Yahui choked out a sound of disbelief and hid the lower half of their face beneath their sleeve. "This has been an absolute mess. First-year initiates could have managed better, and what have we to show for it?" They gestured with their other hand toward the door. "A flood, Senior. A *flood*, and we are perched so precariously atop this little mound and might be washed away at any moment, unless we wish to take to the trees like birds."

"But think," Ailin countered, "of what we have gained. We have catalogued a new species of bird and confirmed the presence of several rare spirit beasts. We have also identified more dreamflower than the sect has seen in quite some time. This is hardly a *mess*."

Yahui's mouth pinched like they'd accidentally eaten a pickled plum. Everything was falling apart—the roof of their tent was bowing under the water, Ailin's incessant positivity was grating on Yahui and fracturing their composure, and worst of all, the area they had spent days cataloguing was now inundated by a torrential rainstorm.

"Everything we've done. All of our work, our effort, for—what?" Yahui sucked in a breath through their teeth. "What will be left once this is over?"

Ailin rested a hand on Yahui's shoulder. "We have studied—surveyed!—an ecosystem before a major event. The information will be invaluable for understanding what it was like before the rain. And we can see how the area recovers. It's perhaps more important than it was before we came out. Our research is important." She ducked her head around, angling herself to meet Yahui's grudging gaze. "*You* are important, because you pushed for this work. And I wanted an excuse to work with you."

"Me?" Yahui jerked their head up. "Why me?"

"Everything I've seen about you, I have liked, Yahui. You are more diligent than many, one of the hardest workers in the sect, committed to everything. The elders speak highly of you. Is it so hard to think someone might wish to be your friend?"

Yahui tangled their fingers together in their lap. It was like they'd swallowed the nest of chime-snakes, uncomfortable twists and wriggles in their stomach and curling up behind their ribs. "I've only ever wanted to do *something* with my life. Something more than picking up broken crockery and sweeping inn floors. Cultivation is competitive. How am I to find time for friendship when I must always stay ahead to earn my place?"

Ailin dropped a hand to Yahui's, the touch cool and reassuring. "You have more than earned your place by skill. The only reservation the elders have is with your distance. You can breathe, take a moment for yourself. As your senior, I can only say that you are clearly remiss in some areas of your education. When we get back, I will get us sweet plum wine and we'll climb up to the roof of the sect library, sing, and practice jumping off and landing gracefully."

A startled laugh bubbled half out of Yahui's throat before they caught it. "You must be joking."

"Hardly," Ailin said. "It is my duty as your senior—but also my pleasure, as your friend."

Friend. The word was like fresh-broken rock before the river had smoothed its cleaved corners away, the edges of it dangerously sharp. But with use, those edges would be less likely to cut.

"I will obey my senior," they said, lifting their eyes from their hands to meet Ailin's gaze, "but I will be happy to spend time thus with my friend."

[Unseasonably heavy rains resulted in flooding and associated weather events, including landslides. Researchers trapped in tent for extended period. Impact survey necessary to understand scope of damage and effect on the ecosystem. Current research team will be extending their stay indefinitely to accommodate this.]

THE CAT IN THE LIBRARY

BETTINA JUSZAK

Tags: fantasy, fluff, library, m/m, misunderstandings, natural disaster (unnatural), non-binary, present tense, third person limited point of view

Despite the size of the library of the University of Forestedge, remarkably few students venture past the first floor of study nooks and general reference tomes. On the quiet upper floors, its age becomes an almost physical sensation pressing on Chief Librarian Galivan's shoulders. He loves the accumulated weight of centuries of history and the atmosphere created by the interplay of age and size and purpose in the vast collection. When he's feeling restless, there are the special collections to comfort him, some noisy with the fluttering of magic-drenched pages, some redolent with scents courtesy of past book-perfuming trends, some kept bright to confine the shadows in forbidden tomes.

His work only requires Galivan to be in the library from the first teaching bell in the morning to the last one in the afternoon, and he *does* usually go home for dinner, but he could happily spend every moment here and never become bored.

All of which to say that Galivan has developed a bit of a sixth sense for the building and its inhabitants, and so it only takes a brief search for him to locate the intruding cat on the third floor, in the meteorology section. It's managed to squeeze in front of the books on "magical weather phenomena," in the middle of a shelf that also holds "weather spells" and "mundane weather patterns." Its tail flicks lazily against the cracked spine of *History of Magical Storms in the Lakes Kingdom*.

Galivan's eyes narrow. Animals are banned from the library—the books are fragile and rare, and the anti-dust charms aren't designed to hold against anything worse than dust or the odd tea spill. Even so, Galivan has to admit that it *is* a handsome cat. Its fur is an unassuming brown that recalls the wood used to construct the houses of Forestedge, except for the paws, which are reminiscent of the worn cobblestones in front of Galivan's home.

The cat is too sleek and clean to be a stray, but there's nothing to denote it a pet.

Cautiously, Galivan reaches out, and the cat *mrrrps*, its soft fur pleasant under his fingers. Galivan smiles when the cat purrs and leans into his touch. Its amber eyes narrow expectantly.

Galivan shakes off the fanciful notion that the cat has sought him out, and steels himself. He has a weak spot for cats, but he's not going to invite disaster upon his books. In one decisive motion, he pulls the cat into his arms.

The cat squirms.

"Be good," Galivan admonishes. "I'm just bringing you outside."

The struggle subsides the moment they pass the library doors. The sad mrrp scratches at his heart, but he's comforted by the thought that such a well-groomed cat must have a home. Cats are smart; it'll find its way back.

He heads for the nearest exit to the gardens, the cat clinging to him. It's with some regret, fuelled by its accusing stare, that he places it underneath his favourite elm tree.

As he steps onto the landing of the third floor on his return, Galivan pauses. That niggling feeling is back. Surely it's not...

He heads back to the meteorology section, breath stalling when he sees the cat.

How?

It hadn't passed him on the way back, leaving only supernatural explanations for its speedy return. Yet it looks so...ordinary. None of the bright colours, strange eyes, or light shows that typically denote magical creatures.

Galivan has no training in magical sight and can't determine the cat's mundanity. But he isn't keen on dragging one of the faculty here to check, in case it *is* just a cat.

Well. Measurability is the soul of experimentation. Galivan steps forward and drags the protesting cat back into his arms. He marches down to the ground floor again, past the elm tree garden to the large front courtyard.

He sets the cat down, brandishes a finger at it, and says, "Stay!"

By the time he has sprinted to the third floor, he's huffing and puffing and t*he cat is there again*, staring at him placidly. Then, it raises a paw to bat at the poor *History of Magical Storms in the Lakes Kingdom*.

"Hey, careful with the books!" Galivan cries, stepping forward to catch the cat's paw. "What are you even *doing* here?"

The cat's ears go back in warning, and Galivan shifts his grip to circle its body. "Seriously, if you want to play, there are much better places."

For a moment nothing happens. Then the cat sags in his grip, making a low, disgruntled sound but no move to bite or scratch him.

He supposes, for the sake of his books, he can spend the rest of the day with a cat securely in his arms. Hopefully tomorrow the cat will have found its way home.

Coat dripping wet from the deluge outside—early in the season but not unexpected—Galivan mentally shuffles through his to-do list: check on the cat, find someone to corroborate its magical or mundane status if it's still there, and put together a list of reading material requested by Professor Ilgon.

One glance into the meteorology section is enough to tick number one off the list—cat very much still present—so he calls his graduate assistant Yunji up to the third floor.

When Yunji appears, the cat's ears swivel.

"This cat," Galivan sighs, "won't go away."

Yunji's expression can only be described as confused. "What cat?"

He frowns. "What do you mean, what cat? It's right there."

"Where?" She squints. "There's some concentration of magic there, but I can't tell what it is."

Galivan steps forward, stroking the cat's back. Yunji's brow furrows, eyes narrowing.

Definitely a magic cat, then.

"You can't see it? Why do you think—?"

Yunji raises both hands as if to ward off evil spirits. "This is above my pay grade. I specialise in linguistics, not whatever this is."

She looks anxious, and Galivan puts his own unease aside; he knows the cat isn't a figment of his imagination, but it would've been nice to have outside confirmation.

"All right, fine, go back to your Old Allyric."

Permission thus given, Yunji beats a hasty retreat.

Galivan stares at the cat.

The cat stares back.

He still hasn't found a single loose hair despite its constant presence.

"All right then," he says, feeling slightly silly, "you win. As long as you don't damage any books, you can stay."

According to the book on cat anatomy he'd glanced at yesterday, the cat is female. He should think of a name—

The library emergency alarm goes off for the first time since he started working at the university.

Water is pouring over the astronomy section from the roof, where old spell-work has developed a fault, driving all thoughts of a to-do list from Galivan's mind.

He and Yunji spend the next three days rescuing what can be rescued, putting aside damaged books for later restoration, and lighting a fire under various university staff in charge of weatherproofing so this will never happen again. If Galivan were a mage, he might've noticed the spells deteriorating, but he'd been upfront about his lack of magical training. His other skills had been enough to get him hired, so they *should* know to compensate. It's no excuse that he's the only non-magical staff outside of admin and hospitality.

At least this happened a few weeks in advance of Golden Autumn

Festival, leaving him the time to fix what he could before the journey to his parents' remote estate. The additional tiredness will not make the three days on horseback any more pleasant, but the challenging journey will still be preferable to the griping that will ensue if he didn't show up. They're already prickly about his constant failure to bring a prospective marriage partner home.

He doesn't have time to investigate the cat, though he does check to make sure she hasn't wrecked anything. The cat's ears twitch, eyes narrowing as she miaows loudly, but he only gives her a quick pet before returning to the fifth floor.

On the fourth day, he's just about caught his breath again.

As he stops to check on the cat, someone unexpected finds him. Alion, youngest professor to ever grace the university, has never, in four years, deigned to set foot in Galivan's domain.

Galivan freezes in his tracks.

There is a strange shimmer in the air around Alion, but Galivan's shock derails when the cat jumps down to nose at Alion's ankles, and the professor looks down at her.

That is an important enough development that Galivan sets aside Alion's attitude for the moment. "You see the cat?"

Alion blinks, clearly confused. "Of course? It's right there, if a little magically bright."

"My research assistant could only see a concentration of magic."

Though he casts Galivan a searching look, Alion doesn't argue. He closes his eyes and does something with magic that goes beyond Galivan's senses. Galivan grudgingly appreciates that Alion takes him at his word; he had braced himself for rudeness. It's not that he has a personal problem with the man. It's just that every time he sees a new publication join the expanding shelves of Professor Alion of Forestedge's corpus of work, he can't help but grit his teeth. If the work were shoddy, that would be one thing, but it's galling for Alion to write so *well*, including all the literature review anyone could wish for, without using the library at all. For *what is the point*, a snide voice in his mind asks in those moments, *of a library, if the best and brightest neither need nor value it?*

The doubt is always momentary, but he doesn't like the feeling.

When Alion's eyes spring open again, there's a hint of gold in their depths, slowly fading. "That's not a cat."

"It's not?" Galivan doesn't curb the dubious note in his voice. He's accepted that the cat is magical, but it certainly *looks* like a cat.

Alion shakes his head, bending down to run a hand along the cat's fur. There's an expression of near-reverence on his face that sits at odds with Galivan's impression of him as aloof and proud.

"It's a manifestation of Forestedge itself," Alion murmurs. "So *that's* why I was sent to the library."

Galivan shifts uneasily. "What?"

"I've been having dreams lately," Alion says, looking up to meet Galivan's gaze. There are indeed faint dark circles under his eyes. Perhaps *nightmares* would be more accurate, if these dreams have disturbed Alion's sleep to such a degree. Galivan wonders if Alion has anyone to talk to about such things. Rumour has it he came to Forestedge unaccompanied from Allyria, living alone in the professors' dormitory. He's the only faculty member from Allyria.

"Of storms," Alion continues, wrenching Galivan away from his musings, "and, well, the library. This floor of the library, to be precise. If Forestedge is here, she must be trying to communicate with you."

Storms. A shiver runs down Galivan's spine.

With a miaow, the cat hops up to her usual shelf. Galivan's gaze follows, and he murmurs, "She first appeared in the meteorology section, and she's hardly strayed from that shelf."

The cat who is, apparently, actually *Forestedge itself*, and Galivan is going to do his best not to think about that fact too hard, miaows and bats a paw against *History of Magical Storms in the Lakes Kingdom* yet again.

Right. In his defence, Galivan surely would have noticed that sign earlier if not for the water damage. He bites his lip to keep the explanation behind his teeth; a side-long glance reveals that Alion doesn't look as if he's judging Galivan for his oversight. Maybe someone with magical talent would have understood earlier that a magical cat was trying to communicate, but then, Yunji hadn't even been able to *see* the cat, so maybe not.

There's no point in regretting the delay now.

"Why do you think *you* were given these dreams?" Galivan asks as he steps forward to tug the book off the shelf.

"My specialism is in genius loci. I'm more attuned to the town's magical signature than most."

"Attuned enough to dream of, what, an impending disaster?"

Forestedge miaows. Galivan has opened the book to the contents page, spine resting against the shelf, and a furry paw taps on the chapter title "Magical Accumulation Storm." He flips to the relevant section and begins to read.

Alion moves closer.

It doesn't sound good. According to the chapter, the town has a history of being hit by strong magical storms from the nearby forest. The why and how are uncertain, though there is a mention of stories of a spell gone horribly wrong a millennium ago. The storms are unpredictable, leading to the theory that the timing is dictated by slow accumulation of chaotic magic until it reaches a critical mass and bursts outward. The chapter records two storms—one that had been averted through "massed power of magic" and one, even further back, that had razed most of the town.

Galivan's gaze lingers on "massed power of magic." It's not exactly *specific*.

The sound of a heavy inhale reminds Galivan that Alion is still there and has been reading over his shoulder.

Slowly, Galivan closes the book, mind blank.

"If that's what's coming…" He swallows past the dryness in his throat. "We need to tell the Council."

Alion nods. Grimness doesn't sit well on his delicate features. "Good idea. Maybe if we go together. I'm not exactly…well, let's just say more senior staff aren't always keen to listen to what I have to say."

There's a hesitancy in his words, as if he's bracing himself for dissent. It seems odd—Alion is so well-known, adored by the students and clearly good at what he does, but Galivan recalls that faculty gossip about Alion always falls in one of two categories: praising him for his looks or his brain, or resentful grumbling about his early promotion.

The silence lengthens, Galivan too distracted to find the right words.

Alion's hesitancy morphs into outright embarrassment. "Perhaps I owe you an explanation. It's been four years, and we haven't properly met."

"You seem to avoid the library." Galivan knows he sounds stiff, but he can't help it. What kind of researcher spurns such a vast and immaculately kept repository of knowledge?

There's a miaow, and Forestedge leaps into in Galivan's arms, a furry head bumping his chin. Automatically, he pats behind the soft ears.

Alion coughs lightly, watching Forestedge. There's a smile in his eyes that doesn't quite fade when he shifts his gaze back to Galivan. "It's not that I *want* to avoid the library. I'm allergic."

What kind of excuse is that? Galivan catches himself before he grips Forestedge too hard. "Allergic to what?"

"…dust." Alion sounds so long-suffering it can only be the truth. "And, for some magic-forsaken reason, almost all the spells used to *repel* dust."

Galivan closes his mouth on a passionate defence that his library is *not* dusty, thank you very much.

"That's why"—Alion makes a vague gesture that sets the air around him shimmering again—"I'm currently maintaining this complex shield spell which is, frankly, quite draining."

"But how do you do your work without library resources?" Galivan bursts out, then pauses as that last sentence catches up with him. So *that's* what the shimmer is about. "Should we go somewhere else?"

"That would be appreciated," Alion says in relief. "And I do use the library. I just…send my research assistant to borrow and return books. I know I shouldn't make them do it, but they promised they don't mind."

"Wait," Galivan says, "is Laia *your* research student?"

Alion nods and, amid a disquieting rush of hot shame, the puzzle pieces that made up his dislike of Alion slot together into a very different picture. His assumptions about Alion were flawed from the beginning— Laia is in and out of the library all the time.

Stepping through the doors into the staircase, Alion lets out a sigh of relief as the shimmer in the air around him disappears. Forestedge jumps onto his shoulder, apparently happy to catch a ride.

Galivan says, "You gave your explanation, and I now owe you an apology. My impression of you wasn't very…favourable, but I didn't have all the facts. Hasty on my part."

"Apology accepted," Alion says, sounding cheerful as he scratches below Forestedge's chin. "It's good there was an opportunity to clear up the misunderstanding."

The smile he sends Galivan past the cat on his shoulder is dazzling.

Feeling a little flushed, Galivan manages a smaller smile in return.

They end up on Galivan's favourite bench in the gardens, underneath the old elm tree.

It's a good place to talk about the potential destruction of their small corner of the world, the sunshine keeping fears at bay. Galivan further busies himself by playing with Forestedge. He had made time before work to acquire a cat toy—feathers tufting out of a ball of yarn—because, at the time, he'd still thought that the cat was mostly a normal cat and not a *town*. But apparently physical embodiments of towns also like batting at feathers, so he hadn't wasted the money. Between tickling at Forestedge's fur and thinking aloud about the storm problem, time slips away. When he looks up, mouth dry from too much talking, he finds Alion's gaze has gone soft. An unfamiliar feeling flutters in Galivan's chest, something warm and hesitant and not at all what he used to associate with Alion. It's unsettling as much as stimulating, and he's glad he doesn't have the time to dwell on the implications of his changing attitude.

They don't come up with anything definitive. The council is just going to have to build on what they have.

It's not easy to convene the full university council on short notice, but Galivan and Alion combining to petitioning for it under the banner of highest urgency has enough clout—or causes enough surprise—to move rusty gears at a speed unusual outside of kingdom-wide emergencies. No matter what Alion says, he *is* a brilliant young talent they pay attention to, and Galivan is notorious for badgering them into dealing with various pressing administrative problems.

Aside from the chemistry department head, who manages to look perpetually jolly no matter his mood, the assembled mages listen solemnly as Gallivan and Alion outline the problem. Forestedge has joined them in the council chamber, sitting primly on the table next to the two stacks of books Galivan brought—all the explicitly storm-related books and a few history books that might give insight. So far no one has commented on the presence of the cat, though there've been some puzzled glances.

"So you're saying that ball of magic," the Deputy Dean says, looking almost pained as he looks at Forestedge, "looks like a cat to you? And is Forestedge? All I can see is a bright knot of power that's giving me a headache."

"Try dialling down your magical sight," Alion suggests from Galivan's right. "I think Forestedge's power is interfering. I saw her cat form because I was maintaining a complicated shield."

There's a shift in the air currents, a sensation Galivan recognizes as indicating that mages are reaching for their power.

"Ah!" the chemistry department head exclaims. "Indeed, a most fetching cat."

Forestedge preens.

Sonya, the head alchemist sitting on Alion's other side, frowns dubiously. "You're sure this is a manifestation of the town?"

"She has the feel of Forestedge's native magic," Alion says, "and I cast an origin spell to confirm it."

Heads nod all around; Alion is *the* expert in genius loci, after all.

It's the dean who speaks next. Galivan has always liked her, a no-nonsense woman with frizzy grey curls who had come for a research stay to consult the library's collection and never left.

"How much time do we have?" Dean Ajuba asks with signature calm.

Some gazes turn to Galivan and Alion but most go to Forestedge. Just as well, because Galivan has no idea whatsoever.

Unfortunately, Forestedge seem no more enlightened. After a minute of awkward silence, Forestedge starts washing one paw, ears flicking. Galivan takes that to mean that cats that are actually embodiments of places aren't particularly good at tracking time the way humans do.

"We can scry for the storm," Ulric offers, his lilting southern accent breaking the awkward silence. He, too, seems calm, but Galivan sees his fingers twitch. "There have been some recent advances in meteorological scrying. They were meant to predict where lightning might hit, but we can adapt the method."

"That's unlikely to be precise," the deputy dean points out. "If the storm is caused by magic, there will be interference."

Dean Ajuba nods in acknowledgement. "It is still worth trying. Either way, we have to prepare as quickly as possible. I doubt Forestedge itself would come to warn us if the threat weren't imminent."

Forestedge nods, ears flicking.

"We need to keep the town safe during the storm's passage." Dean Ajuba gestures to regain everyone's attention. "A shield spell is the obvious solution. If we could extend the Shield of Yang to cover more than a single person…but it would take tremendous power reserves to cover Forestedge. Kabir, what do you think?"

Kabir is the closest thing they have to a combat mage. While they wait for them to speak, Galivan mentally flicks through the last book on shield spells he read. None he recalls seem suited to the situation. Glancing at Alion, Galivan finds him also deep in thought.

"The Shield of Peres is our best option," Kabir finally says, speech slow and grave.

"Why not just extend the Shield of Yang?" Sonya asks, leaning forward. "The energy drain is even larger for Peres's spells. Do you have any idea where she was getting all that power *from*?"

Kabir shakes their head. "The Shield of Peres is the only one that explicitly intends for several mages to overlap their power. We'll need that advantage."

"I've never heard of the Shield of Peres being done by more than five mages at a time—"

The meeting drags on for three hours before people remember they have classes to teach; Galivan's head is buzzing, and he's once again grateful for being a librarian rather than a mage. At least he managed to pass the books on to the dean, who promised to get those more inclined to research to look through them and come to Galivan with questions should any arise.

The rest is out of his hands.

A warning goes out to the university and town the next day:

> Scrying has determined that a large, magical storm will pass over Forestedge within the month. Residents are asked to take precautions. Adult mages at the university with shielding capability must remain available for duty at all times. Senior mages will lead practical seminars aimed at teaching the basics of the Shield of Peres and practice combining their magical powers.

Galivan takes in the announcement in with a sense of forced calm. There is no pressure on him to solve this crisis now, but that also means there's nothing much he can *do*.

Somewhat to his surprise, Alion keeps seeking him out.

"Aren't you needed with the spell design?" Galivan asks over lunch in the dining hall.

Alion shakes his head, spoon dipping back into his soup. "My specialism isn't useful for shield-spell modification. I'll take part in the casting, once it's time, but for now I have little to do until they call me to a seminar." A wry smile flashes across his face. "For once, I can't seem to focus on my research."

Galivan sympathises, having lacked his usual focus since the meeting. Distraction in the form of Alion is rather…nice. The man has turned out to be quite easy to get along with.

He isn't sure why Alion is seeking *him* out, given that there's usually a posse of people trying to get his attention, but maybe Alion wants quieter company. Or to keep seeing Forestedge—he seems to enjoy playing with the cat, for all Galivan knows he's making a study of it to further his academic knowledge.

"You could help me entertain the younger students," he ventures. "We're running events in the library to keep them out of the way. Some of the older ones are helping with research as well."

Alion's expression lights up, and Galivan's heart twinges. Has no one else asked him to join in anything? *Their loss*, he decides, and is proven correct when Alion manages to keep the youngest cohort entertained for a whole three hours that afternoon by telling stories from his homeland and teaching them magic tricks.

A week after the council meeting, the dean comes to the library. Galivan has been looking through increasingly obscure book stock in case there's anything useful to find about the storm or the Shield of Peres. He hasn't had much luck, but the library is vast and there are corners even he hasn't had the time to catalogue.

He's in one of those corners, looking dubiously at a shelf of books bound by dried leaves, when Dean Ajuba finds him.

Forestedge, who disappeared after a curious nose at the leaf books had set her sneezing, reappears at the same time, jumping from a shelf into Galivan's arms. He staggers but holds on to the cat reflexively. He's getting used to being pounced on.

"Dean Ajuba," he greets. "What can I do for you? I haven't yet found anything else useful."

She waves that off. "I'm not here for your research expertise, though we appreciate your efforts." She casts a glance at Forestedge. "May we go to one of the training rooms? I can explain on the way."

"Of course," Galivan agrees, puzzled. When he makes to set Forestedge down, Dean Ajuba stops him.

"Bring her, if she's willing."

Galivan looks down. Forestedge seems disinclined to move, so he shrugs and starts walking. It makes more sense for Dean Ajuba to look for Forestedge than for him.

Alion is waiting outside, looking a little tense, though he smiles at Galivan and Forestedge as he falls in step next to them.

Dean Ajuba explains as they walk, a grim cast to her expression, "We're having trouble integrating enough mages' powers to maintain a shield around the whole town for longer than a few minutes. It's easiest for people who are very powerful and familiar with each other, but most mages don't fit both criteria."

"Why are you looking for me, then? I'm no mage."

"We are hoping," Dean Abuja says, eyes sliding to Forestedge, "that as the embodiment of the town, Forestedge can provide a conduit that can stop personal powers from clashing."

Forestedge makes a *mrrp*ing sound that sounds vaguely considering.

"But you don't need me for that."

Galivan flinches as Forestedge's claws prick through his shirt, not quite scratching but very *present*. When he looks down, amber eyes are staring straight into his soul.

Dean Ajuba sounds amused. "She likes you. Besides, the library is one of the oldest places in Forestedge, and you are a vital part of it. Forestedge may find it easier to connect to you than others."

The cat nods.

A strange feeling sweeps through Galivan. He'd thought he wouldn't be needed anymore, all that *magic* far beyond him. But here they are, and Forestedge wants him, of all people.

He squares his shoulders.

Alion leans over and bumps into him companionably. "Get used to it, Galivan. Once a place adopts you, she won't let go."

Forestedge *mrrps* again, this time sounding distinctly smug.

Darkness gathers on the horizon. Galivan stands in the empty plaza in front of the university gates, and Forestedge sits at his feet, ears alert. Along the outer perimeter of Forestedge, a good mile from where Galivan is standing, the strongest twenty-four mages are spread out in a large, evenly spaced circle. Though he can't see him, he knows that Alion is stationed to the southwest, and his gaze creeps in that direction frequently.

In the blink of an eye, the storm is close enough to see the distortions of magic in the clouds. The emergency gong sounds once, twice, thrice, and the air stagnates as the shield snaps up. Within a breath, the town is encased in a shimmery wall, intangible but present enough to raise the hairs on Galivan's arms.

A soft touch on his ankle diverts his attention.

Forestedge is sitting as straight as any cat has ever sat, forepaws planted firmly on the ground while her tail winds around the exposed skin above his shoe. She is looking straight at the shield, eyes blazing a brilliant gold even as her gaze goes half-lidded. He can't see magic, but he can imagine it running from the earth through her, through him, and upward, joining the clashing colours in the sky until they stabilise, a brown-green tinge covering all.

Looking at Forestedge's eyes makes Galivan dizzy, so he shifts his gaze to the horizon.

One breath. Two. Five.

Exactly a hundred breaths later, the storm hits the shield. It makes no sound, but Galivan's mind conjures one anyway, a heavy *thump* that mirrors his heartbeat. The shimmer pulses and moves, reacting to the storm's shifting forces. Even to him, the air feels charged, and he can't help wondering how Alion is experiencing this, whether his affinity for Forestedge is helping or distracting him.

The shield's movements are harrowing to watch; it undulates like a soap bubble threatening to burst.

Galivan stands rooted to the spot until his feet ache. He'd been warned not to move unless Forestedge directed him to, but his mind drifts and he loses track of time.

It's the dimming of the shield's shimmer that brings him back to himself. Forestedge wastes no time nudging at his leg, asking to be picked up.

"Is it over?" he asks, arms trembling as he lifts her to his chest.

The cat nods. Her eyes are almost back to normal, barely a glimmer of magic lighting their depths.

With a sigh, Galivan sinks to the ground.

Galivan staggers to bed and sleeps for a solid twelve hours.

Back in the library the next day, he finds himself wandering the stacks, a little lost even as he's relieved to see that events have left no mark on the space. With neither Alion nor Forestedge keeping him company, there's a sense of absence in the air around him. He's only known them for a short time, and yet…he almost wishes that Forestedge had left behind even one hair to mark her passing. It feels presumptuous to miss her—a *whole town*—but it's only the truth.

He doesn't hear from Alion for two days.

On the third day, he ventures out to the dining hall and, mustering his courage, asks Laia where Alion is.

After a slightly embarrassing amount of thought, he uses the shared kitchen facilities to bake some cookies and then goes to find Alion where he's resting on a cot in his office, weary and grey-faced.

When Galivan enters, Alion's eyes widen, and he struggles to sit up. "Galivan!"

"Don't exert yourself." Galivan hastily steps forward, pressing him back down. "I thought I'd visit and bring you some cookies. Laia said you were particularly tired."

Alion huffs, expression dry. "As I said, it's not really my area. I'm powerful, but I've never specifically studied shield spells."

"But it worked." Galivan hands him the tin of cookies. "And we're all grateful. *I'm* grateful."

Alion takes the tin but keeps gazing at Galivan, eyes intently solemn. "You contributed as much as anyone, Galivan. Helping Forestedge merge our powers was crucial."

The instinctive urge to deny his own importance presses on Galivan's breastbone. Under Alion's gaze, he breathes through it. He *did* help. Just standing there as Forestedge worked doesn't sound as important as throwing magical power around, but his rationality asserts that helpfulness shouldn't be measured in flashiness.

He makes an acknowledging noise.

Looking satisfied, Alion takes the lid off the tin and peers at the baked goods. "Did you make these yourself?"

At Galivan's nod, he immediately stuffs one of the cookies into his mouth, humming happily. Galivan blushes, gaze fleeing elsewhere.

"Thank you," Alion says, somehow managing not to spew crumbs. "Laia keeps insisting on bringing me boring, healthy food."

"You're welcome." Galivan wills his blush down and takes one of the cookies when Alion holds the tin out.

"You know"—Alion wipes his hands after the last bite disappears—"I was thinking about researching the root of the storm issue. If the forest is cursed, there must be a way to cleanse it. Forestedge might be willing to help."

Galivan hesitates. "I haven't seen her since the storm. I think she's..."

"She's always here." The absolute conviction in Alion's voice tingles down Galivan's spine. "Even if we don't see her cat form again, if we ask for help, she'll answer."

It's a beautiful thought. Galivan finds his fingers nervously rubbing along a seam in his trousers and stills them. "I suppose."

A pause. Then Alion says, less confidently, "Would you join me? It's not my area of expertise."

"Me?"

"You're the one everyone covets for research projects," Alion says. But Galivan rarely gets requests from faculty members. "You know the library best."

That, at least, is undoubtedly true.

It's not that he isn't happy to help, but that Alion is asking *him* implies that—

He hesitates, on the knife's edge of letting the matter drop or asking the question. He's already misjudged Alion once, and Galivan hates working with uncertain data. So he musters up his courage and asks, "You want to spend more time with me?"

Alion smiles, eyes curving into gentle crescents. "Why not? I enjoy your company." The smile droops a little. "It's not...that usual for people to treat me without awkwardness or expectations. Or to really want to know me."

Galivan frowns. A stranger to this country and its culture, no close friends, somewhat intimidatingly handsome and intelligent...

The thought reminds him of another notion that had popped into his head—it's nearly the Golden Autumn Festival, and he knows that Alion is far from home.

"I was wondering," he starts, heart fluttering, "well, would you want to accompany me to my childhood home for Golden Autumn?"

Alion's hand stills on the blanket, eyes wide. In the quiet as Alion digests the offer, Galivan's fingers go back to worrying at the cloth of his trousers.

"Your family wouldn't mind?" Alion asks.

Galivan hesitates. "They might...make some assumptions. About our relationship. They've been a bit overkeen in their attempts to marry me off."

Such an assumption might helpfully curb their enthusiasm for the topic, but he doesn't want that to scare Alion off. While he's secure enough now to call their relationship a friendship, not every friend would go so far as to tolerate his parents' matchmaking.

To his surprise, Alion laughs. "So, I'll be a distraction? I didn't think you had it in you, Galivan."

"I *would* also enjoy your company," Galivan adds tartly even as the corners of his lips pull uncontrollably upward.

Alion sobers a little, but a smile still plays on his lips. "As I would yours. I have no objection to...whatever your family may assume."

Galivan's heart drums, a heady rush that steadies into a drunken sort of warmth. "Then I will procure you a horse for the journey."

Galivan arrives at the library at the first morning bell, mood still bubbly from Alion's acceptance. It's only when he reaches his office that he realises he has a visitor unbothered by locks and magical protections.

Forestedge blinks lazily at him from atop the desk, a proprietary paw on a book Galivan definitely hadn't left there. Five claws are splayed across the canopy of the detailed tree carved into the leather binding.

Laughter rises in Galivan's chest—looks like he won't even have time to miss Forestedge.

Some Strange Alchemy

Rhosyn Goodfellow

Tags: college/university, competence kink, f/nb, first kiss, flirting, horror, humor, magical mishaps, misunderstandings, modern with magic, non-binary, oblivious, present tense, professor, rivals to lovers, romance, scientist, third person limited point of view, washington

Zinnia Hawthorne stares mournfully into the small cardboard box containing all the recovery crew was able to retrieve from her office: two notebooks, her tablet, six pens, and a single piece of lab equipment—an ashmolean alembic she'd used as a prop in yesterday's *History and Philosophy of Alchemy* lecture that she hadn't gotten around to returning to her lab.

She hopes she still *has* a lab.

She'd gotten the email alert just after she boarded the bus that morning. Some idiot grad student mucked up their experiment and summoned a *Vacivea illithus* without constructing adequate containment first. The many-tentacled horror had done enough damage to Emrys Hall that the entire building was closed, and although the email continued with reassurances that the creature had been safely returned to the void dimension and there was no current danger to students or faculty, it also gently suggested that everyone avoid the area until further notice.

150

Alastair Falstaff, head of University of Washington's Department of Metaphysics, quickly let Zinnia and the rest of the metaphysics faculty know that they would be assigned temporary classrooms, offices, and laboratory space to prevent any further disruptions to their classes, and that they could pick up their recovered belongings at the Suzallo Library.

Zinnia tucks the meager box under one arm so she can check her phone, relieved to see another email from Falstaff listing temporary room assignments. At least she'll have somewhere to put her tiny box of things, even if it's not—

Every thought in Zinnia's head comes to a screeching halt as she takes in the information listed beside her name on Falstaff's spreadsheet. She's been assigned to Bagley Hall, which makes sense given that chemistry and alchemy have similar equipment requirements, and although Octavia Maxwell is the last person anyone in their right mind would want to share an office with—the woman is a brilliant physical chemist, but her organizational skills resemble the aftermath of a tornado—that very fact means she's likely the only faculty member in Bagley Hall not already sharing an office.

Zinnia's lab assignment, on the other hand, is completely outrageous. What could Falstaff be thinking expecting her to share lab space with *Evren Wilde*?

Before she'd attended her first faculty mixer at UW, Zinnia had been looking forward to meeting Dr. Wilde. Everyone who spoke of them, students and faculty alike, had only good things to say, and Zinnia had always thought that biochemistry was close enough to her own field of alchemy to make for some fascinating discussions. Plus, Wilde was among the handful of openly queer faculty members, which gave the two of them something else in common.

But then Wilde had the absolute gall to refer to metaphysical science as "a heap of woo-woo nonsense." To Zinnia's *face*, not five minutes after meeting her. Frankly, she thinks she exercised a great deal of restraint by not punching them in their obnoxiously pretty face.

Zinnia takes a deep breath, forcing herself to relax. Clearly, there's been some sort of mix-up. She'll simply talk to Falstaff and get it straightened out. Maybe she can even weasel her way into a better office situation while she's at it.

Falstaff proves remarkably unsympathetic. Zinnia tries reminding him that he was *there* for her disastrous first meeting with Wilde, but he tells her that he doesn't have time to mediate personal disputes between grown adults when he's busy trying to get the Arcane Protection Agency to sign off on reopening Emrys Hall.

It's no wonder he's in such a mood if he's having to deal with the APA, but that does nothing to improve Zinnia's situation. If they have to get the building cleared by the APA, Zinnia has little hope of getting her lab back this week. Possibly even this *month*. The APA are known for being hardasses when it comes to this kind of thing, especially after the Seattle branch so spectacularly mucked up the Fremont Troll incident back in '09.

After the disaster of her new office space—which Zinnia fled immediately after dropping off her things—Wilde's lab is like a breath of fresh air. Each lab station is clean and tidy, and the equipment cupboards are neatly stacked and labeled. A biochemistry lab uses somewhat different equipment than an alchemy lab, but a quick survey shows that she ought to be able to make do with only a few adjustments to the assignments for *Advanced Alchemical Interactions.*

"I'm glad you were able to find your way here all right."

Zinnia jumps at the sound of the voice behind her, whirling to stare, wide-eyed, at Dr. Evren Wilde. "I didn't realize you'd be here." It's hardly the most genial of greetings, but Wilde hasn't earned genial from her.

"I stepped out for a moment to grab a cup of coffee," Wilde explains with an easy smile. "Nobody wants me teaching when I'm not properly caffeinated."

It is, Zinnia grudgingly admits, a nice smile, with just a hint of dimples and a playful twinkle in gold-flecked blue eyes. She can understand why so many are fooled by it.

"I just came to scope out the facilities and drop off my alembic. Now that I have, I'll be out of your way."

"There's no need to rush. My first class isn't until eleven, so you have plenty of time to get settled. It must be a shock to lose your lab like that."

"My lab is only closed temporarily," Zinnia corrects quickly. "I'll have it back as soon as the building is cleared by the APA."

"Still, it must put a crimp in your lesson plans, not to mention your research. You're welcome to use any of the equipment here. Feel free to grab anything you need that's not in use, and if you need something I am using, let me know and we can work out some kind of schedule."

There's that smile again. It's making her feel distinctly off-kilter. "That's very generous of you. I should be able to manage with just the student equipment for my classes."

"But your research?" Wilde presses. "You're probably using a lot of specific equipment if you're still working on aether-state alchemical processes, but I might be able to find you a workable substitute if you tell me your requirements."

The offer sounds so earnest and so unlike their first interaction that Zinnia doesn't know what to make of it.

"I have to go," she says, placing her alembic down on the nearest lab station.

"Oh." If Zinnia didn't know better, she might think Wilde looked disappointed. "I suppose I'll see you tomorrow?"

"Perhaps," Zinnia says over her shoulder as she pushes open the lab door. "But I doubt I'll be spending much time here outside my classes."

She's halfway to the bus stop before it occurs to her to wonder how Wilde knows what her current area of research is, or the equipment required for it.

Zinnia doesn't intend to spend more time in Wilde's lab than neces-sary, but she only manages about ten minutes in the overwhelming chaos of Octavia Maxwell's office the next morning before she's forced to admit she can't focus on her lesson prep there. Gathering her papers, she cautiously makes her way to Wilde's lab.

Her hopes of finding the lab empty are dashed when she's greeted by that warm, oddly unsettling smile.

"I didn't get the chance to ask which lab station you wanted," Wilde says, "so I went ahead and set you up in the front corner. It's the most like a second instructor station, but feel free to move if you'd rather be somewhere else."

Looking over at the lab station, Zinnia is surprised to find not only her alembic, but a full set of tempered glass equipment that Wilde must have conscripted from one of the other chemistry labs—it's not standard for biochemistry—and a digital scale far nicer than the ones provided to students. It's nowhere near as specific as the setup in her own lab, but it's as close as it's possible to get using equipment designed for chemistry rather than alchemy.

There is also, she notices as she moves closer, an insulated coffee mug sitting next to the equipment.

"For you," Wilde explains when she glances over at them. "I was making some for myself, so it wasn't any trouble to make double."

Cautiously, Zinnia opens the mug. The scent is nothing short of intoxicating—rich and fragrant and warm. Intrigued, she takes a tentative sip and can't help the sigh of pleasure that escapes her as the flavor bursts across her tongue.

"I take it this meets with your approval?"

Wilde's tone is teasing, and Zinnia feels heat rush to her cheeks, realizing how she must have sounded. "It's very good. Better than what I usually have."

"It's from a local roaster that specializes in small-batch, single-origin coffees," Wilde explains. "My ex got me hooked on the stuff, and the addiction long outlasted the relationship. It's probably healthier for me, too, even if I do add ungodly amounts of sugar to mine."

"I appreciate your willingness to share with someone in need," Zinnia says, daring to tease back just a little. "Even if you are a heathen who puts sugar in good coffee."

"Milk, too," they say, grinning widely. "I hope it's not *too* much of an imposition to share a lab with someone who thoroughly pollutes their coffee."

Zinnia's eyes narrow. "Have you been talking to Alvarez?"

Chris Alvarez is a professor of arcane crystallography and Zinnia's closest friend. He rarely passes up the opportunity to tease her for what he calls her "coffee snobbery." Zinnia maintains that it's not snobbery to believe any coffee worth drinking should be enjoyed black.

Oddly, Wilde's cheeks seem to color slightly. "I might have asked him how you take your coffee."

"Oh." It's a shockingly thoughtful gesture, and Zinnia resolutely quashes her impulse to feel touched by it. "I suppose if you're willing to go to that much trouble to make sure I enjoy my coffee, I can overlook the fact that you pollute yours. You're already far easier to share space with than Maxwell."

Wilde winces. "Is that who they stuck you with? You have my sympathies."

"I think I managed to talk her out of any overt OSHA violations this morning, at least."

"That woman is a walking OSHA violation," Wilde says, shaking their head. "Every week she manages to go without blowing up her lab is a surprise."

Zinnia wrinkles her nose. "You do realize I have to share an office with her for the foreseeable future? You're not making me feel any better about it."

"Sorry. You're welcome to work here any time, if sharing the office gets to be too much."

"I'll take that under advisement." Zinnia isn't certain how to feel about the offer, or the coffee. Wilde is being so *nice*. She can't help but wonder what their angle is.

The coffee becomes a regular thing—a cheerful, insulated mug waiting for Zinnia at her station every day—and Zinnia finds herself spending more and more of her time in Wilde's lab. She's a bit surprised that Wilde spends nearly as much time there, because their own officemate seems perfectly lovely, but Zinnia finds she minds Wilde's company far less than she expected.

Part of her wants to ask why Wilde is in the lab so often. She would assume they're doing some research they haven't mentioned, but they seem to do more reading and paperwork than anything else. It's odd, and like Wilde's continued friendliness, their curious decision to spend so much time in their lab—specifically when Zinnia is present—is a mystery that plagues her.

Zinnia is glad the repairs to Emrys Hall are nearly complete. She'll miss having regular access to gourmet coffee—and, she can admit in the privacy of her own mind, Wilde's company, to some degree—but she'll at least be spared wondering what Wilde's game is.

It's on one long afternoon when the two of them are both working in the lab, neither having an evening class that day, that Zinnia hears what sounds alarmingly like a human scream. She looks up to find Wilde looking every bit as unnerved as she feels. Their eyes meet Zinnia's, and without having to exchange any words, they're both racing out of the lab just as another scream sounds.

As they rush toward the front of the building, the screams grow closer, and it's clear now that they're interspersed with sobs. Wilde's longer legs mean they make it to the doors first, Zinnia following a few steps behind. She very nearly runs into them, not realizing until the last moment that they've stopped abruptly at the top of the steps.

There is a man wearing work boots and a tool belt kneeling at the bottom of the short stone staircase, face in his hands as he sobs like he's in agony, though Zinnia can see no sign of injury.

"Sir?" Wilde says, inching slowly down the steps. "Sir, are you hurt?"

The man's head snaps up, tears streaming from too-wide eyes. "The shadows have eyes!" He holds out his hands beseechingly. "So many eyes, and they're all opening."

Wilde stops in their tracks, well outside reach of the man's grasping hands.

"Do you know how much the shadows can hear with that many eyes?" the man asks plaintively. "How much they can taste?"

"I don't," Wilde says calmly, sinking down into a crouch so they're nearly eye-level with the man. "But why don't you tell me about it while my friend calls someone to help you? Do you have someone you want us to call? A friend or a family member?"

"No!" the man shouts, scuttling backward. "No, they have to stay away! Keep my family away from the eyes!"

"Okay." Wilde holds out a placating hand, and Zinnia slips her phone out of her pocket. "Okay, we won't ask any of your friends or family to come."

Zinnia opens her phone, intending to call the King County mental health emergency line, but she's interrupted by another shout.

"Over here! I hear another one!"

A few seconds later, two figures dressed in the unmistakable uniform of the Arcane Protection Agency round the corner.

This, Zinnia thinks, can't be good.

Zinnia is exhausted by the time she and Wilde make their way back to the lab after several hours of helping the APA contain the latest disaster at Emrys Hall. The illithus had left behind a hidden clutch of eggs, and the psychotropic pheromones emitted by its newly hatched larvae caused hallucinations and severe psychological stress to everyone in the immediate vicinity. Two students and all four contractors working that day were rushed to a nearby hospital for treatment.

With this latest development, Emrys Hall is closed indefinitely. Glumly, Zinnia wonders if she'll ever get her own lab back.

"Hey," Wilde says as Zinnia slides the last of her things into her bag. "I was thinking of grabbing some takeout, since we worked through dinner. Care to join me?"

Zinnia looks up from her things to find them watching her with an expression she might almost describe as bashful. She's already dealt with a full day of work, the fallout of arcane-induced madness, and the prospect of not seeing her lab again this year, if ever. She cannot deal with whatever Evren Wilde is up to.

"No."

"Of course," Wilde says, shaking their head. "You must be tired."

Zinnia pushes down her annoyance at them for being so understanding, which is only compounded by her annoyance that part of her inexplicably *wants* to get dinner with them.

"Thank you, Dr. Wilde," she forces herself to say. "For the invitation, and for your help with the containment."

"You're most welcome, Dr. Hawthorne," Wilde says solemnly. "But I think after seeing me in a hazmat suit covered in amniotic sludge, you're more than entitled to address me by my first name."

"Well." Zinnia isn't at all certain what to do with *that*. "Thank you,

Evren."

Evren's answering smile is so wide that there's no missing those dimples. Zinnia tells herself that the speed at which she leaves absolutely does not constitute running away.

Zinnia only makes it halfway across campus before she course-corrects, heading instead toward the university library. She cannot stand another month of Evren Wilde and their strange friendliness, let alone however long it takes the APA and Cryptic Creature Control to find a way to safely relocate the larvae. She's uncertain if she can take another *week*. She'll just have to find a way to deal with the larvae herself.

In the back of her mind, she knows she'd have better luck asking for help from someone with more experience in cryptid or void-dimension biology. She'd also have better luck if she let herself get a good night's sleep first. But she's too keyed-up to sleep, too anxious about whatever is going on with Wilde—with *Evren*—to even think about anything else without some kind of solid plan for getting her life back to normal.

It takes nearly two hours to find what she's looking for, by which time the library has already dimmed the lights twice to indicate they'll be closing soon. Zinnia has just enough time to print out a copy of *Void Dimension Biological Compounds and Their Effects on Human Neurology* and shove it into her bag before a haggard-looking library assistant is gently coaxing her and a few other stragglers toward the exit.

She pages excitedly through the paper as her bus trundles its way down the hill. Although the paper doesn't mention illithus larvae, there's an entire section on the specific neurotoxin excreted by the mature illithus. She really ought to consult an expert before trying anything, though. Cryptobiology is an adjacent field to alchemy, but she'll need to pull someone like Blevins in on this. Or perhaps one of the authors of the paper, if they're available and willing to consult.

Zinnia flips back to the cover page, which she'd skipped in her haste to get to the research. Her eyes land on the byline, and she freezes, the whole world seeming to tilt on its axis as her brain scrambles to make sense of what she's reading.

The second author listed is *Evren Wilde, PhD.*

Evren isn't in the lab when Zinnia arrives the next morning, a good hour earlier than usual. This isn't entirely unreasonable considering the excitement of the day before, but Zinnia finds herself unwilling to simply wait. She has, after all, been waiting all night.

Evren's office door is halfway open when she gets there, so she doesn't bother knocking. She feels slightly guilty for the alarmed look this prompts from Evren's officemate, but she's quickly distracted by Evren's usual warm smile.

"You're in early this morning. I'm afraid coffee's not ready yet. I'm still waiting for the kettle to boil."

"I'm not here for coffee," Zinnia says hotly, slamming a mess of printed pages down on their desk. "What is this?"

Out of the corner of her eye, she sees Evren's officemate quietly gather his things and head for the door. Zinnia makes a mental note to grab him a couple of those salted-caramel-chip cookies he likes as an apology later.

With a confused frown, Evren picks up the printout, glancing through it quickly before looking back up at Zinnia. "It appears to be a research paper I published several years ago."

"You know that's not what I meant," Zinnia snaps.

"I really don't." Evren sets the papers back on their desk and rises to check on the electric kettle sitting atop a nearby bookshelf. "Can you explain it to me while I finish making our coffee?"

Their calm only serves to irritate Zinnia more, but she pushes the feeling down and forces her voice to remain steady. "I'm asking why *you* wrote a paper involving void-dimension compounds, one that specifically addresses illithus secretions and their effects on humans, and then completely failed to mention this research when we were dealing with the effects of illithus toxins yesterday."

"I wrote the paper because I collaborated with a former colleague on the research," Evren explains as they portion out fresh coffee grounds into two pour-over filters, "and I didn't mention it yesterday because we were busy with cleanup and I didn't think bringing up old, only-possibly-relevant research would help."

It's an obnoxiously reasonable point.

"Well, it could help now. If we know the exact mechanism by which the larvae's toxin affects the human mind, we might be able to brew a synthetic pheromone to counteract it."

"Which would allow CCC to safely remove the larvae without endangering their agents," Evren concludes. "I see where you're going with this, but the larvae's pheromones could be significantly different from mature illithus secretions. Besides, I'm not sure the APA would be happy with a couple of academics getting in the middle of their operation."

"The APA is more worried about avoiding bad press than they are about reopening Emrys Hall," Zinnia argues. "They were all too happy to let us worry about cleanup yesterday once they'd dealt with the immediate threat. They didn't even leave anyone to investigate! Besides, you've studied illithi and how their pheromones affect humans, specifically. It's not like there are a huge number of void-dimension experts in the world, and I doubt the APA just happens to have one in the Pacific Northwest."

Evren sets the kettle back on its stand as the coffee slowly drizzles into their mugs. "This is really important to you, isn't it?"

"It's the only way to get my lab back."

Evren nods. "I can't promise I'll be much help, but I'll do what I can."

"Thank you." Zinnia smiles in relief. "Do you want to get started now? The sooner we can figure this out, the sooner you can have your lab to yourself again."

It might be Zinnia's imagination, but Evren's answering smile seems dimmer than usual.

Evren is surprisingly easy to work with. Even when their experiments are miserable failures—which most are—the work is satisfying in a way her research hasn't been in a very long time.

"The problem is that aether-state matter only resembles void-dimension matter under laboratory conditions," Zinnia says, erasing an entire section of their shared whiteboard. "It's fine for experimentation, but it won't work in an uncontrolled environment."

"We can run our experiments with the aether-state compounds we have on hand and then switch in comparable void-dimension compounds when we want to test on the larvae."

"That still leaves us with the problem that we don't *have* any void-dimension compounds," Zinnia points out. "Not unless you count the larvae themselves."

"So we grab one of the larvae and see if we can extract what we need," Evren says with a shrug.

Zinnia gapes at them. "Are you seriously suggesting that we sneak into an APA-quarantined area and *steal* an illithus larva?"

"It's not really stealing if the eventual plan is to send them back to the void dimension anyway, is it?"

It's an absurd suggestion, but Zinnia can't help the grin that creeps over her face. She is, she realizes, having *fun*. More fun than she's had working with another researcher since she was in undergrad, taking *Fundamentals of Alchemy* with her then-girlfriend. Evren is nothing like Liliana, but there is perhaps some hint of similarity in the careful, almost elegant movement of their hands, and they both have such striking eyes, though Liliana's had been brown to Evren's gold-flecked blue.

It clicks then. The reason Evren's friendliness has put her so on edge. Probably the reason she reacted so strongly to their careless insult when they first met, if she's honest with herself.

She's *attracted* to Evren Wilde. She's attracted to their competence and the warmth of their smile and their throaty laugh and even to that little crease they get between their eyebrows when they're thinking.

"Is that a no to stealing one of the larvae?"

Zinnia realizes she's been staring and swallows down the embarrassment that threatens to throttle her throat. "I thought you said it wasn't stealing."

Evren laughs, and yes, the warmth that curls through her is definitely attraction. How dreadfully inconvenient.

This time, it will work. Zinnia is certain. Their last attempt partially neutralized the psychotropic compounds in the larvae's secretions, but Cryptic Creature Control refused to let them try a larger dose when it appeared to be thinning the protective mucous barrier around the larvae.

"You have ten minutes." The APA agent tasked with overseeing their experiments says the words by rote, just like they have the last half-dozen times. "And if there's any change in the creatures' appearance or behavior, you stop immediately."

Zinnia spares them a curt nod as she pulls on her protective gear, reminding herself that they've been perfectly pleasant and are in no way responsible for the bureaucratic hoops their superiors keep insisting she and Evren jump through before continuing their work.

When they reach the door to the auditorium that houses the larvae, Zinnia sets her bag on the floor and opens the flap to reveal the industrial spray bottle within.

"Would you like to do the honors?" she asks Evren.

They shake their head. "This project was your idea."

"It was a collaboration." Zinnia holds out the spray nozzle.

Instead of taking it from her, Evren places their hand over hers in a gesture that feels oddly intimate given the two sets of thick gloves that separate them. "Together, then."

"Together," Zinnia agrees, glad that her respirator mask disguises the faint tremble in her voice.

With her free hand, she pulls open the door to the auditorium, and together they cover the closest larvae in a fine mist. As per their agreement with CCC and the APA, they wait a full minute to observe the larvae for any negative effects before moving on to the next cluster of larvae.

It's quick work, and they're able to cover the entire auditorium in just under the five minutes it took to start seeing effects in the lab. They split up then, heading to opposite ends of the auditorium to measure the levels of psychotropic compounds in the air as well as monitoring the larvae surrounding them.

"Levels falling fast," Evren calls. "No sign of any negative effect on the larvae."

"Same on this side," Zinnia reports. "Nearly down to negligible levels already."

A minute later, Evren says, "And down into the safe zone."

Zinnia checks her own readings. She doesn't bother to report them, simply pulls off her mask. She knows she's grinning like an idiot, but she can't help it. They actually did it.

Evren crosses the room in long strides, pulling off their own mask as they do and grinning every bit as wide as Zinnia.

"You," Evren says, pulling her into a fierce hug, "are brilliant."

Much like their hand on hers earlier, the layers of protective equipment do nothing to lessen Zinnia's reaction to the touch, and she has to force herself to let go after a few seconds rather than sink into the embrace like she wants to.

"One of us should stay here to keep an eye out for any negative effects on the larvae while the other takes our findings to the APA," she says.

"I can stay with the slimy little buggers," Evren offers. "You'll have more fun than I would telling the APA we did their job better than they did."

It's true. She's going to enjoy every little bit of smugness she can muster. If the APA had done a thorough job in the first place, the eggs never would have gotten the chance to hatch.

"Thank you." Zinnia is horrified to feel a lump welling up in her throat. It's such a small thing, but the fact that Evren noticed her petty smugness, that they're willing to stay with the larvae so she can indulge it, makes the fact that this is perhaps the last time they will ever work together—the last time they're likely to spend any notable amount of time together—that much more painful.

She turns away before Evren can see her blinking back tears.

Zinnia hasn't seen Evren since they neutralized the larvae pheromones nearly a week ago. She's been busy helping Falstaff and the rest of the metaphysics faculty restore the classrooms and labs. Her own lab had sustained significant damage, thankfully concentrated on the side of the room that housed the student lab stations rather than the one where the equipment and materials were stored. The notebook containing the notes she hadn't yet transferred to her computer was covered in plaster dust but otherwise unharmed.

So it's not as though she's had the time to swing by Bagley Hall. She just also hasn't bothered to *make* the time. The fact that Evren hasn't come to see her either should feel like vindication, but instead makes her feel slightly ill.

She arrives just as the students from Evren's afternoon class begin trickling out of the lab. Evren is engrossed in a discussion with a few students, so Zinnia quietly makes her way to the lab station she'd begun to think of as hers and begins collecting her things. Perhaps it's better this way: simply moving on with no protracted goodbyes.

She's in the process of carefully packing her alembic into the box—the last thing to go in so it won't get damaged—when Evren approaches her, a small box in hand. The students, she notes, have all gone.

"I got you something," Evren says shyly. "A sort of 'thanks for being a good lab partner' gift."

Curious, Zinnia takes the box and opens it to find a bag of Evren's fancy coffee and a pour-over set.

"For your office," Evren explains. "So you're not forced to rely on the swill they offer on campus."

"Thank you." Zinnia finds herself unable to stand the question that's been whirling around in her mind since she first set foot in Evren's lab. "Why have you been so nice to me?"

Evren frowns in confusion. "Do I have a reason not to be nice to you?"

"You certainly seemed to think so when we met." Zinnia's tone is perhaps a bit sharper than she intended, but the confusion and anxiety of the past two months have become too much to bear.

Evren's frown deepens. "You mean that faculty party?"

"Yes, at the faculty party," Zinnia snaps. "You know, when you called the field of metaphysics a heap of woo-woo nonsense?"

"When I *what?*" Evren sounds truly bewildered. "Putting aside that I don't think that even a little bit, I'd have to be a complete asshole to say that to someone whose life's work is metaphysics—"

"I certainly thought so."

"—and while I won't deny I can be a bit of an ass sometimes, I'm pretty sure I'd *remember* saying—" They stop suddenly, a look of dawning horror crossing their face.

"Has your memory returned, then?" Zinnia asks icily.

"No," Evren murmurs. "I mean, yes, I remember, but that's not—" They run a sheepish hand down their face. "Wow, I really put my foot in, didn't I? I wasn't calling the *field of metaphysics* woo-woo nonsense. I was talking specifically about George Abercrombie's claim that most of the 19th century spiritualists were simply misinterpreting psycho-metric phenomena as messages from beyond rather than engaging in intentional fraud, which I maintain is an absolutely outrageous claim given the evidence."

"Oh," Zinnia says softly. "That was. Not clear when you said it. Not to me, at any rate."

"I'm so sorry," Evren says earnestly. "I feel terrible that you've gone all this time thinking I'd say something so awful to you."

"You're forgiven," Zinnia says quickly. "I'm relieved it was just a misunderstanding. Although I'm surprised the way I stormed off after didn't give you a hint that I'd taken you the wrong way."

"Oh. Well." Evren grimaces, and Zinnia thinks she can detect the faintest hint of a blush on their cheeks. "I assumed I'd just—overdone it a bit. I know I can be a little much when I get talking about things I'm interested in, and it's even worse when I'm nervous."

"Nervous?" Zinnia doesn't quite know what to do with that. "What were you nervous about at a faculty party? It's not like *you* were the new face on staff."

"No, that was you." Evren's flush deepens. "Zinnia Hawthorne, world's leading expert in quantum alchemy, first person to definitively prove Holst's thesis on the interdependence of photons and prima materia."

"You were nervous…about meeting *me*?" It sounds ridiculous even as she says it, but there's no other conclusion to draw from Evren's words.

Evren smiles ruefully. "I can't really be the first person to be intimidated by your body of academic work."

"Well, no, but." Zinnia shakes her head. "It's just. You're *you*. Everyone loves you! I think I heard more about you my first week here than I did about my own department."

"Being well-liked is hardly the same thing as being *brilliant*," Evren argues, and now it's Zinnia's turn to flush. "I'd been following your work for years, and I was trying to make a good impression by showing off my knowledge of your field. Instead I made a complete ass of myself. I'm sorry."

"I already accepted your apology," Zinnia says gently. "And I may have jumped to conclusions. You may not have noticed, but a lot of scientists in other fields can be extremely dismissive of metaphysics. If I'd been a little less defensive about it, maybe we would have had the chance to work together sooner."

"Or if I hadn't been too embarrassed to just tell you how much I admire your work," Evren says ruefully. "I really have enjoyed working with you these past few weeks, and sharing a lab with you before that."

"As have I." Zinnia bites her lip, considering, and then takes a deep breath and says, "Would I be crossing a line if I were to ask if your admiration was entirely academic?"

"Not since about ten seconds after we met," Evren admits. "I thought I was terribly obvious. My officemate called me out on it the first day you came by."

"I admit I did wonder, but it didn't make sense in light of our first meeting, so I was just confused. Now, though"—she sets her gift aside and steps forward, bringing them closer together than could ever be mistaken as professional—"I think we've cleared things up. I don't suppose you know if making out in a chemistry lab would constitute an OSHA violation?"

"Oh, absolutely," Evren says, grinning as they draw her closer.

As their lips meet, warm and soft with just a hint of desperation simmering underneath, Zinnia decides that her life could use the occasional OSHA violation every now and again.

FAIR WINDS AND FORTUNE

MAGGIE PAGE

Tags: bipoc, bisexual, character injury (non-graphic descriptions), death of a lover, demiromantic, demisexual, doctor, elf, f/m/m, fantasy, flirting, hurt/comfort, interspecies relationship, magic use, nobility, past tense, polyamory, pre-relationship, third person limited point of view, veteran

"**M**ay I?" Zara asked, tipping her hand toward Bastian's chest. Bastian unbuttoned the left strap of his tunic and scooped his hair away from his neck and wings, careful not to catch his feathers. He tilted his head to offer a clear view of the bright-red score spanning from the meat of his shoulder and across his collarbone. After three weeks as a patient in the University of Vismark's Halls of Healing, he performed the process by rote.

Zara stooped to examine the scar. "Looking good. Is the salve helping the itching?"

"It does dull it, but it never goes away."

"We can do better than that. Feeling achy? And don't tell me it's manageable."

Bastian conceded with a scowl, which earned him a light swat to the bicep. He affected being wounded, then admitted, "Yes, I'm achy. I miss

167

moving without so much effort."

The nature of his wounds made progress slow. Wyvern claws and scales contained a rare property that nullified magic, which made for superb weapons, shields, potions—and terrible injuries. The lesions could carry a magical deadzone for another three months, inhibiting spells that would have healed him in minutes under normal circumstances.

Zara hummed sympathetically. "I know. It'll come back quickly. You've been up and about volunteering in the medical gardens already. That's been helping, hasn't it?"

"Mhmmm, thanks to you. It has helped." In more ways than one.

After the accident, Bastian hadn't made it through three days of wakefulness before begging for something to do. Luckily, Zara's skills as a healer included cheering up restless patients. She'd loaned him books to read, invited him to assist her in mixing remedies and studying for classes, and introduced him to the horticulturalist who tended the greenhouse in the central atrium. Watering, replanting, and harvesting herbs was different from the work he was used to, but it was nice.

"Would you like to venture outdoors soon?" Zara asked as she crossed the room to the cabinets holding medicines and supplies. Her movements displayed an easy grace Bastian admired. "We can find plenty of things to do on campus."

"I'd like that a lot," Bastian said. Spending time with Zara outside his sick room would be wonderful, and it pleased him that she suggested it again, now that it was possible. "Probably can't handle the city yet, but I'd love to see all the places we've talked about."

Itinerant employ as a wandering knight kept Bastian on the move, so he hadn't spent so long in the company of a single person in years. Though affection was a distant memory, he believed Zara's rapport with him revealed more than an exceptional bedside manner. Kindness was part of her job, but…

He could ascertain Zara's interest when he was himself again. If his hopes weren't wishful thinking. If he regained full function of his limbs. For what was an Avolan who could not fly?

Zara returned with a bottle of absorption solution and a dropper.

Bastian bared his arm before she could ask, and Zara spread the fluid below his elbow, then placed a flat sheet of herbs on top before it dried. "This is the usual willow bark and feverfew for pain." She added a second strip. "Witch hazel and chamomile for the itch." The patches were remedies prepared with magic and, when combined with the solution, activated for rapid relief.

Bastian sighed as the stiffness that had invaded his limbs eased. The sudden absence emphasized how much energy the pain had leeched from him. "Thank you."

"There's no need." Zara clasped his hand, squeezing appreciation and reassurance into his palm. "But you're very welcome." She released his hand and dragged a chair up to the bed. "Dr. Torik discussed your options for when the rest of your sutures come out, right?"

The doctor had removed the stitches from his chest two days ago. The thread sealing the lacerations on his wing would stay in for another week out of an abundance of caution. Even if all the cuts healed perfectly, Bastian would have to wait for the magic-canceling effect to fade to determine if his severed flight feathers could be regrown. And if he couldn't fly…

It didn't do to borrow trouble, as Zara had reminded him in periods of anxious agitation. Bastian nodded, shaking off his fears and centering himself in the present. "He says I'm well enough to check out of the Halls of Healing, but I'm free to continue lodging here because I've got frequent follow-up care."

"Do you know what you'll do?"

"As long as there's room available, I'm content here."

Zara nodded. Her face held an uncharacteristic graveness underscored by a more habitual resolve. "I'll be reassigned to the general rotation then, too, so we won't get to see one another constantly anymore. I don't want the next few days to be the last we see of each other."

Warmth swelled in Bastian's chest, setting his heart aflutter. "I don't either. I'll miss you."

Zara leaned forward and rested her forearms on the mattress, which brought their hands within inches of contact. The space between them tingled with energy. Bastian imagined their hands clasped, more intimately than they had been moments ago: his sun-bronzed and weapon-roughened fingers interlaced with her deeper brown ones, which were soft and well-tended, giving no hint of her repetitive, manual work. Ensnared by the thought, Bastian almost missed Zara's question.

"We're fast friends now, wouldn't you say?"

Bastian straightened, repositioned his wings within the bed recesses, and met Zara's eyes, exuding all the earnestness he could muster. "Absolutely."

"Brilliant." Zara rucked her sleeves up and folded her arms. When she settled against the bed again, her elbow brushed Bastian's wrist, pressing their arms together. Neither of them moved away. "I've been thinking that you'd like my friend Emory. After my shift ends tomorrow, do you want to meet him?"

"Emory, the charming mage from your stories?"

"The very one," Zara confirmed, her words colored by a fond grin.

Her anticipation felt thick enough to taste, and Bastian craved to understand the flavor. "You make him sound so dashing I can't help but be intrigued. Where should I meet you?"

"By the south entrance. There's a fun way we can show you around without tiring you out too much."

Bastian remembered little of his trip from Rookvale to the Halls of Healing. Pain and shock had blurred the flashes he could recall and did no justice to the scope and beauty of the University of Vismark's grounds. Buildings and walkways melded seamlessly into the surrounding woodlands, utilizing trees and foliage as part of their design. The architect at work here had evidently respected and cherished nature. The overall effect was as impressive as it was lovely.

Zara called his name, and Bastian turned toward her voice. He spotted her easily, but her appearance stunned him; he'd only seen her wear the pale-blue healers' robes with their navy sash and gold embellishments—Vismark's colors. Now she wore an emerald top with a sheer collar encasing and accentuating everything from her collar bones to her throat, paired with black pants. Copper jewelry adorned her wrists, ears, and neck. Though Bastian had always thought Zara pretty, her personality shone through with these informal clothes in a way her uniform hadn't allowed.

Zara waved and walked toward him. When she stopped, a tall, elegantly dressed elf stepped up beside her. He cut a striking appearance with midnight silver skin, violet eyes, and exquisitely fitted clothing consisting of a plum doublet over a lilac tunic and gray pants, all embroidered with black and gold floss. The tips of his long, slender ears poked out of loose black curls. Something in his angular face, especially those brutally high cheekbones and the strong line of his nose, struck Bastian as familiar.

"Bastian, this is Emory," Zara said, presenting her companion.

A bright, sincere smile disrupted Emory's serious countenance. He tapped the fingertips of his left hand on his chin, lowered his hand in a deliberate forward arc, and extended his right hand to shake. "Calm skies, clear words."

Taken aback and touched, Bastian automatically completed the traditional Avolan greeting, which conveyed well wishes along with a promise of genuine intentions and honesty. "Fair winds and fortune."

Zara, looking pleased, dipped her head toward Bastian and tucked her hands in her pockets. "I've told him about you."

"I've heard so much about your kindness, intelligence, and curiosity. Though I must say your plumage is even more handsome than I imagined." Sonorous and silky, Emory's voice curled around the words and heated Bastian's cheeks, which made Emory's eyes crinkle with delight. "It's my pleasure to meet you."

"Zara makes you sound like the lead in an adventure story, so I expected debonair. You don't disappoint."

Emory laughed. "Perish the thought! I've had my share of exploits, and I always welcome more." He shifted and nudged Zara with his elbow. "Ready to reveal your plans?"

"It's Bastian's first time here," Zara said. "We have to take him sculling."

"Sculling?"

"It's the term for riding the campus ferries," Zara explained. "Vismark is built around a deviated branch of the Periwinkle River, so you can get anywhere by boat."

"A sculler steers each ferry," Emory added. "The motion of the oar used for propulsion is called sculling."

"I see. That sounds nice, but—" Bastian partially spread his right wing. "Will I fit?"

"Oh, no worries," Zara said. "There are elevated seats. Between students and tourists, the ferries get plenty of winged visitors."

Emory pointed over Zara's shoulder. "Here's one coming now."

A long, narrow, gray boat bearing passengers rounded the nearest bend in the river.

"Perfect. The Halls of Healing have a dock right over here." Zara gestured toward the riverbank, where the roots of the willow trees lining the water formed a short barrier, stairs, and a banister leading to a platform. "Shall we?"

As the ferry neared, Bastian observed ornamental carvings on the stemhead and the railing enclosing the sculler akin to those he'd seen around campus. The handle of the oar bore matching details at the top. Once the boat moored, they boarded, sitting together where a low seat and a raised one faced one another.

As they situated themselves, Bastian said, "I haven't met many people versed in Avolan niceties since leaving home."

Emory inclined his head and stared toward the shore. His face pinched with his thoughts before softening again. "I grew up in the capital." His voice seemed strained with a forced nonchalance. "Politics and diplomacy are my family's bread and butter. I picked up a few things."

Zara rubbed a circle in the middle of Emory's back, soothing whatever old wound he was remembering.

"Thank you for the courtesy," Bastian said, deciding a brief acknowledgment might offset any awkwardness. "It was thoughtful." The last time someone had exchanged those words with him, they had marked a solemn farewell at Lirim's funeral. Grief still cast shadows over Bastian's life, but he wouldn't linger on the loss of his lover today.

When no probing questions ensued, a small, relieved smile quirked Emory's lips and his shoulders relaxed. "So, Zara tells me you've been devouring books as fast as she can check them out. Have any favorites?"

"I love Horatio Glen's mystery series."

A spark of something Bastian couldn't name ignited in Emory's eyes, and his focus turned magnetic. "Cyrus and Barker's shenanigans are such a treat," he said, slouching into a more inviting posture. "What do you think about their relationship?"

Bastian mulled over the question. Zara had undersold Emory's charm, and Bastian wanted to make a good impression. "I appreciate their bond. Their willingness to protect each other is admirable, and their affection is so…clear. Relatable. I wish Barker would tell Cyrus the truth about what happened during the robbery."

Zara made an emphatic noise. "Absolutely! If he doesn't, I'll find a way into the book and shake him, I swear."

Bastian and Emory both grinned at her enthusiasm.

"He has to," Emory agreed, "especially if they're moving in together. I hope Glen makes them a couple."

"Do you think he will?" Bastian asked, uncertain and intrigued. He had noticed hints of romance in the text but wasn't sure if he was reading too much into the story, yearning for a similar dynamic.

Emory shrugged and tilted his head back and forth as though weighing possibilities. "There are indications that point that way. Subtle ones. But it seems more like purposeful foreshadowing than empty promises."

"Unlike Farris Cline," Bastian added.

Zara pulled a disgusted face. "Ugh, Cline. We don't like him."

Emory snorted. "Definitely not."

Literary chatter interspersed with comments about significant campus sights carried them until they stopped at another dock. A sycamore tree towered above the bank. A marvel of construction—shaped like a giant almond balanced on a point—protruded from the sycamore's base. Slats formed by wooden planks lined up at precise intervals, allowing glimpses of the interior of a café. Where the tips of the structure met the tree trunk, the boards curved into curlicue flourishes.

"What is this place?" Bastian asked, studying the odd building.

"Honeydew Hutch," Zara said. "Eating here is another Vismark must-do. They specialize in comfort foods—if it can be baked or put on bread, you can get it here. Excellent drink selection, too."

"They also serve a rotating variety of soups that I can't recommend enough," Emory said. He strode toward the staircase that looped around the tree trunk and into the restaurant.

A touch on his wrist spurred Bastian forward, and Zara's knuckles skimmed against his as they rushed to catch up.

"Get anything you like," Emory said as he glanced over his shoulder. "I'll cover us. Any excuse to spend my father's money." He twisted, spritely, to face them, continuing to walk backward and revealing a sardonic smirk. "He has plenty of it, I assure you."

They hovered away from the line, allowing Bastian time to peruse the menu. As he scanned the offerings, he saw a section devoted to Cinora teas. His village had kept at least three pots brewing at all times, ensuring the staple Avolan beverage would be available. Bastian's favorite of the many varieties called for boiling the beans with spices to make a syrup later added to milk. To his pleasure, Honeydew Hutch had this preparation listed. He'd welcome a taste of home.

After they ordered, Zara drifted toward a pair of shelves piled with games. "Wanna play something?" she asked.

"I'm down." Emory looked to Bastian for his opinion.

"Me too. What's something we all know?"

"They've got fiddlesticks, trick-track, about 500 dice games..." Zara scanned the seating area. "A couple of tables for marbles are free."

"I loved marbles as a kid," Bastian said. "There are special tables?"

"Yeah, let's grab one!" Zara stepped forward, hesitated, and whirled around. She wore a severe squint and held a threatening finger up to Emory. "But you can't cheat."

"Me? Cheat?" Emory scoffed, pretending offense. "That would be a misuse of magic. Besides"—he coughed pointedly—"I'm not the one who steals pieces like a professional pickpocket."

Zara sniffed dramatically. "I only do that when you deserve it." She continued across the room without waiting for a reply.

A disbelieving noise escaped Emory, and his expression pleaded for commiseration.

They gathered at a round table that had a sunken center lined with felt and marked with a boundary. Several semi-circular trays housed different-colored marbles, each including a large shooter.

Bastian traced the board with a finger. "This is neat."

"You start first," Zara suggested.

They played a few amicable rounds before their drinks arrived, but conversation soon dragged their attention away from the game.

"If you want something to do, maybe you'd like to run some tests for my research?" Emory asked.

Bastian propped his elbows on the table, cradling his mug. "What are you researching?" He sipped his drink, savoring the rich, creamy flavor. Lirim had made better, but this was the closest second he'd found so far.

"I'm creating a reusable teleportation charm. A natural ability for it, like mine, is rare, and various mages have tried to mimic it throughout the years. All the extant spells are limited in some way: by distance, by number of passengers, or by energy expenditure. I want to eliminate the need for a mage. And that requires copious trial and error to refine the variables."

During an attack of carnivorous beetles, Bastian had once been among a party transported out of a cave by such a spell. The mage had exhausted herself with the feat and remained unconscious for two days afterward.

"Not ambitious at all, is he?" Zara asked. Though her tone was teasing, she was obviously proud of her friend.

Bastian nodded. "A revolutionary undertaking. I'd be delighted to help."

Emory's cheeks flushed a darker gray. "I've got *Advanced Mending Theory and Applied Transmutation* on Monday and Wednesday mornings," he said, not-so-subtly dodging their admiration. "When would be a good time to get together again?"

Bastian paused by the mirror pool in the entryway of the medical building, examining his reflection. Dr. Torik had extracted the final sutures and replaced the imitation skin magically supporting and shielding his wing injury this morning. A patch of feathers had been removed to access the wound, and Bastian was relieved that the protective seal matched the fern green that predominated the upper edge of his plumage, making the bald spot less noticeable. The teal tunic Zara had gifted him complemented his hazel eyes without creating an overwhelming monotone with his wings.

Satisfied with his appearance, Bastian continued outside and found Emory lounging against one of the awning pillars. He resembled a fashion advert from some city publication come to life even in casual clothes. Nice as Emory was to look at, his vibrant nature made Bastian eager to spend more time with him.

Emory pushed to his feet as Bastian approached and met him halfway. "How'd it go?"

"No trouble. Though I've got follow-up appointments every five days."

"I'm glad you're well." Emory transferred his weight to one foot, inhaled deeply, and scrutinized Bastian. "Are you certain you want to collaborate? I can get intense. Science and magic often cause mishaps. I want you to be prepared."

Bastian couldn't repress a chuckle. "I've made my living running into danger and fighting where others dare not tread. I can handle you."

Emory's eyes sparkled and flitted down before meeting Bastian's gaze. "I don't doubt it. We'll stop by my place so I can show you the charms and my evaluation process. I could teleport us, or we could catch the ferry—whichever you prefer."

Had he looked at Bastian's lips? Bastian couldn't feel desire so quickly, but he didn't mind Emory's interest. The attention was gratifying given his confidence-shaking circumstances. "I don't mind either way," Bastian replied, refocusing on the conversation. "You mentioned you're trying to emulate what you can do with the charms, so it might be good to have the comparison."

"True, but I didn't want to assume. Some people view direct magic use as an intimacy acquaintances shouldn't share." Emory dithered and bit his lip. "And it works by touch."

"Clear words, right?" Bastian asked, invoking the meaning of the Avolan greeting Emory had offered: a vow for genuine intentions and truth.

Emory smiled. "Assuredly. Though I don't quite travel by sky, it should be calm enough. It's usually easiest to maintain balance if we hook our arms together like attendees at a ball." He lifted his left arm, and Bastian linked their elbows obligingly. In a blink, they stood in the woods near a forked dirt track.

Bastian had never seen this place but could hear the familiar sound of the river behind them.

"This way." Emory canted his head toward the curved path.

Bastian spied a structure's warm red wood amidst the foliage as they walked. Sooner than expected, a clearing emerged, revealing a multi-level cottage with a deck adjoining the top story. Flaring, leaf-shaped roofs crowned each level and lent a whimsical air to the building.

"You live here?"

"I do. With Nelas. He's—an archmage. My mentor. His rooms are on the first floor, our lab and library occupy the second, and my rooms are up top."

Emory fished a key out of his pocket, let them inside, and led them up the stairs near the entryway.

Half the second floor was a library, walls lined with bookshelves filled to the brim. Two squat, sturdy armchairs upholstered with rusty brown fabric huddled on opposite sides of a small table in the middle of the room. End tables snuggled against each chair, crowded with more books.

Cabinets bordered the other portion of the room. A long table dominated the space, with open books, sheaves of paper, pencils, and a slew of magical implements dotting the surface. At least twenty stones lay in orderly rows atop labeled cards at the far end. Four of the stones sat apart, closer to the table's edge.

Emory drifted through the room and relocated two of the many stools surrounding the table. His bearing evinced a new lightness that made Bastian realize abruptly that the Emory he'd met in public—while appearing effortlessly confident and relaxed—was a mask, one he'd shed in this personal setting.

Emory beckoned Bastian closer.

"I've tweaked the spell and gotten it to transfer into a physical charm. The problems I'm having are with longevity and durability." He ran a finger over the separated stones. "These four are my most promising attempts. Quartz is sturdy and accurate but drains quickly. Obsidian holds the spell reliably for a few trips but becomes brittle and volatile afterward, shattering frequently. Beryl is good with long distances but is imprecise, unlike jasper, which is exact if you're traveling a mile or less."

"So, you're experimenting until you find the right base object?"

"Yep. Another set of hands will help immensely, if you're sure about all this."

"I'm happy to be of service."

"Fantastic. Let me explain how I'm recording data, then you can do some trials with a couple of short-range charms and fill out the documents at your leisure."

While teleporting with Emory had been seamless and instantaneous, the charms Bastian first tested had produced a suspended sense of floating accompanied by a twinge of vertigo.

Since then, Emory had modified the spell twice based on Bastian's evaluations.

Today, Bastian had some time to himself. Starting on the third set of charms could help him multitask. Bastian closed his eyes and imagined the woods near Emory's home, envisioning his feet treading the worn trail. Though the magic still distorted time, no disorientation lingered. He opened his eyes to find himself exactly where he'd pictured. Bastian continued down the path, seeking a place sequestered away from campus and Pheasant Run, the student housing across the river. The solitude settled him, centered him. As much as he cherished Zara and Emory as companions, he had spent the majority of the last three years in his own company. He wasn't accustomed to fully relaxing around others.

Bastian found a glade shielded by a dense copse of trees and brush. Standing in the middle of the expanse, he flared his wings to their full span and began a sequence of stretches isolating the muscles used in flight. If—*when*. He would be strong enough to take to the skies *when* his pinions regrew. No alternative was acceptable. He kept up the repetitions, three counts of fifty for each muscle group, before moving on to some basic sword forms, keen to rebuild his stamina.

When Bastian finished his exercises, the ball of stress he'd borne, which had felt ready to crack his ribs, seemed shrunk to the size of a walnut.

Two months after Bastian's injury—the earliest point when the wyvern-inflicted deadzone might have faded enough for magic to heal him entirely—Dr. Torik's first attempt at regrowing his feathers failed. But his friends refused to let him stew in a low mood. Just as Zara had engaged and heartened him during his convalescence, she and Emory conspired to keep his spirits up.

Tonight, Bastian and Emory planned to meet Zara at the library, from where they would take the ferry to visit Wisteria Grotto. Eschewing speedier modes of transport for now, they walked a meandering route from one side of campus to the other, soaking in the seep of afternoon toward evening. Shoving aside a pang of longing each time a bird swooped nearby, Bastian managed to enjoy it. The occasional, light bump of Emory's shoulder helped, reminding him of their closeness.

They slowed as they neared Alchemist's Green, a grassy expanse interspersed with herb planters that ranged along one side of the promenade bisecting the campus. The library was a massive building visible from a distance with three spires rising above the trees. Pointed trefoil arches and kaleidoscopic stained-glass windows afforded the impression of a sanctuary bursting with knowledge. Over the entryway, an iron sign, emblazoned with scrollwork and script, proclaimed the name: Lark Library.

Emory followed his gaze as he examined the architecture and paused, staring at the sign with an intensity that made Bastian's eyebrows scrunch before Emory drew his shoulders back—seeming to steel himself—and kept walking.

"Built five centuries ago by Edril Lark," Emory commented, tipping his head toward the stone façade. "My great-grandfather."

Oh.

Bastian had seen it in his cheekbones, his nose, the shape of his eyes—all like a face he'd seen on flyers tacked to notice boards and in newspapers. Reminiscent of the city, indeed. "I almost recognized the similarities when we first met. The duke is your father?"

"Yes. My brother, Oriah, is Earl of Vismark."

"Is this a secret?"

"Not exactly. I try to avoid notice, but my family's prominence makes it difficult. I don't talk about it much." Emory clenched his hands behind his back. "I never had the best relationship with my father. My brother and I used to be close but grew apart as he had to focus on training to the exclusion of everything else, even me. Being spare to the heir is awkward."

"I can't imagine. I'm surprised you're permitted to study what you want."

"My temperament makes me unsuited for any position my father would have approved of. Once that was plain, he didn't have much use for me. So, I found ways to amuse myself. Nelas was one of the archmages who consulted with the council. He took me under his wing when I exhibited an aptitude for magic, and he became more a father to me than Titus has been in years."

"I'm glad you had him."

"Me too. I shudder to think what would have become of me without him."

Bastian tangled their fingers together, offering a reassuring pressure. Such gestures had become common with Zara. It felt natural to extend the same familiarity to Emory. "Thank you for telling me."

Emory leaned into him with unmistakable fondness on his face and kept hold of his hand. "Thank you for being you."

The three friends exited a sparsely populated ferry near one entrance to Wisteria Grotto, a quirky botanical feature connecting two campus bridges. It included a tunnel over the sidewalk and waterway, a small amphitheater, and multiple cloistered seating areas.

As they climbed the stairs leading away from the dock, Emory said, "Zara, this new bag of yours is fancy."

The scenery stole Bastian's attention as they strolled inside a canopy of vines and cascading purple petals. Dappled light filtered down. The dimness, the sense of envelopment, and the beauty of the place begged for reverence.

"Thanks! My sister embroidered it."

"Oh, wow. Does she take commissions?"

Zara laughed. "Baz said the same thing this morning!" She blinked, surprised the nickname had slipped out. "Is it okay if I call you that?"

Bastian's distraction delayed comprehension and left him unguarded for the realization that he *had*, in fact, heard that dear diminutive.

"I—" Bastian's voice fled as memory seized him, a bittersweet ache clutching his heart at the reminder of his lost Lirim. Did he mind another person using the same endearment? He took a deep breath and began talking, hoping to sort his thoughts with the explanation. "You know Avolan society has a communal structure? Like dwarves."

His companions nodded.

"Though my parents had no other children, I grew up with a peer group who were like my siblings. I shared a special bond with one of them. Lirim. When we came of age, we began traveling and picking up work wherever a warrior was required. Fighting together and living in what was, for us, isolation, created greater intimacy. Within three months of departing from home, we became lovers. The life we made together suited us perfectly, and we were happy." Bastian cleared his throat. His voice had gone wobbly. "For years."

More words wouldn't come.

After a swift deliberation, Emory led them into a secluded niche. He and Zara sat on either side of Bastian, their arms flush against him. Only then did Emory prompt him: "What happened?"

The hushed, gentle understanding of his tone lent Bastian the steadiness he needed to continue. "One winter, an ice storm isolated Plessen. While we sheltered there, a sickness struck and spread too rapidly for the healer to make headway. Lirim caught it. He was one of a dozen people who died."

Bastian dabbed at his cheeks and found them wet. He hadn't known he was crying. "He called me Baz. Started when we were kids."

"Oh, Bastian," Zara breathed. She took his hand, nestling it between her palms. "I'm sorry."

Bastian shook his head. "Don't apologize. I'm grateful to hear it again. Lirim would be pleased to know I have friends close enough to show casual affection. I'll miss you both when I leave."

Emory hooked his fingers together at chest level and began sweeping his thumb along his knuckles, an anxious, pensive motion he fell into regularly. "Do you think you'll visit?"

"I can, if you'd like."

"We would," he confirmed, confident as an edict, inspiring a few quiet moments. Without raising his eyes, Bastian knew Emory and Zara had initiated a wordless conversation above his head. They'd intended to play a board game at one of the tables here. But that no longer fit the mood. Where would the evening go now?

"Yes, I think so," Emory said—surely answering Zara's raised brow.

She reached down, disrupting the anxious jiggle of Bastian's knee. "Can I ask you a serious question?"

"Of course."

"You described life as a wandering knight as perfect—with Lirim." Zara grasped his hand. "Is that true now? Do you want to devote the rest of your life to that pursuit?"

Bastian exhaled sharply, stunned. "It's what I know. What I'm good at."

"I'm good at adopting and discarding flawless court manners from one blink to the next," Emory said. "That doesn't mean I enjoy it. Or that I should build a career on the skill."

"That's fair. But not the same. I chose warrior work for myself. It's an important job that means a lot to me and lets me help others."

"It's not the only way that you could do good," Zara said. "You have other skills that could be cultivated for pursuits that are just as worthy. You don't owe it to anyone to remain a warrior, especially if it doesn't fulfill you anymore."

Bastian couldn't deny Zara's assertions. Stability and companionship were potent cravings, yet closing the door on that part of himself while flightless felt like a betrayal. "If I choose another course now—with the uncertainty of my recovery hanging over my head—I think I'll always feel like I was running away from facing the future."

Zara's brows furrowed as he spoke. "I don't understand."

"You feel compelled to confront what you'd do if you can't fly again?" Emory asked.

"Yes." Stated outright like that, it sounded harsh. And foolish. Bastian crossed his arms, shoulders and wings drooping. "I don't know who I'll become if I become flightless. I'm afraid of that possibility and that person."

Zara hummed thoughtfully. After a beat, she asked, "Do you think you're holding on because you have so little left of him?"

"I—" Bastian blinked. "Maybe." He drew his legs up, braced his elbows on his knees, sank both hands into his hair, and fell into contemplation.

Emory and Zara didn't budge from his sides, providing companionable, silent support.

Time frayed, unraveling in a thread too thin to grasp. Bastian stretched and then gathered his hair into a bun. "That feels true," he said, finally, measuring the taste of honesty on his tongue. His belief lifted a weight—an unknown but bosom presence—off his back.

"Then could there be another way to honor Lirim? Would he have wanted you to continue with a job that no longer brings you joy?" Zara asked, redirecting his thoughts to more positive avenues as she so often did.

"No." Of course he wouldn't have. Bastian had known that but never allowed himself to face it. "He would have told me to be kinder to myself."

"Maybe you can let us be kind to you now," Emory said. "I don't mind waiting for you to catch up."

Zara draped her arm around Bastian's shoulders and hugged him. "Neither do I."

Bastian laughed and laughed. Sprinkling humor atop the release of heavy emotions turned the sound uncontrollable and tugged Zara and Emory along with him. Their chorus of mirth rang out, lovelier than Vismark's tower bells.

Days of intimate company had melted into weeks. And now, the day had finally come.

At noon, he would know if he could fly again. A pleasant, drawn-out dinner with Zara and Emory had kept his fretting at bay the previous evening, but this morning, they both had classes. With no diversions, impatience warred with anxiety inside him.

Bastian followed the bend of willow roots lining the embankment, his mind distant and tread slow. He took deep, measured breaths, counting them with his footfalls. By the time he traversed the bridge into the woods encompassing Pheasant Run, he'd wrangled his thoughts into a semblance of calm. Performing his customary workout coaxed out true mental peace.

When he finished, Bastian sat by the tributary of the Periwinkle River that ran through Rookvale, giving himself space to curl his wings comfortably forward. He combed through his feathers, cleaning section by section and removing loose quills.

Bastian reached out with the handful of feathers he'd gathered, intending to scatter them over the water. A sudden urge stalled him. He wanted to keep two of the feathers—the comeliest ones. A pair of his secondary coverts would serve nicely: the tops carried the mossy green of his coverts and scapulars but merged into the white-scaled browns of his largest feathers.

Carving a wooden ornament, trimmed with a shed feather, was the first step in an Avolan courtship. It was too soon now, but the time would come to use them to make gifts for Zara and Emory.

As the tower bells pealed out one hour past noon, Bastian gripped one of the teleportation charms in his pocket and thought of the path to Emory's house. He appeared at a distance considerable enough not to draw attention, but from where he could see Zara and Emory waiting for him on the upper deck as promised. Bastian smiled, unfurled his wings, and launched himself toward the balcony. His landing was soundless. But his reception echoed with joyous congratulations as Zara and Emory rushed toward him, throwing their arms around him. He pulled his companions closer, one tucked into each side and sheltered by the drape of his whole and hale wings.

$C_8H_{10}N_4O_2$

Mina Kramek

Tags: alien, bilingual, f/nb, getting together, illness, interspecies relationship, misunderstandings, non-binary, past tense, science fiction, scientist, third person limited point of view

"Are you certain that you will not require any tissue, Doctor of the Lim-Moreno?" Ckarik asked through her translator, a circular device suctioned to her throat. She pointed at the base of the smallest of her three flexible, bulb-tipped fingers. "If I cut here, it will take only five daylights to regrow."

The Vrn had recently built their first space station, but their unparalleled regenerative capacity meant they'd had little need for—and in some regions, a cultural taboo against—medical research. Now the two of six total Vrn species that reproduced parthenogenetically were experiencing a population decline, and their planetary government had allowed off-world research in the hope their findings could help reverse the trend.

"Your saliva sample will be sufficient," Adriana rushed to assure her. Responding too slowly to a similar question had already resulted in one spindly Vrn appendage in her lab's freezer.

Sarcasm did not yet translate from Spanish to Vrn common, but the station's linguist, Dr. Ezekiel Laferty-Gonzolez, was working on it.

Ckarik blinked her large, white-less black eyes. "If you're certain. My sister, Ckitik, has been scanned by Doctor Seyel of the Amirl. Is more information required? If I may borrow a knife…"

"No," Adriana said tightly. "No, that's quite all right." Though volunteers seemed to have no trouble finding Seyelamirl, the Madraki xeno-immunologist, Adriana had yet to pin down their schedule.

Adriana peeked into the lab next door. As usual, Seyel was absent. She banged her head against the door and groaned. The Vrn government, unaware of the long, painstaking process of medical research, was expecting rapid results, but Ckarik's sample was her first from a parthenogenic species. Her sister's near-identical data would be invaluable, but without Seyel's cooperation, Adriana couldn't access it.

This was the first real attempt at collaboration between humans and Madraki since the end of the First Contact War between the Teegarden-Jovian Alliance and the Madraki Central Government, and to say it wasn't going smoothly was an understatement.

By the time Adriana reached her office, her face was dripping with sweat, as the Vrn required humidity of greater than 80% to keep their skin moist. Reaching for the towel she kept by the door, Adriana wiped off her face—and blinked at sight in front of her. The current bane of Adriana's existence was perched on the edge of her desk sipping bubble tea. Seyel was impossible to find if one went looking, but they could always be counted on to show their face whenever Adriana was least prepared to deal with them.

"Hello, Adriana," Seyel said, blinking their impossibly large, round eyes. "I tried a new flavor today. What is a rose and why does it taste sweet yet also bitter?"

Despite the semi-aquatic nature of Madraki and terrestrial nature of humans, the two species possessed remarkably similar internal physiologies and diets. Madraki could easily be mistaken for human at a distance, but up close the short, dense hair and storm patterns covering their bodies were distinctive. Seyel's storm patterns were bright-pink lines amidst a sea of grayish-brown hair, flowing across their head and neck and continuing beneath their clothes. The markings were like tattoos, a permanent color change at the root that represented their lineage and personal interests.

"Roses are a flower from Earth. We grow them in greenhouses because they spread like wildfire in Teegarden's soil."

"Edible flowers, and you put them in tea!" Seyel inspected the murky brown liquid in their cup. "How did your flowers decide to be edible?"

"I don't think the flowers did it on purpose," Adriana said dryly.

"Do I have the wrong word?" Seyel blinked their big, round eyes, and switched to Madraki. "I meant the process of becoming."

"The word you're looking for is 'evolve.' I don't think you have an exact equivalent, but we'd have to ask Zeke. You implied the flowers themselves *chose* to be eaten."

Seyel's laugh had a rough, honking quality. "Flowers choosing to be edible, what a thought!" To their tea, they said very seriously, "Thank you for sharing yourselves with me, roses."

Sharing. Just like that, Adriana remembered why she was irritated. "Is the work we do here worth sharing?"

"Imagine the benefits for all our peoples if we succeed!" Seyel said.

"I do." The potential medical techniques were mindboggling. "I also imagine being sent home if the Vrn representative inspecting our work tomorrow doesn't like what he sees."

Seyel shrugged, unconcerned. "There is no need to worry. He will."

Before Adriana could place a nice, professional request to be serious for one damn minute, Seyel swept out the door.

They were so *nice* and yet determined to be a pain in Adriana's ass. Trying to have a serious conversation felt like trying to shout through a sound-proofed wall.

It was possibly Adriana's fault Seyel didn't want to work with her. She hadn't exactly made the best first impression. In her defense, just before she arrived on Skyforest Station, Adriana had received peer review feedback on her research paper on differing rates of genetic disease in children born on Teegarden, Mars, and the Jovian Stations, and Reviewer 2 had asked her to add not one, not two, but *five* unfeasible experiments.

Seyel had stepped forward, offering their hand. "Hello, I am Seyelamirl, or Seyel, named for summer downpours in equatorial waters. I am the immunologist for our project." In an awkward beginner's Spanish, they added, "Pleased to meet you."

Adriana failed to take their hand, focused on controlling her temper to the exclusion of Seyel's rapidly dimming excitement.

"Is this not the appropriate greeting among humans?" Seyel started to draw back their hand, and something in the disappointed crinkle of their eyes broke through the overwhelming desire to throw a dinner plate at the reviewer through hyperspace.

"I—yes. Dr. Adriana Lim-Moreno, xenobiologist." Adriana shook their hand and just as quickly released it, touching her forehead automatically to offer the simplest of Madraki greetings. "Please excuse me. I have things to do."

At the time, it had seemed critical to extract herself quickly so she could write an eviscerating response to Reviewer 2 and avoid snapping at her unexpected new colleague. But she could have phrased it better.

Adriana sat down at her desk, intending to look through the data her bioinformatics student, Ximena, had sent. Her fingers brushed over an object resting on her console. She looked down to find a shell balanced there.

It was of medium size, partially rolled on one side, with a rough black exterior. She flipped it over to see the smooth, obsidian interior, flecked with slivers of an iridescent pink.

She unlocked a drawer in her desk and stared at the shells of varied shapes and sizes within, all sorted into categories based on their physical characteristics. Since a small, mottled-purple shell had been placed on her tray in the canteen when she was distracted by Seyel exclaiming over their very first bubble tea, not long after her arrival, she had accumulated over fifty, each one appearing after an equally confusing conversation with Seyel, who never said a word to acknowledge them.

Adriana started to shift the shells to make room for the new one, and hesitated. Eleven months, and she felt no closer to solving the problem of Seyel. If tomorrow's inspection didn't go well, she might not have a twelfth. And that, despite everything, would be almost as much of a shame as her career going down in flames.

This shell, she placed in her pocket. It was past time to ask for a second opinion.

"I'm hardly an expert in Madraki culture, but I doubt this is a sign Seyel secretly despises you," Zeke said as he turned over her latest shell. His project on the station was a collaboration with Vrn archivists to produce a more complete Vrn-to-Spanish dictionary. Thanks to the dusting of freckles and large round glasses, he was an oblivious heart-throb to the student researchers. Adriana had never told him. "If they were human, I'd guess they had a crush."

"No way," she dismissed, a beat too late. "Since when are you into interspecies relationships?"

"Hey, I said, 'If they were human.' " Zeke waved his hands. "Guess you'll have to try communication." He grinned.

"If Seyel won't even share their data, I doubt pressing them about cultural traditions they're clearly hiding will get me answers. *Your* work is progressing nicely, at least."

"You say that now, but one of my team will program the wrong intonation into the translator and I'll call someone's entire family line no better than fire slugs, ruin our shiny new trade agreements, and get myself thrown out of an airlock."

"I do not believe airlocks are a traditional punishment for insults among the Vrn," Seyel said, appearing out of nowhere at Adriana's side. "Dueling with acid-based projectiles is a tradition in some territories."

"Don't worry, Zeke, dueling was outlawed decades ago," Adriana told him when he blanched. "Mostly."

"And on that lovely note, the arbiter of our fate has arrived." Zeke gestured to where a pair of Vrn were preparing the airlock.

Representative Glick of the Etlunki was a rather eye-popping shade of orange his species considered the peak of attractiveness. Among the Vrn, it was considered polite to greet a stranger by standing straight-backed and still while holding their gaze for fifteen seconds, unblinking. Adriana's eyes burned by the time Glick moved on, but she hadn't failed the first hurdle.

Zeke exhaled sharply and slumped when his turn was over, and as Adriana thumped him on the back, Glick's gaze flicked back with what she thought might be amusement. "Well met, some of you," he said through his translator. "I hope the value of your work far exceeds your courtesy."

"We look forward to sharing. I have found some very interesting cell activity that may help explain your people's healing," Seyel said, clapping their hands together.

"I know well what *you* get of this station, Doctor of the Amirl," Glick said. "I wish to know how the Vrn benefit from two warlike peoples sitting in our skies."

"Our governments have respected the agreement not to bring weapons-capable ships into your system," Adriana reminded him.

"For now," Glick said. "I would like proof you are fulfilling your grand promises."

Seyel tilted their head. "Is scientific advancement not sufficient reason?"

"To me, no," he said. "Where do we begin?"

Glick did not seem particularly impressed by the FTL or ecology groups, much less the economics team's rambling presentation. By the time Glick declared they would be taking a break, the small of Adriana's back was aching.

Then Glick added that biology would be next. Figuring an attempt to improve his mood couldn't hurt, Adriana offered to show the representative where he could find the insect smoothies.

"This contraption is unnecessarily complicated." Glick complained. "Is this even fresh?"

"I'm not certain of the details as my diet does not include"—she squinted at the screen—"stinging trillipedes, but it is fresh. I can call the canteen staff if you'd like."

"What good is a 'biologist,' as you say, if you do not know how food is made?" Representative Glick stared at her, and she held his gaze as long as her eyelids could hold out.

"Do you expect the person who designed your house to build a rocket, Representative? I will be happy to tell you about my specialty shortly."

"You held my gaze easily for a human, yet do not respond to insult. Very strange." He hummed. "Have you considered that you are too courteous?"

Adriana blinked, and when Glick swept off to the table, forgot to follow for a long moment. Courteous? Her? When she lost her temper on a regular basis?

She slid into the remaining seat between Seyel and Zeke, who seemed to have made the mistake of asking Glick his opinion on the station. Seyel pushed an extra mug over to Adriana, smiling with what Adriana thought might be sympathy. She took a sip, bracing herself for Seyel's over-sweetened tea…

Double espresso, black. When had Seyel noticed what Adriana drank when she was stressed?

"You keep it far too dry in here. System, increase the humidity by 5%," Glick was saying as he reached out absently, grabbing a cup and taking a sip without looking at its contents. He grimaced. "What is that? How terribly sweet."

"Oh, that's my coffee. I'm sorry, Rep—" Zeke began.

A hacking, mucosal cough burst from Glick's throat. His long fingers wrapped around his neck as he gasped for breath, spilling the cup along the way. His translator was knocked loose, and any words turned to gurgles of distress.

Adriana leaped out of her seat, rushing to him.

"Do you know what's wrong with him?" she demanded of the nearest Vrn.

"I've never seen anything like this. Is he dying?"

Another Vrn grabbed the first's arm and started speaking too rapidly for the translator.

Adriana muttered a whole-hearted *fuck* before snapping, "Someone get me a med kit!"

Faster than she would have thought possible, Seyel knelt next to her with an open kit. "What do you need?"

"Oxygen tube," she said. Though from the way Glick's skin was dimming in shade, Adriana would bet a swelling throat wasn't his only problem. "What do you make of this?"

Seyel's response was unexpectedly steady. "From the inciting incident and symptoms, I would say anaphylaxis, but the Vrn don't produce histamines *or* epinephrine."

"We need to get him into your stasis chamber. Now." Adriana couldn't be certain it would work on Vrn physiology, but if she didn't take the chance, Glick would likely be dead in minutes.

Seyel was already assembling the kit's foldable stretcher and directing the stronger members of the audience to carry Glick while Adriana monitored his vital signs.

He was alive when they loaded him into the stasis chamber, so—

So.

Adriana sank into the nearest chair and laughed bitterly. Putting a government official in a coma was sure to get her full marks on the performance review.

"Are you all right?" Seyel asked, their hand hovering over her shoulder as if to touch.

"What do you think the odds are that we'll get kicked off this station before dinner?"

Seyel frowned. "Why do you assume we will not succeed in curing Representative Glick? I believe if we—"

We, they said, and the tight rein Adriana kept on her temper snapped. "Oh, now you want to work together? Now, and not anytime over the eleven months we've been on this station?"

Seyel flinched, and their expression shuttered. They flexed their webbed fingers, angry as Adriana had never seen before. "I did *not* cause this."

Zeke raised a hand, saying weakly, "It was my fault—" but backed away when Adriana stood, stepping close enough to Seyel that she had to look down to meet their eyes.

"*This* was an accident. But maybe I would have the *slightest* idea how to treat him if we had been working together like we're supposed to!"

Seyel blinked, stepping back. "You *wanted* to work together?"

"Have you *ever* listened to a word I've said? If half of my prospective research subjects hadn't told me they already gave samples to you, I wouldn't believe you ever set foot in your lab!"

"I had a few ideas about where to begin with Representative Glick's treatment, but if your opinion of my worth is so low, perhaps you will solve this without my assistance." Seyel tilted their chin up imperiously, turning to go.

Adriana caught them by the hand. "That is *not* what I meant." Somewhere within her were the words to express the months of frustration, the worry that it was her own fault that they had run out of time. Adriana couldn't find them.

"I will go." Seyel pulled out of Adriana's grip, careful not to scratch her with their pointed claws even now.

A flash of orange—something falling from their pocket, skittering to a rest at Adriana's feet.

Numbly, she bent to pick it up, her fingers wrapping around it before Seyel could retrieve it. Their eyes met as they straightened. It was another shell, a nautilus, nearly as bright as Glick and sparkling with an embedded mineral. Adriana loved it immediately, though she was uncertain if it had been meant for her. "Seyel, what do these *mean?*"

As Seyel hesitated, the comm system went off.

The incoming call was from the Arbiter, the sacred judge of the Vrn government. Reluctantly, Adriana picked up the call.

"I have received a report that Representative Glick has come to harm during his audit. An accident, I am told," the Arbiter said, conveying her displeasure despite the translator's monotony. "Representative Glick is my favorite aid. I am told his condition is deteriorating rapidly. You are here to provide us with healing knowledge, yet it seems you know nothing."

"We don't have a cure—*yet*—because no one knew this could be a problem." And because medical research was a lengthy process, but she could hardly say that to a semi-religious planetary leader's face. "He's alive, and we can keep him that way indefinitely. Given time, we can figure out what's interfering with his regeneration and reverse it."

The Arbiter blinked once, slowly. "One of yours endangered him, and you wish to use him as a test subject."

Well—yes, if the Arbiter had to phrase it in the most uncharitable way possible. Adriana took a deep breath, set her shoulders, and threw diplomacy out the window. "I'll be blunt. We may be able to save his life, we may not. But without our technology, he would already be dead. What is the harm in letting us try?"

"'Us'?" Seyel whispered under their breath.

"Very well," the Arbiter said after a long moment. "You have three days before we revisit this station's continuation."

Adriana took that as a win.

"Anaphylaxis without the molecules involved," she muttered. Could the universe never just leave her to research *theoretical* medical mysteries in peace?

Seyel made a grunting sound, the Madraki equivalent to clearing their throat. "The Vrn immune response occurs much more quickly than ours, with a higher immune cell count in every tissue. I believe a compound in this drink blocked the initiation of the reconstructive response—"

"—trapping him in uncontrolled acute inflammation. So, you do intend to help?"

Seyel nodded. "I would like cell samples from his blood, lymph, and multiple positions along the digestive tract. Dr. Zeke, what was in your drink?"

Zeke took a break from panicking to say, "Just coffee and almond milk."

"It would help to analyze the exact composition." Adriana should have thought of it earlier.

"I grabbed it." Zeke handed her the cup in question, a bit of liquid remaining at the bottom. "I had the presence of mind for that, at least."

"That's great," Adriana replied. "More than I expected after your accidental assassination attempt."

He sighed. "And I was trying so hard not to think about acid duels and airlocks."

"A sibling or spouse would have grounds to challenge you if he dies," Seyel mused, causing Zeke to turn an unnatural shade of green.

Adriana patted Zeke on the shoulder. "I'm prescribing you three shots of tequila and a long nap."

"Now those are doctor's orders I'll gladly follow," he said, and practically sprinted out the door, leaving the problem to Adriana.

And Seyel, who was looking at her, perplexed. "That does not sound like medically sound advice."

"You'd be surprised." Adriana looked down at the cup in her hand. "Shall we get to work?"

Seyel's answering smile was small, but it was a start.

Adriana had portable equipment brought to Seyel's lab while she and Seyel collected samples from Representative Glick. Once Adriana had the samples in genome replication chambers, she looked up to find Seyel hovering over her.

They set down a metal object in the shape of a spiral of about ten centimeters in diameter.

"Is this…?" She reached out to trace the spiral with the tip of her finger.

"All of the data my team has collected over the past eleven months and seven days, yes." Seyel said.

The data from Ckarik's sister could lead to the breakthrough Adriana was chasing. "Finally," she breathed, but was taken aback by the hurt expression on Seyel's face.

"Why did you never—?" Seyel began, but an eruption of irritated chatter cut them off as their respective students, Jaime and Teket, began arguing over the cell-sorting system.

The readout showed fewer dead cells than Adriana might have expected, alongside a large quantity of a rare inflammatory cell-surface protein. Hmm. She directed the students to start a new set of experiments and left them to their bickering.

Clearly, Adriana had been willfully ignorant and a poor example of professional behavior. She hadn't expected Seyel to simply hand over the data, especially after she nearly drove them away. Now she feared she would find herself without Seyel's unique perspectives even if they succeeded in saving Glick's life.

Adriana could admit to herself that she would miss that. Miss *them*.

She took a deep breath and returned to Seyel's side. "I apologize if I overstepped. And I'm sorry I…implied you weren't doing your job."

"Only implied?"

"Said," she admitted.

"You are being unusually straightforward today. Please continue." Seyel tilted their head in that familiar, amused way, and Adriana's heart constricted.

Too courteous, Glick's translator had said. But perhaps a more accurate translation would be *indirect*. "I think we've been misunderstanding each other for a long time. We should talk about it."

"We should," Seyel agreed. And, after a brief hesitation, said, "If you wished to collaborate, you could have begun by sharing your data with me."

Adriana stared until Seyel's ears twitched and lay back against their skull. "I did," she said slowly. "I've been giving you drives containing my team's reports and raw data every week for the last eleven months."

It was Seyel's turn to startle, and they gradually shrank back, eyes lowering, until they asked in a small voice, "Not the— Are your drives small metal disks?"

Adriana had one, in the small protective pouch attached to her belt. She fished it out and held it up for Seyel to see. She plugged it into the attachment that, yes, had been properly installed, the files coming up on screen.

Seyel stared at the data too blankly to be taking any of it in. "I—I should show you something."

Something was apparently elsewhere. They checked in with the students and gave approval to start the next experiment before departing. Adriana let Seyel lead her to their destination in silence. Seyel kept looking at her and then away without ever meeting her eyes. Adriana didn't like it.

Their destination was Seyel's room. Taking up the bulk of the space was a pool indented into the floor, designed so the water lapped at a shallow sloping ledge, padded with an algae-based fabric for a bed.

A dry space lined with open shelving stood close to the door, upon which rested the driftwood sculptures that would have been gifted to Seyel by family and mentors as they grew to adulthood. Among them was a structure that reminded Adriana of a half-built sandcastle, composed of small flat circular disks that glittered gold and bronze and silver.

It took her until Seyel gestured at the castle-in-progress, their gaze lowered and sheepish, that Adriana realized those were her data disks. "I did not know what these were. It was my understanding that individual achievement is important for humans in research, and in general."

"That's...true," she admitted. "But we also collaborate, and we tend to get better results when we do."

"I would be amenable to future collaboration if we succeed, Dr. Lim-Moreno." And yet they seemed, somehow, distinctly disappointed, still not meeting Adriana's eyes.

Adriana clasped her hands behind her back to prevent herself from reaching out to grasp them by the shoulders and beg them to look *up*. "To be clear, the shells you've been giving me aren't another form of data storage, are they?"

"They are not," Seyel said, quietly. "Please do not concern yourself further with my…cultural misunderstanding."

"And if I want to know what they meant?" The *gift* of those disks had meant something to Seyel, something they had responded to with dozens of beautiful shells, each of them unique. She stepped closer to Seyel with a dozen questions on her lips, almost daring to hope—

"Ah," Seyel said, pulling out their handheld communicator. "The analysis of Dr. Zeke's coffee is complete."

Zeke's coffee was just coffee, but it was poison, nonetheless.

Vrn tissue continued to grow and expand in culture conditions, so it was a relatively simple matter to synthesize the remaining chemicals and use their tissue models to identify the culprit.

"It much simplified the process of creating tissue models for skin and bone, though internal organs are more complex to obtain," Seyel explained. "My request for organs of the recently deceased was denied as disrespectful."

"No offers to let you perform untrained open-heart surgery?" Adriana asked.

She wasn't surprised when Seyel's response was a half joking, "Oh, several."

She *was* surprised by the warmth that flickered through her when Seyel smiled at her openly before ducking their head and returning to work.

The compound that had poisoned Representative Glick was nothing more than caffeine. The Vrn could heal rapidly from injuries that would kill a mammal instantly, but a single sip of coffee could kill.

With the experiments complete, the data showed that almost all of Representative Glick's first-responder cells had collected in his gastrointestinal system—rather than distributed through his body—impairing his natural wound-healing process.

From there, Adriana had Ximena run computational analysis to produce a series of synthetic antibodies compatible with Vrn biology and capable of binding to caffeine.

While the analysis processed, Adriana made a coffee run to the canteen where yesterday had gone so wrong. She filled a large cup with enough caffeine to kill thirty Vrn—maybe even enough to keep her awake. After a brief hesitation, she grabbed a bubble tea for Seyel.

When she returned to the lab, Seyel was removing their gloves and stretching their shoulders, seeming slightly dazed from the long period of focus. The white of their lab coat set off their storm patterns, high-lighting a set of diamonds above their right ear.

She offered them the cup, and Seyel took it hesitantly and sipped. "This is rose again."

"I figured one accidental poisoning was enough," Adriana joked.

"Perhaps for the whole week," Seyel agreed. They cradled the cup between both hands and gazed into the murky brown tea like it could divine the answers they sought.

"You like that one, right?"

"I do," Seyel said brightly. "On my home world, caffeine is produced by common seaweed and eaten raw. It is an effective stimulant, but I have never liked the texture."

"Well, I'm glad I can indulge your sweet tooth and energize you at the same time." Adriana was *not* flirting, because they were in the middle of a crisis. She couldn't be *that* out of practice.

"If we are not exchanging tokens, it isn't— You do not *need* to." Seyel rolled the cup between their hands. Nervously?

"And if I want to?"

"You—you may. Excuse me, I must—I must check on the patient."

There was nothing the stasis room monitors could tell them that wasn't already being transmitted to their lab.

Adriana stared after them, bemused.

With less than twenty-four hours remaining, they identified which of the synthetic antibodies bound best to caffeine, stopping further damage when injected into the blood vessels in the tissue cultures.

"We have a problem, however," Seyel said. "The culture still isn't repairing itself."

While Seyel had been busy testing the antibodies, Adriana had been following her own leads. "There are extremely high levels of inflammatory cells, proteins, and oxidative stress in Representative Glick's digestive tract. Vrn immune systems aren't prepared for a prolonged response, and their cells continue to respond as if to a completely new injury."

"A standard non-steroidal anti-inflammatory drug combined with that antioxidant protein you identified might be well-tolerated," Seyel said, their eyes sparkling.

Adriana had slept for perhaps three of the past however-many hours, yet she felt like a fire had been lit within her, and not just from all the coffee she'd been guzzling. *This* was what she'd wanted all for all these months. Or at least part of it.

Glick had to be taken out of stasis to receive treatment, leaving him on assisted breathing.

"At least we can't kill him harder," Adriana muttered as she prepared the injection.

Seyel giggled, then covered their mouth with their hand.

With the sound of Seyel's laughter in her ears, Adriana pushed the needle into the vein that ran down the front of Glick's neck and depressed the plunger. She held her breath in anticipation, reaching out subconsciously to take Seyel's hand.

Miracle the first: they squeezed back.

Miracle the second: the medication worked.

Almost too quickly to believe, Representative Glick's heart rate stabilized, and he began to breathe on his own, allowing Adriana to remove the tube from his mouth. He coughed, sucked in a deep breath, and opened his eyes, sharp and black as ever.

"What happened?" he asked. "Where am I?"

"It seems your people are less indestructible than previously believed," Seyel said.

"Indeed?" Representative Glick asked, his tone unreadably bland as ever.

"Our medicine saved your life," Ariana told him. "If your people want to go to the stars, it could save countless more. That is, if your beliefs don't prohibit it."

Representative Glick bowed his head as if amused. "I am not one of those who believe death is preordained. Rather, I must thank you for saving my life."

"Does that mean we pass the inspection?" Adriana asked.

"I see you are more direct. I still wish to see your progress. But yes, you have shown the value of your work. The linguists, on the other hand…" He trailed off, making a clicking noise that Adriana chose to interpret as a joke.

Representative Glick was reluctantly persuaded to rest in the treatment room overnight, and they left him speaking to the Arbiter.

Outside, Adriana gave in to the urge to hug Seyel, releasing them when Seyel stood stiff in her arms, only for them to grab her forearms before she could pull away. She grinned at them. "Drug development in less than seventy-two hours. That has to be some kind of record."

"Legend has it the great hero Yriikiirl made an elixir to cure the first plague in one day and one night," Seyel said softly, brushing their fingertips down the side of Adriana's face, not seeming to realize what they were doing. "But they cannot be said to have followed scientific methods."

"We skipped a few critical steps ourselves," Adriana murmured, lifting her hand to cover Seyel's.

They snatched their hand back as if stricken. "I apologize."

"What does this mean?" Adriana reached out to mimic the gesture, but Seyel evaded her touch.

"Nothing." They refused to meet Adriana's eyes. "Do not concern yourself. I know you did not mean it."

"You can't know that," Adriana said softly. "Because I don't."

Their lips parted as they looked up at her, eyes wide with surprise and hope. Adriana swayed toward them, magnetized despite all logic warning her that words, not action, were needed. Seyel's head tilted to the side, not reciprocating the gesture, and Adriana snapped back into herself, stopping with her nose just shy of brushing Seyel's.

"You really want to," they started to say, only for the sound of footsteps to startle them apart.

"Sorry to intrude," said Zeke, who was making a habit of intruding. "I heard Representative Glick woke up?"

"You will not be summoned to an acid duel," Seyel informed him.

"But you *may* want to do some extra preparation for your inspection," Adriana added. "Fair warning."

Adriana wandered back to her rooms, nearly asleep on her feet and yet lost in thought. The shells must have been courting gifts. The growing feelings Adriana had been ignoring were mutual. And yet, when Adriana had tried to return what she guessed was a romantic gesture, Seyel froze.

Seyel seemed to like when she was straightforward. Maybe she could find it in herself to be straightforward about her feelings, too. Experience had taught her that asking if she could kiss a date was generally an effective way of moving from conversation over coffee to—well.

Did the Madraki even kiss? She spoke the word into her dictionary and got 'the press of lips together' for a translation, which wasn't promising.

So: exchanging tokens. If Adriana meant to act on this wild, reckless feeling, a courting gift was in order. She probably wouldn't be promising herself in marriage with a single gift.

Probably.

Adriana yawned, and the world swam before her eyes.

Make that a courting gift *after* she got some sleep.

Seyel had not lost their talent for disappearing on a space station of supposedly limited size. It was nearly a week before Adriana managed to corner them. She finally managed it by waiting in their office.

"Ah," Seyel said. "Hello."

"You've been avoiding me," she accused.

Seyel didn't deny it, shifting from one foot to the other. "Once the crisis was over, I did not know how to face you. I misinterpreted your intentions."

"Are you sure about that?" Adriana dropped a string of pearls into Seyel's hands. "It's not a shell, but I hope it's acceptable."

Seyel held the pearls up to inspect their imperfect shapes and iridescent shine. "This is…?"

"I'm not sure of the steps of your courting process." Adriana had spent an irresponsible amount of time looking, but Madraki databases offered limited access to humans. "I want to find out. So this is, I hope, a token."

Seyel gasped, clutching the pearls close to their chest. "It— Yes, this is *wonderful.*" Their ears twitched, but they moved closer, standing almost between Adriana's legs. "We exchange tokens as we explore a partnership, beginning with shells and progressing to more intimate gifts as we learn each other's hearts. I should not have assumed that you knew, simply because you know more of my language than I yours." They paused before heatedly confessing, "What I have learned of human courting is utterly confounding."

"*Humans* often find human courting confounding. We have many ways of courting, but one of the most common is to go for a coffee. You could say we've done that. And after, if we like each other, we kiss."

"Kiss," Seyel repeated. Then in their own language, "This is the thing I have seen in your films, yes? Pressing mouths together. It has never been our practice. But I would not be opposed to the experiment."

Adriana drew them closer, tilting her head up to capture their lips. Seyel grasped her shoulders to steady themself, responding with inexperienced enthusiasm as she kissed them gently, until Seyel took the initiative to climb into her lap. Their momentum nearly tilted the chair over, forcing their lips apart as they regained their balance. Seyel stared down at her, dazed and a little breathless, but most importantly, smiling.

"I think it's safe to say the experiment was a success." Adriana said, more than a little smug, enjoying the weight of them on her thighs, her arms locked around their waist.

Seyel tilted their head, the mischievous grin Adriana had not seen in far too long playing across their lips as they traced Adriana's jawline with their fingertips. "We will have to repeat it to make sure."

THE LIFE CYCLE OF LEAF SPRITES

ZEL HOWLAND

Tags: california, dragon, epistolary, f/f, first person point of view, interspecies relationship, library, minor character death, modern with magic, norway, past tense, present tense, scientist, speciesism, trans woman

February 6th, 2023

This is ridiculous. If the administration is so married to their corporate sponsors and wringing every bit of silk out of these leaf sprites, they shouldn't punish me for my so-called "misuse of funding" by separating me from the flock. They aren't getting *anything* from these sprites without me to take care of them.

But sure, send your only researcher with any expertise on leaf sprites on a forced sabbatical. That makes sense.

February 7th, 2023

Fuck it.

February 8th, 2023

Yes, I know, I'm not supposed to be on campus. Sue me. I wanted to check if Brendan had actually been feeding the sprites their spectral moths, not just crickets from The Pet Company.

The parking lot is by necessity *not* within the boundaries of the Bosque de la Bendición International Enchanted Forest, where magic has it out for any technology with more moving parts than what a medieval peasant could put together. It was a toss-up whether the campus would even be *there* when I arrived—the forest has a habit of disappearing and showing up somewhere else, or straddling two places while legally not being in either.

I haven't actually violated the terms of my sabbatical. Yet.

The forest *is* here today, but only barely. The edges of it blur as it transitions in and out of some place cold, judging by the slushy snow spilling into the parking lot.

Nobody here cares, though. They're more focused on the old Spanish bell tower that has managed to survive dozens of wildfires, earthquakes, and god-knows-how-many pissed-off victims of Spanish missionaries, but is now crumbling under the weight of the giant fucking dragon clinging to it.

"Giant" might be underselling it. I'd say it's about 35 meters long from snout to tip-of-tail, roughly on par with the largest dinosaur skeletons ever discovered. I didn't think dragons *got* this big. No idea if that's my failure to remember my undergrad degree in magical zoology, or if nobody else knew that dragons could reach this size either.

I'm writing this entry from inside my car, and I can see the dragon's opalescent white scales through the trees, hear the crunch of crumbling concrete, smell the acrid brimstone of the bright-blue liquid flames dripping from its mouth.

A van just pulled in with the logo for the "Free-Lance Knight of Santa Cruz County—Magic, Monster, and Cryptid Pest Control" splashed on the side. The guys in full plate armor stepping out of it look as prepared to go up against this dragon as any small-town exterminator trying to take down Godzilla would be. (Why not normal body armor? Magic messes with *mechanisms*, not materials.) They haven't entered the forest yet—from what I can hear, there's a question of jurisdiction when the forest is straddling California and Norway.

I don't know what to do. Of all the obstacles I thought I'd hit in getting to my leaf sprite flock, a dragon taking over the Archive never crossed my mind.

I should go. The sprites will probably die, but at least I won't die with them.

February 9th, 2023

Miraculously, the sprites haven't been crushed. They are extremely stressed, and five of them have died, leaving 286 out of my original 300. All of them have returned to standard variability. If I want to continue the study on extending pre-swarm adaptations for the purposes of silk harvesting, I would need at least another week of calmer conditions for the sprites to re-enter their pre-swarm state.

I can't move them, as much as I dread having to sneak onto the Archive campus again. I got lucky today, since the dragon seemed pretty occupied with its Free-Lance Knight barbecue and my colleagues were all preoccupied with running away from certain death, so nobody noticed the idiot in hot-pink platform heels ducking through the side door. The sprites are dependent on the magic of their home forest to survive, and there's no way I can look after them loose in the forest.

I could let the sprites go. I'm already in hot water with the dean. It can't get much worse than it already is. But who knows when another flock will be spotted, let alone caught and kept alive for study? This is the first time scientific observation has been made of leaf sprites. In the wild, sprites are so adept at camouflage and shy of other creatures that making observations of a single leaf sprite is nearly impossible, let alone an entire flock of them.

I don't have the fresh foliage they need for their nests or any spectral moths to feed them. I'll just have to keep coming back. I'll let the sprites out of their individual enclosures and give them free reign of my office so they can return to a stable condition more easily.

Yeah. I'm gonna die.

February 11th, 2023

The sprites are rebounding from their neglect surprisingly quickly. They're still pickier than usual about their nesting foliage and sites, a possible stress response, but they're at least building nests. They've also resumed occasional bonding songs—the flock is improving.

I'm glad they've started singing again, I really am. But god almighty do I wish they hadn't started the exact moment I opened my office door to leave for the day, right when the dragon was shouldering its way through the now-open-air hallway. The bonding songs, while beautiful in a "haunted house" way, are apparently pitched at exactly the right frequency to be heard over the crunching of concrete walls and ceilings. The dragon swung its head around at the sound, and I swear it actually *made eye contact* with me.

Eye contact. Hah. Just *one* of the dragon's eyes is bigger than my entire head.

I bolted, obviously. I don't know how I'm still alive. Even *my* adrenal system, usually stuck firmly on "fight," wimped out in the face of a goddamn dragon. But it's not like I can outrun dragonfire, especially not in this dress, and this dragon hasn't been shy about spitting flames. The only reason the entire woods aren't a smoldering ruin is because there's enough ambient magic here to smother a volcano—and even that wasn't enough to keep those knights from turning into charcoal briquettes.

So why haven't I?

February 12th, 2023

Somehow, I'm still not dead, and the leaf sprites are doing better than ever. I've never been so confused in my life.

The dragon definitely knows I've been coming and going, and has definitely spared my life.

Today when I arrived, I tried to sneak in like I've been doing, only to find that the dragon was perched in the multi-story foyer, right on the balcony for my floor. To get to my office, I had to walk directly in front of it, fully in its field of vision the entire time I picked through the maze of rubble.

I couldn't help but hesitate at the intersection of the balcony and the partially destroyed hallway, where I would have to turn my back on the dragon to get to my office. We looked at each other for a long, long time. Me, clutching a Safeway bag full of fresh leaves and a Tupperware full of live moths, sweating through my makeup; and the dragon, huge, ancient, and inscrutable, with the remnants of liquid fire oozing out between its massive fangs.

That's when the sprites started singing, probably hearing me approach and getting impatient for their breakfast. The dragon looked behind me down the hall, and then, unbelievably, opened its mouth and *sang in response.*

Barely anyone in all of human history has even heard a dragon *speak* and lived to tell the tale. Nobody has ever reported a dragon *singing.*

Sprite songs are high-pitched and tuneful, like a parrot imitating the sound of a theremin. The dragon song had something of the same tenor and tune, but it was so deep and resonant I could feel it vibrating in my chest cavity and in the broken concrete around me. Even the ambient magic of the forest hummed like a plucked piano wire.

It was the most beautiful sound I've ever heard.

The music continued for a long time after I walked into my office.

February 15th, 2023

There's always been speculation about some common ancestor between dragons and silk drakes, given the similarities in their appearances and the overlap in their observed habitats. There has never been any such discussion about dragons and leaf sprites—why would there be? It would be like wondering if ants and elephants are in the same genus. Once it was discovered that silk drakes weren't individual creatures but rather the magically swarmed form of leaf sprite flocks, the speculation died.

Now I'm wondering if we should bring it back. The leaf sprites and the dragon have continued singing to each other intermittently, and the flock has been rebounding far more rapidly since they started. The sprites are not quite in pre-swarm, but it's not impossible they'll transition to pre-swarm within the next few days. I've previously noted—as supported by observations from Lopez et. al.—that the sprites' bonding songs play an influential role in their physical health; now I believe that the dragon singing to them has had an exponentially beneficial effect on the health of the individuals and the flock as a whole.

I wish I could just *ask* the dragon what it knows about leaf sprites, without getting spit-roasted in the process.

February 20th, 2023

It's…nice. Knowing that another person cares about these leaf sprites' well-being, and not just how to monetize them. Even if that other person is a dragon. With a…different understanding of contracts and fiduciary responsibility.

Lately, I've been struggling to get the sprites their preferred fresh-caught moths from the forest. The magic on the nets wears off within a few uses, and without the magic, spectral moths can phase in and out of the trap without getting stuck. Normally I stockpile the nets in my car, but I haven't been able to afford more since my sabbatical started.

The minute the sprites saw me holding a bag of gross crickets instead of their favorite meal, they stopped singing and started flying around the office in agitation, chirping their disapproval.

To my horror, the dragon's head then poked into my office.

"Why did they stop?" the dragon asked.

I might have squeaked. Or maybe I screamed. Something to that effect.

The dragon lowered its head and softened its voice to a mere rumble through the floor. "They're unhappy about something," it said.

Numbly, I held up my inadequate meal service.

"Crickets," I said, like an idiot.

The dragon looked at the pathetic, smelly bag, then snorted. A wave of hot smoke blew over me and settled on my office ceiling. I held in the hacking cough that tried to escape my throat.

"They prefer the moths," the dragon told me. "Why change to crickets?"

"The nets," I said hoarsely. "For the moths."

"Nets?"

"They're expensive."

The dragon snorted again. Some emotion played across its face, but I couldn't say what it was.

"I see," the dragon said.

It lowered its head farther so that it could fit more of its crest and horns through the door to look around the space. I can't guess at what it thought—a tiny office made even tinier by the giant, opened terrarium, the rows of much smaller individual terrariums, and the plethora of sprite nests on every available surface in defiance of their intended enclosures.

"This space is too small for them," the dragon declared. Its eyes focused on the terrarium. "Do you enclose them in there?"

"Only for feeding," I said hastily, finally catching a thread of disapproval in the dragon's tone. "I'm not supposed to let them out of the terrarium at all—well, I'm supposed to be keeping them in individual terrariums so I can study if their pre-swarm state can be maintained over long periods of isolation, to make silk harvesting easier. But while they're recovering from…uh, stress…it didn't feel right to separate them, so I've let them socialize normally for now. I've hypothesized that their singing resonated with ambient magic in the air to actually kickstart their swarming abilities, so if they aren't singing to each other then— Um. Yes. The space is too small for them."

One gargantuan blue eye stared straight into my soul as I rambled. When I mentioned separating the sprites, the eye flicked over to the small, lonely glass containers.

"Come," the dragon said, withdrawing its head from my office. I think it might have been addressing the sprites, because they all took off and fluttered around the dragon's head. But I couldn't not obey a magical apex predator that had already grievously wounded at least a dozen knights.

I'm glad I did, because as soon as the last sprite cleared the door, the dragon reached through the doorway with its talons and gently knocked a wall down.

I backed away in a cloud of panicking leaf sprites as the dragon meticulously destroyed the wall separating my office from Brendan's, and the one on the other side that cut me off from Dr. Nguyen's lab. As terrifying as it was, the dragon's dexterity and eye for structural detail bowled me over. It made sure the doors and walls bordering the hallway were untouched and left in a load-bearing support beam, but the rest of the walls were cleanly removed. The rubble was scooped out of the office and unceremoniously tossed into the foyer by the dragon's tail—the terrariums along with the drywall and concrete.

The dragon stuck its head through the door once more to examine its handiwork—clawwork?—then sat back with what I assume to be a satisfied expression. It whistled at the leaf sprites, communicating *something* to them. Their distress forgotten, the sprites immediately flew into their new digs, chirping and singing in delight.

"They will need plants to fill the space," the dragon told me. "Perhaps those structures used by your domesticated felines."

"Cat trees?" I said, barely managing to produce words instead of more open-mouthed staring.

"I have seen pictures. They will be good for nesting."

"Well, it's just…I don't even have enough money to get them moths. Cat trees are—"

The dragon turned away before I finished my sentence, its tail twitching. I swallowed my words and ducked into my newly expanded office.

I'm glad the sprites are happy with their new space, and that the dragon seems to genuinely care about their well-being. I'm also terrified the dragon thinks I'm an idiot.

February 20th, 2023 (con't)

I thought that was the end of things with the dragon, but just now as I was leaving for the day, I nearly tripped over an antique golden goblet sitting in front of my office door. When I picked it up, there were clear scratches on the surface from a dragon claw. Given where it was, and the conversation from earlier…I have to assume it was a gift from the dragon.

I can't believe that a dragon just…*gave* me a piece of its hoard. I could have sworn that dragons were magically bonded with their hoard and couldn't part from it. I almost don't want to part with it myself, it feels so significant. Then again, the sprites need their moths, and I need more nets.

February 22nd, 2023

The expansion of the sprites' habitat has had an enormous impact on them. As of this morning, all of them have entered the pre-swarm stage, characterized by the beginnings of silk production at the tips of their claws and tails and the addition of special aerial dances to their bonding songs. With the individual enclosures destroyed and not enough money to buy more even after pawning the goblet, I won't be able to sequester the sprites as planned. Oh well! My investors will be angry at me, but what can they do? I'm already on involuntary sabbatical, and there's a temperamental dragon between me and them.

February 23rd, 2023

The leaf sprites will almost certainly begin a swarming dance within the next few hours. I have moved into the Archive for the time being so that I can be present for it. The dragon claims that swarming dances can be of varying lengths depending on the size of the flock and their conditions, which is supported by the handful of accounts from those who've seen the dance in the wild.

February 23rd, 2023 (con't)

The sprites have swarmed! The resulting silk drake is smaller than most specimens that have been recorded, about 60 centimeters from snout to tail, which I'm guessing is due to the limited size of the leaf sprite flock that formed it. Its coloring is a mottled blue, almost the same shade as the dragon's eyes. I wonder if that was intentional, since none of the sprites were that color on their own.

Based on the preponderance of silk that the drake is producing, I believe it is male. If it begins creating nests, then I'll know for sure.

The swarming dance was beautiful, though short. The dragon seemed to know when it was about to happen—based on the songs, maybe?—and pushed its head through the door to watch with me. Neither of us spoke, but when the newly formed silk drake raised its head, the dragon rumbled in a sound that reminded me of a cat's purr.

March 1st, 2023

Now that I'm living in the Archive, I'm having a hard time restraining myself from following the dragon around to take notes. The silk drake and the dragon are so similar that there *has* to be a connection. The drake looks *just like* a miniature dragon, except for the fluttering, papery texture of its pseudo-scales compared to the pebbled true scales on the dragon. Even their mannerisms are similar, and I'm getting better at reading both of their expressions and body language.

I haven't been following the dragon around. That would be stupid. Most *humans* would be angry if I did that to them, and they can't kill me with a sneeze. If I've taken the silk drake on maybe a few extra strolls around the Archive, I don't think the dragon can fault me for *that*.

Unexpectedly, the dragon seems to be interested in the books and research materials available in the library. I don't know if it's looking for something specific or just browsing; but I suspect the dragon's distemper has less to do with the humans jousting at it and more to do with being a massive creature trying to use human-sized facilities.

Now that I think about it, it *is* a little ridiculous that we have this library ostensibly open to the public located within an enchanted forest, but absolutely zero accommodations for magical creatures who might want to use it.

I wonder if I can help.

March 2nd, 2023

I cobbled together a dragon-sized magnifying glass out of materials left behind by my colleagues and with the plethora of silk my drake has been producing. It looks like garbage, but I'm pretty sure it's sturdy enough for the dragon to use, and I *think* it's functional.

I left it in a spot I've noticed the dragon favors for its afternoon naps, and just now I spotted the dragon bringing the glass into the library. Fingers crossed!

March 3rd, 2023

Allowing the leaf sprites to swarm into a silk drake has given me so much more insight into these incredible creatures than I would have guessed. Snorfle (yes, I named the drake, I couldn't help it) is extremely affectionate with both me and the dragon, in a way that flies in the face of the general wisdom that silk drakes are too temperamental to domesticate. Given how intelligent Snorfle is, I wonder if the difficulty in monetizing his species is because silk drakes refuse to be taken advantage of. I can't help but admire that.

March 6th, 2023

I saw the dragon fly today. I've never seen anything so beautiful. Its wingspan is staggeringly large, and when it flies in front of the sun, you can see the tapestry of its iridescent veins branching along the webbing, casting rainbow shadows on everything beneath it.

Snorfle has taken to searching out the dragon on our walks, and he seemed especially driven this morning. When we entered the library, I could see why: the dragon's size was working against it again. Half the stacks on this level had been knocked down like dominoes. The dragon was whirling around in anger and frustration, flames frothing at the corners of its mouth. It took off before the fire could touch the books and furniture, crashing through the ruined roof to wheel overhead and roar in frustration.

Snorfle whined and whistled in distress. I may have my problems with the Archive administration, but I still know how amazing a resource this library is, enough to feel uncomfortable with this much destruction. I started gathering the hundreds of books that had fallen to the ground, to at least get them in some semblance of order.

I was contemplating whether I would be able to lift a bookcase into place on my own when the dragon returned. I felt the heat and heavy weight of it landing behind me; I did my best to keep working and not acknowledge its presence. I doubted it wanted a human gawking at it when it was already having a bad day.

The dragon snorted, then made the rumbling noises at Snorfle that meant it was speaking with him. I let them finish their conversation— is it a conversation? Can Snorfle meaningfully communicate with the dragon, in a way that he can't with me?—before I said, as casually as I could, "Which book were you looking for?"

The dragon fell silent.

It was a gamble, based entirely on my ability to read the body language of a dragon, which was in turn based on my harebrained theory that silk drakes and dragons were similar. But if Snorfle had tilted his head downward like that, shuffled his feet, and huffed as much as the dragon had been doing—then I would know that he was being shy, reserved, and frustrated.

"I don't know yet," the dragon said finally, its voice shockingly quiet. "I've been trying to browse, but it's hard to manage the paper."

I finally looked at it. The dragon had lowered its head so that we were more or less eye to eye, and the tip of its tail still twitched with leftover irritation.

"Is there a particular topic you're interested in?" I asked.

"I've... wanted to learn about modern technology," it said. God, have all its interactions with humans been at the point of a lance? "My knowledge is out of date. I had no idea humans had built flying machines until I nearly crashed into one."

"Oh, airplanes?"

"How do they stay in the air without flapping?" the dragon asked. "Even eagles move their wings sometimes."

I bent down to dig through the books I'd been sorting. The dragon had been in the right section, at least. "It has to do with the shape of the wing, I think," I told it as I searched. "I'm not an expert, though. Ah, here!" I held up my prize, a hefty book definitely not current with the latest in aircraft advances, but at least published within the past two decades. "Maybe this will answer your questions?"

The dragon held out its front—hand? paw? limb?—to take the book, but it looked so absurdly small next to it, I couldn't bring myself to hand it over. Instead, I dragged a chair out from a nearby table, sat down, and said, "Get comfortable, and tell me if you get bored."

My voice is sore from reading out loud for several hours. It was worth it, though, to hear a dragon purring in contentment.

March 11th, 2023

I have the beginnings of a theory. I don't even want to write it down. But the more time I spend with the dragon, the more I think there is some connection between dragons and silk drakes.

March 19th, 2023

The dragon's name is Hrafnhildr. She finally told me today, and from the weight in her tone, I gather that the exchanging of names is more significant in her (draconic) culture than it is in my own. I kind of understand. It's been eight years since I fully transitioned, and I still feel a thrill when I introduce myself as Jadzia. I wonder if dragons also choose their own names.

We've been reading together every day, and when my voice gets too tired, Hrafnhildr takes over with stories from her centuries of life. I don't think she's had anyone to talk to for a long, long time, and now that she's started, she doesn't want to stop. Not that I'm complaining. I've never met anyone as intelligent, insightful, and thoughtful as Hrafnhildr.

I finally asked her today what brought her to the Archive. She hesitated before answering, but I'm learning that she never responds to direct questions right away; she takes the time to think over every angle of her answer before she speaks.

She told me that she'd grown bored of hoarding gold and treasures, and she'd become interested in different forms of wealth after interacting with some humans who had ties to a museum. "Knowledge," she told me, "is a far more elusive and valuable treasure than any gemstone or precious metal. When I was young, it was nearly impossible to collect without being attacked. But you humans have been so industrious these past few hundred years, with your printing presses and your gramophones, that I've finally been able to add my real interests to my hoard. Though the attacking is still a problem," she added, nodding at a singed sword a knight had dropped on his narrow escape.

I took that as confirmation of my earlier impression. All of her interactions with humans until now have been fraught, if not outright violent.

Another thing we have in common.

March 30th, 2023

Things have been going so, so well, and I'm worried. The forest never stays in one place for long, let alone straddling two places at once like it has been. Once it fully makes the shift to one location, there won't be any more jurisdictional issues keeping the Archive administration from summoning a fucking army to get rid of Hrafnhildr. If we end up in Norway it's bad enough, but if the forest fully shifts to the US, we're screwed. The magic of the forest messes with technology more complicated than a bow and arrow, but the Archive is at the very edge of that boundary. A bullet flying faster than the speed of sound isn't technology, it's physics.

Hrafnhildr seems resigned, but I'm not ready for this to end.

March 31st, 2023

Snorfle has covered the entire Archive in silk, but without any female visitors to his nest, he's begun exhibiting some unexpected behavior. He is hunting more food than he needs and wrapping the extra in silk to stow inside the nest. More strangely, he has been doing the same to small objects that he takes a fancy to, like a crow collecting shiny things. He already has a decent-sized collection of buttons from my cardigans, pieces of foil, and torn pages from an illustrated book. He is extremely protective of his trinkets and won't allow me nor the dragon to get near them.

I've also noticed that he curates this collection carefully, and places more importance on the overall composition of the collection than on the individual pieces. One day he'll be very invested in a particular button or hair tie, displaying it in a place of honor. But the next day, if he finds two candy wrappers that he likes better, he'll switch the previously treasured item to the back of the collection or throw it out altogether. He no longer guards the items he's thrown away, and shows no interest in them even if I present them to him later on.

The food I can understand as preparation for leaner times, or perhaps some kind of hibernation, but the trinkets are baffling to me.

I am glad, though, that he's got this stash. It means he'll be able to survive even after I'm fired and the administration tosses him back into the forest.

April 3rd, 2023
The forest fully shifted to Santa Cruz.
Fuck.

April 3rd, 2023 (con't)
Snorfle doesn't like the sound of helicopters, and frankly neither do I. I guess the administration was ready for the forest shift. The helicopters have been hovering for an hour now, and I've glimpsed what look like actual tanks in the parking lot.

I told Hrafnhildr that the writing was on the wall.

She just looked at me.

"You've been shot at before, right?" I asked. "Cannons in castles, that kind of thing? This is much worse."

"I can fight worse," she said. Her voice was low and quiet and sad.

"You won't have a *chance* to fight back," I told her. "We have to get out of here while we still can. You, me, and Snorfle. We can go deeper into the forest. There are places we can hide where they'll never find us."

Hrafnhildr shook her crest in a chuckle. "You, in the forest? No, my friend, you should go back to your home. Snorfle will find his way to safety in the forest, and I will take care of myself."

She didn't give me a chance to respond, just flew away. She's sitting in

the library now, using the magnifying glass to read a book. As if nothing's the matter.

If I were smarter, I'd do what she said. But I can't bear to leave her alone.

I want to help, but what the hell can I do?

April 3rd, 2023 (con't)

Apparently, I can do a hell of a lot.

I feel like a goddamn action hero. I am *awesome*. If anyone is out there negotiating world peace, let me know. I'll fucking nail it.

It didn't start out that great, of course. I managed to catch up to Hrafnhildr in the library and tried to persuade her again.

"You have *wings*, Hraf! Just fly away!"

Her tail lashed like an angry cat's. "I cannot," she said. For the first time since I'd heard her speak, she put all her booming, awe-inspiring force into her voice. "I have made these Archives my hoard, and I cannot abandon it."

"It's just *things*, just a place! Please, Hrafnhildr."

"A dragon's hoard isn't only a collection of things or a place," she said. "It's part of me. Haven't you noticed that I don't need to eat as you do? I am a magical creature, sustained by magic, and that magic is produced by my hoard. If I had understood the rules of human hoards and ownership before I came here, I would not have made the transfer from treasure to knowledge, but now that it has happened, I cannot so quickly undo it."

She lowered her head to the ground so she had to tilt her eyes upward to look at me. The deep resonance left her voice, leaving her usual gentle tone. "I cannot leave, but Jadzia, *you* do not have to stay here. You should go back to your own kind and be safe."

"I'm not leaving you," I said. "You need a friend on your side."

Hrafnhildr looked genuinely touched. She pushed her head forward so that her snout butted against my elbow, and I bent down to hug her. For a moment, the only sound was her maelstrom breath and the incessant drone of the helicopters overhead. But eventually, she drew back up to her full height.

"At least get Snorfle out of here," she commanded. "His hoard is still small enough to take with you. Get him to safety."

"But you—"

Then that word hit me.

Hoard.

Hoard. Snorfle had a *hoard*.

Suddenly my baseless suspicions had a whole lot more bases. I'd practically scored a home run.

"Hrafnhildr," I said slowly. "Question for you. By any chance…are dragons actually just mature silk drakes?"

The dragon stared at me. For a long time, she said nothing, and I went through all five stages of grief about my newly vocalized hypothesis. Surely she would have said something if she'd begun her life as a swarm of leaf sprites. Surely someone in the long history of human-dragon interactions would have proposed this. That they hadn't meant it wasn't true, and I was an idiot for thinking it. I was a terrible scientist—

"Yes," Hrafnhildr said finally.

I screamed.

I was right—*I was right*—I had so many questions, and thoughts, and theories, and I hardly knew where to start. There were archers lining up outside and an army sitting just beyond the tree line and I couldn't care less. *Dragons and silk drakes were the same species!* I jumped up to hug Hrafnhildr's snout again and impulsively planted a kiss on her cheek. I have no idea if kisses mean the same things to dragons as they do to humans, but she looked as bashful as I felt when I finally pulled away and caught my breath.

"It's some kind of hibernation, right?" I gushed. "That's what the hoard is for, to tide you over through—"

"We don't like to discuss it," Hrafnhildr said sharply. Smoke spilled from her nose and mouth. "It's…impolite. Besides, is this really the time?"

"Right, sorry," I said. "I just have one question, then, sorry that it's rude—but I swear, it's relevant."

She hesitated longer than usual, but nodded.

I thought about Snorfle's carefully curated collection—his hoard!—and of the behaviors I had catalogued all this time. "When you took the Archive into your hoard," I said, "did you discard your gold and treasures from it?"

She looked at me curiously. "I would not have been able to come here otherwise," she said.

I grinned. "Then I know what to do."

Running full-tilt through an enchanted forest in platform heels, with a dragon at my back and a hundred-odd soldiers aiming bows and guns in my direction, was the most terrifying thing I've ever done. But I didn't care. I was right, I was *fucking right*, and even if I died, I would die with the satisfaction of knowing that my life's work had culminated in this moment.

I didn't get shot, obviously. Not surprising, since the black-ops guys were aiming at the very large dragon, and not at some woman clearly running away from the dragon. More challenging was getting them to focus on me, put their horrible weapons down, and listen instead of shooting the best friend I'd ever had.

They did listen, in the end. The possibility of vast amounts of treasure will catch anyone's attention, I guess.

I've spent the last four hours negotiating with the dean and a few of my colleagues who were brave enough to show up. It was annoyingly difficult to force them to understand, but I think we've finally come to an agreement that will benefit everyone.

A dragon doesn't value bits of their hoard that they had released, but humans still find centuries worth of treasure completely irresistible.

June 14th, 2024

The expanded Archive campus looks amazing. My lab space is huge now, and worth the extra wait while the construction crews adapted the space for a dragon to use. Now that it's finished, I finally get to work on my next project: studying silk drake and dragon physiology to further our understanding of arcanazoologic medicine.

I don't foresee a lot of investors taking interest in this project. But it's fine. Who needs grants when your research partner is an ancient dragon with a former hoard she's just giving away?

QUEENRIGHT

LEE PINI

Tags: bipoc, commoner/royalty, first kiss, fluff, has a disability, library, m/m, military, mistaken identity, past tense, romance, royalty, science fiction, smoking (casual), third person limited point of view

M arcus hadn't needed a cigarette this badly in weeks.

No—it wasn't a need; he'd kicked the addiction months ago, but nerves were making him want to do something with his big hands while he waited for the garrison commander to arrive and clear him for his new posting.

It was nothing to be nervous about. It wasn't like he was being assigned to the first in line to the throne. To keep his hand from creeping toward the pocket where he kept his emergency cigarettes, he clasped his hands behind his back. It was just library duty. So what if the youngest prince spent the majority of his time in the palace library? So what if library duty was more akin to being the personal guard to Vespasian Quintus Appius?

The crunch of gravel under boot heels made him straighten his spine. The unit commander, Hesperus, rounded the corner of the building and raised an eyebrow. "Bright and early, huh, newbie?"

"Still learning my way around, sir. I didn't want to be late for this morning's shift." That was an understatement. Marcus had never realized how huge the royal palace was. Not just huge: grand, ornate in parts, and cleanly, expensively simple in others. History weighed heavily on the palace, and it felt by turns oppressive and exciting.

The house he grew up in back home had always seemed special because the foundations were 500 years old, and the palace had entire wings that were older than that. That kind of history made a thrill thrum deep in his chest.

As he followed Hesperus into her office, she said, "You must not have come through South Gate. We'd be waiting on you for hours."

Marcus made a mental note to pull up a map of the city on his personal holo when he had a free minute. "Is something going on there?"

Hesperus didn't bother sitting at her desk before she conduited into the palace holo. The office was downright cramped, with equipment and hard copies of paperwork everywhere. Or maybe it only felt cramped because of Marcus's tall and wide build. Hesperus didn't seem to mind it as she flipped through holo screens and said, "Bees. Bees are happening."

"Bees, sir?"

"Bees," Hesperus agreed. "As in buzz-buzz honey-making bees. I've had so many concerned citizens reporting them, you'd think the city was about to be invaded. Now! Your orders."

The subject change came too fast for Marcus to offer to help with the bees. Tending the hives had been his job on his parents' farm since he was 12 years old, so he felt pretty qualified to give advice. He'd been recommended for the palace unit because he was a good guard, but he was probably a better beekeeper.

Minute, rapid flicks of her eyes made it clear that Hesperus was pulling up his orders from the palace holo. After a second, they appeared in front of Marcus's eyes. Library posting—as expected—with special attention given to the safety of Prince Vespasian.

"Everyone calls him Ves," Hesperus said, interrupting his perusal of the orders. "That's not in there. He hates the name Vespasian. Thinks it makes him sound like a senile colonialist who stopped being relevant 60 years ago."

Marcus bit back a smile as he put his digital signature to the orders to accept them. Last night, he'd tried to find pictures of Vespasian. Ves. The most recent was from last year, with Ves obviously trying to sidle into the background to avoid the camera's attention. The photo gave the impression of a slight, bookish young man, which was exactly the way every media channel portrayed him.

Once he was dismissed for duty, Marcus projected a path toward the library wing with his holo and made his way. He managed not to take any wrong turns, but there were a few close calls where he had to study the map for a minute to determine why it was suggesting three circuitous routes when there was one that went straight to his destination. It became quickly clear to Marcus the architects had taken the aphorism "It's about the journey, not the destination" to heart.

The overnight guard nodded as Marcus arrived to relieve her. "No badge yet?" she asked, touching her own where it was pinned to her collar.

The palace security badges were sleek, quicksilver-bright darts that Marcus had coveted for most of his life—and certainly since he'd gone into the security corps. With a regretful shrug, he replied, "Delayed in transit."

"Oh, yours is in that shipment?" She gave him a cheerful thump on the shoulder. "Hopefully the bees don't hold it up much longer!"

He almost laughed at the stir the bees were causing. As they walked in opposite directions, she the way Marcus had come and Marcus down the hall toward the library, an explosive sneeze echoed down the stone and carbon-fiber corridor.

"Bless you," Marcus said without thinking, only realizing as the words left his mouth that he'd arrived in the open door to the library, and there was a young man sitting at a table who bore a striking resemblance to the youngest prince.

Those brain cells that had gotten him transferred to a prestigious posting at 26 years old kicked in. The young man sitting at the table *was* the youngest prince. A shaft of light illuminated blond hair in need of a trim, skin a shade of lighter brown than the rest of his family, and clothes so rumpled that he might have slept in them. A haze of dust, likely from the ancient book laid open before him, was settling on his clothes and hair. Marcus hadn't expected the sharp, pristine line of his jaw or the way his shoulders filled out his shirt. Or maybe Ves had done some work to cultivate the intriguing breadth there.

Marcus pinched his leg through his pants to remind himself that ogling the prince wasn't included in his job description.

Ves's hand was halfway to his mouth, his eyes round. Stepping into the library, Marcus said, "Nice to meet you, Your Highness. I'm Marcus."

Ves shot to his feet. A bright grin split his face. "Marcus! I didn't think you'd be here so early! Wow, okay! Um—stars, I had a whole thing, but that was before I found this book and this is so much more interesting—oh! And the 'Highness' stuff—you don't have to do that. Ves is fine. Everyone calls me Ves. *Please* call me Ves."

While he barreled on, Ves crossed from the table to the doorway, hand extended. Marcus shook it, which was the kind of protocol you got in a constitutional monarchy that didn't take itself too seriously.

Ves's grip was warm and firm, and his handshake was enthusiastic. Marcus hadn't expected Ves to know he was coming. That was... flattering. Marcus also hadn't expected to be flattered.

Up close, Ves's eyes were gray, the same color as the fog that sat over the fields on the farm on cool autumn mornings. There were two freckles under his left eye. Light from the high transom windows caught the edges of his eyelashes and turned them gold.

Marcus made himself stop noticing all of it.

"No 'Your Highness'-ing," Marcus repeated. "I can do that."

Their hands were still clasped, so Marcus let go. Ves took a step back and rocked on his heels. "I'm so happy you're here; you have no idea. This is the most exciting thing to happen to me all *year*." He paused and his eyes went wide again. "That's too much, isn't it? You can tell me I'm too much. Everyone does."

He said it too cheerfully for it to register as sort of sad, at least until Marcus thought about it for another few seconds. "Of course you're not too much."

To Ves's other point, had Marcus heard him right? A new guard was the most exciting thing to happen to him all year? That couldn't be right.

"I won't get offended if you change your mind. How was your flight?"

"Oh, I didn't fly in."

With a puzzled frown, Ves said, "I guess the drive from Adastra Spaceport lets you see some of the country," which almost made Marcus frown in confusion, too. Why would Ves think he'd use the spaceport? If he *had* flown in, he'd have gotten a shuttle to the local airport because it was the oldest continuously functioning airport on the planet.

Before Marcus could figure out a way to politely voice his confusion, the prince touched his forearm. "I hope you don't mind me changing our plans, but I think I might have found an adventure for us. Er." He looked chagrined. "If you're up for an adventure, that is?"

For some reason, what came out of Marcus's mouth was "Yes?" instead of "Wait, have you somehow mistaken me for someone else?"

The luminosity of Ves's smile made him not regret it—that was the worst part. Was he possibly the most terrible guard ever? How had he gotten this job if all it took to distract him was golden hair, gray eyes, and a sunshine smile?

Ves flushed. "Sorry, can I say something? I'm just—you don't look the way I thought you would. I thought you'd be…older? Yeah, definitely older."

"I'm 26," Marcus said.

The flush on Ves's face deepened. "I wouldn't have guessed. You seem so much…you know what? It's not important! Here, come look at this amazing thing I found this morning. Your expertise is definitely going to help. Maybe you'll even be able to write a paper about it, if it's important enough!"

If this had been anyone but the prince, Marcus would have laughed and stopped them. His expertise? Write a paper? Unless it was about beekeeping methods, he wasn't qualified to write a paper about anything. Did Ves really think security was a scholarly profession?

While he mulled over that, he followed Ves to the table covered in books, most in some state of decay One small folio was surrounded by red leather detritus that had flaked off the binding. Others were blotched with age or water or mold. Another looked like it had done time as a chew toy in the royal zooarium.

Ves moved all of those aside and opened a thick clothbound book. The title flashed in metallic black on the cover: *Twenty Centuries of Masonry in the Royal Palace of Verulam.*

The two of them were close enough for Marcus to smell Ves: citrus and resin and beeswax, and a hint of something that reminded Marcus of rain swam around the prince. The top of Ves's head and that tousled golden hair were level with Marcus's nose.

"Here it is. Look!" Ves pointed to a black-and-white photo on a page from the back half of the book. The picture showed an undercroft, the walls composed of tightly joined stone blocks.

"See how there's an inscription?" Ves asked eagerly.

Marcus squinted. "It's too small for me to read."

"Me too, so I fiddled with it on my holo—here." A magnified version of the carved message flickered up between them.

The inscription was written in a simple but archaic script. "'Do not open until the queen returns,'" Marcus read. "What does that mean?"

"No idea!" Ves said happily. "But I want to try to find out! I bet we can track down that room and open whatever secret door is in there."

"How do you know there's a secret door?"

"Well, there has to be, right? I mean, who goes to the trouble of inscribing this on a wall if there's *not* a secret door?" There was an excited sparkle in Ves's eyes as he closed the holo projection. "I haven't had any time to think about what might be hiding behind it."

Marcus scanned a few lines from the book. "It says this style of masonry is over 600 years old. Are there any parts of the palace that have been around that long?"

Ves's face fell, but he brightened again just as quickly. "I'm pretty sure there was a huge renovation about 600 years ago, so there's a pretty good chance all of those parts of the palace are still around." He splayed his hand on the table to prop himself up, and his pinkie finger brushed Marcus's. "And I think it was a queen that started the renovation. Did she die before it was finished…?"

"Maybe that's the reason for the inscription." Marcus fingered the corner of the book. "Maybe there was something important she was having built, but she died before it was finished."

With a gasp, Ves rocked back to look at Marcus. His enthusiasm and excitement were so charming. "You're right. I bet that's it."

"What do you think it is?"

"Hm." Ves drummed his fingers on the table. "Maybe the answer to a historical mystery. Like the Heir's Disappearance—that was around the same time."

"Wasn't that more like 800 years ago?" Marcus said.

"Yeah, I think you're right. And I guess I don't know why the queen returning would be the right time to reveal that."

"So, wait"—Marcus turned to face Ves, an elbow on the table—"do you think it's a queen who's returning or the queen? Is this a ghost thing?"

"Do you believe in ghosts?"

"My house is haunted." After Marcus's first boyfriend had laughed at him for saying he'd seen a ghost of an old woman with a pet forest cat who sat in the rocking chair on the porch on sunny winter days, he didn't make a habit of telling people. Unless their name was Ves, it seemed.

Delighted, Ves said, "No. Haunted, really? You're not messing with me?"

So Marcus told him, and that conversation led to another, then another, and the next time Marcus checked the time, his shift was nearly over. Would it look bad if he were to be found sprawled on his stomach on a dusty rug in the library, paging through an old book with Ves at his side?

He sat up, and Ves followed suit, a stripe of gray dust swept across his forehead. Marcus had to look away from him before he did something stupid like rub it away with his thumb. "Should we start looking?" Ves asked.

Marcus hesitated. Could he convince Hesperus that since his job was basically to watch Ves, he should do so outside the library, too?

He hedged. "It's my first day here, so I need to—"

"I'm so sorry." Ves looked guilty. "I'm going on and on, and you just got here. I do that; I get going and…" He made a sailing motion with his hand before his eyes drifted to the windows, which were dark with the oncoming night. "I monopolized your whole day."

"Don't be sorry." Marcus almost took his hand because he looked so dejected. "This was great. I couldn't have asked for a better welcome."

Ves touched Marcus's hand. Marcus tried not to let the explosion of butterflies in his stomach show on his face. "Thank you so much for coming. People don't usually make a special trip to see me from the other side of the city, let alone the other side of the galactic sector."

Wait. What did he mean, people didn't come from the other side of the galactic sector to see him? Before Marcus could ask, Ves's skin darkened with a flush, and he hurried away. The spot where he'd touched Marcus thrummed.

Marcus found Hesperus still at her desk, holo screens full of numbers and text wrapped around her like amber forcefields. When he explained the situation, she seemed relieved that he *wanted* to act as Ves's personal guard. "Most people think he's too much," she explained. "It's good he took to you, though. He must have been disappointed that professor of his had his trip delayed."

"He didn't mention anything about a professor."

With a fond eye roll, Hesperus said, "Found something more interesting than checking his messages, I imagine. You'll hear about it tomorrow. Everyone who's spent any time with Ves over the last six months knows all about Professor Marcus Vytina. We think he has a crush."

Several things clicked into place. "Ves was expecting someone today named Marcus?"

"We adjusted all his clearances for his new arrival date next week. Don't worry; I'll give you all the info once you need it." Hesperus flicked her fingers. "Go on. Get some dinner, and get some sleep. Sounds like you'll be tramping all over the palace tomorrow."

It was a clear dismissal, so Marcus did as he was told. On his walk back through the city toward his rented apartment, he stopped for a kebab at a food stall and let the motherly woman running it talk him into sesame cakes for dessert. The two teenagers stationed at the grill were talking about the bee swarm, which had moved deeper into the city instead of out to the surrounding countryside.

The sesame cakes were worth being talked into and distracted him from feeling like an idiot for not realizing Ves had mistaken him for a different person named Marcus—at least until they were gone. He'd have to explain about the mix-up right away in the morning. Obviously, Ves would want to search for the room and inscription by himself. He'd probably be livid that Marcus had pretended to be someone else, even though it hadn't been intentional.

A thick slug of disappointment settled in Marcus's stomach, but what else could he do?

When Marcus entered the library the next morning, Ves pushed a sweet bun and a currant roll slathered with honey butter into his hands. "Good morning! I pulled historical plans of the palace last night, and I'm pretty sure I know exactly where to start looking."

Marcus felt every inch the hulking palace guard as he stood there holding food in his giant paws for hands, gawping down at Ves, who, mysteriously, wouldn't stop beaming. "Good morning?" Marcus finally managed.

Ves's smile faltered. "Oh, no. You don't like currant rolls, do you? My sisters hate them too."

"No, I like currant rolls." Marcus took a big bite to prove it. "Did you, um. Did you read your holo messages last night?"

Ves wrinkled his nose. "No. Your messages are the only good things in there. Otherwise it's all keep-Ves-busy work from people with better things to do than pretend they want my input. My fathers are good at making people do things like that."

"So you haven't read any of your messages at all since…?"

"A couple days ago." Ves frowned. "It's irresponsible, I know. Not a good look for a prince."

"No, it's not irresponsible!" Giddiness surged through Marcus. If Ves hadn't checked his messages, then he had no idea Marcus was a palace guard!

"It is. I shouldn't keep them waiting, even if they don't need my help. I'll do it tonight."

Tonight. That meant Marcus had all of today to hold onto Ves's interest.

Wait, no. He was supposed to come clean. It was an accidental lie before, but if he didn't fess up now, it became purposeful. He definitely needed to tell the truth.

He finished the breakfast Ves had brought for him. "Where do you think we should start looking?"

That made the hesitant smile on Ves's face bloom to fullness. "The residential wing."

As they made their way there, Ves pulled up the plans on his holo. Walking and staring at a holo had always made Marcus queasy, and walking while following Ves's rapid-fire flicking and zooming around the plans made him feel like he was back in basic, white-knuckling his way through emergency shuttle scenarios.

They paused outside the palace kitchens to look at the photo again. Ves pointed to a fuzzy, dark patch and said, "Does this look like the shadow of an amphora to you?"

"Zoom back out."

Ves was right. The dark patch, which Marcus's eyes had passed right over, had the shape of the person-sized jugs which held everything from wine to cooking oil to cleaning solutions.

"Where are the palace stores?" Marcus asked. "And—"

"Are they on these plans?" Ves finished. When Marcus nodded, Ves flicked the palace plans up alongside the photo and traced a finger through a series of long, narrow rooms. "I think they're here. I don't usually go into the palace store rooms. Ugh, that makes me sound, I don't know, like I'm too good for storerooms, doesn't it?"

Marcus thought of the house he'd grown up in, its ancient foundations deep in the sub-basement. "Sometimes you have to think about looking in places you don't expect there to be anything interesting."

Knocking an elbow lightly against Marcus's, Ves said, "I guess that's why you're the researcher."

Marcus's chest panged at the reminder that Ves thought he was someone else, someone *interesting*. Someone who wasn't the kitchen storeroom of the people in his life.

"Sorry," Ves said. "I shouldn't just touch you like that, should I? I'm the touchy-feely one in the family. Once I get to know a person… But I shouldn't. Sorry."

"But you hardly know me." At this rate, Marcus wouldn't make it until the end of the day. He'd give himself away with that kind of stupid comment.

"After yesterday, I feel like I've known you forever."

How was Marcus supposed to respond to that? Not the way he wanted to, certainly, with a wondering "You feel that way too?"

Before he figured it out, Ves cleared his throat and strode into the kitchens. The back of his neck was flushed dark.

They took a half-flight of stairs on the opposite end of the kitchens, which made a partial turn around a stone pillar and spilled onto a wide, well-lit hallway lined with doors.

They went through the rooms one by one and reached the end of the hallway, both sweaty and disheveled after needing to move heavy stores in several rooms. Ves had opened his jacket; the sweep of his collarbones was visible above the line of his shirt.

"Anything?" Ves asked. When Marcus shook his head, Ves sighed and hung his head.

"There's still a lot of palace to explore, though," Marcus said bracingly.

Ves fisted two handfuls of his own hair and thunked his head back against the wall. "I know. I was just really sure it would be down here."

Without thinking, Marcus put a hand on Ves's shoulder. "So we keep looking."

Ves raised his eyes, but on the way to meet Marcus's, they detoured, trailing up Marcus's torso and finally locking gazes with Marcus. Suddenly everything seemed extra bright and extra loud. His skin prickled, and the space between them crackled. Marcus dared not close the distance.

He dropped his hand and his eyes, clearing his throat. "We'll find it," he said, which felt so inadequate that he winced.

Just beyond where they stood, the hallway turned a sharp corner and narrowed to a flight of stairs leading upward. Ves took the stairs, and Marcus followed, fiddling with his lighter. As Marcus pulled his hand from his pocket to grab the railing of the narrow spiral staircase, he fumbled the lighter, sending it clattering to the floor.

Above him, Ves paused. "Are you okay?"

"Yeah, I just dropped something." Marcus descended again, scanning the floor. He ducked under the stairs and kicked something; it sounded an awful lot like his lighter, skittering deeper into the gloom.

Swearing under his breath, Marcus stooped lower, groping in the dark and hoping the nearby spiderwebs weren't occupied. Finally, with the tips of his fingers, he felt his lighter. As he strained to reach it, the heel of his hand caught on an uneven piece of floor. Marcus felt around it. It was a lip—no, a deep groove. A smooth, evenly cut groove, into which Marcus was able to reach and find a handhold.

"Ves, I think you should see this." Marcus shoved the lighter into his pocket as Ves came down the stairs. When Ves crouched next to him, Marcus took his hand and placed it on the floor.

Excitement vibrated around Ves's words as he said, "That feels like a handle to a secret hatch."

"On three?" Marcus said, heartbeat ratcheting up with his own excitement.

The only way for both of them to hold the handle was for Marcus to fit his big hand over Ves's slender, bony one. Marcus opened his mouth to apologize, but the words died in his mouth when Ves turned his head, a shy smile on his face.

Marcus's heart beat even faster.

On Marcus's count of three, they pulled with their combined strength. Marcus's shoulders strained as he fought time and inertia's grip on the hatch. Next to him, Ves grunted.

With a protesting squeal, the hatch swung open.

Marcus and Ves tumbled into each other, Ves's hands landing on Marcus's chest as Marcus sprawled on his ass. Their eyes caught, and for a second that seemed to last forever, the adventure didn't matter. *Nothing* mattered except the way Ves's knee was pressed into Marcus's hip, the way his palms pressed harder against Marcus's chest.

Ves scrambled to his feet and offered Marcus a hand of assistance. A set of stone stairs came into view. "No one's set foot on these for hundreds of years," Ves breathed.

Marcus nudged him. "Until you."

With a flicker of a grin, Ves led the way down. The light from the room above faded as they descended, so both of them projected their holos. Their illumination was thin, but it was enough to see where they were putting their feet.

The stairs ended in a narrow corridor, dark and smelling of mildew and earth. They followed it, whispering occasionally as it sloped gently upward. It might have been an unsettling place for some people—dark, claustrophobic, underground—but it reminded Marcus of exploring the foundations under his childhood home.

Abruptly, the corridor opened into a dead end. If the inscription was down here, it had to be in this room.

Ves walked the perimeter, using his holo to shed light on the walls. Halfway along the longest stretch, he let out a triumphant crow, his voice bouncing around the room. "We did it!"

The inscription was right there. Around it was a thin seam in the stone, outlining the shape of a door. Marcus ran a reverent finger over it. "Let's find the handle to open this."

After going over the wall inch by inch, though, there didn't seem to be a handle. There were two irregular shapes and a slot carved into the stone and some holes that didn't do anything, even when Ves tried poking a pencil through each one. The slot seemed promising until Marcus inserted his pack of cigarettes into it and all that happened was a mysterious *click*.

They tried pushing, they tried tracing the carvings, and, in case the door was voice activated, they tried as many likely phrases as they could think of. The door remained stubbornly, silently closed, and as the hours passed with no progress, Ves became increasingly frustrated and dejected.

Finally, after another fruitless attempt to unlock the door, Ves flopped onto the floor, sprawling on his back with his hands over his face. "Why won't it *open*?"

Marcus kicked the door lightly, staring at the unidentified shapes. He knew he was seeing patterns where there weren't any, but it was striking how much they looked like two essential beekeeping tools. The long, thin line with a square at the end reminded him of a utensil for opening hives, and the cylinder looked like the smoker that beekeepers used to calm bees.

He snorted at himself. He was seeing things that he wanted to be there. If knowing something about beekeeping would open this door, then he'd be the perfect companion for Ves. Instead, he was a farm kid-turned-guard pretending to be a professor—a professor who would probably know exactly what to do to get that door open.

Guilt and shame crashed over him. What was he doing, lying to a prince? To someone he was supposed to be protecting? Maybe he was looking after Ves's physical safety, but it was only a matter of hours until Ves found out that Marcus wasn't who Ves thought he was. How could Ves trust him after that?

He had to tell the truth. Now.

Marcus swallowed hard and sank to the ground. There was no point in tiptoeing into a confession. Trying to soften it wouldn't make Ves hate him any less. He squeezed his eyes shut. "I'm not Professor Vytina."

There was a rustle of fabric, and when Marcus opened his eyes, Ves was sitting up. "What do you mean, you're not Professor Vytina?"

"I mean…" This was harder than he'd thought it would be. "I'm a palace guard. I was assigned to the library. Yesterday was my first day."

Ves's throat bobbed. "You said your name is Marcus."

"It is Marcus." He hung his head. "I didn't know you were expecting your friend, and by the time I realized you'd mistaken me for someone else…"

There was a long, fraught silence. Marcus wanted to sink through the floor, but for some reason, instead of getting up and walking away, Ves remained where he was.

"I can't go off-world," Ves said. "When you asked me why I don't go off-world to study, and I said my family needs me here? That's not true. It's because I have a"—he made a face—"*condition*, where my body can't handle different atmospheric concentrations. That's why I wanted an adventure close to home. So you're not the only one who kept something to yourself."

"Your thing was personal, and you didn't need to share it with a stranger." The urge to sink into the floor was getting more intense, not less, the further they got from his confession. "My thing was me just…being afraid."

"Afraid of what?"

It was embarrassing, but Marcus owed Ves an answer. "That you'd think less of me for just being a guard."

Without any hesitation, Ves said, "I'd never think less of you."

"You don't even know me."

"Weren't you listening before?" Ves turned so he was facing Marcus. "I *do* feel like I know you. I spent eight hours with you and felt like we'd known each other forever."

"Me too," Marcus said quietly. Tentatively. It seemed impossible that Ves didn't hate him, but there was something soft in his face. The green threads in his eyes looked more like the pale gold of honey in the combined glows of their holos.

Ves laid his fingertips on Marcus's knee. "And I got my adventure, too."

"Even though it was pretty anticlimactic." Marcus gestured at the inscription, the carvings, the stubbornly closed door.

"I guess we needed an actual queen to see what's behind there," Ves sighed.

Realization crashed into Marcus. *Do not open until the queen returns.* The carvings that looked like beekeeping tools.

"Bees," he said.

Ves's forehead crinkled. "Huh?"

Marcus stood and strode to the sealed door. Certainty coursed through him. All he needed was smoke. His emergency cigarettes! He fumbled for them and his lighter as Ves joined him. "If I'm right, we have a queen. She's just not here yet," he said, knowing it was cryptic but unable to make his excitement settle enough to explain properly.

He raised the smoking cigarette to the holes in the door and blew gently to waft the smoke through them. He held his breath. From within the wall came a whirr. Heart in his throat, Marcus slid his pack of cigarettes into the slot on the door again. This time, the *click* was followed by a series of *clanks* and one heavy *thunk*.

The door swung open.

Daylight blinded Marcus, Ves said excitedly, "Boxes! Er, which do…what?", and Marcus finally blinked the spots from his eyes.

He took in the small courtyard, from the riot of weeds and wildflowers to the nine wooden boxes standing above the blooms. The silence of the space struck a discordant note with the busy hum Marcus was used to surrounding those boxes.

"Beehives," he said, a little amazed that he'd been right.

"Beehives," Ves repeated. He craned his neck to look at the palace rising around them. They were hemmed in by walls, domes, and turrets, but above was clear sky. This little patch of wildflowers with no obvious door must have been overlooked as the palace had grown up around it.

Ves looked at Marcus, a grin spreading across his face. "All we need are some bees," Ves said.

Marcus wondered if reports of the city's bee swarm were still pouring in. "I know where we can get some."

If beekeeping was an art, then enticing a wild bee swarm to move into empty hives was sitting an orchestra down and having them sight-read a symphony. The process wasn't quick. Marcus had to lure the scout bees to the garden, wait for them to lead the swarm there, trap them, and get them settled in the hives. It took Marcus and Ves more than a week.

When Marcus asked Ves if he was sure he wanted to help, Ves gave him that same bright smile that had made Marcus helpless from the beginning. He'd decided it reminded him of wildflowers blooming where no one expected them to be.

Then Professor Vytina arrived.

Of course he did—his trip had only been delayed by a week. Because he'd traveled all the way to Lyraith Prime to see Ves, Ves went to spend his time with him. The Marcus he'd been excited to meet in the first place.

Of course he did.

So that was it. It had been stupid to develop a crush on a prince. For a glorious week, Marcus had held Ves's attention, and then the adventure fizzled out. Ves moved on to the next thing.

After a week, Marcus inspected the hive. The bees were docile, buzzing lazily around him, and he quickly found eggs. Beautiful—the colony was queenright. Maybe next year, he could split it and populate some of the other hive boxes. It wouldn't take much of his time; he could manage it on top of his guard duties.

"You should ask for a raise if you're going to be the palace beekeeper on top of being the library guard," a voice said from behind him.

Marcus turned to see Ves standing in the open mystery door. His heart hummed, and something he couldn't attribute to honeybees buzzed deep inside him.

"You're here," he said.

Wildflowers brushed Ves's shins as he came toward Marcus. "Of course I'm here! I told you I'd be back as soon as I had time."

"But Professor Vytina—"

Ves made a disgruntled sound and reached up to grab a fistful of Marcus's shirt as he drew close. "Professor Vytina is a very interesting man, but he's not an adventurer."

"He seems too old to have an adventure," Marcus said, trying to be fair. From what he'd seen of the professor, staying up past his bedtime probably qualified as an adventure at his age.

Laughter flashed through Ves's eyes. "I also don't want to kiss him."

The buzzing in Marcus's chest coalesced into a single bright chord, each note humming together in perfect harmony. Hope circled like bees on air currents. "Does that mean there's someone you *do* want to kiss?"

Ves bounced impatiently on his toes, so Marcus laughed and leaned down, meeting Ves's mouth with his own.

Bees hummed among the flowers, the sun shone bright, and Marcus couldn't wait to see what the next adventure was.

PARTNERED UP

CASSIA KING

Tags: college/university, elf, f/f, fantasy, first kiss, fluff, interspecies relationship, lesbian, magic use, orc, panic attack, past tense, pining, professor, romance, third person limited point of view, trapped together

Professor Bridget Nightstar opened a book, but she wasn't happy about it. Given the choice, she'd much rather lead her students through a grueling weight circuit at the university athletic center. The faculty lounge was too quiet, too still, and reading never gave her the sense of accomplishment that came along with a new personal best. Even with her petite elvish build, she'd built up significant muscle, and she was proud of it. Still, it was the books and research and studying that increased her *magical* strength, so she put in the effort there too.

Across the lounge, Professor Ismanna Urzoth, head of the languages department, had taken over a low table with the textbooks and assigned readings for her literature courses. The purple-skinned orc's bulky form was currently hunched over a tiny chapbook, quill in hand and notes within reach. Two hard horns curved upward from either temple. Her thick black hair was tied up in a queue. She pushed a tiny pair of glasses up the bridge of her nose. Tusks jutted from between her full lips. She was handsome, but quiet.

Bridget had no idea how Professor Urzoth survived that department. Too much sitting, not enough doing.

Not that it mattered. Their paths rarely crossed. Bridget had talked to Professor Urzoth exactly once, and it had consisted of "What day is it?" (Bridget), "The third of the month" (Urzoth), "Thanks" (Bridget), and then dead silence (Urzoth). Thrilling stuff, truly. She almost preferred the way guests at the athletic center ignored each other altogether as they went about their business.

Ah, the athletic center. Her personal oasis, peaceful and quieting. She hadn't gone yet today, and she itched for it.

Wait, what was I doing? Book. Right. Ugh.

With a hefty sigh, Bridget returned her attention to the chunks of text on the bound parchment before her, already bored.

Luckily, that was when the president blew through the doors, pamphlets in his translucent blue hand. He came right up to Bridget's armchair, and she was happy to ignore her book and ask, "How's your day, sir?"

"I've had better." President Mistral Bluebreeze, an air spirit from the north of Zephyria, handed her one of the folded papers. "I'll be announcing it this evening at the faculty meeting, but you can get started early if you like."

Normally Bridget was pretty good about keeping up with other people's thought processes, but this time she was lost. "I think I missed something. What are you announcing?"

President Bluebreeze gusted over to Professor Urzoth and held out a pamphlet. "Faculty research projects," he said loudly.

Professor Urzoth jerked upright as if she hadn't noticed him standing there. Cautiously, she took the paper, which crinkled between her thick fingers.

The president gestured between Bridget and Professor Urzoth. "You two are my first pair. Pick a topic, do your time in the library, and present a research paper on the first of the month."

Bridget's jaw dropped. That was only a week away. "Uh, are you sure—?"

"Maybe you mean the first of the month *after* next?" Professor Urzoth offered. It was the first time Bridget had heard her husky voice all morning, and she sent up silent thanks for some sense. Surely President Bluebreeze had to listen to that, had to realize his time frame was absurd.

But he waved off the attempted correction. "Next week!" He pinned a large flyer to the notice board at the front of the room, and he breezed out the way he'd come in with no further clarification.

Abandoning her halfhearted studies, Bridget hopped to her feet and made her way over to the notice board. The president's neatly hand-printed poster hung right in the middle, still swinging a little on its pin.

A shadow fell over Bridget, and she looked up. Professor Urzoth loomed over her, studying the same paper.

"So it's you and me?" Bridget said, leaning back to see Professor Urzoth's face, to try to suss out how the orc felt about the sudden (and absurd) assignment.

Professor Urzoth's brow was creased; her lips curved downward over her tusks. Her thick arms akimbo, she heaved a sigh. "I suppose so," she said, tone heavy.

Perfect. They were on the same page, then. "I'll ask him to reassign us to better-fitting partners."

Professor Urzoth looked down at Bridget then, and her cheeks flushed a pinkish-violet. "We can make it work," she said quietly, unexpectedly.

Bridget's eyebrows jumped. "You don't mind?"

The surprisingly adorable flush darkened. Professor Urzoth shook her head.

"Huh. Um, all right then. We can...make it work." Bridget held precious little confidence about working well with the quiet, standoffish literature professor, but the project was mandatory and she liked her job most days, so she'd do what needed to be done.

After her last class, Bridget entered the grand assembly hall for President Bluebreeze's announcement and details about the faculty research projects. Wall sconces of blue fairy-fire cast flickering shadows on the faces of her coworkers. She headed down the aisle to sit with her friends from the athletics department...but in the back sat Professor Urzoth, alone and silent, her nose in a book. With a sigh, Bridget came to a stop. Backed up.

"'Scuse me," she muttered.

Professor Urzoth looked up from her book, startled. Her eyes went wide behind her glasses. "Professor Nightstar?"

Bridget indicated the empty seat beside her. "May I?"

"Um…"

"I thought we might as well get used to spending time together," Bridget said frankly.

"Oh. Right. Of course." Professor Urzoth stood and awkwardly leaned back while Bridget inched past her and took the seat.

When it became clear Professor Urzoth wasn't going to say anything else, Bridget huffed and stuck out her hand. "Let's try this again. You can call me Bridget, if we're gonna be in close quarters this week."

Professor Urzoth hesitated, but then gripped Bridget's hand with a gentle strength, her oversized purple hand practically swallowing Bridget's slim peach one. The touch was warm but not clammy, firm but not domineering, and it lingered longer than Bridget had expected it to. The orcish professor gave Bridget a real shake, not a dainty, too-careful one like she might break. No, she treated her like an equal. Not many people thought of a petite elf that way, no matter how much she bulked up.

"You can call me Ismanna, then." The orc dropped Bridget's hand a second too late, and the warmth of her touch lingered on Bridget's skin. She flexed her fingers in an effort to dispel it. She didn't need that quiet strength clinging to her hand or any other part of her, thanks.

President Bluebreeze was gliding toward the front, so Bridget sat forward, ready to figure out what in the four hells was going on with this faculty research project nonsense.

But Professor Urzoth—Ismanna—leaned toward her, so close Bridget could feel the heat of her muscles. "Meet in the library after this?" Ismanna asked lowly.

Bridget, for once, couldn't summon any words. She just nodded.

Then Ismanna straightened, leaving cool space between them, and Bridget kind of wished she hadn't.

Wait, what?

She pushed the thought away. She'd never had any connection with Ismanna before, never thought anything of her; what did a handshake and a first name do to change that?

After a too-long assembly in which President Bluebreeze admitted he was aiming to garner more funds for the university, Bridget and Ismanna walked together, in silence, to the university library, where they made their way to the back of the private research section. Blue-flamed lamps hung from the ceilings, enchanted to stay safely within the confines of their frames. The bookcases rose high above Bridget's head; rows of book spines would be out of reach even if she jumped—and she could jump quite high.

"So we have to choose a topic," Bridget said, sitting backward on a straight-backed wooden chair. "Do you have any ideas? Anything in mind?"

Ismanna perched her massive frame delicately in a square armchair. She barely fit. "Er, maybe we can find a middle ground between our disciplines? Something we're both interested in learning more about? If we can manage to increase our magic with only a week of study, too, it'll look good for the university, but I'm not as worried about that at this point."

In Zephyria, innate magic was leveled up by study and research. Everyone, no matter their race or gender or other personal characteristics, was born with the ability to harness magic, but those who wanted to harness more than average or do more fantastical things with it had to study, to improve themselves. So institutions of higher education, like the University of the Four Winds, were as much about strengthening one's connection to the magical realm as about the learning itself.

Bridget's preferred area of research was, obviously, the physical form. Anatomy. Musculature. Learning what each type of body could do, and pushing bodies to the limits to hone and improve them. By contrast, Ismanna preferred literary feats and silence.

"A middle ground would be nice," Bridget admitted, even though she wasn't sure what that middle ground would be. "What about…? I don't know." Where did physicality and intellect intersect? She spitballed a few ideas, hoping she didn't sound like an absolute idiot. "What about the long-term effects of reading on the body? On the brain, even?"

Ismanna sat back, thinking. Or silently judging Bridget. Could have been either.

"Or, I don't know if there's a difference between the mental work of writing a story and that of a poem. Like, does the brain do different things? Or we could look at how much someone remembers if they're being read to while they work out? I'm just thinking out loud. It doesn't have to be any of those ideas. Maybe you can think of something better." Bridget was rambling now. That was never a good sign.

Ismanna took pity on her and offered, "Those are perfectly good places to start. Let me think. Is there a connection between magical strength and physical strength? Or how about seeing if the topic of study affects the rate of magical improvements?"

Those were good options too. "By the gods, I wish we had more time," Bridget muttered. "Time to pick a topic, time to *do* the research...I think we'll have to just pick one and move forward."

Ismanna made a *go for it* gesture. "Take your pick."

Bridget wasn't afraid to choose a solution at random and move on. As department head, she made a lot of tiny decisions that way. But part of her was curious what Ismanna was thinking. The orc professor was so quiet all the time; Bridget suspected she had one of those brains that was always turning things over, always thinking. "What interests *you*?" Bridget asked instead.

"Me?"

"Yes, you. What are you thinking?"

That pinkish-violet flush darkened Ismanna's cheeks and spread to her neck and pointed ears. "Who says I'm thinking anything?"

"I don't know you very well yet..." The *yet* slipped out by accident; Bridget didn't take it back. In truth, she *was* already interested in getting to know Ismanna better. "...but I can already tell you're a thinker. Which is why we'll make a good team."

"Why's that?"

"'Cause I'm a doer, and thinking and doing are the two stages of making things happen. The thing is, I need a thinker, and you need a doer. So here we are." Bridget planted her hands on her hips.

For the first time all day, Ismanna cracked a smile. Her tusks gleamed in the blue light of the lamps, and her eyes were soft, pensive but not judgmental. They were a deep brown, rich and warm and welcoming like the earth itself. Bridget had always liked blue irises, like her own, but something about Ismanna's eyes made her suddenly very fond of brown.

"What about the memory of what's read aloud during exercise?" Ismanna suggested. "That seems like something we could reasonably research in the time we have. And it certainly combines both our interests."

"Sounds good." Bridget was flattered that Ismanna had selected one of Bridget's suggestions, but not overfull of herself. Having an idea was simple. The actual research would take both of them to complete on time and well.

They brainstormed the topic together for an hour, sketching out the details of how they might research what had already been studied on the subject as well as how they might conduct new research of their own. Once they had a good starting point pinned down, they rolled up the parchment and tidied the workspace.

"I think we're going to make a good pair on this," Bridget said as they exited the library. "I look forward to working with you." She kept the words formal, platonic. They were two coworkers and nothing more; the University of the Four Winds had rules about fraternizing with fellow faculty. She didn't mean anything more by it. She couldn't.

But Ismanna flushed anyway, one hand going up to her right horn. "You too."

Bridget watched the violet blush travel down under the neckline of Ismanna's simple day dress. She didn't think about it. She didn't take the mental image of it home with her.

She would never.

The next evening after classes ended, Bridget made her way to the back of the university library. Ismanna was already waiting for her there, a few books spread open on the table. She had her nose in a leather-bound novel.

The orcish professor looked up at Bridget's approach and smiled tentatively, firelight glinting off the wire frames of her glasses. "Welcome back."

"Evening." Bridget took the seat beside Ismanna, and their knees brushed. Bridget pulled back, trying to be respectful, but she missed the contact.

Ismanna settled back in, tucking her book away, but Bridget for some reason felt she needed her to look up again. She blurted out in a low voice, "What were you reading?"

Ismanna did look up, and Bridget warmed all over when their gazes met. "A romance," Ismanna said quietly, and of course Bridget *had* to lean in to hear her better. Her arm and thigh brushed against the solidity of Ismanna. As big as she was, she was soft. Warm. Touchable.

And Bridget rather liked touching her.

"Well, is it any good?" she prompted.

Ismanna stilled. "I—I'm enjoying it." She sounded a little defensive, as if maybe she'd been teased for this before.

But Bridget only said, "Nice. You'll have to tell me about it sometime."

Ismanna nodded. Even as she lowered her hand and redirected her attention to the research texts, she said, "Tell me about you. What brought you to the University of the Four Winds?"

Bridget wanted to offer some interesting story, but she only shrugged. "I needed a job. They had an opening. What about you?"

Ismanna lit up. "I did my graduate studies here, actually, and I loved it so much I took a position as assistant to the head of the literature department, and then I just worked my way up, I suppose. I've really enjoyed my time here. It's hard to imagine going anywhere else."

"Oh." That seemed...so much better than Bridget's take-it-or-leave-it attitude.

"My favorite part is when I get to help students see a part of themselves or the world in a piece of writing they didn't expect to connect with."

"That's fantastic." Bridget looked at Ismanna, really looked. The orcish professor was warm and vibrant, truly enthusiastic about her position here at the university. It was...well, it was adorable. Something thrummed in Bridget's chest.

They chatted as they researched earlier studies on their topic, learning about each other's lives. Bridget couldn't absorb enough about Ismanna, even as she felt the magic welling inside her. The magic had to come from the books, of course. What else could she be studying?

It was dangerous, though. That old rule from the foundation of the university: Faculty shall not be romantically involved with one another.

It had never been a problem for Bridget before now.

As they reached the end of the existing studies, they started creating their own research. Bridget got on the floor and did pushups as Ismanna read to her, and then after the reading was over, Ismanna quizzed Bridget to assess her memory and comprehension of the story. They took extensive notes on all of it.

Bridget tried to focus on her pushups. There was nothing for her here, nothing to be gained by allowing whatever feelings were simmering to see the light of day. Even if the now-familiar, husky voice reading to her scratched an itch she hadn't known she had. Even if stealing Ismanna's undivided attention warmed Bridget from the inside. Even if she was starting to wonder if every rule was worth following.

She got up, dusted herself off, and sat next to Ismanna at the table to finish up their notes on the exercise. The night was dark outside the library, but here in the flickering light of fairy-fire, with the reassuring bulk of Ismanna beside her, Bridget didn't want to leave just yet. "So tell me about your romance book," she suggested. "As much about it as you've read so far, anyway."

"I can tell you already, it's very dramatic," Ismanna said with a smile. "Winds whipping in the moors, cliffside confessions of love, and all that. I love it. Maybe because my life is so quiet."

Bridget liked that contrast—the shyness of Ismanna in public, the drama she enjoyed for herself in private. Bridget was honored to know about it. "I've never been bookish," she admitted. "Maybe it'll go better if you're reading to me while I work out. We could try it again with one of your stories. As part of the study."

Ismanna leaned in, brightening. "I can pick out something you'll like. Something adventurous, I would guess?"

"I'm that easy to read?" Bridget nudged the orcish professor's shoulder teasingly.

Ismanna turned a lovely pinkish-violet that Bridget was beginning to recognize. "No—well, perhaps."

Bridget laughed, too loud for the library. Someone hushed her from afar.

But Ismanna didn't seem bothered by Bridget's vivacity. If anything, she seemed pleased by it.

"I'm an open book. Got it."

Bridget had been trying to get another smile out of her companion, but tragically, Ismanna averted her gaze. "No, it's more that I'm a…book opener."

"I'm not sure I understand."

"I've noticed you," Ismanna blurted. "For a while. When they hired you, it was hard to miss you. You're just so…"

"Muscular?" Bridget suggested. That was what most people knew her for.

"*Interesting,*" Ismanna whispered. "You shine. I can't look away."

Heat bloomed in Bridget's cheeks, crawling down her neck and up to the tips of her pointed ears. No one ever thought of her like that. Like she was worth something just for existing. She hadn't given Ismanna the same courtesy before the research project, but now…she was enjoying Ismanna's company so much more than she'd expected.

It was dangerous, how much she was enjoying Ismanna.

Bridget should've kept that to herself. But, like a fool, she admitted, "I'm not the only one."

It wasn't the best compliment to give a beautiful, intelligent woman. Bridget normally had no trouble wooing a lady she liked, but it was different here, now. Her words wouldn't cooperate, awkward and unimpressive.

Ismanna smiled anyway.

The fairy-fire lamps went low, all at once. Not fully doused, but dim for sure. Bridget looked around, surprised. "Is the library closing? Did we miss an announcement?"

Ismanna peered into the stacks. "Maybe someone's having trouble with their maintenance magic. If they were closing, wouldn't a librarian have come back here and told us to leave?"

"You would think so." Bridget still felt not quite right about the lights, but she returned to the work at hand. They compared their notes, made plans for another workout reading session the next day, and then got distracted chatting again because it turned out Ismanna had never even stepped inside the university's athletic center, and Bridget started babbling about her favorite circuit, the best equipment to use, the best times to work out to avoid the crowd.

"Maybe we could go together sometime," she offered. "I can show you around."

Ismanna beamed. "I'd like that."

Bridget smiled back, lost in soaking up the look of Ismanna. The gleam of her horns and tusks, the waves in her thick hair, the fullness of her lips. And as if her being pretty weren't bad enough, she was *smart*. She knew so much about so many things, and Bridget wanted to absorb it all. Preferably with mouth-to-mouth osmosis. And the idea of kissing Ismanna lit Bridget up from the inside, warmed her all over.

But those feelings were dangerous. Those feelings were unacceptable. Those feelings were…dangerously close to bubbling over. And now she'd let too much time pass without saying anything.

"What are you thinking about?" Ismanna asked.

Bridget had no good way to say *you*, so she scrambled for something reasonable. "How fun it'll be to show you the athletic center."

Ismanna seemed unconvinced, but she let it go.

After they finished up their research work for the night, they packed up and headed, together, to the front of the library. No other patrons were around this late, which made sense (normal people needed their beauty sleep), but oddly, they didn't see any librarians either. No one stocking shelves, no one cleaning up, no one even at the front desk.

"Hello?" Bridget looked around, but no one appeared. "The librarians are gone. I think they did close for the night."

"No, they must just be in the back." Ismanna tried the doors. They rattled, remaining firmly shut. But there was no visible lock; magic sealed the doors.

Panic rose in Bridget's throat. "We're trapped in here. No one knew we were still in the back, and they left us."

"Wait, wait." Ismanna drew Bridget away from the doors, but Bridget was starting to breathe too quickly. "Follow my breaths. We're okay." Ismanna breathed in deeply, and Bridget forced herself to follow suit. She held her breath as long as Ismanna held her own, exhaled long and slow as Ismanna did. And as her body learned to cooperate, her mind calmed too.

"Look at me," Ismanna said softly.

Bridget looked up, deep into her research partner's earth-brown eyes.

Ismanna watched her in return, calm and serious, and Bridget steadied. Her heart was still pounding, her belly aflutter, but it didn't feel like anxiety anymore. It felt like appreciation and admiration and *ache*.

Bridget was holding on to Ismanna. She ought to have let go, but instead she tugged lightly, drawing Ismanna in toward herself. And Ismanna followed, moved into Bridget's space as if in a trance.

I need to end this now. Whatever this is.

Except Bridget didn't want to.

Her hands skated up Ismanna's biceps, over the arch of her shoulders. Ismanna's glasses gleamed in the low light. Ismanna was watching Bridget, eyes wide, lips parted, breaths shallow, and with every detail Bridget absorbed, magic welled up in her. She was learning *Ismanna.* If it were anyone else, it could've become her faculty research project. But it was Ismanna, and professional research was the last thing on Bridget's mind as she admired her partner.

The orcish woman smelled of ink and parchment, as if her very being had absorbed all those books she liked to bury her nose in. This close, the scent intertwined with the cinnamon perfume potion Bridget dabbed onto her pulse points every morning.

Ismanna's hair was loose today, and Bridget threaded her fingers through it, relishing the silky softness of the black waves. Then, without really meaning to, she cupped the back of Ismanna's head and drew her down as Bridget rose up on her toes. Their foreheads touched, and they lingered in the connection, Bridget's eyes fluttering closed. Ismanna was warm and strong and safe in a way Bridget had never experienced before. Usually she had to take on the role of safety-giver, comforting partners and acting bigger than she felt. But here, with Ismanna…Bridget could just be Bridget.

Inhaling the reassuring ink-on-parchment scent of Ismanna, Bridget opened her eyes. "Ismanna?"

Ismanna blinked down at her, full lips curving in a slight smile. "Bridget."

Bridget met her gaze and found heat there that encouraged her to whisper, "I was thinking about kissing you."

"An hour ago?"

"And right now."

Ismanna quieted, but her eyes fell to Bridget's lips.

It had been a long time since Bridget felt so self-conscious, and her mouth ran away with her. "But it doesn't mean you have to, there's no pressure, I'm just happy to have gotten to know you this week, and I guess I read into it, so if you're not—"

And then Ismanna was kissing Bridget, her tusks satisfyingly sharp against Bridget's mouth, and Bridget clung to her with a happy sigh, cupping Ismanna's chiseled jawline with one palm to keep her close and holding the back of her head with the other.

Bridget had never felt so *much* before this. She'd had her share of romantic partners, both serious and casual, but never with a connection like this one. It had been, what, two days since she'd started spending time with Ismanna? It was hard to believe she was here already. Here, ready, aching for all of Ismanna.

Ismanna was a careful kisser, probably so that her tusks wouldn't scrape Bridget, but Bridget wanted her, all of her. The library, the university, all of Zephyria spun around them, and Bridget's only anchor was the feel of Ismanna in her arms. Pure perfection.

She sighed and sipped at Ismanna, taking and giving in equal measure. Magic itself seemed to spark everywhere they touched. Bridget arched for more, but a warning bell was clanging in the back of her hazy mind. Something about this wasn't perfect, something she ought to know. Then it came to her, and her eyes flared open.

The old rule about no faculty fraternization.

Bridget didn't want to think about it, but if they were caught…

"Ismanna," Bridget murmured.

Her mouth moving to Bridget's jaw, Ismanna hummed an affirmative, an approval for whatever Bridget was asking for.

The sound buzzed happily in Bridget's belly, but she pulled away, dropping back to the flats of her feet. "Ismanna, we can't."

Ismanna stared down at Bridget blankly, extending a lavender hand. "Why not?"

Bridget didn't take it. "The university doesn't allow faculty relationships."

Ismanna swallowed.

"That kiss was…" Mind-blowing? Magic-altering? Bridget couldn't admit how far she had fallen, so she let the end of the sentence fall away. "But it would cost us our jobs if anyone found out. I mean, I suppose we could sneak around, but…" The suggestions felt disgusting on her tongue. Ismanna deserved better than to be someone's secret.

Indeed, Ismanna grimaced at the suggestion. "It doesn't feel right to hide. But I—I could leave."

Hurt clenched in Bridget's chest. Ismanna was that ready to forget her?

"I could put in my resignation," Ismanna offered. "Find another teaching position somewhere else."

"Wait, what? No!"

Ismanna huffed.

"Absolutely not. You love your work here."

"I'm quiet. I keep my head down. No one will miss me."

I'll miss you. "You're not quitting."

Ismanna took Bridget's hands in hers. She didn't insist on anything, simply held them. "This is worth tending," she said quietly. "It's just a bud, but it could bloom into something beautiful if we let it. A job's not worth that."

If it were anyone else, Bridget would have cracked a joke to break the tension. If it were anyone else, Bridget wouldn't be considering the solution that had crept into her head.

If it were anyone else, Bridget wouldn't have been here to begin with, holding hands in the library foyer, freshly kissed and thinking about making the stupidest move of her life.

Ismanna was right: a job wasn't worth their budding relationship.

"Don't quit," Bridget insisted. "I'll take care of it."

Ismanna smiled, and everything was worth it.

The next morning, after a librarian had returned and dissolved the special locking enchantment, Bridget knocked on President Bluebreeze's office door. She held a folded piece of parchment in her other hand, worried at the edges. She'd read the handwritten words so many times, the inked symbols were burned into her mind. Her eyes were starting to burn; she blinked away the feeling.

The door opened, and President Bluebreeze hovered on the other side. "Professor Nightstar! Happy morning to you. Come on in."

Bridget edged into his office. He blew into his desk chair and gestured for Bridget to take a seat. She sank into the guest chair, and her stomach sank with her as she held out the letter.

"Oho, what's this?" He plucked it from her fingertips. With a raised eyebrow, he unfolded the parchment, but as he scanned the inked words, his playful confusion faded. He looked up at her, disappointed. "You're resigning?"

Bridget nodded, once, quickly, trying not to tear up. She hadn't realized how much she'd miss the job until it was filtering through her fingers like sand. "I enjoyed my time here, but I, er, found something else I want to pursue." *Someone* else. And yes, she would use the time off to immerse herself in her magic studies, but in the end, this was for Ismanna.

"That's a real shame. There's nothing I can do to persuade you to stay?"

"I don't think you can change the university rules," Bridget blurted, which was more than she'd meant to let on.

President Bluebreeze leaned in. "Which rule is giving you trouble?"

Bridget flushed warm; she didn't want to get Ismanna in trouble, but she couldn't get in trouble if Bridget was quitting, right? "No relationships between faculty?"

President Bluebreeze's hair whipped in his personal wind as if they were outdoors. Interest lit up his pale blue eyes. "I see."

"Nothing happened," Bridget lied quickly, maybe too quickly. "You can't fire her. I'm leaving."

"No one's getting fired," President Bluebreeze assured her, which was only true because Bridget was in the middle of resigning. "Let me see what I can do about that rule." He held out the letter.

Bridget had no faith that anything would change, so she shook her head. "Keep it."

He frowned but tucked the creased parchment into a desk drawer. "Don't pack up your office yet. I'll speak to the board and get back to you by the end of the day."

Bridget nodded, but that was a lie too.

She barely survived her classes for the day, anxiety thrumming under her skin as she taught. She avoided the faculty lounge out of fear that she'd run into Ismanna and have to admit what she'd done. When she wasn't in class, she hid in her office with the door closed. She was supposed to meet Ismanna at the athletic center later, but how was Bridget supposed to pretend everything was fine? Pretend everything was the way it had been before the kiss that had changed everything?

In an effort to distract herself, Bridget worked on the research. She compiled her notes and drafted the paper about what they'd found so far. It would've been better if Ismanna had written it—cleverer, clearer—but Bridget didn't know how much time she had left here, and she wanted to make Ismanna's job as easy as possible.

A knock reverberated against the office door, and Bridget looked up, startled. "Come in?"

The door creaked open, and Ismanna poked her head in.

Bridget's heart fluttered, but her stomach plummeted.

"How's your day going?" Ismanna asked, quiet and tentative.

"I've had better."

Brow furrowing, Ismanna stepped fully into the office and closed the door behind herself. "Why? What's wrong?"

Bridget had meant to keep her resignation a secret, but the words fell from her mouth. "I took care of it."

Ismanna looked at Bridget, really looked, and her shoulders slumped. Her dark eyes went soft and sad as she realized what Bridget had done. "I told you I would do it."

"But you love this position, this place. I can find somewhere else to work." Bridget pushed herself to her feet and reached for Ismanna, who hesitated but finally took her hand. "I'll miss this, but I'd rather have you."

Ismanna's lips parted, but before Bridget could draw her around the desk and into her arms, someone else knocked on the door. Quickly she dropped Ismanna's hand and stepped back, away from her. "Come in," she called.

President Bluebreeze whipped into the now-borderline-crowded office. "Afternoon, Professor Urzoth. Good to see you. I hope your day is going well."

Ismanna glanced at Bridget. "I've had better," she said pointedly.

"I was just about to show Ismanna—Professor Urzoth—my first draft of the research paper." Bridget held up the ink-covered parchment. "It should give her a reasonably good start."

"And you should see it through to the end," the university president declared with a smile.

Bridget lowered the paper. It shook in her hands. "Pardon?"

"The board has offered to rescind that statute. It was an old principle, no longer useful to the way we want to run this university."

Oh gods. Bridget's lips parted in shock, and her legs threatened to buckle. She'd been so ready to lose what she wanted, to know she wasn't worth chasing by one or the other. Her throat went thick at the possibility that everything she wanted in her life wanted her in return.

When she said nothing, he sobered. "If you still wish to go, you're not obligated to stay. But if this was the only thing shoving you out the door..."

Trembling, Bridget looked from President Bluebreeze to Ismanna. "I can stay, and we can—?"

Ismanna took her hand and squeezed, her brown eyes alight with hope.

"Indeed. Your choice of partner is officially no longer the university's business. Now, should I keep this, or...?" President Bluebreeze held out a familiar worried paper.

Joy expanded in Bridget's chest, filling every crack. She yearned to stay, to keep both her job and her partner. But it wasn't just her in this. Would Ismanna prefer she leave or stay?

She looked to the literature professor, who only said, "Where do you want to be?"

Bridget took the letter, looked over the handwritten resignation, and dropped it into the hearth. Blue flames curled and darkened and shrank the parchment until it disappeared.

"I want to be here," she said firmly. "Tomorrow, anyway."

Ismanna quirked a brow. "Tomorrow?"

"Tonight, I'd like to take a beautiful orc out to dinner." Bridget smiled fondly at Ismanna, who blushed.

"Congratulations, you two." Beaming, President Bluebreeze blew back out the door.

Ismanna still held Bridget's hand, and she took the other as well. Softly she admitted, "I'm glad you're not leaving. I just got you."

Bridget drew her in close. "You've definitely got me now. But that has nothing to do with whether or not we work together."

Ismanna looked away and smiled.

Bridget turned Ismanna's face back toward hers. "What do we think about a kiss before that dinner?"

A quick, eager nod was all she needed.

She pressed her lips to Ismanna's, smiling into the kiss despite herself.

Sharp tusks and soft lips. Quietness, boldness, calm, drama. There was so much to her. Bridget appreciated every facet of Ismanna she'd learned this week, and she looked forward to learning even more. For as long as she had her, Bridget would keep learning Ismanna.

LATE OR NEVER

E. V. DEAN

Tags: bisexual, college/university, death of a spouse, elderly, f/f, family, fraught family dynamics, ghost, parenthood, present tense, second chances, third person limited point of view

If she overlooks the sea of gray hair and bald spots stretched before her, Janine almost feels like a real college freshman. Dr. Vamer's magnetic voice fills out the uselessly spacious lecture hall, spinning tales of spirits plaguing misty moors. The chemical scent of a brand-new book of folklore wafts into Janine's nose with each turn of the page as she's trying to keep up with note-taking.

In nearly half a century, she's gotten a little rusty at it—not scribbling fast enough. Some people in the hall have brought laptops, and they type away swiftly, as if they have a lifetime of office work behind them. Janine never learned that black-magic trick, so she's stuck with pen and paper, and with the slender set of highlighters her daughter Mary gifted to her—a sort of olive branch—before Janine left. Mary swore they're indispensable when studying. And she was right; they make the information pop up and settle easier in Janine's ancient brain.

Janine can only hope that her son David's parting words will not also prove correct.

"There's not going to be a pop quiz, you know?"

255

Janine barely spares a glance at Susan, who's resting her chin leisurely on her bejeweled fist, her notebook starkly blank.

"Well, I'm here to learn, not for the mixers," Janine puts enough amusement into the bite not to offend her new friend. They have different incentives for enrolling into the University of the Third Age—Susan's incentive being, namely, finding the third husband—but that doesn't mean they can't enrich each other's lives.

Susan laughs a little too loud, drawing the attention of the students sitting nearest.

"You call our little meetings mixers? You must have not been to a good college mixer before."

She's right; in fact, Janine hasn't been to *any* college mixer. Her first college adventure ended too quickly for her to taste the night life. And thank goodness she'd found out early enough, before she poured fountains of alcohol right into Mary's tiny body already nested inside her belly.

"Thing is," Susan adds, ignoring Janine's silence, "Vamer's fables are better enjoyed if you just relax and listen. You'll remember them better, too, promise."

Janine gives her a skeptical look, but thanks to the distraction of their conversation, there's now a gaping hole in her notes. If she'll have to borrow notes to copy anyway, she might as well try a different approach for the lecture's remainder.

She sits back and shifts her focus to Dr. Vamer. She's a beautiful woman, somewhat younger than Janine—or maybe she only seems younger, emanating brightness and energy in every movement, every passionate word. Her long, braided hair is unabashedly gray; Janine could bet she's never tried to hide the silver strands with dyes. Her dark eyes shine, surrounded by lovely crow's feet and decorated with the gentlest makeup.

She talks about Arthur Conan Doyle's nosedive into the mad world of mediums and seances like she's his biggest fan defending him from a crowd of skeptics, but Janine's learned by now that it's not the author that Dr. Vamer's so enthused about, but the stories of ghosts, ghouls, and vampires that she's passing on to her students.

Now that she no longer has to stare at the page, Janine lets her eyelids drop, just to rest her eyes for a moment. The warm air of the last days of summer engulfs her, and Dr. Vamer's voice, the scribbling, and the tapping of the keyboards become distant.

A buzzing in her pocket startles Janine. She rubs her eyes and looks around to see if anyone caught her snoozing, but luckily, no one's paying attention to her.

She discretely pulls out her phone and reads the text from Mary: *Zoey's in labor. We've just arrived at the hospital.*

A warm flush of excitement mixed with anxiety washes over Janine. She sends back a wish for a quick and light delivery for Zoey and health for the baby she can't greet in person. She hadn't been planning to drive home until next weekend when the baby was due.

She's beaming when she turns to Susan. "Looks like I'm going to be a great-grandma—again—tonight."

She recognizes the gleam in Susan's eye. "Ain't that just the best occasion to celebrate."

Janine doesn't protest. She'd much rather wait for the good news surrounded by people than sit alone in her room.

When the evening lecture ends, she and Susan go to knock at Armando's door.

He greets them with a glass of fine whiskey already in hand and a few guests sat around the table. His room is almost twice the size of other rooms, which makes him a perfect, and very willing, host.

Janine joins the relaxed yet lively atmosphere, but as the evening progresses, the worry persists: should she be on her way to the hospital, four hours away, instead of enjoying her glass of red wine?

She confirms that her phone's ringtone is turned on before making herself refocus on Armando's story of a trip across the Balkans he took as a young man.

"What a shame back then we didn't have smartphones with cameras. Oh! The photographs I would have taken..." he muses, ending his long tale.

"You would've been one of those travel vloggers my grandniece watches all the time," Susan says.

Armando leans forward with curiosity. "Vloggers? What on Earth is that?"

As Susan explains the term, a preppy jingle of Janine's phone steals her attention. There's a picture attached to the message: the sweet, wrinkly face of the newest member of her family.

Lana's here, happy and healthy!

Janine lets out a delighted sound and, as all eyes turn on her, she boasts of her precious great-granddaughter by showing the picture to each of her friends and accepting their congratulations.

"How do I put it on the background?"

Her screen has shown the same picture of Edwin for the last five years. It's one of the last pictures she had taken of her late husband, dear to her heart, but it's time for a change.

"Let me…" Susan takes the device from Janine and twiddles with it. "I can figure it out."

"My sons always make fun of my ancient phone with buttons," chimes in Anne. "Those new ones have so much going on."

Armando laughs. "I heard next semester's technology class will be about smartphones. Maybe we'll learn a thing or two."

"Oh—"

Janine looks at Susan, concerned, expecting her phone to have imploded in her hands, but Susan's lowered gaze as she returns the device suggests a different kind of mishap.

"I'm sorry, I didn't mean to read it."

One look at the message explains Susan's reaction: it's another text from Mary.

What a shame you decided not to be here to greet her.

Janine's heart drops.

Her upset must be visible because the silence in the room grows heavy. Everyone's trying not to look too curiously at her, but Janine knows they're a nosy bunch.

"I've mentioned that my family wasn't happy about me coming here," she explains.

Anna rolls her eyes. "Let me guess—you should sit at home and be an on-call free nanny."

"It's not like that," Janine protests. Of course when her grandkids were little, that was often the case. But now they're grown, and it's David's and Mary's turn to care for their respective grandchildren. She's only a back-up option. "They're used to me being around. I'm lucky that my children and grandchildren want to spend time with me."

"It doesn't mean you can't do other things."

"It's just not the best timing," she repeats the old excuse.

"For now, they're stuck in the hospital anyway," Susan says. "At best you'd see her through the glass."

Anne nods. "Let them come home first, then visit."

"I suppose…"

"Besides, you don't want to bring any germs to the baby," Armando says somberly. "You're looking under the weather."

Janine touches her cold forehead. She's feeling perfectly fine, but she knows Armando wouldn't offend someone for the heck of it.

"I didn't want to say it," agrees Susan, "but you have been quite pale."

"Oh, I haven't slept well the last few nights," Janine explains and, as if on command, yawns. "In fact, I think I'll go now, get some early sleep."

Her friends try to stop her, but she's made up her mind. She doesn't feel like moping around, hoarding attention.

She expects to fall asleep as soon as her head hits the pillow, yet her eyes remain wide open. Is she being selfish? Like David said, even if she succeeds and gets to the end of the program, the diploma won't mean a thing, not really. It won't give her any jobs—she's long retired anyway—and isn't that the whole point of having a degree?

"No one puts 'BA' on their gravestone." David's words ring in her head.

A waft of chill air brushes Janine's shoulder. Disgruntled, she sits up and reaches to the windowsill to adjust the towel she put there last week. She needs to ask the janitor to get the window fixed. She wraps herself with her duvet, hoping the room won't get colder.

Or maybe the leaky window is a sign, too old to properly fill its role, and the cold is telling her to leave. Her own home is always warm, and the windows are brand new; David saw to that after Edwin's death. He wanted his mom to be comfortable in her last years, healthy and safe, and she'd rejected that for this drafty old building, with noisy pipes and mice in the walls.

'Cause it must be mice, that scraping coming from the corner, beneath the wardrobe. It always starts so quiet, at night, that Janine's worn-out ears can hardly catch it. But as she tosses and turns, it grows louder.

Or closer.

Like it's stepping, ever so slowly, toward her bed.

Janine's stare is fixed on the floor drowning in the darkness. The curtains block out the moonlight, so she's left with useless eyes and perked-up ears. The desk light is too far, but her phone is in the pocket of her sweater on the chair. Close enough for her to reach.

She pulls her arm from under the covers and outstretches it over the darkness beyond her bed.

The cold crawls across the bare skin. It wraps itself around her forearm like a set of long, icy fingers.

Despite thrills running up her spine that have nothing to do with the temperature, she pushes forward until the tips of her fingers touch the fabric. She pinches it and pulls it closer, then feels for the phone. Finally, she manages to yank it out and bring her arm back to safety. She frantically turns the device around in her hands, searching for the right button.

The screen lights up, shining bright into her eyes.

Bang! Something smashes into the floor beside her. Janine jumps and a small, startled scream tears out of her mouth.

She shines the light toward the ground and finds the chair toppled over. The room around her is still completely empty.

Janine laughs.

The chair fell because she pulled it. Is she a little girl scared of the dark? There's nothing in here besides herself and a mouse looking for crumbs.

Sadly, the mouse will have to be dealt with, and if Janine's to get any sleep, it'll have to happen tonight. She's dressed in a coat and outside the door before she even realizes how late it is, but she knows there's someone at reception; perhaps they'll be able to find a mouse trap in the broom closet.

Somehow the high, empty halls flooded with moonlight don't bring Janine the same sense of fright her own room did.

The reception's on the other side of the building. Janine wraps herself tight with the coat before she opens the door to cut through the courtyard, but outside, the air that envelops her is warm and pleasant.

Spacious and green, with flowering bushes and many benches, the courtyard is a beloved spot for hanging out between classes. Surprisingly, one of the benches on Janine's path isn't empty. She approaches it cautiously to find the person on the bench is Dr. Vamer.

She's not planning to stop for chit-chat, but Vamer's soft smile and bright tone is so inviting as she muses, "Beautiful night, isn't it?"

Janine follows her gaze to the multitude of stars in the ink-black sky. "Haven't seen this many stars since I left the countryside as a teenager."

"We're far enough from downtown to miss most of the light pollution. One of the reasons I love it here," Dr. Vamer says, then as an afterthought, "and the full moon makes it magical."

"Shouldn't we watch out for werewolves?" Janine asks lightly, remembering last week's lecture.

Dr. Vamer laughs. "I think we're safe. I haven't heard of any werewolf attacks in the four years I've been here." She shifts to the side, inviting Janine to sit with her. "How are you enjoying college?"

"It's wonderful. Great people. Interesting classes. Your lectures especially are fascinating, Dr. Vamer."

"I wasn't fishing for a compliment, but thank you," Dr. Vamer says. "And it's Carol outside the lecture hall."

Janine nods and, encouraged, asks, "Why did you choose to teach old folks instead of shaping young minds?"

"I do teach at the local college twice a week," Carol says, then goes quiet. Janine expects that's all she'll get, then— "I like the atmosphere. I've taught in many places and found that there's something unmatched about the passion people approach school with when they don't only care about the degree."

"Some say it's pointless." Janine barely hides her bitterness. "Why put in all this work just to die not much after?"

Carol ponders, then gives Janine the most mischievous smile. "So that you can be a very smart ghost."

Janine bursts out laughing, and Carol joins her. Their laughter fills the night. For the first time in a while, Janine feels carefree.

"Is that why you chose to teach folklore? Because you believe in ghosts?"

" 'Believe' is a strong word, but I'm not a skeptic," Carols says. "No luck meeting one so far."

"If you'd like to, there's a fifty-percent chance my room is haunted." Instantly, Janine is mortified; she's invited Carol into her bedroom. "The other fifty percent says it's a mouse," she adds, and gets up. "Actually, I was going to ask someone for a mouse trap. A few nights now, it won't let me sleep."

"My wife would always put bait in a bowl and pour in oil to make it slippery. She hated killing the little rascals."

Janine doesn't miss the past tense, but they're not close enough to bond over dead spouses. "I never heard of that method. I'll try it."

"Good luck. I don't want you falling asleep in the classroom again."

Janine, embarrassed, leaves and goes to the common room to gather the materials for the contraption as instructed. Then she sets up the trap in her room, hoping the mouse is caught quickly. She lies in bed, and luckily neither the mouse nor the unhappy thoughts about her family keep her awake.

The trap is empty the next morning. It stays empty throughout the day and into the evening, the bait untouched.

Janine braces herself for another sleepless night. She changes early in hopes that if she can fall asleep before the scratching starts, maybe it won't wake her.

As soon as she lies down, her phone rings.

"I'm sorry about that text yesterday, Mom. I was too harsh," says Mary. "David riled me up. He's still unhappy with your leaving."

Janine sighs. Mary's got a lifelong habit of blaming David for things she's done, whether it's breaking a vase or ruining holidays.

"I certainly remember what he thought about it."

"You know he only wanted to hurt you in hopes it would stop you."

"And what about you?" Janine asks to steer the talk back to Mary.

"Well...I still don't understand why it had to be that school. There's plenty of places here that do classes for seniors."

Janine looks around her room, at her neat desk, at her books lining the shelves, at the window looking out at the lecture hall. She would not have this at any other school. Every weekday, she'd be riding half-way across the city in a crowded bus for a lecture among strangers she'd maybe exchange a few sentences with over a cup of bad coffee from a vending machine. Afterward, she'd return to an empty house.

Truth is, she didn't just enroll here to study. She wanted to get as close to the full experience she'd missed out on as possible, including the noisy dorm room and, despite what she's told Susan, the mixers.

"You know I've always wanted to do this, Mary."

The sudden coldness in Mary's voice feels like a punch, her words even more so. "I'm sorry for ruining your life."

Janine stiffens. "I never *once* thought that."

How dare Mary claim David wanted to hurt her then do the same!

"I gotta go," Mary says as if nothing happened. "We'll talk when you're here."

She hangs up before Janine can say goodbye.

Janine buries her face in her hands. All this time she believed she'd managed to raise Mary without making her feel as if she's cost Janine anything. She never regretted having her. She only regretted not returning to school when Mary was older. First there was Edwin's doctorate, then David was born, then Janine's mom got sick. And after that, it seemed too late. She'd had a good job that hadn't required a degree; there was no reason to make life harder for the whole family just because she craved some college fun.

But then Edwin died, and despite her family visiting often, at the end of the day she was on her own. All the excuses went out the window. She didn't want to die with regret.

Yet in the place of one regret came another. She's fulfilling her lifelong dream at the price of her family, and it's not fair.

Janine pulls her suitcase out from under her bed and starts packing her clothes. She'll visit Zoey and the baby, stay for a week or two, and then decide. Maybe that senior program in the city wouldn't be so bad?

Despite all the friends she's made here, all the lecture notes she's taken, not a day has gone by when she hasn't doubted her choice. The relief might be worth it.

She runs out of steam before she gets to packing her books, so she leaves them for tomorrow. With the new resolution, she might sleep a little better. The curtains stay open, letting the moonlight in to shoo away the darkness. It's much nicer this way. Illuminated, the luggage reminds her she's not an awful mother, even if her children think so of her these days.

She can see the mouse trap, too, still empty, as the scratching begins.

With a disgruntled groan, Janine grabs her phone, gets out of bed, and slowly moves toward the wardrobe where the noise is coming from.

She doesn't have a plan for what she'll do when she finds the mouse.

A part of her already knows there is no mouse.

She gets on her knees and bends to light the space beneath the wardrobe. It's empty, yet the scraping persists. It scuttles beyond the bookshelf, under the desk. Janine follows it with the beam of light until it grows frantic, jumping from one side of her to another. It's in the walls and behind the door. It's under the wooden floor right beneath her feet. Janine rises, as fast as her knees allow her, to run back into her bed and hide under the covers... but her bed's occupied by the pale, translucent silhouette of a young woman.

Janine freezes. Despite every instinct telling her to scream and storm out the door, she remains strangely calm, facing the bespectacled apparition. Dark hair frames her hollow cheeks, the frame of the window visible through her chest. She stares at a real ghost, and the ghost stares back at her. And then, in a blink, it's gone.

Janine's own words echo in her head: *there's a fifty-percent chance my room is haunted.* The very last thing she expected was to be right.

Even if the ghost isn't threatening her, the thought of sleeping here brings chills up Janine's spine. Her choices are to count on Susan's hospitality or to evict the ghost. Given the likelihood that Susan already has a guest over, the latter sounds like a more plausible option. Besides, she can't let some other grandma get a heart attack from the encounter after Janine leaves.

Logic suggests that if the girl's ghost haunts the dorms, she died on the school's premises. It's as good a start as any. The internet should have some information about her death or her identity. That is, if ghosts even follow logic.

Janine puts on her coat and leaves the room. Tension lets off her shoulders as soon as she closes the door behind her.

A few students are lounging in the common room, but the computers are luckily not in use. She goes through the learned motions of turning one on and getting on the internet, then she asks the search engine about deaths at the college in the last few decades. She finds a few fatal accidents, a few suicides, but the descriptions don't match and none of them mention the dorms.

She's about to give up when her eye catches an article about the downfall of the private college that used to operate in this building. The death of the daughter of a prominent lawyer prompted him and many other sponsors to withdraw their financial support. She died of pneumonia in her dorm room. No one even noticed until she started missing classes.

Janine moves on to looking for a way to get rid of a ghost, but the endless advertisements and popping-up windows make the websites near unusable. Even when she manages to scrape out information, it's either lore from some movie or adverts from mediums too sketchy even for her elderly, naïve mind.

She turns the computer off.

She's got a much better source of ghost lore at hand.

Hopefully, Carol will be in the courtyard again. Otherwise, Janine'll have to wait until tomorrow.

She goes straight to the same bench where she met Carol yesterday. Carol's there, basking in the moonlight.

"Hi, Janine," she greets her cheerfully. "How's mouse-hunting?"

Janine sits and takes a deep breath. She's about to sound ridiculous, and it hardly seems worth it, now that she's leaving. Then again, after she leaves, she'll never meet Carol again, so it shouldn't matter what Carol thinks of her. And yet it does.

"It wasn't a mouse," she says at last.

"A ghost, then?" Carol asks, like seeing a specter in one's room is completely normal.

Janine nods. "It appears so."

Carol laughs, lightly; for a moment until she realizes Janine isn't joking. "Why do you think that?"

"Have you heard about the daughter of Joseph Ashcroft, named Alice? She died in the dorms."

Carol hums in confirmation. "Awfully sad story."

"Well," Janine starts slowly. "I've seen her."

"You've seen her ghost in your room." Carol doesn't sound like she thinks Janine has lost her mind.

"Bright and clear."

A silence falls as Carol appears to mull Janine's words over. Janine expects to be told that she was only dreaming—a thought that's crossed Janine's mind a hundred times since she left her room.

Carol surprises her by asking a different question. "Were there any other signs besides the noises? Like moving objects or drops in temperature?"

"My window gets awfully drafty."

"In weather this nice?" Carol gives her a meaningful look. Janine could have put that one together herself. If the fluctuating temperature had been a sign of the haunting, could the toppled chair also have been not of Janine's doing? "What do you plan to do?"

"I was hoping you'd tell me."

A sly smile lights up Carol's face. "Only if you let me tag along," she says. "I won't get another chance to see a real ghost."

Janine barely hides her relief. She won't have to try to banish the ghost alone. "I'd love some backup."

Before hunting the ghost, Janine and Carol hunt down a few protective components. They borrow white candles from the meditation room, then pillage the kitchen for spices and herbs that, according to Carol's books, have warding or purifying qualities.

"The problem is, we don't actually know what works on ghosts because there's no solid proof they exist," Carol explains, vigorously mixing the ingredients in a bowl. "This is guesswork based on folktales."

"So it might not work," Janine says.

"Did you feel like Alice was threatening you?"

"Not at all." Janine recalls the strangely serene moment she'd shared with the ghost. "We just stared at each other, then she was gone."

"Then let's hope this is merely a precaution and doesn't need to work," Carol says, setting the wooden spoon aside. "Let's go."

They discuss their plan on the way to the room. First, coax the ghost out of the hiding, then guide it to the afterlife with a few sentences copied from one of Carol's books.

"Are you sure you don't want to bring in equipment to register the ghost activity? You could write papers about it. Or become a ghost vlogger," Janine suggests as they hesitate outside her room.

"And become a pariah and the laughingstock in my field?" Carol dismisses the idea. "Believe me, many have tried."

"Maybe they were right."

Carol presses her lips tight. "Only one way to find out," she says, pressing the handle.

The room is calm and quiet, just as Janine left it. Somehow it hasn't occurred to her until now that Alice's ghost might not show up when they call her. Carol's trusted her near blindly. Will she be disappointed or relieved if this whole thing turns out to be a bust?

"Getting ready for the weekend?"

Janine follows Carol's eyes to the suitcase standing by the wall.

"I'm leaving a little early," she simply says. Her plan is to head home, then deal with the formalities of withdrawing over the phone. Everything she forgets to take home, she'll ask Susan to send over.

"You won't miss any of my lectures, so I'm not—"

A book flies off a shelf.

Janine throws her arm up, at the last moment protecting Carol's lovely face. Another book, Carol dodges, then she bends to pour the herb mixture in a protective ring around the two of them.

"I don't think this will shield us from books," Janine says while struggling to light the candles on the table.

"Talk to her!"

This wasn't the plan. Janine isn't the one with the magical notes in her pocket. She'd barely glanced at the book Carol was copying, let alone memorized it.

She has to improvise.

"Alice, stop this!" she calls in her most "stern granny" voice.

The attack halts.

"You know my name?" Alice's form appears by the bookshelf, her hand still raised. Her voice is strangely solid for a see-through apparition.

"I do," Janine says. Behind her, Carol stands up, the ring around them finished. Janine doesn't feel any protective power emanating from it. "And I know you've been stuck here for a long time."

"I've always been stuck here." Alice's anger simmers.

"We want to help you," says Carol.

"No lectures!"

Alice glitches out and reappears before them. Janine steps back in their tiny ring, almost colliding with Carol. Somehow, her palm lands right in Carol's hand. Carol gives it an encouraging squeeze. Janine's on her own, but she's not alone.

Then she gets it: Alice's anger at the professor, throwing books. Being stuck here, at school, *always*—not only in death but while she was alive, too.

"Who chose for you—your father?"

"He wanted a lawyer daughter," Alice snarls. "Read, study, memorize, repeat!" She yanks a few more books from the shelf, but she slams them on the floor instead of hurling them at their bones. "I was too dumb to get accepted anywhere, but Dad's money got me in here."

"You weren't dumb," Janine says. "You can't excel at a thing you despise."

Alice pushes a finger behind her glasses to wipe away a ghostly tear.

Janine fights back the urge to leave the ring and approach her, to comfort her in any way she can. Best she can offer is the softness when she asks, "What did *you* dream of?"

"I wanted to travel," says Alice quietly. "More than anything, I wanted to see the whole world."

She slumps on the bed, head hung low, one book still in her hand. Ironically, it's the book of essays about South America that Janine borrowed from Armando.

"I wanted to see Machu Picchu," she says, pointing at the cover before dropping the book on the mattress. "The Colosseum and Baalbek. I wanted to walk the Great Wall of China. To eat Maqluba in Ramallah. To step-dance in Galway. To touch the meteorite in Namibia." Her emotions build in every word. "But instead I was stuck here. So I studied all the time—I told myself that once I had a good job, I'd be able to—" She swallows an angry sob.

Janine knows what comes next. There never came a spring break nor summer holidays when Alice jumped on a plane and visited any of the places she'd dreamed of. Did she even get a chance to go abroad? Taste the food and a culture different to her own?

The numbness in Alice voice says it all when she adds, "And then I died."

Janine feels the girl's scorching grief in her own heart. Though it isn't fair to compare her own frustrations to the ghost's—unlike Alice, she got to live a long and good life; she loved every second of being a mom. Yet, she too felt stuck, a part of her always unfulfilled, always waiting for better timing, in fear of disappointing her family.

Now, she's abandoning her dream, same as when Alice would have to leave her beloved world behind, guided by Carol's spells.

What if she didn't have to?

"Then go," Janine says. "See the world."

Alice stares at her like she's said something incredibly stupid. "I can't. I'm dead."

"So?"

"I'm stuck here. I can't leave."

"Have you tried?"

Alice shifts uncomfortably and doesn't answer.

"Look. It won't be the same," says Janine, no longer afraid to step out of the ring. "You can't do all the things a living person can. But you can still see those beautiful places. You can listen to the music, dance, and laugh. You can dive with the angler fish and climb Mount Everest, maybe even hop on a rocket to space. And hey, you don't even need money anymore."

Janine gets so close to Alice that the pale, ghastly light illuminates her clothes.

"So what's stopping you, really?"

Alice looks between Janine and Carol. Then, she moves toward the window. "I don't know if this will work," she says, pressing her fingertips to the glass as cautiously as if there's a fire writhing beyond it.

"You won't know until you try."

With her eyes squeezed shut, Alice pushes her arm through, as if the glass doesn't exist. She waves her hand on the other side, making sure it's still whole. Encouraged, she floats to the windowsill.

"All this time…I could've just left?" Her voice cracks.

Janine knows something about the ache of waiting for too long. An old cliché is best she can offer. "I've heard it's better late than never."

Once again Alice looks at Janine with eyes clear and bright. "Thank you."

With that, she jumps out the window into the grass bathed in moonlight. She runs to meet the world outside the college walls as if for the first time.

"How did you know that would work?" Carol still pants from the excitement, her hand pressed to her chest. "There's extensive lore about spirits being tied to the place of their death."

Janine grins. "I must have slept through that part of the lecture."

They turn on the light and collect the tossed books into a pile. Carol begins putting them back on the bookshelf.

"Leave them here. I'll be packing them tomorrow." Janine doesn't bite her tongue in time.

From the change of expression on Carol's face, she knows there's no use offering a calming cup of chamomile.

"So you're not just leaving for the weekend?"

"I'm not sure," Janine admits. She'd hoped Carol would stick around a little longer, have a chat about the metaphysics of ghosts into the late-night hours. But it was all a sweet dream that would be gone in the morning. "I love being here, but it's not the right time."

Carol blows out the candles and collects them into the now-empty bowl before turning to Janine again. "And here I was thinking everything you said to Alice came from the heart."

Janine doesn't answer. Carol hardly knows her; how can she know anything about her heart?

And yet, she's right.

Carol takes her silence as a cue to leave.

"Take care, Janine," she says. "Thank you for an incredible experience."

Next morning, bright and early, Janine knocks at a door in a brightly lit hallway. She double checks the plaque: Dr. Carol Vamer, Department of Culture. She couldn't wait until office hours, so she hopes she can catch her before classes start.

"Come in!" comes from the inside. Janine's heart beats faster.

Carol sits behind her desk, reading some papers. At the sight of Janine, she smiles. "Did you sleep well?"

"Not really," Janine admits as she takes a seat. "Had a lot to process."

"I'm guessing you don't only mean the world-altering revelation about the existence of ghosts."

"That was certainly part of it. How about you? Still not planning to write a book about it?"

It's not every day that one discovers the secrets of the afterlife without crossing that road for good. For someone who has spent their life study-ing ghosts, gods, and monsters as nothing but made-up creatures from bedtime stories, it must throw a new light on everything she's known.

"No," Carol says decidedly. "But I might have to look at the works of my disgraced colleagues from a new perspective. What have you decided?"

"That I'd like to be a very smart ghost one day."

Carol laughs her sweet laugh.

"So you're not leaving?"

Is that relief Janine hears in her voice?

Janine had spent the sleepless night weighing her options. Alice's grief for her life lost had been so palpable that it left a mark on her. The last thing Janine wants is to experience the same on her deathbed, or beyond it.

Mary and David are adults; they don't need her to be on call, and she's still so near. There's nothing wrong, or selfish, about doing this one thing for herself after five decades of giving. She's not abandoning anyone—including herself. Maybe it's too late, and maybe it seems pointless to them, but it's not pointless to her.

"I'm leaving, but only to visit my great-granddaughter," Janine says. She's terribly excited to meet little Lana. But there's another thing she's almost as excited for. "How would you feel about having a coffee with me on Monday? We could do some of the processing together."

Carol smiles her wide, gorgeous smile and places her palm on top of Janine's. "I would be absolutely delighted."

A CLOCKWORK WARMTH

JESSICA MASON

Tags: attraction at first sight, classism, clockpunk, college/university, first kiss, getting together, library, m/m, meet cute, pining (mutual), present tense, romance, science fiction, student (undergraduate), third person limited (alternating) point of view

"**C**an I open the window?" Laurie addresses his question to the frost-coated glass rather than look back at where Professor Simon is scowling from his desk.

Beyond the window, a thin layer of snow covers the university grounds. The gray clouds are thick and heavy, and the entire world of Barlow College looks even more muted and monotone than usual.

Except for the birds: delicate bits of clockwork that still manage to reflect the dim light off their tarnished brass shells.

One of them perches on the icy window ledge and cocks its head, staring in at Laurie. It's the size and shape of a small sparrow, moving in short, fluttery bursts. One of its legs is bent at an awkward angle, forcing it to balance precariously on the other. Beneath its breastplate, an exposed gear stutters over every fifth click as it turns.

"Excuse me?" Simon responds, incredulous.

"The birds," Laurie explains. "They get cold."

Outside, fresh snow falls. Inside, the heat from the old radiator is almost as stifling as Professor Simon's judgment. "They aren't *real*, Laurence."

Spark of Life laws would argue otherwise, but few seem to care about the legalese that classifies these creatures as more than the sum of their mechanical parts.

More real than a bunch of smoke and mirrors, Laurie wants to say, but he holds his tongue. Shuffles his feet instead. Taps his fingers nervously against the book of poetry he's been annotating since he was a boy, the pages now interspersed with letters from his mother. Scribbled notes about her menagerie of clockwork animals back home, and detailed sketches of their innerworkings.

In the corner, a Basset Hound hologram flickers, yawns, and shakes its head, multi-colored pixels fizzling around it until the image of the dog settles into its original, pre-programmed position.

"My office hours are limited," Simon says. "I'm not keen to spend them arguing over spare parts."

The sentiment is nothing new, though it sets Laurie's teeth on edge. The mechanical animals are a holdover from a generation ago, back when the wealthy filled their gardens with shiny, expensive novelties. Now that bolts and gears have gone out of fashion in favor of holograms, the animals are left to fend for themselves out in the wild. Or, if they're lucky, in sanctuaries like his mom's.

"Sorry, Professor." Laurie moves from the window to the bookshelves lining the walls. Rather than physical books, they're filled with projections of text. He reaches for one of them idly, and at his touch, the display blinks out of existence.

Laurie clears his throat and retreats to hover over the chair facing the desk. Simon glares pointedly until Laurie finally sits down.

Immediately, Laurie's knee starts bouncing.

"You have such potential, Laurence. But the difference between your assignments now and those at the beginning of the semester is...concerning."

Laurie settles a hand over his bouncing knee to still it, only to have the other knee take up the effort.

"If the material has gotten too challenging for you..."

"It hasn't. I've just been...distracted." That's one word for it, he supposes.

Laurie had jumped at the chance to attend Barlow a few months ago, excited to continue his studies in a place with more than just the one bookshop, where he could access information quicker than sending away for texts on the weekly ferry to the mainland and learn from professors in person rather than by post.

But university life is much lonelier than he'd anticipated. Filled with far fewer books and far more projections that hurt his eyes and give him headaches.

Part of the allure of studying the classics was in making the past tangible. Holding a piece of history in his hands. But even the *present* doesn't feel tangible in this place. Like everyone prefers to keep the rest of the world at a distance, turning reality into something transparent and flimsy.

There's no risk of caring about anything when the things aren't really there.

Simon's frown softens with a touch of sympathy. "Given the caliber of your work before that 'distraction,' I'm reluctant to fail you. But I'm also hard-pressed to find anything of merit in the final paper you've submitted."

The Hound hologram huffs a preprogrammed breath without sound. The text display on the shelf blinks back to life, marred now with lines of static. A typewriter on the desk has a glowing speech-to-type device hovering over its keys, and an unused fountain pen rests beside a well-used touchscreen calendar. The juxtaposition of the traditional and modern leaves Laurie feeling wrong-footed and tongue-tied.

He's been homesick ever since he got to the mainland, but he suddenly misses the island where he grew up with an intensity that feels like a physical injury.

"Rewrite the paper," Simon says. "Show me that you can turn this around. I'll give you until the end of break."

It isn't until Laurie's back in his dorm room that he feels like he can breathe again.

He opens the single window, and an icy breeze scatters the papers on the desk beneath it. The cold air is bracing, his dying radiator no match for it. His fair, freckled skin has been chapped pink since winter began, the color clashing with his auburn hair, which was already a sore thumb in the middle of this homogenized campus of grays and browns.

Still, he stands there waiting, shivering, tapping his book of poetry against his thigh, until a small brass bird lands on the ledge and hops inside. Moments later, two more follow.

Laurie runs careful fingers along their backs, noting where they've been breaking down with time and where they've been patched up with odds and ends not designed for the job: a pen nib, a deconstructed bulldog clip, a broken strike bar. Evidence of someone's inexpert, but dedicated, care.

Evidence that maybe Laurie isn't as alone as he feels.

The low murmur of voices on the other side of the office door barely registers as Beck works. He prefers when the job is outside booming lecture halls or crowded classrooms, where the background noise to playing handyman is something interesting and educational. But the quiet of the English Department is a walk in the damned park compared to where he was a year ago.

So he keeps his head down and his hands buried inside the wall, where rusted pipes are leaking onto the sleeves of his last clean shirt.

The office door opens, and Beck hears a soft voice in a subtle accent he doesn't recognize. Catches a glimpse in his peripheral vision of unexpected red hair and patched corduroy.

But when he risks a glance up, he's met with exactly what he's come to expect from students at Barlow College. Two of them stand over him, all the same brown hair, charcoal coats, gray electronic devices wrapped around wrists and projecting constant static right in front of their faces. "You going to Rockwell after this?"

Beck grits his teeth and re-focuses on the pipes. There's nothing foreign about their voices, nor the expensive black shoes getting uncomfortably close to where his canvas tool roll lies open across the floor.

"The dean said our dorms would take priority over break," the other says.

"Then go ask the dean where I'm headed next."

"How about I ask him who's replacing you?"

He's used to the entitlement at this point, which always seems to go hand-in-hand with empty threats and a generous helping of condescension. Still, a prickle of fear that Beck prefers to call "self-preservation" makes his shoulders tense at the idea that anyone could impact his entire life with a single word to the right people.

"Rockwell's on the list," he says shortly. "So's Collins and the Union." Not that he plans to start on them until after the incoming snowstorm lets up. But it's enough to get the students to leave him alone, stepping over his tool roll and leaving scuff marks across the waxed green canvas.

Beck finishes his work with steady, calming breaths, reminding himself that, whatever the obstacles, they're worth it to get out from under his father's thumb.

He runs a hand back and forth over his close-cropped black hair, calloused fingers rough against his face when he drags his palm down. His wet shirtsleeves cling to his forearms, highlighting the uneven tan still lingering from a summer of patching holes in the roofs of every building on campus.

Well, every building except the library. Why waste funds protecting the aging physical copies of what's already been scanned into the college's database?

The books remain, gathering dust on the shelves, but the librarians have all retired, and no one seems to know how to find texts that don't automatically appear as projections when they speak their query aloud. Students still use the space to study, wires and electrodes gradually encroaching on the communal areas. A monument to the past slowly being overtaken by the electronic present.

Maybe that's why the dean put Beck up in the drafty library attic. A place as out of sight and out of mind as is possible at Barlow.

Maybe that's also why the birds make their homes up there with him.

"This is only temporary," Beck says later that evening as he finishes attaching a fountain pen nib to one bird's wing.

It's perched patiently on the overturned wooden milk crate that acts as Beck's worktable and chirps happily in reply. An odd facsimile of a bird call that sounds more like metal keys clinking against each other.

"Best I could do for now, but you should still be able to fly."

Another chirp. Two of its friends flit down from the rafters to land beside it and hop about the crate, examining his handiwork. He's not certain how much they understand but likes to err on the side of mutual respect, especially where Spark of Life is concerned.

People are another story. In Beck's experience, most don't deserve the same deference.

"I'll find something for that foot as well," he tells the bird with the bent leg. Beck has been particularly worried about that one; its gears stutter a little too often.

The bird chirps back, delighted, with seemingly more faith in Beck than he has in himself.

On the floor by the bed lies a stack of Spark of Life schematics that Beck had found in the rubble when he'd first moved in. He studies them religiously but doesn't feel qualified to fix anything less superficial than feet and feathers.

A particularly icy draft hits, startling the birds into brief flight before they settle again. They've been getting slower as the temperature drops, their chirps quieter. At night, they huddle together around the old vent in the floor that delivers heat from the building below.

"Sorry," Beck tells them. He's never been one for apologies, but he thinks these little guys are overdue for a few of them.

The wind outside intensifies, shaking the rafters and sending more birds swooping down to find hiding places amongst Beck's things. The one with the broken leg hops toward him, and he takes it in hand automatically, lifting it up to cradle against his collarbone.

The bird settles the top of its brass head against the underside of Beck's jaw, and he can feel the vibration of its gears turning against the sensitive skin there. On every fifth click, the gear stutters a second too long.

Beck would never admit it, but his breath catches every time.

Two days into winter break and Laurie hasn't seen a single other person. The dormitory around him is eerily silent without the usual bustle of other residents, and the world beyond is muffled by the snow that falls with increasing persistence. He's been living on peanut-butter sandwiches and instant coffee and the soul-crushing malaise of not knowing how to rewrite this damned paper.

It shouldn't be this difficult. His source material is poetry from a hundred years ago. His thesis champions the application of historical knowledge in modern spaces. Laurie *thrives* on this stuff.

But his head is too muddled by his heart, and his heart doesn't know why it should bother.

A part of him wishes he'd gone home for the break like everyone else. Except he couldn't stomach the expense and couldn't say with certainty that he'd actually return to Barlow if he left.

"Besides, where would that leave you?" he asks the broken-legged bird that's remained with him these last two days, despite Laurie's attempts to shoo it off to join its brethren, wherever they're currently hiding. He hopes it's some place warmer than here.

Laurie pulls a sweater over top of the one he's already wearing and paces his room, rubbing cold hands together. The cast-iron radiator seems to have reached the end of its slow death just in time for the height of the storm.

When the power also fails, it feels like a matter of course.

The frost on the window creeps along the inside of the glass. Between the fading daylight and the thickly falling snow, Laurie can't see anything beyond the nearest tree.

The bird chirps at him from inside the scarf nest Laurie has made on his desk.

"We could try the dean's office? See if the power's on there?"

Brass plating can only convey so much emotion, but Laurie gets the distinct impression that the bird is unimpressed.

"All right, how about the library?"

He doubts the place has power, but it's only two buildings over, and there's a large fireplace in the back. The flames are digital projections, but the stones housing those images are real enough. He might be able to do something with that.

The bird looks decidedly more interested in this option.

So Laurie bundles up and carefully tucks the bird into the front of his jacket. He can feel the gentle vibration of its gears against his chest, with an added vibrato from shivering. He grabs his book of poetry and mechanics, setting off into the storm.

The library is dark and nearly as cold as the outside. Rows of book-shelves go on forever around him, disappearing into the darkness and continuing upward several floors to vaulted ceilings and stained glass currently blacked out with snow. Laurie heads to the back, encouraged by a flickering light that becomes brighter the closer he gets. Apparently, he wasn't the only one with this idea.

Then he sees the birds.

They're perched in a line that spans the whole oversized hearth. There must be forty or fifty of them, the firelight dancing across the undersides of their brass bodies and making them look otherworldly. Almost magical.

The shadowed figure standing before them is just as captivating an image. Backlit by the fire, all Laurie can make out are the sharp angles of him; the toned muscle and rigid posture of someone always on high alert.

Between the cold, the darkness, and the days without human interaction, something about the scene feels ethereal. "Oh," Laurie says with a dreamlike, dawning realization. "Are they yours?"

The man turns, fists clenched, and doesn't relax even when he sees the lack of threat that Laurie poses. "…I didn't know anyone else was here," he says, voice rough and low but somehow gentler than the rest of him. There's a caution behind it that speaks more of vulnerability than of violence.

"I didn't either. Are you a student?"

Rather than answer, the man takes a slow step forward and narrows his dark eyes in an assessing sweep of Laurie's person.

Laurie is struck by the deliberateness of his movements, the calculation and compactness, versus Laurie's careless energy. He imagines himself through this man's eyes, and it all comes up short. The layers of patched and mismatched clothes, the book gripped tight in one frozen hand, the lump of something moving beneath his coat cradled by the other.

The man's brow furrows. "You brought a book with you?"

"Uh." Laurie taps nervously against the book cover. "Yes."

"To a library."

Laurie fidgets. The snow in his hair has started to melt down his neck. "It's a good book."

From within his jacket there is a sharp, metallic chirp.

Those dark eyes turn hard. "What do you have?"

"Oh. Um…a friend?"

"A *friend.*"

"My radiator broke. And he was cold. So." A tiny brass beak pecks at the top of Laurie's coat zipper and chirps again.

The stranger's hard edges soften in response. Like Laurie has said the magic words. Or else the bird has.

"Well." Another, deliberate step forward. A hand offered to shake. "You better come closer to the fire, then." The sleeves of his shirt are rolled up, exposing tanned, dark-haired forearms. Recent scrapes and older scars. A tendril of black ink that might be a tattoo disappearing beneath fabric. "I'm Beck."

As Laurie hesitates, Beck nods toward the birds on the mantle. "Seems you already know the others."

"Laurie," the man says with that slight accent that Beck remembers from the hallway in the English Department.

It isn't the only noticeable difference between Laurie and the rest of the Barlow student body. His hair, for one, could be spotted a mile away, mussed in too many directions to be intentional, the firelight making the red tones look even redder. There's also his patched, corduroy jacket, his practical work boots, his frenetic energy.

But his face is the most striking. Fair skin, more pronounced for all the freckles. Large eyes, constantly in motion. Angular features, at once boyish and elegant.

Beck holds Laurie's hand for longer than he means to.

Remembering himself with a jolt, he plays it off by lifting their arms to examine Laurie's wristwatch. "There's no projector?"

It's just an old-fashioned timepiece with a leather band. Not particularly special, but Beck finds himself amazed by its existence. By the fact that someone in this place is wearing it.

"No. I'm useless with electronics," Laurie says.

Beneath the delicate skin on the inside of Laurie's wrist, Beck can feel a rabbiting pulse against his thumb. Laurie's fingers are long and slender, faint freckles across the knuckles, smudged ink stains fading into the grooves.

"Me, too." Beck clears his throat and forces himself to let go just as another chirp erupts from inside Laurie's coat.

Laurie lowers the zipper enough for the bird to poke its head out and make several excited noises when it spots the others.

Beck laughs softly. A rare thing, but a damned better option right now than the bewildering swooning his heart would prefer. No matter how out of the ordinary Laurie appears to be, he's still a student, still as far from Beck's reality as is possible to get, even when standing barely a foot away.

He ushers Laurie closer to the fire, sidestepping the mess of wires that he'd ripped out of the fireplace to create it.

Laurie's cheeks flush dramatically with the heat. And Beck can't help but stare as Laurie's expressive hands deposit the bird from Laurie's coat onto the mantle, then work to remove a few layers of damp clothing.

"Have you been studying them? The birds?" Laurie asks. "I didn't realize Barlow still offered Spark of Life coursework."

"It doesn't. But I have some old drawings…" Beck shrugs. He's never said it out loud before. Has only revealed this particular interest when caught out by his father, back before he left that closet above the auto shop. Trading one attic for another, knowing that doing so meant he could never go back.

The part of Beck that enjoys digging into a textbook as much as digging into a car's engine was never going to garner his father's approval. But poring over diagrams and equations more often than he indulged his father's friends for a drink had gained the man's outright scorn.

The only thing worse than bowing out of customary masculine rituals was doing so for the wrong reasons. And the only thing worse than studying was studying "fancy, over-priced abominations."

"It's just a hobby," Beck finishes lamely.

Laurie runs a gentle finger along one bird's dented breastplate while it chitters at him with obvious affection. "A worthwhile one."

Maybe this storm was sent to test Beck in more ways than one.

"Are you interested in clockwork too?" he asks, trying to get a handle on his renegade emotions.

"Oh. Uh, no. I'm in the English department. Classical…well, classical *everything*. Much to the chagrin of my professors."

"Your classical professors don't like that you're studying the classics?"

Laurie laughs, a musical sound that the birds add to with a burst of tinkling chirps and ruffling metal feathers, like a living windchime. "They don't like that the only way I know how to do it is classically. I guess philosophy, history, and poetry are all better when projected in bright lights and static, rather than plain text on a piece of paper."

Beck's eyes return to the ink stains on Laurie's fingers, the worn book he's still holding like a security blanket.

"I like paper," he says, feeling like an idiot as soon as the words are out.

But Laurie turns to him with a grin, and Beck feels suddenly like he could conquer the entire world.

They shove an old couch close to the fire and sit on opposite ends, several birds flitting down to nestle into the space between. Though one perches on the couch back and presses its head into Laurie's sweater, between his shoulder blades.

"Should I be offended that they've found a new favorite?" Beck asks, though offense is so far from the feeling currently expanding inside his ribcage.

"They must recognize a kindred spirit." At Beck's look, Laurie adds, "I don't really belong here either."

"You could say the same about me."

Laurie regards him critically for a lengthy moment that has Beck, for perhaps the first time in his life, struggling not to fidget. "Fair enough. They must recognize a bit of my mother in me, then."

Beck raises an eyebrow, and Laurie lays his book open on the middle cushion amongst the birds. "This is mine." He points at the annotations in the margins of the poetry, then at the loose-leaf schematics sticking out every few pages. "And these are hers. She used to build them. Not just birds, but all kinds of animals."

"Not anymore?"

"Now she just collects them. Gives them a home. Kind of like you."

Beck shakes his head, but Laurie continues. "Mom says that creating things comes with responsibility. And that too many machinists took that for granted. No one thought about who would care for the animals beyond their intended use."

"She's right. It was cruel not to consider the consequences. What happens when their purpose no longer exists? Where are they supposed to go?"

Laurie frowns, and his knee starts to bounce.

Without thinking, Beck reaches a hand across the birds to still it.

Laurie freezes. The large hand is a warm, comforting weight on his thigh. He glances at his other leg, but it remains still as well. His body has never felt so…quiet before.

He swallows thickly, and his next words come out a little hoarse. "I think she's too wrapped up in *fixing* things to contemplate deeper meanings."

Beck draws his hand back slowly, a determinedly inconsequential motion. But Laurie can see the panic in his tight jawline, in the way his other hand is now a fist against his own leg. "That's more your area, right? Poetry or whatever."

"Yeah." Laurie bites back a smile. "Poetry or whatever."

The bird against Laurie's back hops onto his shoulder and then down to land on the open book. It pecks at a page corner before glancing up at Laurie's face like it's asking a question.

"Their purpose is to exist," Laurie says, eyes on the bird. "To live. They shouldn't need to do anything beyond that to be worthy of care."

When Laurie looks back at Beck, he's surprised to see the gutted expression there. Like Laurie has said something profound.

Abruptly, Beck blinks and stands, jostling the birds. He turns away to break off another leg from the demolished chair being used for kindling.

Laurie watches him toss it into the fire and tend the blaze with an iron poker. Through the thin fabric of Beck's shirt, Laurie can see how defined the muscles are, carving out sharp grooves and prominent slopes along his back, each adjusting in a seamless dance as he reaches and flexes.

It is a heady thing to behold, someone so at home in their own skin that their body has shaped itself around what they require of it. Rather than, in Laurie's case, awkwardly trying to shape himself around whatever his body will allow. Adjusting his life to make room for his own constantly fumbling and twitching limbs.

"What dorm are you in?" Beck asks, his back still to Laurie. "I'll come by once the storm is over and fix your radiator."

"You don't have to do that. I'll head to the maintenance office in the morning."

Beck's shoulders hitch. "Just. Tell me the room. So I can check in."

"Collins. 302."

Beck nods once, then returns to his place on the couch. The same place, but it feels farther away somehow.

Maybe it's because Laurie's already half asleep, sunk down low in the couch, surrounded by warmth and the clicking of gears that remind him of home, but he has a desperate urge to bridge that distance.

Slowly, he slides his hand across the cushions, through the huddled brass bodies of the birds, until his fingers meet the untucked end of Beck's shirt. He takes hold of it in a tight grip.

Beck jerks his head up to stare at Laurie, wide eyes made more intense by the thick frame of lashes around them.

"You should visit the island sometime," Laurie says around a yawn. "Meet the other animals. My mom would love you."

A smirk tugs at Beck's lips, but it looks sad. "I'm not someone mothers tend to love."

"Mine would."

Beck leans toward Laurie then, taut frame hovering above the birds between them. But he stills before reaching him. Closes his eyes like it hurts. "Go to sleep," he whispers.

As Laurie does just that, the entire world narrows to this single patch of warmth surrounding them. The darkness beyond is vast, the wind still howling outside, but this space by the fire, the birds huddled close inside the edges of the light, feels intimate and safe and forever.

Nothing about the golden glow of this room is gray.

It can't last, though. Laurie knows this. And when he blinks awake the next morning, he isn't surprised that the only company still with him are the birds.

In the early morning hours, Beck spends more time staring than sleeping.

Laurie's frantic energy doesn't quite extinguish in slumber, but it does get softer. There is a fragile vulnerability in the way his fingers still occasionally twitch and his slack mouth mumbles incoherently on random exhales. His arm remains settled across the couch between them, a loose grip on Beck's shirt.

Beck finally turns away to scan the room as the sun starts to rise. The fire's died but the power's returned, the electric heaters interspersed throughout the building humming again.

He extricates himself from Laurie's hand, shushing cheerful greetings from the birds as he goes.

Then he heads out to the Collins dormitory to fix a radiator.

The winter break ends, a couple thousand bodies return to campus for spring semester, and Beck goes back to keeping his head down, his hands busy. He listens keenly to the professors in their classrooms as he does his repairs. He reminds himself that this is better than the alternative.

If, in his periphery, he catches a glimpse of red among all the gray...if he lingers near the English Department more than any other building...it doesn't have to mean anything.

Beck has always been an expert in denying himself, dividing the important parts of his life up into what he can realistically keep and what he'll need to sacrifice to do so.

Still. Every time he thinks he spots some color in the crowd, his body betrays him. He sets his tools down, forgets his work, searches for the source before realizing it was just wishful thinking.

At night, he combs through the random parts he's managed to collect, hoping something will stand out as a magical fix for the birds more broken than the others. Hoping the old schematics he's studied so thoroughly that he has them memorized will suddenly feel less intimidating to apply to the real-life models.

The Basset Hound hologram in Professor Simon's office raises its head as Laurie paces closer to it. On instinct, he reaches down to pet the dog, only to trip as his hand passes through the projection. Bursts of static fizzle around the interruption, but the image doesn't notice.

Laurie winces and paces back toward the window.

"I should've had you wait outside," Simon mutters as he reads Laurie's essay.

A "sorry" is on the tip of Laurie's tongue, but he grits his teeth against it. He's been handing out too many apologies since he got to this place, like his mere existence requires one, and he's done with it.

That night in the library had awakened a few realizations. Most notably, that stifling the pieces of himself connected to the reason he wanted to come to the mainland and study is probably what's been chipping away at his resolve to stay here and continue that study.

A fact obvious in hindsight, but so hard to notice when floundering blindly through the feeling.

Simon lays the last page down on his desk. "It's certainly...interesting."

"But?" Laurie asks, leaning against the windowsill and tapping fingers against his thighs. He feels bold prompting a professor like this, insisting that there should be more. That he deserves more.

Simon peers at Laurie over the top of his glasses. "*But*," he says, "not inadequate."

Laurie pushes off from the wall and makes an embarrassing display of excitement that Simon dutifully ignores.

"Your ideas have merit, Laurence, they're just terribly antiquated."

"Good thing all the books they're based on are a couple hundred years old."

Simon huffs an aggrieved sound that's almost a laugh.

Laurie considers this a win, just as he does the package from home that arrives a week later. It's wrapped in thick, brown paper and tied, not with twine, but with the copper-coated wire Laurie's mother uses in her workshop. Beside the scribbled address is a rough sketch of a bird's innerworkings.

"That's you," he tells the bird perched on his desk.

It cocks its head to one side, skeptical, as another bird peeks in through the open window. The temperature outside is still freezing, but Laurie keeps the heat up full blast, tempting fate at breaking the radiator again, and drowns himself in extra layers of clothing so that the birds can come and go as they please during the day.

He has a hunch where they spend their nights. And with whom.

"Doesn't change anything, though," he mutters.

Both birds chirp at him, impatient, then flit outside to dart back and forth between bare tree branches.

They keep trying to lead him back to the library.

Laurie watches the stark bits of color against the gray backdrop, taking stock of all the new places where they've been patched up. They chirp again, scolding. And he doesn't have much excuse at this point.

"All right," he sighs. "All right, I'll go."

Impossibly, Beck is even more handsome in the daylight. A body that isn't only capable, but also intrinsically aware of its surroundings. Dark eyes that aren't merely assessing, but also unfathomably kind.

Laurie finds him descending a rickety set of stairs buried deep in the book stacks and can only stare soundlessly until Beck notices and stops short just above him.

"The birds brought me," Laurie says, apologetic. "You live here?"

Beck is silent. Then he dips his chin in a single, reluctant nod.

"I'll leave you alone, I swear. It's just..." Laurie offers the package from home. "I asked my mom to send whatever parts she could spare. Some tools and drawings, anything she had on aviary machines. I thought it might help."

Beck stares at the box with wide eyes, like he doesn't know if it's going to bite him or grant him a wish. Like it's something equally as wondrous as it is dangerous.

The same way he then looks at Laurie.

He clears his throat gruffly. "...I'm not a student."

"Oh. Yeah, I figured that out. Honestly, I should've known from the beginning."

Beck flinches, so Laurie quickly amends, "Because if you were a student here, you wouldn't listen to me like what I say is worth a damn."

Metallic chirps echo from the rafters overhead. Laurie draws in a deep, fortifying breath. "Because when you look at me, and when you look at those breaking birds, it's like you actually understand the risk of caring. Like you'd rather that reality over an empty projection of it."

Beck draws in a matching breath, though sharper. Painful. "It's not a risk I'm prepared to take."

A bird perches on the staircase railing, and Laurie glances pointedly at it. "I think you already are." He moves forward, up a step, and holds out the box between them. "So. Will it help?"

"Laurie." Beck shakes his head ruefully. "I don't know how to fix more than feathers."

"Yeah, you do. You *will*."

Hesitantly, Beck takes the box.

Laurie smiles, though it feels less like a victory and more like a good-bye, and begins backing away.

"Wait." Beck's tone is raw, his shoulders tense, and Laurie has never witnessed anything so brave as when he whispers, "Open it with me?"

Upstairs, Laurie is met with a scavenged but intimate home: a twin bed piled high with extra blankets and neatly folded laundry, an over-turned milk crate covered in nuts and bolts, a heating vent in the floor surrounded by pillows and birds.

They join the birds there, where it's warmest, and unpack everything together. Tools, instruction manuals, pristinely cut feathers, beaks…and legs.

The bird with the broken one chirps enthusiastically, landing on the edge of the open box.

"Yes," Laurie chuckles, "that's for you." But when he looks for confirmation, he finds Beck distracted by all the new gears and screws.

Beck holds one up to the bird's breastplate, near the gear that's stuttering, and nods thoughtfully. "I think we can help him."

For one long moment, Laurie can hardly breathe. And then, per usual, his body reacts before his brain can intervene.

He tackles Beck into the pillows in a hug.

Beck's response is just as careful and calculated as any of his other movements. And all the more appreciated for its decisiveness. He wraps strong arms tightly around Laurie's narrow frame. Kisses him. Pulls them both back up to sitting. Kisses him again. Laughs. "We have some reading to do first," he says, reaching for the instruction manuals.

Laurie nods, flushed and breathless and jittery with every emotion erupting inside of him. "Excellent, my specialty. Good thing you have me."

Beck nods seriously and repeats, like a promise, "Good thing I have you."

And for the first time since coming to the mainland, Laurie feels perfectly at home.

Though the landscape is new, the sum of its parts is more grounding than those parts would suggest. An open window. An icy draft. A circle of fragile warmth, chiming brass, and turning gears. Laurie's hand in Beck's shirt, but closer to Beck's heart this time. Beck's eyes sharp on the words scrawled out across pages of yellowed paper as Laurie reads them aloud. The mechanics of clockwork sounding like poetry in an attic above a cold, gray campus.

A Curatorial Puzzle
of the Heart

Robin Huntington

Tags: bipoc, bisexual, dubious consent (mild), historical with magic, love declaration, m/m, museum, new york, present tense, puzzles and games, romance, third person limited point of view, veteran

There's nothing in the world like the scent of the museum's collections—the way the ancient, slowly decaying paper, wood, leather, and fabric mingle together, undercut by the pungent smell of moth balls and something that only imbues the magical artifacts wing. That particular collections smell hits his nose the moment he steps through the door leading from the museum's grand rotunda into the staff-only areas beyond, and only becomes stronger as he weaves his way through the dim corridors. Magic is supposed to be odorless, but Hank swears that there's another note in the air here, one absent from his colleagues' halls on the other side of the sprawling New York History Museum.

Hank has only been the assistant curator of these collections for a few months, but he doesn't think he'll ever grow so accustomed to the aroma that it'll stop being special. For so long, it represented something out of reach, an impossible dream; he still sometimes has to pinch himself when he comes in and sees his name on the heavy brass placard next to his office door.

Coming from a non-magical family of immigrants, he'd had to fight tooth and nail to get here. His English father, an army physician and inveterate skeptic, viewed magic as little more than a novelty best suited for party tricks, and his Indian mother regarded it with deep mistrust. To say that they hadn't been enthusiastic about Hank's desired career path would be putting it mildly. In the end, the academic side of magic proved more acceptable in their eyes, and now—well, it's hard to argue with a position as pre-eminent as this one.

Today, as he does most days, Hank bypasses the curatorial office suite and descends farther into the bowels of the museum, taking the staircase at the end of the hall that leads down to the collections storage facility. Juggling the paper bag he's carrying, he fishes out his keys and lets himself into a cavernous room packed with an endless maze of cabinets and shelves. Here, the collections scent is overpowering, and it brings a smile to Hank's face as he traces a labyrinthine but familiar path past unassuming, plain metal cabinet fronts concealing unspeakable wonders within. Paper labels identify the contents along his route as *Edged Weapons: Assyria–Carthage* on one side of the aisle and *Amulets: Strength and Fortitude* on the other.

Near the back of the collections, he passes through another door, and, in a narrow space between the artifact room and the library, he finds his goal: a door left slightly ajar, indicating that *Jonathan Talquist, Collections Manager*, as the nameplate reads, is within. Also that he isn't keen on being disturbed, but that's Jonathan's fundamental state and not particularly indicative of his actual availability.

Hank gives the wood a quick rap with his knuckles, waiting for the beleaguered, "Yes, Dr. Ashford?" in reply before he pushes the door open and steps inside.

"How many times do I have to tell you to call me 'Hank'?"

"At least another dozen," Jonathan says, dry as a desert. It's impossible to tell if it's meant to be a joke, but Hank smiles like it is.

"Ah, well, I suppose I'll have to weather it a bit longer, then," he replies as he finds a place to stand next to the desk in the cramped office.

Jonathan reaches up to adjust his glasses as he sits back in his chair, his penetrating green eyes skittering over Hank as if judgmentally cataloging every stray lock of dark, wavy hair that escaped his attempts at taming them with a comb that morning and every wrinkle in his clothing that evaded the iron. Hank is well aware that he's not the neatest or most careful dresser, but he'd never thought twice about it until he found himself under the regular scrutiny of someone as meticulous as Jonathan. Hell, half the time, Hank's tie finds itself crammed into a jacket pocket before the end of the day, which always elicits a disapproving hum when they cross paths.

It's possible that Hank *sometimes* does it to try to get a rise out of Jonathan. Not that he'd admit such a thing.

"What can I do for you, doctor—" Jonathan breaks off at the look on Hank's face and sighs. "Henry."

"That's still not 'Hank,' you know."

Hank could swear Jonathan's full lips twitch like he's suppressing a smile, but he's probably imagining things.

"I'm rather busy today," Jonathan says instead of correcting himself again. "Did you need something?"

"Only to deliver this," Hank replies, placing the paper bag in an open spot between a pile of neatly stacked books and an assortment of papers spread across the desk. Jonathan eyes it warily, as if Hank doesn't do this nearly every day. As if he doesn't already know what's heralded by the ornate *Pâtisserie Céline* logo adorning the bag. "It's pistachio and chocolate. I thought, since you liked the almond one…"

"Did I?" Jonathan asks, his eyebrows barely quirking upward.

Now Hank is *sure* Jonathan is fucking with him, though whether he's amused or just annoyed is still up for debate. Hank hopes fervently for the former.

"Yes, you did," Hank says confidently. Jonathan always saves the pastries Hank brings him to eat during his mid-afternoon coffee break, which means that Hank can sneak glances into the tiny department kitchenette and catalog the subtle expressions crossing Jonathan's face. The almond croissant had netted a fleeting smile, which had buoyed Hank with triumph for the rest of the day—and the evening, too.

It's possible he's a little too invested in thawing his colleague's icy exterior.

"Well, then. Thank you, Dr. Ashford," Jonathan says crisply, already turning back to the papers on his desk. A clear dismissal.

Hank bites back a sigh. "See you later, Jonathan."

He must not be hiding his disappointment very well, because Laila *tsks* at him from her secretarial desk when he walks into the suite containing the curators' offices.

"I don't know why you insist on inflicting him on yourself every morning," she says. "A good way to ruin a perfectly good day before it even starts."

"Be nice," Hank chides, though he can hardly blame her.

When he'd been hired, he'd discovered that everyone in the department gave Jonathan a wide berth. Even Laila, with her unfailing good cheer and grandmotherly affection for anyone even slightly younger than her, didn't have much positive to say about him besides he was good at his job. This, of course, just made Hank more determined to befriend the man.

"I'm perfectly nice, which is more than I can say of him," she returns as she shuffles through the notes on her desk for his messages. "Director Rivers called to remind you about the fundraising gala next week and wants to know if you'll be bringing a guest."

Hank doesn't miss the pointed look on Laila's face as she delivers the latter part of this message. "I'm not bringing anyone."

"You know, my granddaughter Nadia is such a *lovely* girl and so interested in history," she starts.

"Didn't she only just turn twenty?" he asks, aghast. He only knows these things because Laila talks about her granddaughters endlessly, dropping unsubtle hints about their beauty and marriageability, despite Hank doing everything in his power to discourage such conversations.

Laila smiles unrepentantly. "And not yet betrothed; can you imagine?"

"Heaven forbid," Hank says flatly, unsure of how to politely say that he's not interested in marrying a girl sixteen years his junior. Or anyone, really; he's far too busy, and after the rotten luck he's had with relationships, he's not sure he's meant for such things (much to his mother's chagrin). He clears his throat. "Any other messages?"

"Mr. Davidson called, this time about a box," she reports, tapping her finger on the notepad. "He said you'd definitely be interested in this one."

The antique store owner couldn't always be relied on to judge the merit—or, indeed, the magic—of some of the artifacts he received, but it was probably worth a look. "Ring him and tell him I'll come by at lunch," he tells Laila. "Until then, hold my calls."

For once, Mr. Davidson had underestimated the item that had come into his possession—sold to him, he said, by a man cleaning out his father's attic. The box itself was almost shockingly plain, appearing at first glance like little more than a block of polished wood, but a closer inspection revealed nearly invisible seams. A puzzle box, then, and judging by the way the wood hummed under Hank's fingertips, an extremely magical one. These days, the bulk of historical magical items still in private possession were no more than trinkets, with only trace levels of magic, but this one was in another league.

Not that Hank would let that on to Mr. Davidson, who didn't have the training to determine such things. Knowing that he'd never get a good price for such a seemingly boring item in the antiques market, Mr. Davidson let it go for a song. Dr. Rivers would be pleased.

The box's humming gets stronger when Hank returns to the museum, which isn't unusual; put high levels of certain elements next to each other, and they'll trigger a positive feedback loop that accentuates their natural reactivity. It's why certain items had to be stored in special lead-lined cabinets and isolated from those of similar power. Hank will have to figure out what the box has been enchanted to do before he'll know whether or not it needs special storage, and to do that, he'll need some help.

"Dr. Ashford," Jonathan says, not bothering to hide his exasperation, when Hank finds him again in the collections. Afternoon sunlight filters in through a partially shaded window, bringing out coppery highlights in his chestnut hair. "A rather unusual time of day for a pastry delivery, isn't it?"

"Sorry, no pastry this time," Hank says as he digs the wrapped box out of his bag. "Try not to be too disappointed."

Jonathan rolls his eyes, but he follows Hank to a nearby table with a lamp anyway, perhaps curious enough to overcome his natural disdain for, well, everyone. Setting the box on the table, Hank flips on the light and gestures toward the still-wrapped parcel.

"Would you like to do the honors?" Hank asks.

"What is it?"

"C'mon, where's your sense of mystery?" Hank teases. "Would you ask someone what's in a gift before you open it?"

"Yes," Jonathan replies bluntly, but he looks intrigued. "So, it's a gift?"

Hank opens his mouth and closes it again. "Well, technically it belongs to the museum now, but sure, if you want to think of it like that. Go on."

Stepping forward, Jonathan reaches out and tugs on a loose end of the twine holding the muslin in place. The bow gives way, and the cloth slips quietly off the smooth, featureless surface of the box.

"Oh," Jonathan breathes. He's staring so fixedly at the box, fingertips trailing lightly over the surface, that Hank can't read his reaction.

"It seemed to me to have quite a bit of innate power to it, though I haven't gotten it under the instruments to check the magic intensity levels or determine the exact chemistry yet. Obviously the work of an extremely skilled craftsman, so the potential is high that it's a significant object. And, well, puzzle boxes were never my forte, so I figured I could use some assistance—"

"You want my help?" Jonathan asks, blessedly interrupting Hank's rambling.

"Er, yes? You wrote your master's thesis on the Harvard Box, right?"

"I did," Jonathan confirms. His eyes narrow. "How did you know that?"

Hank shrugs helplessly. "I looked up your work when I started here," he admits. "It was a brilliant thesis. Why didn't you ever go for a PhD?"

Jonathan's already closed-off expression somehow shutters further. "What else? The war." He reaches up to rub at his left arm just above the elbow, and the pieces fall into place.

Hank had noticed Jonathan's left hand wasn't as strong or dexterous as his right, but of course he'd never *asked*. The lingering effects of a combat injury, then. It takes every ounce of Hank's self-control not to ask a thousand questions—chief among them, why Jonathan hadn't been assigned a non-combat position in the divisions devoted to magical counterintelligence, as Hank had been—but he manages to hold his tongue. Barely.

"The point is, it's still the best treatise I've read on puzzle boxes,"

Hank says instead, forging on as best he knows how. "So, if you're willing, I'd appreciate your expertise."

For a moment he thinks Jonathan is going to beg off, but then he gives a nod so small that Hank might have missed it if he hadn't been watching so closely.

"All right," Jonathan says. "I'd like that."

As one might expect from a puzzle box, Hank's new acquisition doesn't yield its secrets easily. Apart from taking it to the spectrophotometer labs for testing, he leaves the box with Jonathan. The benefits of this are two-fold: Jonathan is the subject-matter expert, and it also gives Hank an excuse to visit even more frequently than before. What's more, those visits no longer seem to be an annoyance; at times, Jonathan almost looks *pleased* to see him, and Hank valiantly tries to ignore the thrill that shoots down his spine.

He's never pretended that Jonathan isn't gorgeous, at least in the privacy of his own mind, but there was never any danger of it becoming an issue, seeing as the most he ever thought he could hope for was Jonathan's tolerance. However, that was before *this*—before spending hours, days, *weeks* together pouring over historical records and ancient spell compendia, before he'd witnessed the spark of excitement in Jonathan's eyes when he uncovered something new, before their conversations expanded beyond the box and into their own personal histories.

That was before he could interrupt Jonathan while he's concentrating on his work and get a *smile* rather than a scowl.

"I've got something for you," Hank announces when he finds Jonathan hunched over the box at their, now, usual work bench in the collections. It's late, and everyone else in the department has gone home for the day, but he'd been pretty certain he'd find Jonathan still here. He deposits a *Pâtisserie Céline* bag on the table—a chocolate-hazelnut tart inside—but holds back his real delivery.

"No food in the collections," Jonathan replies automatically, though there's no bite to his words. Instead, he looks sort of fondly amused by Hank's usual antics, which Hank feels precisely nothing about.

"You're not going to eat it until later, anyway," Hank says. "That's not what I meant, though." With a dramatic flourish, he pulls the slim folder out from under his arm and drops it in front of Jonathan. "I got the lab reports."

"And?" Jonathan asks, quickly opening the folder and paging through the papers within.

"High natural amounts of Merlinium, which isn't surprising given the wood is mostly rowan. It was probably made in England before the Industrial Revolution, based on the carbon signatures. There are some peaks here, though"—he leans forward to point out the trace on the graph—"that suggest there's something containing Circium buried under the outer layers."

"A different wood, or an object inside?"

Hank shrugs. "Hard to say. Any luck on the next challenge?"

They'd gotten past the first only last week, finally detecting a minute variation in the wood on one side that triggered the opening of a panel to a puzzle of sliding slips of wood marked with unusual symbols. Eventually, they'd found a reference to them in an ancient, obscure text, and it had been pretty simple to solve after that. Completing that puzzle had revealed an ornate silver device set into the wood, and, so far, its solution has been opaque.

"Not exactly," Jonathan admits, disappointment and frustration coloring his tone. "I figured out some of the movements, but I don't think it's possible with only two hands."

Hank stares at the metal device, tipping his head as Jonathan demonstrates the moving parts. "What about more?"

"I'll be sure to let you know when I grow another."

"I mean, what if the puzzle is meant to be completed by more than one person?"

"Why didn't I think of that?" Jonathan asks, frowning.

"Because you hate other people?" Hank teases.

Jonathan rolls his eyes. "Give me your hands," he demands, grabbing onto Hank's wrist and tugging him closer before Hank knows what's happening.

Jonathan's hands are warm, and his fingers strong and sure as they manipulate Hank's into place, pale skin contrasting against rich brown. It's the most contact they've ever had, and Hank's stomach swoops. They're so very close now, Jonathan's face only inches from his as he bends over the box. Fortunately, Jonathan is so focused on the puzzle that he doesn't notice that Hank can't tear his eyes away from the way his eyelashes fan over his cheeks or the fine stubble dusting his jaw.

"Are you listening?" Jonathan asks peevishly.

No, in fact, he hasn't been.

Hank swallows hard, trying to focus. "Run through it again?"

It takes them several tries, and more than a little bickering about the order of operations, but finally the mechanism shifts under their fingers. There's a satisfying *click*, and a little jolt of something like static electricity stings Hank's fingertips. He yanks his hands back, but Jonathan doesn't seem to have noticed the shock.

"It worked," he says breathlessly, and looks up at Hank with such an ecstatic grin that Hank forgets all about the stinging in his fingers. In fact, he forgets everything other than the warmth spreading through his chest at the sight of that smile.

He made Jonathan smile like that, and now the only thing he can think of is that he desperately wants to do it again.

They work for a while longer, carefully taking notes on every aspect of the puzzle solution, until finally Hank pulls them away from the work and insists Jonathan at least eat the tart, because Hank *knows* he skipped dinner. Jonathan, in turn, cuts the tart neatly in half and won't accept no for an answer when he offers a piece to Hank. They eat standing in the department kitchenette, a heavy cloak of silence surrounding them.

"I don't hate everyone," Jonathan mumbles as he polishes off his half. He's leaning his hip against the counter, jacket discarded somewhere downstairs and his shirtsleeves rolled to his elbows to reveal pale, muscular forearms, his normally neat hair slightly mussed from how he'd run his hands through it in frustration earlier. As if that weren't enough, he lifts his hand to his mouth to lick the lingering chocolate off his fingers, and Hank's mouth goes dry.

"Don't take this the wrong way, but you do a very good job of making it seem that way," Hank manages once he's torn his gaze away to focus on the floor.

"I just prefer to keep to myself. It's easier that way. Safer."

"Sounds lonely."

Jonathan shrugs. "I don't mind."

"I couldn't do it," Hank says, shaking his head.

"You don't say," Jonathan drawls sarcastically, a teasing note in his voice that Hank's never heard before. "I've never met someone so doggedly determined to befriend everyone he comes across."

"Hey, I can't help it if I'm a naturally friendly person," Hank replies. He raises his eyebrows pointedly at Jonathan. "Even to people who refuse to be friendly back."

"*You* just couldn't stand that someone might not immediately fall for your charms and had to make it a personal mission," Jonathan counters.

"Excuse me?"

"You heard me."

Hank grins, crossing his arms over his chest, and doesn't miss the way Jonathan's eyes track the movement. "What I heard is that you think I'm charming."

"Please," Jonathan huffs, his attempt at a glare severely undermined by the dusting of pink that appears on his pale cheeks. Hank is floored. "What you are is a pest."

"But a charming pest."

"Good *night*, Dr. Ashford," Jonathan says firmly as he pushes away from the counter and heads toward the door.

"I know you know it's 'Hank,' Jonathan," Hank calls after him. In fact, Jonathan had finally come around to using Hank's first name recently, but somehow, said like *this*, Hank finds he doesn't mind the teasing formality.

Jonathan stops in the doorway, one hand on the frame. "Jonah," he murmurs, almost inaudible. His back is still to Hank.

"What?"

"You can call me 'Jonah,' " he says, finally looking over his shoulder. "That's what I go by with…friends."

"You have friends?" Hank says, the ribbing words out of him before he can stop them. The weight of that permission is heavy, and so is the way Jonah had said "friends," loaded with meaning that Hank can't begin to contemplate. Much easier to hide his feelings about it behind a joke.

Fortunately, Jonah laughs. "Shut up," he huffs, ducking his head as his cheeks darken. When he looks up again, though, his expression is serious. "Not many people call me that anymore. Not since the war. But…I'd like it, if you would."

"Oh," Hank breathes. The weight is back, pressing on his chest. He swallows hard, meeting Jonah's green eyes steadily. "Of course. Good night, Jonah."

Hank will be thinking about the soft smile he gets in return for a very long time.

For once, Hank is the one holed up in the collections, bent over the now partially opened puzzle box and a thick volume on early Celtic puzzle box construction that recently arrived, courtesy of a colleague at Oxford. In return, Jonah has been packaging up a loan of witch-trials-era amulets, on top of managing the regular visiting scholar requests and dealing with a recent donation of a collection of "magic wands" that have mostly, but not entirely, turned out to be no more than poorly carved sticks. Hank had been hoping to have something new and exciting to reveal about the box's origin or purpose, but so far, he hasn't uncovered anything.

They'd gotten through a few more puzzles, most of which either required or were made easier by the participation of two people. It seemed to be something of a theme of the box, which wasn't a conceit either Hank or Jonathan had come across before. Presumably, it had something to do with the underlying spell, but that was another thing they hadn't figured out. Something about collaboration, perhaps. "Many hands make light work," or so the saying went—folk aphorisms often had an origin in early spell-making—except four hands weren't exactly *many*.

Hank flips past a section on using a puzzle box to bind a spirit to the mortal plane and ends up in a chapter detailing the use of puzzle boxes as tokens in love spells. He almost skips that one, too, except an engraving catches his eye. Two pairs of hands, twisted together, not unlike Hank's and Jonah's had been when they'd opened the silver mechanism, with the simple caption: "Completion of an entanglement spell."

"Find anything interesting?" a low voice purrs, shockingly close, and Hank nearly jumps a mile. Then a firm hand slides onto his shoulder, hot through the thin fabric of his shirt, and Hank finds himself scrambling to his feet before he can stop.

"N-no, nothing yet," he stammers, the book clutched to his chest like a shield as he takes a step backward.

Jonah tips his head. The smile slips off his face, replaced by a bemused expression that creases his rugged features. "Everything all right?"

"Yeah, of course," Hank says quickly. "I just remembered—I have an appointment to get to."

"It's seven in the evening."

"Dinner meeting," Hank lies. "I, uh—I'll see you tomorrow?"

"Sure," Jonah agrees, but he's frowning. His eyes drop to the book. "Are you taking that?"

"Thought I'd do some reading later," Hank says, his fingers tightening around the spine of the book. "I'll let you know if anything turns up."

With that, he flees before Jonah can ask any more questions.

Jonah's smart. There's no way he'd miss something like this, and Hank can't let that happen before he figures out what the hell is going on. Because to Hank, it looks like they've stumbled into working on some kind of *love magic puzzle box* together and that is, in fact, terrible. It's not that the idea is objectionable. Rather, the problem comes from the fact that Hank has spent *months* trying to work his way into Jonah's good graces, and now it seems increasingly probable that Jonah's warming to him had nothing to do with him actually liking Hank, and everything to do with a fucking *spell*. The increasingly flirtatious banter. The familiar touches. The soft smiles. All things you might expect from a love charm.

What's worse, Hank can't even be sure of his own feelings. Yes, he's felt himself falling for the prickly collections manager as they've gotten to know each other. He'd already known Jonah was brilliant and absurdly gorgeous, but now he's experienced Jonah's dry humor and his biting wit, heard him speak with passion about music and art, felt a warmth kindle in his chest when Jonah laughed, and he'd thought—

Well. It's hardly a given for him. Hank makes a lot of friends, and he's never had problems finding the company of either sex when he wanted it, but the kind of connection he's felt with Jonah is rare. It felt…special.

What if it's not even *real?*

Hank's fingers tighten around the book still in his hands as he hurries through the museum's dark halls. One thing's for sure: he wasn't lying when he said he'd be doing plenty of reading tonight.

Hank isn't proud to admit that he's been hiding for the past three days. He'd called in sick to the museum, begging off when Laila offered to send one of her granddaughters by with some soup, and has been shut in his apartment ever since. He spends most of his time reading and rereading the book, trying to look for any hint that the box isn't what he fears. Instead, he becomes more convinced.

The combinations of wood and metals, the design, the fact that most of the puzzles were made for two people—it all points to a box designed as a love spell. What's more, Hank's accidental *gifting* of it to Jonah, even though he meant it as a joke, likely set the spell in motion.

Christ. He's certainly made a mess of everything.

What he hasn't been able to figure out yet is how to undo the spell. It has to be possible, but the thing about puzzle boxes is that the spells imbuing them aren't complete until they've been solved, and it's rarely possible to unravel an incomplete spell. Jonah might have an idea of how to get around it, but Hank doesn't think his heart can handle being around the collections manager right now. As it is, he misses Jonah in a way that one might ungenerously call *pathetic*, considering it's only been three days. He almost hopes it *is* a spell, because if it's not, he's got even bigger problems.

Early—*very* early—on the fourth day, the doorman to Hank's building calls to say "there's a Mr. Talquist here to visit," and Hank is too shocked to do anything other than tell him to let Jonah up. A few minutes later, three crisp raps sound on his front door, and Hank opens it to find an annoyed-looking Jonah on the other side with a suspiciously sized rectangular package tucked under one arm.

"How did you know where I live?" Hank asks, somewhere between a polite "Hello" and what he'd really like to ask, which is "What the hell are you doing here?"

"I bribed it out of Mrs. Nasir," Jonah replies, meaning Laila. What Hank wouldn't give to know the details of *that* exchange. "Can I come in?"

It's a reasonable request, but Hank hesitates. Inviting Jonah into his home feels like a treacherously slippery slope, no matter how much Hank wants him here. Then again, the alternative is having a conversation about this in public, which is hardly optimal. Plus, Hank is still in his pajamas, a situation he sorely needs to remedy. With a bitten-down sigh, he steps back and lets Jonah in, trying not to wince at the current state of his apartment.

"I promise I'm not usually this messy. It's just the illness," he tells Jonah, which nets him a raised eyebrow. Hank tries for a probably unconvincing cough. "Really, you shouldn't be here if you don't want to get sick—"

"You're not sick, Hank," Jonah says flatly as he looks him up and down. "You're avoiding me. Avoiding this," he adds, jiggling the box under his arm. "And I think I know why."

"You do?" Hank manages weakly. Jonah nods, and Hank pushes a hand back through his wild curls. "Christ, I can't have this conversation in my nightclothes. I haven't even had any coffee."

"Go get dressed," Jonah tells him. "I'll make the coffee."

Too tired and overwhelmed to argue, Hank leaves him to the percolator and heads back to his bedroom, desperately hoping he'll find some scrap of composure tucked into his closet amongst his clothes. By the time he returns wearing a pair of slacks and a simple button-down shirt, the aroma of coffee fills the apartment and Jonah has seated himself on Hank's couch, the book from Oxford that Hank had foolishly left out cradled in his lap and open to the marked section on love spells.

"I can explain," Hank blurts, resisting the urge to go yank the book out of Jonah's hands. "It's kind of funny, really, because you asked if it was a *gift*—" The percolator dings. "Erm, coffee?"

He doesn't wait for a reply before bustling off to the kitchen and busying himself with pouring two mugs. He's so wrapped up in making sure Jonah's is just right—lots of cream, two sugars—that Hank doesn't even notice that the man himself has followed him until a soft touch brushes his shoulder.

Hank jumps back like he's been burned, narrowly missing upsetting the coffees and *actually* hurting himself. "Sorry, sorry," he says, wincing at Jonah's exasperated expression.

"Hank," Jonah groans, wiping a hand over his face. "For fuck's sake, calm down and stop apologizing."

"Sorry," Hank says before he can stop himself. He sighs. "This *is* mostly my fault, though."

Jonah does not look mollified. "I don't know how you came to that conclusion," he says, which makes Hank frown in confusion. "Look, you didn't set off the box by 'gifting' it to me any more than I did by accepting it."

"So you read enough to know what it is," Hank surmises. He doesn't know whether to be relieved or worried that Jonah doesn't seem more bothered.

"No," Jonah says. "I mean, yes; the confirmation was nice, but I already had my suspicions."

"For how long?"

Jonah bites down on his lower lip, looking uncharacteristically hesitant. "A while. Since the first two-person puzzle, at least."

"Since…" Hank trails off. It's been over a month since then. A month of late nights and close quarters and growing ever closer. A month of falling in love. "And you let us keep going?"

"Was I wrong to do so?" Jonah counters. Hank can't understand how he's being so nonchalant about all of this.

"But it's—it's—it's a trick. It's not real," Hank says, then realizes maybe that's the whole point. Maybe Jonah is comfortable because he *knows* none of it is real, so he can write it all off as a silly side effect and focus on the research. Meanwhile, Hank is slowly losing his mind. The thought that he's the only one in this, the only one it matters to, makes something cold and hard settle into his gut.

Jonah's watching him now with an evaluating expression that makes Hank struggle to keep from squirming. "Is that what you think?" he asks, then shakes his head. "How much do you know about love spells, Hank?"

"Not much."

"Right. I might have guessed that."

"*Hey,*" Hank huffs despite himself. He didn't get the curatorship for *nothing*, after all. Love magic is a pretty niche field of study.

"I don't mean it as a slight," Jonah says, a fondly amused smile playing on his lips. "Even scholars who have devoted their lives to their study don't entirely understand how they work. Everyone thinks they're simple—give someone an object with a love spell on it, and they fall in love with you. But feelings are tricky. The spells are notoriously unpredictable because the recipient's reaction matters as much as the gifter's intention."

"So, the recipient has to be…open to the idea." That's at least some-what promising. Not that Hank's allowing his mind to run wild down those paths.

"In a manner of speaking," Jonah confirms. "Most of the time, love spells cause little more than a fleeting interest. Sometimes, a short infatu-ation. But they never last long."

Hank turns this new information over in his mind as he starts pacing across his tiny kitchen, trying to fit it together with what he already knows. "Okay, but the box's spells are complicated," he argues. "There are layers. The puzzles must prolong the effects."

Jonah catches Hank's wrist to arrest his restless movement and tugs him close. So close that he's looking up at Hank through his pale eyelashes, his voice low when he says, "And that would still mean noth-ing if we were nothing more than colleagues."

Something catches in Hank's throat. "If we were…"

"Christ, Hank. For a terrible flirt, you are *hopeless*," Jonah bemoans, then he grabs Hank's face in both hands and drags him down into a kiss.

It's so utterly unexpected, even given their conversation, that it takes his brain several moments to catch up. When it does, he gets about as far as the warmth of Jonah's mouth and the smell of his sensible soap on his skin before he gives up trying to make sense of it and lets himself sink into the sensation, his hands finding Jonah's waist to draw him in until the firm lines of his body are pressed against Hank's.

"I love you," Jonah murmurs when they finally part. Hank's still dazed from the kiss, which keeps him from losing it over the fact that Jonathan Talquist just confessed to *loving* him. Jonah pulls back a little farther and stares Hank dead in the eye. "I've *been* in love with you since before the goddamned box, but it was…*safer*, to keep you at a distance. Until you made it damned-well impossible, that is."

"Oh," Hank breathes.

"Now's when you say you felt something for me before the box."

A slightly hysterical laugh bubbles out of Hank's throat. "Of *course* I did. Do you think I'd bring pastries for just anyone?"

"In a misguided attempt to win their friendship? Yes, absolutely," Jonah says, but he's laughing, too, a brilliant smile on his face that Hank doesn't know how he'll survive.

"Shut up," Hank retorts, then kisses him again, just because he can. "Not from *Céline*, though."

Jonah makes a little, pleased hum, then tragically lets Hank go and steps away. "Now, can we finish opening the box?"

On one hand, *yes*, but also: "What will happen when we complete the spell?"

"If I'm right? Nothing."

"Nothing?"

Jonah shrugs, his smile soft. "We're already in love. The magic might have pushed things along, but it was there before, and it'll be there after the spell is gone."

"All right," Hank agrees, letting his own grin take over his face. "Let's go solve a puzzle box."

He holds out a hand to Jonah, but there's no tingle of magic when their fingers twine together; it's only them.

FAMILY MEAL

SHANNON LIPPERT

Tags: bipoc, break-up (past), chef, ethnocentrism, f/f (past), food (graphic descriptions), found family, friends, past tense, science fiction, space ship, student, third person limited point of view

First impressions mattered, and Station 17, with its earsplitting klaxons and flashing red lights, didn't exactly endear itself to Meena when she stepped onboard. The cacophony was overwhelming, especially after Meena's solitary trip through the dark expanse of space.

"Just a fire drill," Niamh, the exuberant welcoming committee, shouted over the sirens, adding to the sensory onslaught. Niamh's long black braid swayed as she waved her tattooed hand in the direction of the ceiling. "Well, not a *drill*. The junior test kitchen is on this wing—that's where you'll be. Sometimes the smoke triggers the alarms. When you see your fellow chefs running toward the evac chute, *that's* when you need to panic."

"Great," Meena muttered as the sirens cut off. "Sorry, where did you say we were going? I couldn't hear over the—" She gestured toward the alarm.

Niamh grinned. "First, we're going to drop off your bag with one of the courier bots, then I'll show you your classroom. Sound good?"

It sounded no better than any other option, but Meena wasn't going to say so. Niamh was clearly excited to have a new face on the station, and Meena wasn't going to sour that, even if it did make her feel even more out of place than she already did.

Meena had never dreamed of becoming a chef; she barely cooked anything beyond ramen. Her one dream—thoughtful people coming together to share what they loved in a space she had created—had turned into a lonely, miserable nightmare she'd badly needed to escape. The culinary school orbiting Venus on Station 17 had a vacancy, one as far from Earth as it was possible to get, and a self-paced program that meant she could start right away. Applying to the Venusian Cultural Council's Development Program had been a leap for a lifeboat from a sinking ship.

Just take it easy and figure out your next step, Meena told herself. *Don't get overinvested.*

"Here's the courier bot hub," said Niamh, gesturing at three neat rows of glossy, wheeled machines. "Have you used one before?"

Meena shook her head.

"They're very cute," Niamh continued, a smile adding a flush to her pale cheeks. "Their paint makes them look like they're wearing tuxedos."

Meena looked down at the row of robots that stood about three feet high, black with a white strip down the front where the control panel lay. Meena thought it…*might* look like a suit if she squinted, but Niamh seemed really into the idea.

"Yeah. It's just missing a bowtie," she offered.

"You get it." Niamh nodded. "Hello, C-105," she said to one machine, reading its designation label. "Our new friend Meena just arrived with luggage. Can you bring it to her quarters?"

The courier bot beeped in what Meena assumed to be the affirmative, because Niamh gave it an affectionate pat before reaching for Meena's bag. "So clever," she said as she placed the bag in the robot's arms. "The hub indexes all of the passenger manifest data, so the bots know where you've been assigned. If you ever get yourself turned around, just tell one you're a parcel that needs to be delivered!" Niamh chuckled, though Meena wasn't entirely sure it had been a joke. So far, the corridors had all been an identical shade of drab, functional gray.

The little courier bot scuttled away, and Meena found herself thinking it looked rather determined as it carried the weight.

"Right!" Niamh clapped. "Test kitchen. Let's go."

Meena trailed along, listening with half an ear as Niamh detailed the various classrooms, labs, and storage closets that lined the corridor.

"On the right is the library. Do you want to take a peek inside?"

Meena didn't much care—until she saw the room.

The library was vast and illuminated by starlight. Automated electrics hummed to life when they sensed Meena's approach, casting a warm glow on shelves of books two-stories tall. *Physical* books. Meena had expected capacity on Station 17 to be limited, for everything to be digital, but this library was all analog and brimming with books—thousands of them! Neat stacks of dense, glorious books, and Meena could smell the pages and soft leather bindings. That wasn't all; the room itself was beautiful, with delicate lights glowing to life above an airy, open space with beautifully carved wooden desks. It looked so…old-fashioned, in the best way.

But what really took her breath away was the planet. Venus was *bright*, vivid and beautiful through the wall of windows. The segmented glass sprung from the floor and arched overhead in a dome, giving Meena the sense that she was standing not in a starbase but in airless space, floating outside the planet's atmosphere as it shone, golden light reflecting off its surface.

"It's…"

"Something else, right? This was a meteorological observation room during the first stage of terraforming, then repurposed when the Stations were converted to intellectual hubs." Niamh was smiling. "Surprised me, too. And not just because I was terrified the window was going to crack and kill us all."

Meena blinked. Caught up in the sight, she had forgotten she was on a station. "It…won't, right?"

"Kill us?" Niamh laughed. "Nah. It's not really a window, it's part of the solar paneling that looks like one solid piece but is really hundreds of tiny panels collecting energy. The seams are too small for us to see. There's a secondary layer on this side, too, compartmentalized so if there's a breach the section can get locked down before we're in danger. You're lucky," she added. "We're rotating, so you don't always get a view this good."

"Thanks," Meena said, though she wasn't sure why.

Niamh smiled at her. "Kitchen's one more down. That's where you'll be!"

The test kitchen was utilitarian but no less beautiful for it. Stainless steel appliances gleamed underneath the bright lights, and the white quartz countertops looked glossy and smooth where they weren't covered with mixing bowls and clear square containers of sauces, vegetables, and other ingredients Meena couldn't identify.

A triumphant cheer greeted Meena and Niamh as they arrived, though the raucous chorus clearly had nothing to do with them.

"You did it!" shouted a short white man with a curly beard. "These are beautiful!"

He held a small, round bright-yellow wafer in his hands. Across from him, a tall woman with dark, pin-straight hair was grinning. Two more student chefs stood with them, admiring the yellow wafers. Their blue aprons were covered in flour, and all four were flushed with excitement.

"They taste even better." Glancing behind the bearded man, she made eye contact with Meena. "Hi. Are you the new student?"

"Um, yeah. Hi," replied Meena, glancing around the room. The tall woman placed one of the wafers on a plate upside-down, then reached for a piping bag. She squeezed pale cream onto the wafer, and then added another on top. She handed the plate to Meena with a smile.

"Perfect timing. I finally got my macarons to come out right. They're honey flavored."

Meena accepted the plate with a shy smile, picked up the cookie, and took a bite. Despite the hard-looking shell, the wafer was chewy before it practically melted. The cream was sweet and smooth, blending together with the nutty richness of the meringue. It was gone before Meena knew it.

"Wow," she said. "That was really good. You made that?"

"Sure did! I'm Jeonghee, senior culinary student and teaching assistant for the junior chefs. I supervise the introductory courses along with Chef Lupe."

"Meena," she replied. "Is Chef Lupe—?"

"She has some friends visiting. You'll meet her tomorrow. I know she's sorry to miss your arrival. Do you want another macaron?"

"Gotcha, no worries," Meena said. "And sure."

Jeonghee grinned. "What every cook wants to hear. How about you, Niamh?"

"Maybe a few for the road. Gotta report back to Personnel. Do you have everything you need, Meena?" The way Niamh asked, it sounded like she was ready to jump through every hoop imaginable if there was something Meena *did* need. The sincerity was overwhelming. Back on Earth, everyone Meena had known was obsessed with looking helpful, but *being* helpful wasn't nearly as important.

"I think I'm all set. Thank you," she added, meaning it.

"Great," Niamh smiled. "If you do need something, don't be afraid to ask!"

"We'll take excellent care of you," said the bearded guy as Niamh departed.

"Corentin, you set off the smoke detectors less than an hour ago. *Again*," said a dark-skinned Black man with a cutting board in his hand.

Corentin shrugged with a good-natured grin. "If I wasn't supposed to play with fire, I wouldn't be in a kitchen."

"That's not how it works," Jeonghee snickered. "Chike, what are you doing?"

Meena followed Jeonghee's gaze; the man with the cutting board was wielding a sleek knife with remarkable precision while chopping carrots into neat sticks.

"It's an important rite of passage."

"He's right," said Corentin. "It's tradition. We have to welcome Meena."

"Oh, don't go to any trouble," Meena said.

"It's just Never-Have-I-Ever," said Jeonghee with an eye roll betrayed by the fondness in her voice. "You know the rules, right? Instead of taking drinks or holding up ten fingers, we use carrots. When we lose a point, we eat the carrot."

"Oh. Why carrots?"

"Because carrots are delicious," Chike said as he snapped one between his teeth. "And because we always get too many carrots in our shipments. Apparently they grow really well on Venus."

"How about we offer her something *real* to eat, first?" asked the last student, who reminded Meena of a 21st-century Persian actress she'd had a crush on as a kid. She had dark brows, a wide smile, and a steaming quart container of something that smelled *amazing*. "Here," she said, handing it to Meena. "It's not an assignment, just my lunch, so no fancy plating."

"Oh! I couldn't take your lunch—"

"Don't worry about it. I made plenty. I'm Noor," she said, offering her hand for Meena to shake.

"Thank you." Meena looked down at the bowl. "It's chicken?"

"Zereshk polo. I've been craving it, so I got the saffron sent special. I have lots leftover, so if you have any ideas, please help yourself."

Meena took a bite, and then she had to close her eyes.

"Good?" asked Noor.

"*So* good."

"Excellent." Noor grabbed a stool and offered it to Meena. "Sit, eat, and I'll bring your carrots so we can play."

The others pulled up their own seats while Chike distributed carrot sticks. Meena realized quickly that the game was to help her get to know the group, as well as an opportunity for some gentle ribbing. Chike opened with "Never have I ever set off the smoke detectors twice in one day," clearly targeting Corentin, who cheerfully ate one of his carrots.

Jeonghee went next. "Never have I ever been to Earth," which knocked out a carrot for everyone else in the group. "Venus native," she explained. "My parents worked on the second phase of terraforming. I was actually born on Station 5. But I spent most of my childhood planetside."

After several rounds, Meena was ahead of most of the group with seven carrots left.

"We need to catch you up," said Noor, considering her own turn. "Never have I ever...learned to drive."

"A car?" Chike asked.

Noor nodded. Chike and Jeonghee ate a carrot.

"Not you, Meena?" asked Noor.

"Sorry," she shrugged. "I've always lived near a Metro hub. Am I next?"

The others nodded.

"Um. Never have I ever...started a *successful* business?"

No one touched their carrots.

"Wait," said Corentin. "A successful business? I feel like there's a story there."

"Oh." Meena looked down at her carrots. "I guess."

"You don't have to explain if you don't want to," Chike said. "Corentin is very nosy."

"It's not some big secret." Meena shrugged. "I tried something; it didn't work out."

"That sounds rough," said Jeonghee. "Was this recent?"

Meena leaned back, the cool countertop pressing against her back. Maybe sharing wouldn't be the worst thing in the world. "My girlfriend and I opened a bookstore last year. And then things got a little intense—"

"Intense?" Chike asked.

"Okay, *I* got a little intense." She'd had this grand vision for the shop—a community space, where people could come together and find their home away from home—but she'd always been stressed out, over-thinking things. It always felt like she was unintentionally driving people away. She'd poured her heart and soul into building a space but never found her people. "I spent all my time working. My girlfriend started to resent it. I'd figured we were there together, that counts as quality time, right? Anyway, now I'm here, with no store and no girlfriend." *And no idea what I'm doing with my life*, Meena thought. She looked around at the suddenly somber group. "And I feel like I should eat a carrot for bringing down the mood. That's gotta be a penalty, right?"

Noor snickered. "Definitely. Penalty carrot."

For the next couple turns, Meena gave her new friends a few hints to help them, like her allergy to seaweed and love of classic cinema. Once the game was finished, the group dispersed to their individual worksta-tions, where they each had their own projects. Jeonghee gave Meena a quick safety overview before leading her to her new space.

"I know it's a lot to take in. When you meet with Chef Lupe, she'll work with you to get started with the fundamentals and propose some potential first projects for you to try out. We're all staggered, so you'll be able to build your own program once you master the basics. Usually new folks take the first few days to get acquainted with the equipment and try out some beginner recipes like soup stock or roux."

Meena thought for a second. "Can you show me how you made those macarons?"

"You're diving right into the deep end," Jeonghee laughed. "Macarons are delicate; most students don't tackle them until the end of the pastry module. I see what you meant about being intense. I *love* it," she added with a smile.

The routine on the station became comfortable nearly overnight. Each of the departments and programs—the dental school, the engineers' union, and the multifaith seminary—ran on a different schedule. The junior culinary school was on the earliest shift, nearly in sync with the schedule that Meena had kept on Earth. It made the transition easier, and she enjoyed that the corridors were quiet and dimly lit when she arrived at the kitchen for class. It felt like walking through a twilit world with the sunrise just breaking when she reached her workstation.

Lupe, the culinary instructor, led daily lessons on food prep, knife skills, equipment safety, timing and measurements. Meena learned to braise, sauté, grill, poach, and roast, with labs on alternating days to practice and demonstrate her new skills. The self-paced structure meant each student could spend as much time as they needed on each of the modules. Outside of these lessons, students could select recipes based on what they wanted to discover, with Lupe's and Jeonghee's encouragement.

A guest chef joined them every month to teach a new technique, with a practical exam at the end of the module. There were several days when Meena ate nothing but omelets as she struggled to create the neat, silky half-moons the French chef had demanded. Corentin, despite his track record, managed not to set off the smoke alarm as they practiced the dish.

Jeonghee also showed them how to make gyeran mari—a rolled version of an omelet with carrots and scallions.

"Jeonghee's the egg whisperer," Noor said "Whenever there's an egg dish, she makes it look easy while we all struggle."

Remembering the macarons from her first day, Meena could only nod. Those little cookies had been impossibly tricky.

The days passed quickly, even with the school's built-in downtime. Despite the temptation of the station's wide range of leisure activities, Meena found herself absorbed by her coursework, returning to the library whenever she wasn't in the kitchen. Most days it was a quiet, comfortable sanctuary filled with books on food chemistry and flavor profiles. It was strange to discover that people had studied the techniques and ingredients that went into making dishes she'd had a thousand times growing up.

She'd talked to Noor about it shortly after arriving on the station.

"It's weird, right? Seeing your family recipes dissected in a book," Noor said, making a funny face. "On the one hand: respect. On the other hand: did we really need to be told we were worthy of respect?"

"That's—yeah. You put it into words." Meena sighed. "That's a huge debate in publishing right now, too. Who decides what's worthy of being on a bookshelf? Does everyone even *want* to be seen as 'worthy' by someone who doesn't understand them? I guess I thought food would be…"

"Exempt?" Noor chuckled. "Nope. Food nourishes the body the way stories nourish the mind. It's complicated. You have to be the biggest, loudest version of yourself with no apologies."

After the tumultuous year she'd had, Meena wasn't sure that there *was* a big or loud version of her anymore, but she was beginning to like the way she felt in the kitchen. It wasn't just the satisfaction of following complex recipes or the skill it took to chop vegetables into uniform pieces; her curiosity was finally returning, bringing with it the joy of trying something new with a dish. At least once a week, the junior chefs would sit together at the long steel pass station and share their creations in one big family-style meal. Meena looked forward to the days when she had something to share, hoping that whatever she cooked would make her fellow chefs excited to try it.

One day, Niamh dropped by the library while Meena and Chike were studying techniques for making ice cream. "I have news! The station president is going to come by for a visit next month."

"Last time she was here, Noor made those duck-fat potatoes…" Chike sighed. "I *dream* about those potatoes."

Niamh grinned. "Why do you think I came to tell you all as soon as I heard? Oh, Meena, don't worry," she said, switching gears, "President Tākiri just likes to make sure we have everything we need. You don't even need to make a dish if you don't want to."

"She's really friendly," added Chike. "Venus is investing in programs like ours to make the planet into a cultural hub, so she makes herself available for feedback. A nice meal is just a bonus." He winked.

Meena assured them she was all right, but her mind was already racing. While Niamh and Chike went to get some tea, Meena flipped through the pages of the nearest recipe book. It didn't matter that the president's visit wasn't to test them. Meena would make her friends on Station 17 proud.

Thus began a series of nearly sleepless night-and-day cycles. When Meena wasn't in class or the library, she was at her workstation in the kitchen, frantically measuring ingredients, watching the stove, and marking off containers for storage in the fridge. Conveniently, there were regular food deliveries from Venus. Its fully automated farms were apparently overflowing with abundance, so Meena could easily place orders for ingredients she needed to experiment with new recipes.

Her classmates noticed—it was impossible not to—but they didn't interrupt her. A few extra plates of their own dishes appeared on Meena's counter with notes of encouragement. Meena ate them with gratitude, sampling Corentin's buckwheat crêpes alongside Chike's bitterleaf soup.

One night, hours after the rest of her classmates had departed, Meena was carefully arranging squares of chocolate fudge on a platter. Since it was off-cycle, the kitchen was dark, and Meena had leaned into the moodiness of the space by activating only half of the lights. It made her feel like a mad scientist, working from the glow of the burners. She was reviewing the recipe for the caramel drizzle when the kitchen door opened and Noor walked in, more lights turning on automatically as she did.

"Hey, Meena," she said. "You're up late. Or early, depending."

"Yeah. I…may have gotten a little absorbed in what I was doing."

"It smells good," Noor said.

"Wanna try one?"

Noor nodded, taking one from the pan and pinching her nose as she tasted the fudge.

"Helps you pick up the nuances in the chocolate," Noor explained. "Those are *nice*, texture is spot on."

"Thanks," Meena grinned. This was her third batch, and she'd been pretty sure she'd finally gotten it right. "What are you working on this late?"

"Dunno yet. I'm only up because I wanted to call home. Maybe I'll surprise everyone with breakfast. I'm gonna stare at the shelves in the walk-in for a bit and see if inspiration strikes."

With a smile, Noor retreated toward the back of the kitchen while Meena focused on her caramel. *Low and slow to start,* she reminded herself.

Noor returned in time to watch Meena carefully drizzle the caramel over her fudge. When Meena reached for the salt container, Noor made a choked sound.

"Can I make a suggestion?"

Meena bristled. She'd always had a hard time accepting unsolicited advice and didn't like the defensive way it made her feel. But Noor was her friend, right? After a few moments of inner turmoil, Meena nodded. Noor reached into a cabinet at her workstation and brought Meena a small blue container.

"Use the fleur de sel, not table salt."

Meena glanced at the recipe.

"Will it make a difference? The recipe says—"

"Try both. Trust me."

Meena carefully sprinkled salt onto two pieces of fudge, each with a different kind. She tasted the one with table salt first; the texture and flavors melded together beautifully, and she felt satisfied that she'd finally lived up to the recipe. But then she tried the second piece, the one with the fleur de sel still sparkling on the surface of the caramel. While the chocolate and creamy caramel remained the same, there was a mineral sweetness to the fleur de sel that felt bright, a contrast to the dense fudge and thick sauce.

"Oh," Meena said.

"Right? It dissolves quicker, so you get more flavor. And visually it adds a little something, too. See the way it sparkles?"

Meena nodded.

"Just a touch of presentation. You could do that with a regular sea salt, too, but I prefer the complexity of a fleur de sel." Noor tapped her finger on the recipe. "You should always try it the way other cooks have done it, see what they did, and retrace their steps. But you also need to make it your own."

The day of President Roimata Tākiri's visit finally arrived.

Classes had been cancelled to allow the instructors to meet with the president, so students from most of the programs were at their leisure. The test kitchen, however, was bursting with activity. Noor had a container of goat meat marinating in the prep fridge and was busy chopping vegetables. Chike carefully inspected the delivery of catfish and plantains. Corentin had set off the smoke detectors while sautéing onions, but everyone had accounted for that eventuality and no one was terribly off schedule.

Jeonghee and Meena watched from their own workstations, handing their classmates utensils and offering encouragement.

"You're not making anything?" Meena asked.

"Nah," Jeonghee shrugged. "Chef Lupe's with the president, so I'm here to support and supervise. And the last time she visited, I worked myself into a frenzy for days making banchan—eight dishes, at least."

"It was nine," Noor interjected.

"That sounds…familiar," said Meena.

Jeonghee laughed. "You get it. I used to be pretty intense too. But I'm almost ready to matriculate, and I guess I don't feel like I have anything to prove. I'm actually going to take a break before I decide what's next. Finally going to see Earth!"

Meena smiled. "That sounds good."

"It *feels* good. I'll miss everyone, but I'll make plenty of excuses to visit." Jeonghee smiled. "What about you? I thought you were cooking all week for this."

Meena nodded. "Everything's prepped in the freezer. I'll need to whip some egg whites into a Swiss meringue while the main course is being served, but other than that, I'm ready to go."

"Egg whites?" Jeonghee's eyebrows went up. "Do you want a hand?"

Meena paused, grappling with her instinct to say no. "That would be really nice, thank you."

"Of course," Jeonghee bumped into Meena's shoulder with her own. "Any time."

As soon as Jeonghee said yes, Meena felt a warmth blossoming in her chest. She was still nervous, but she didn't have to do everything on her own.

Meena gathered mixing bowls and several cartons of eggs at her workstation. They settled into a methodical rhythm of cracking shells and dropping whites and yolks into separate containers.

As the dinner approached, the scent of rich foods combined into a heady stew. Meena helped her classmates by laying out dishes for them to plate their creations. Students from the other programs had volunteered to help with service, but all of the cooking belonged to the culinary students. Chike, up first, garnished his catfish pepper soup with fresh efirin. He thanked Meena with a wide grin.

"I'm not used to making so much! It's tricky getting the timing right."

Corentin was up next: kig ha farz with a side of caramelized potatoes. Chike wiped down the pass station to make space for Corentin, and they exchanged a fist-bump. When the last of Corentin's dishes disappeared through the kitchen door, Niamh stuck her head in.

"Just letting you know that everything is going *great* so far. The president looks really happy. All of our guests do!" She departed with a friendly wave.

Corentin took his turn wiping down the pass station, smirking up at Noor. "You ready to blow them away?"

Noor's eyes were sparkling as she gave her dish one final taste. "It's perfect." She'd volunteered to make the main course and chosen a mutton biryani. The entire class helped her carefully portion out the dish before, as a finishing touch, Noor garnished each bowl with fried onions and a sprig of fresh cilantro.

Standing beside the stove, Meena was gently warming the alcohol that would be the finishing touch on her dessert when her stomach rumbled.

"Did you forget to eat?" asked Noor. "There's plenty left. I can make you a plate."

"No, thanks," Meena said. "I want to get my dish ready. I'll find some leftovers after."

Turning back to her workstation, she reached for the egg whites and sugar. Jeonghee appeared by her side without a word, and together they whipped the ingredients into stiff peaks. As soon as the meringue was ready, she and Jeonghee spooned it into piping bags.

Right on cue, a courier robot beeped by the kitchen door.

"What's that for?" asked Noor.

"Just a little touch of presentation," said Meena.

Her classmates helped Meena wheel her trays out of the freezer, each one holding a carefully layered dessert made of cake and ice cream, frozen overnight to keep everything stiff. There was one platter for each table—they would need to be sliced and served tableside to keep the layers from turning into a melted mess.

The final touch was the meringue, which she and Jeonghee piped over the top of each dish like a cap, then Meena browned the meringue with a torch. She set one platter aside, wanting to save it for the surprise at the end. As she prepped, the serving plates felt heavy in Meena's hands, like maybe she'd gone a little over the top. She swallowed down her nerves, ladling the warmed liqueur into her porcelain serving pitcher.

"Are you going to go out there to do the last one?" Jeonghee asked.

Meena nodded while arranging a platter with the last unbrowned meringue on the robot's outstretched arms. "But only if you guys come with me." She paused. "I might need some help serving once we get to the tables."

"Of course! I want to see this," said Chike, and the others agreed.

The group walked together down the corridor from the kitchen to the grand dining room, led by the dutiful courier robot and its precious cargo. Meena had given it a real bowtie for the occasion, and Niamh let out a delighted gasp when she saw it.

"That's so adorable!"

The dining room was an imposing space, with walls painted forest green and five round tables. Meena followed the robot to the head table where President Tākiri was seated. She was a slight, broad woman with moko kauae and a pleased expression decorating her face. She eyed the dessert happily.

"You students are too good to me. I hope I'm not putting you all to a lot of trouble?"

"Not at all," said Jeonghee, by Meena's side. "We like having the chance to show off. Meena?"

Meena took a breath, reaching for the lighter in her apron pocket. At her cue, Corentin dimmed the lights, and Meena carefully poured a measure of liqueur into the concave indent she'd made at the top of the meringue.

"This is my take on a baked Alaska."

She flicked the lighter.

The fire burst to life as it consumed the alcohol, to a delighted gasp from the guests. Corentin cackled. Meena carefully ladled more of the liqueur onto the flame. It trickled down, flashing bright orange and blue, toasting the meringue. The president clapped, and the other guests followed suit.

"That is marvelous!"

"I used a torch on the others," Meena said, suddenly shy. "This is the traditional way."

"A brilliant idea," President Tākiri said. "And I'm sure it tastes even better."

"I have plates for everyone," Noor chimed in, hoisting them, a serving knife placed on top. "Meena, do you want to do the honors?"

Meena anxiously picked up the serving knife. In the months she'd spent on Station 17, she must have used one a thousand times. But no one had been *watching* her before.

She looked up at her classmates. At her *friends*. She wanted them to see what she'd created. So she made the first cut.

"The first layer is a saffron ice cream," she explained as she lifted slices of her creation onto the plates. "The second is gajar halwa, a carrot and cardamom pudding. And the base is a salted caramel cake. Topped with a meringue and ginger liqueur."

The president took the first bite, closing her eyes to savor it.

"Incredible," she said. "Well done, all of you. Excellent work!"

After the remaining tables were served, the trip back to the kitchen was a blur. They passed the library, with its soft golden lights and carefully maintained stacks. Meena was in the center of the group, everyone laughing and shouting.

"You found a way to use up the saffron!" Noor said.

"And the carrots. *Finally*!" Chike added.

"You got the meringue just right," said Jeonghee. "That's really difficult! Such a step up from your first day."

"All those orange and gold layers looked a little like Venus," Noor said thoughtfully. "Did you do that on purpose?"

"No," Meena replied, surprised. "I guess all that time I spent in the library admiring the view had an impact."

"I can't believe you set it on *fire*," Corentin half shouted. "You get it! Why be in a kitchen if you're not going to play with fire?"

They quickly tidied the kitchen, foregoing the next day's prep work for the first time in weeks. They'd all worked hard, and it was time to celebrate.

Jeonghee had some leftover japchae in the fridge, and there were plenty of boiled potatoes from Corentin's dish. Chike and Noor set about mashing them with garlic, curry, black pepper, and thyme. By the time they were finished, Corentin had made several omelets, and Meena had scooped what remained of her saffron ice cream into bowls with a few shredded carrots as garnish.

It was an incongruous, chaotic meal.

It was also the best dinner Meena had ever enjoyed.

When Meena had arrived on Station 17, she'd felt like a misshelved book in a genre that nobody could place. And then her classmates made space for her. They'd helped her channel her tendency toward overenthusiasm into a passion for cooking. And the kitchen felt like home.

HISTORIANS

INDIGO J. H.

Tags: : bipoc, college/university, f/f (background), found family, ghost, has a disability, library, mystery, non-binary, present tense, queerplatonic relationship, student (undergraduate), third person limited point of view, washington

"**I**s it weird to look at the history of a building *while we're inside it?*" Echo ponders from their position on the floor of the library's study room. "What if we find out someone was murdered right where we're sitting?"

Contrary to popular belief, as a ghost, they have no way of knowing if someone died in any given place by just getting a *feeling* about it. If they did, they'd probably get a lot of those feelings. There have been a lot of people in a lot of places.

Jasper, who's much more sensibly seated at the lone table in the room, snorts and turns another page of the giant book in front of zir. "I doubt they would put that book on display if that'd happened. At least not on this floor. Feels like it would be kinda morbid."

"…fair enough."

Echo turns their attention back to their own book and skims through another mind-numbing chapter before their eyes glaze over. The words blur together into meaningless lines and blobs. It's frustrating. Jasper seems to have no issue with researching for hours on end. Echo's a little jealous of that ability, but it isn't how they like to learn. They find history so much more interesting when they can actually *go* places and see things. Or talk to people, even if it's only through Jasper. That's what really gets them invested. That's when the words on a page will actually mean something to them. It's why they're taking classes as a ghost—it's not like they can get a proper degree, or *do* anything with it, but they want to know more.

It's exciting—with the exception of moments like these. This assignment is on local history, which should be the perfect opportunity for them to find a topic they can really sink their teeth into, but so far they haven't found anything that grabs them.

Meanwhile, Jasper's probably finding something in a footnote to become zir next obsession for two months—something with little relation to what ze's actually looking for. Echo'll be perfectly happy to listen to zir explain it in intricate detail when that happens, but for now, it's not going to capture their interest. It likely won't even capture the *professor's* interest.

They turn around so they're lying on their back on the library floor, staring up at the stained-glass windows high on the walls around them. They spend a few minutes trying to make out the pictures in the stained glass, the book abandoned by their head.

"Hey, check it out. I found something weird," Jasper says. "Can I see that book you've got?"

Echo shrugs. "Go ahead. It's not like I'm getting anywhere with it. What did you find?"

Jasper picks the book up from the floor and sets it on the table next to zir laptop. "Is there a map of the building somewhere in here? Like a blueprint, building plans, anything like that?"

"I think I saw something like that in the first chapter. Why?"

"Because the version I found in the other book doesn't quite match the one on the website, and I want to see if this one does."

Echo gets back to their feet and leans over Jasper's shoulder. "What doesn't match?"

Jasper finds the page ze was looking for. It says it's the original building plans for the space. Echo looks between it and the picture Jasper has open on the laptop.

Jasper points at the map on the website and then at the same spot on the book. "There's an extra section in the basement, right there."

There's an extra room—or multiple rooms, Echo can't quite tell—shown in the basement in the book, and the website has no mention of them.

"Huh. Maybe they planned to build it but never did? Budget issues, or something structurally was the problem…" Echo starts walking in circles, thinking. "But if that were the case, they'd have made up different plans. Why are these the ones they published?"

"It's weird," Jasper says.

"Let's go check the map in the lobby! See if it matches the website or the book."

Echo takes off without an answer from Jasper, but ze'll follow them anyway.

When they get there, Echo is moving so fast they almost phase right through the lobby map. "Perfect, here it is! Directory…"

Jasper shows up a moment later, zir uneven gait audible because of zir forearm crutch on the left side. "I'll check the other side."

Echo can't find the basement at all on the map, but then Jasper says, "Look over here."

They see more floors of the library on that side, including the basement. A basement that, according to this map, also doesn't have the extra section that the building plans do.

Huh.

The only way to settle this, they conclude, is to go down to the basement and see for themselves.

They find the spot that should have, according to the original plans for the building, opened up to another wing of the basement.

They end up staring down a completely normal-looking wall.

"I can phase through it and see if there's anything on the other side," Echo says.

"Are you sure?" Jasper sounds worried.

Echo hates the act of phasing through things. Nothing—no objects, not even the ground they stand on—is real to them; if they don't pay attention to their surroundings, they'll just fall through. They don't tend to offer it as an option on their own, and Jasper doesn't ask.

This time, Echo's decided it's worth it. "I'm sure."

Echo closes their eyes and steels themself, then they step through the wall.

When they open their eyes on the other side, they find the room right where the book said it was.

They were *right*.

It's nothing spectacular at first glance, just an abandoned basement. Small cobwebs hang in the corners of the ceiling, and a few dusty, spare pieces of furniture are scattered throughout. Nothing betrays the room's intended purpose.

Echo paces in a circle. What are they missing? There has to be a *reason* this room was left off the building maps.

They don't want to deal with phasing back through the wall to talk to Jasper, so they just call out, "Okay, I'm in. I don't see a door, or anywhere you'd be able to get in, except..." Echo spots a small window on the opposite wall, a few inches above their head. It looks to be at ground level outside.

"Except what?"

"Okay—go back up and go outside—there's a window."

"You want me to climb through a window?" Jasper's tone is incredulous.

"It's the only way in!"

Echo hears nothing from Jasper's side of the wall for several minutes, so they assume ze's gone around to find the window despite zir protests. Just in case, though, Echo has an idea. The library is big, and Jasper probably won't have any idea where Echo is from the outside. Therefore, they need to get creative.

Echo's only done this once or twice before, but it's intuitive enough that they're fairly confident it'll work. They grab hold of the connection between themself and Jasper—the one neither of them can quite understand—and they *pull*. Jasper should feel the tug, and it'll direct zir toward them.

After a minute, Jasper appears in the dirty window. Through the smudged glass, Echo can't see much more than a pale face and dark hair standing out against the green of the trees outside. They can't even see

Jasper's distinctive piercings, but there's no one else it could be. Especially when ze stage-whispers: "All right, I'm here. How are we supposed to open this?"

Echo certainly can't. "Use your crutch!" They match Jasper's tone and reply in the same stage-whisper, even though no one can hear them.

"How?"

"Just—smash it. Quietly."

"I think that makes this officially breaking and entering," Jasper says.

"Not if the property doesn't technically exist."

Jasper sighs, and zir feet turn in a little circle—checking to see if ze's being watched, maybe? Then, ze shoves zir crutch through the window and shatters the glass.

Echo cheers zir on. Jasper brushes aside loose pieces of glass from the window pane with zir shoe and carefully pulls zirself through as zir crutch drops to the ground.

"As long as we don't stay too long, we should be fine. Someone's probably gonna notice the broken window soon, though." Ze looks up at the impossible distance between the floor and the window. "Not that I have any idea *how* I'll get out… Let's look around quickly."

The dim light from the window and Jasper's phone flashlight is all they have to work with. It illuminates the dust particles in the air, and Echo waves their hand through them, watching them stay motionless. The place is clearly old, and the amount of dust suggests that no one's been down here for quite a while.

That assumption comes into question when they walk farther and spot a lamp sitting on a side table, glowing cheerily.

"Who the heck's been down here to turn on a lamp?" Echo whispers.

"No clue," Jasper says. "Let's keep going."

After they've gone through two different doors—this place is a maze if Echo's ever seen one—they hear something other than faint footsteps from floors above.

Music.

Jasper and Echo trade confused glances.

It's not a song Echo recognizes. It's something with a scratchy, older sound to it—maybe swing music?—like it should be played on a record player. Maybe it *is* coming from a record player.

Jasper steps more cautiously as the music gets louder, making zir footsteps quieter. Echo keeps pace with zir, even though part of them is itching to rush ahead and find out what all of this means.

Suddenly, an older man bursts through a door on their left. A door Echo's sure they didn't see open.

He's calling out to somebody behind him, "Yeah, yeah, I'll be back in a minute."

He turns toward them and freezes in place.

Jasper and Echo are already frozen.

The man's face is twisted somewhere between shock and wariness, deepening the lines on his forehead, but that's not what catches Echo's eye. What hooks them is the translucent quality to his skin—same as Echo's.

For the first time ever, they're face-to-face with another ghost.

"Who're you two?" The words are said to both of them, but the man looks at Jasper as he says it, watching as if ze's about to attack.

"Sorry!" Echo doesn't know what they're apologizing for, exactly, but it seems like the right thing to say. "Uh, my name is Echo and that's Jasper. We were just...uh—" Echo looks to Jasper for help, but only gets a panicked shrug in response.

The man lets out a frustrated sigh. "Let's talk."

The tone allows no room for argument.

He ushers them away from the door. Echo's wringing their hands and practically bursting with questions—who were the others in that room? Why are they down here? What was this place even made for and why isn't it on any of the maps?—and the man's eyes narrow.

"We don't get any members of The Living down here." He looks pointedly at Jasper. "And that's by design. What are you doing here?"

As he talks, Echo hears a trace of an Irish accent.

"Uh...Jasper got in through the window," Echo says. The man doesn't say anything to that, and his unimpressed stare stays in place. "It was my idea, though!"

"We don't mean to cause any trouble, really!" Jasper cuts in.

Echo nods vigorously. "We have an assignment about local history, and we got curious about what was down here and—well—I've never had the chance to talk to another ghost before. They tend to keep to themselves. And I understand why! I just—" Echo glances at Jasper and lowers their voice. "We both have a lot of questions."

The man considers them for a moment before his face softens, just a little, and a touch of his intimidating demeanor falls away.

"I probably can't tell you everything you want to know myself—I don't spend much of my time here, not like these folks do—but I might be able to answer a question or two. My name's Desmond."

"Can you tell us what this place is?" Echo bursts out as soon as he's finished. "How did this get built without anyone knowing? Did it always have ghosts, or did you find it later?"

"I can tell you the basics of what I know... *if* you keep it to yourselves," Desmond says. "My story ties directly to this place. If that were to get out, we'd have to leave."

Jasper and Echo both nod as Desmond sits on an armchair in the corner. There's a coffee table in front of it with another chair on the side. It makes Echo feel like they're conducting some kind of *professional interview*, and they sit up straighter than usual when they take the seat next to Jasper.

"You said you noticed this area wasn't on the maps? That's on purpose. When I was a boy, my father had a job working on building this place. He was a little like you." Desmond nods to Jasper, and Echo leans in closer. "He could see ghosts, maybe was even friends with a couple. He and some others arranged for these rooms to get wiped off all the maps—he wanted to create a safe haven for the ghosts of the time, and ghosts in the future, like us.

"It didn't get used so much at first, but some people trickled in and made it their home. Toni and her wife came here eventually, and the two of them have really built this place up."

Echo's enthralled, and out of the corner of their eye, they can see Jasper listening as intently. When Desmond's done talking, ze turns to meet Echo's eyes. "Hey, Echo... this might be perfect for our assignment. If these ghosts have been here for decades, they *have* to know about local history. It'll be a more unique topic than anyone else in the class."

Echo considers. It's true. It's also true that there might only be a few ghosts willing to speak with them—they aren't likely to trust either of them much, especially Jasper. But finding out what the ghosts here have to say would be... pretty incredible. "Okay. We should at least try."

They both turn back to look at Desmond; this certainly isn't something they can do without his help. He looks skeptical.

"We wouldn't share anything without explicit permission, and we can use pseudonyms for anything they say on the record, if they'd like," Jasper says.

"All right," Desmond agrees. "Suppose there's no harm in introducing you to some people. Come back in a few days, and if there's anyone willing to answer a couple of questions, I'll bring 'em here to talk to you."

A shout comes from behind the closed door, and Echo abruptly remembers they'd heard a *party* going on in there. They wonder what they can do to get an invitation to the next one.

"Well, that's my cue." Desmond stands. "I'll see what I can do about getting the others to speak with you."

"Thank you!" Echo stands up, too, and promptly remembers how they came in. "Is there a better way to get out of here? Jasper came in through the window and—uh—it's not a great exit plan."

Desmond smirks, and it's the first time they've seen a hint of humor from him. "There's a door that only unlocks from this side. I'll show you two where it is, and leave it unlocked for next time." His voice goes hard. "As long as you don't tell anyone else it's there. We've kept it well-hidden for decades now."

"We won't. Promise," Jasper says.

They follow Desmond to the exit. As they leave, Echo takes one last look behind them, already buzzing with excitement for the next time they come back.

It's their first proper interview. Jasper sits on the couch with zir legs crossed underneath zir and zir crutch folded at zir side. Ze has zir favorite notebook on zir lap and a pencil case resting on the arm of the couch. Jasper's color-coded note-taking system isn't something Echo can even begin to figure out, but ze assures them the system makes perfect sense to zir.

Jasper and Echo decided it would be easiest during the interviews for Jasper to take notes and Echo to ask their list of questions, along with any follow-ups they think of.

Their first interviewee arrives by walking into the room straight through the wall on the left. Echo jumps in their seat, and Jasper's head snaps to attention. They'll have to get used to that.

The ghost walks confidently to the chair Jasper has set up, and they smile at the two of them in a way that's a nice change from Desmond's wariness. They've got long black hair, a leather jacket, and big platform boots with creases on the top. Echo's a little jealous of the outfit.

"Thanks for being willing to answer our questions!" Echo says.

"It's no trouble at all," the ghost says. "I'm glad there are still folks like you two out there who're interested in hearing about us."

Echo has a list of questions written in Jasper's notebook—they memorized it beforehand, but they keep glancing at it anyway as their nerves rack up. "Uh—" They peek at the notebook, then shake their head; obviously they don't need the list for this question. "Would you mind telling us your name?"

The ghost smiles warmly. "Mo Gonzales."

Echo nods. "Pronouns?"

The ghost's—Mo's—mouth twists as they think about it. "I never much minded what people called me in that sense. You can use whatever you'd like."

Echo nods and smiles back, and their nerves slowly dissipate. It occurs to them that they should mention their own pronouns—a strange concept to Echo, but a welcome one. There aren't many people who refer to them, other than Jasper.

"I use they/them, and Jasper usually uses ze/zir." Echo gestures to Jasper as they speak, and then turns back to Mo. "I have some questions about your past, but first I wanted to start with your present. What makes you stay here, when you could go anywhere you want?"

Mo smiles, and that gives Echo a bit of confidence. "Some ghosts travel the world, and some ghosts never leave the house they grew up in. I spent some time wandering at first, but I always found my way back here. It's my home—the city I lived in most of my life, but far enough removed from the places where I actually spent time that I'm not seeing echoes of the past around every corner. Once I found out there were other ghosts here, especially ones who were *like me*, I felt like I had found my family. And so I've been here ever since."

Echo knows what they mean. It's not dissimilar from how they felt when they found Jasper; they knew that with zir was where they were meant to be.

"If you wouldn't mind, could you tell us when you passed?" Echo's not going to ask how; Mo can tell them if they wish, but it's personal.

"It was in the early '60s. My memories from those first few years are fuzzy, but there are some moments from before that I remember like they were yesterday."

"Could you tell us about some of those moments?" It's the first question Echo didn't already have scripted, but the words come out easier than they expect them to. Maybe they're getting the hang of this.

"My best friend. She introduced me to the Grand Union. It was my first time in a lesbian bar, and I had no clue what I was getting into." Mo smiles fondly. "She led me to this door under an overpass—no sign over it, no nothing—and I thought she was *out of her mind*. By the time the night was over, though, I knew it wouldn't be my last time.

"I made new friends pretty quickly after that. There was a group of us, and I'd see them all the time. Lucy would have these parties and we'd all gathered at her place, and it was nice to have somewhere to go after a couple nights when cops raided the bars."

Echo leans forward. "How often did that happen? Were you ever arrested?" They catch themself, worrying the question might come off as invasive. "I mean, if you don't mind me asking."

Mo shakes their head lightly, and Echo hopes that means they don't mind. "I got taken in once, but they let me out not long after they took us to the station. Nothing came of it, but I was terrified at the time. The raids didn't happen often, but they were often enough that we had plans in place for when they did. That's where Lucy's house came in.

"It might be an exaggeration—but it really felt like every queer person in the city spent time there!" Mo laughs. "I met my first girlfriend at a party in that house, and even if it didn't last long between us, it was something I'll never forget. She had been a student here for a while, actually, and she and I almost got caught making out in a stairwell on the other side of campus."

The three of them laugh, even Jasper while ze diligently takes notes, and Mo tells them about how they lived their life. Jasper ends up asking a few unplanned follow-up questions on zir own, and ze turns to Echo partway through, with the same excitement in zir eyes that Echo's feeling. "Honestly, I feel like we could do our whole assignment just on Mo."

Echo agrees. "I know. And we already have other interviews lined up—imagine how much more we're gonna find out."

At the end, Echo only has one more question for Mo. "Is there any one thing you wish young people today knew about life sixty years ago?"

"I don't think there is. I wish people had curiosity toward the past, if only to be sure not to make the same mistakes over again. But there's more than that, too. There's so much beauty to be found, anywhere you go. Sometimes I think all the bad and the scary parts of our history can overshadow that. So I think…what I wish is for more curiosity about the joy that we found. Yes, there was fear, but there was also so much love.

"I want the love to be what we're remembered by."

Their next interview is with an elderly woman named June with light-brown skin and shocks of bright white in her salt-and-pepper hair. She had been a student at the university during her life, and had often used the library as a meeting spot to organize with her friends. "We used the fifth floor to plan a sit-in, protesting the lack of accessibility. This was before the ADA, you understand.

"It wasn't easy—that's for sure. And we didn't always win, either," she says. "To be honest, most of the time it felt like we weren't getting anywhere. But we were a part of something bigger than ourselves, and I wouldn't change anything I did if I could go back."

She tells them about the events she had put together, meetings and protests and book clubs, along with the incredible people she had the pleasure of meeting at each one. Echo even learns about old campus gossip, though they hadn't been planning to ask.

When the interview ends, they say their goodbyes, promising to speak more with June another time. Echo suspects they've only scratched the surface of the stories she has for them.

They turn to Jasper after June leaves.

"I don't think I realized how much there would be to say about this campus—or even this building—alone," Echo says. "It's definitely more than we can use in just one assignment."

Sitting perched on the arm of the couch, Jasper hums zir agreement and flops down on the seat cushions. "There could be a whole *class* for this stuff."

"There could be. It wouldn't be the same without learning it from the ghosts themselves, though," Echo says. "I don't know how a professor could teach it."

The next day, they meet the first ghost who's closer to their own age. Mariana is bright and bubbly, with long black hair that goes almost down to her hips. She plays with it as they talk, running her fingers through the strands and getting at least five questions out of her mouth before Echo can ask one.

"Do the people in your classes really not care that you're a ghost? Do professors actually grade your assignments? Oh—do you ever help Jasper cheat on tests?"

Echo blinks a couple times as they process the questions being thrown at them. "Uh—I wouldn't say they don't *care*; they're definitely curious, but for the most part they're all right with me being there! As for assignments, it depends on if I can get Jasper to type them out for me. It's not like I'm officially in the school's system, so I can't get *real* grades, but they'll mark my stuff for me if they can. And no—I don't help Jasper cheat on tests. I don't want to, but it wouldn't be worth the risk even if I did."

"Is there anyone else on campus who can see us?"

Echo can't think of any, so they look to Jasper to answer the question.

"There might be a few—there probably are—but I don't know them. Most people don't make it public knowledge," Jasper says. "I'm a weird case that way, since everyone knows about Echo."

"Huh. I wish there was a way I could let them know I'd like to meet them," Mariana says. "If they want to, that is. I know Desmond and some of the others don't trust The Living, but I think it could be really fun to get to know some of them."

Echo meets Jasper's eyes, communicating a silent question. Mariana could be right, and if The Living and ghosts had more ways to communicate, they might be able to break down some of those walls of mistrust.

"We'll see if we can come up with some way to make that happen. I don't know how, but...we could try," Echo says.

Jasper's eyes go wide—surprised, but not disapproving.
Echo grins.

Their last interview is with two women Desmond mentioned when they'd first met: Toni and Faye. Desmond said they were the leaders of their community in some ways. They reach out to newer ghosts who appear lost and offer them whatever help they can give. They also do their part to keep the ghosts safe from any members of The Living who might pose a danger.

Toni gets a fond smile on her face as she looks at her wife. "Faye and I owned a bookstore together. We did our best to make it a place for our community—somewhere people wouldn't be afraid to be who they are. It was like this place, in a way. That might've been what drew us here. The store was controversial, and running it wasn't always easy. We had neighbors on that street that wanted us gone—but it was ours. We were proud of it. We still are."

"How did you two find the library?" Echo asks.

Faye answers, "It didn't happen right away. We spent some time disconnected—we still had each other, but not much else. We had some good memories here, from before, and when we came to visit, we ran into Desmond. He was alone too. So were most of the other ghosts we'd come across. When Desmond mentioned a place at the heart of campus, one The Living didn't know about, it sounded like the perfect opportunity to bring us together."

The interview keeps going, longer than the others. Somewhere along the way, the structured questions dissolve into conversation between friends. Echo's thoughts stray to the party they crashed when they first discovered this place, and how they've gone to the university for two years and never known about this beautiful world hiding beneath their feet.

They think about how they could have gone years longer without finding out.

"So how did you two meet each other?" Toni asks. "I hope you don't mind that I ask. It's rare to see such a trusting relationship between one of us and The Living—on both sides."

"Oh," Echo says. "Well, it wasn't too long after I became a ghost. I did a lot of exploring, people watching, that sort of thing."

Jasper picks up the story. "They were at a bookstore café when I met them—I didn't realize they were a ghost at first. Not many people knew I could see ghosts back then— it doesn't happen too often, and as a kid I just assumed the people I could see were really there. The only giveaway that *Echo* was a ghost rather than any other pink-haired college student was them reading a novel over some guy's shoulder. Occasionally they'd say 'come on, hurry up, turn the page' and the guy never reacted."

Echo cuts in. "And *now* I can read novels over *your* shoulder, and I actually have some say in what we pick. Some of the books I read back then were so *boring*." They throw their head back dramatically for emphasis.

Toni chuckles. "It sounds like you two meeting was for the best, then."

Even though it's not a question, Jasper answers it like it is one. "I never thought I would even *speak* to a ghost, or get to know one, before Echo and I became friends. My family never liked ghosts; I never told them I could see them. I was prepared to go my whole life without acknowledging my ability. And I would have missed out on *so much*."

The smile Jasper gives Echo is precious, and Echo tries to memorize its lines before turning back to Toni and Faye.

The same nerves from their first interview creep up on them; they have some plans they've been thinking over for a few days, but they won't go forward if the ghosts don't all like the idea.

"You know, if the two of us meeting was for the best, I'm sure it wouldn't be just us," Echo says. "If we had a way to open the lines of communication between ghosts and The Living more—not enough to put the ghosts in jeopardy, just enough for the ones who want to get their stories out there to be able to do so…I think it could be really good for a lot of people."

Echo pauses, taking in their reactions. Toni is wary, but not closed off. Faye seems considering.

Echo presses forward. "Maybe there could be a way for both groups to ask each other questions. I have a few ideas I was hoping we could go over with you, and maybe you could tell us what you think?"

"Oh wow. That's…a lot of people." Jasper's looking out at the crowd for the University of Washington's very first ghost tour. Despite the dreary weather, they have a turnout of almost fifty people gathered by the library's entrance. Echo and Jasper peek at them from around the corner.

Implementing a question box to facilitate ghost communication in the library had been their first step, but this is something else entirely, at least for Jasper. This is *real live public speaking*.

It's taken a few months of hard work and negotiation with the university admin and the ghosts themselves—plus an almost perfect score on their history assignment—to get to this point, but these people are proof that the work has been worth it.

Echo turns their attention from the crowd to Jasper. Ze's fidgeting with the button on zir right sleeve with the same hand; the other one is occupied holding zir forearm crutch. That type of fidgeting is usually the kind they only do when they're anxious—it's a small enough motion to mask, most of the time, but frantic enough that it means ze's itching to make bigger movements.

"Well, it's the first weekend of the semester," Echo says. "Guess we've got a bunch of people here who want to check it out. Plus, the question box has been getting traction. I heard that even *Desmond* has started writing down answers for the board whenever he pops in."

Echo does, too—or at least they have Jasper write answers for them, and Toni's promised to teach them how to move objects on their own soon. Echo's already got some back-and-forth notes with people in their classes. It feels weird to have friends other than Jasper. It's a good kind of weird, though.

"So they either have high expectations, or *I'm* their first impression of the school?" Jasper asks. "Cool. That's great. No pressure at all."

"You'll do fine. You know what you're talking about, and Toni knows what she's talking about when she tells us this stuff. And even if you freeze up, I'm here to remind you."

Echo has complete confidence that they'll figure this out. That said, they tend to have confidence in *all* their ridiculous ideas—but for the most part they *do* work out!

"That's easy for you to say! You're not the one standing up there talking in front of them." Jasper gestures to the crowd with one hand.

"I mean—I *could* get up there if it would make you feel better. Make some silly faces at them before you go on."

That makes Jasper smile, but ze quickly schools it into an unimpressed scowl. It doesn't matter anyway; Echo can see through it. "You know it's not that same when they don't know you're there."

"Potato, patahto."

"That's not even how—"

If they don't get in front of those people right now and do some proper ghost tour-ing, they're going to start late, so Echo makes an executive decision and takes off, trusting Jasper will be right behind them. "Come on! You and I were born for this."

When Echo looks back, they see Jasper finally give in to the smile ze's been fighting. "Yeah, yeah, all right. Let's do it."

ESCAPE THE STACKS

VEE SLOANE

Tags: college/university, dwarf, fairy, fantasy, halfling, humor, inter-species relationship, library, m/nb, non-binary, past tense, private detective, third person limited point of view

"Quint!" barked the daffodil intercom from the corner of the office. Quint Guff, library detective, did not fall asleep on the job, and they certainly didn't startle so hard they almost fell out of their chair. "The director wants you!"

The daffodil punctuated its announcement with a sneeze of pollen.

"Bless you," Quint muttered. They brushed a bit of dust from their practical coat and strode from the office with purpose.

The Barnabas Memorial Library of Twinkleburg University was a charming, sprawling place that called students from every magical walk of life.

Neither magical nor a student, Quint had been called nonetheless.

All around them, enormous bookcases—adorned with bright, multilingual, and occasionally scented signage—stretched toward the stained-glass dome roof. The majority-bewinged student body zipped and fluttered through the stacks and alighted on the shelves, engaged in the intense work of discovering the limits of magic.

Sometimes, the showy beauty made Quint's long, slow days almost worth it.

Other times, like when they were taking the stairs to avoid the affectionate vines that worked as elevators, or dodging flying, giggling students as they slogged along on the ground, they questioned all their life choices.

The director's office was by the front entrance, carved into the base of a fairy-sized mushroom. Quint had to crouch to knock on the door, and when it swung open, they had to get even lower to enter.

"Good morning, Quinty-dear!" chimed Director Berrybottom. Her glossy wings were decorated with tiny yellow flowers to match her cheery glasses. "Please have a seat."

Quint sat right on the floor in front of her desk. They'd only had to break one chair to learn their lesson about fairy furniture.

"Good morning, Director," they said, wishing for their long-departed dignity to return. They used to have heaps of dignity.

"I know you're terribly busy, but do you think you could look into a small matter for me?"

"Yes, of course, ma'am. What can I do for you?"

They did not get their hopes up. In the ten moons of their employ, they had been called down to this office one hundred and forty-seven times. Fifty-six of those had been a request to help a student get a book down from a high location where flight wasn't allowed, forty-eight of those had been to help a staff member with the same thing, thirty-three had been reminders to attend weekly staff tea parties, and ten times had been assignments for their actual job. Seven of those had been solved within an hour. Three of them in less than that.

The library did not so much need a detective as it did a ladder.

"Elsa reported a missing title."

Quint sat up straighter. "A missing rare book?"

"Yes, let's see…" She shuffled through a stack of catalog cards. "Ah, yes! *The Grimoire of Color and Folly*. It walked right out of the rare book room yesterday."

"The newer security system I recommended—" Quint started.

"Oh, the library knows better than some newfangled alarms," the director tsked. "In any case, it seems a student disappeared along with the book."

Quint stared at her. When she said nothing else, they asked, "Do you mean no one has seen this student since they took the book?"

"Borrowed," Director Berrybottom corrected. "I'm certain he didn't intend to take it."

Considering how many students Quint had seen using their magic to steal from the vending machines, they had their doubts.

"So you want me to track down the student?"

"Just the book!" she said with a wide smile. "I'm sure the student isn't missing."

"You said no one had seen them," Quint said patiently.

"If I don't see you all day, I don't assume you're missing," she sniffed. "Here's the information!"

Taking the card, Quint gave her a tight nod, then crawled out of her office. Who cared about dignity when they had a case!

The card had the book's information, and crammed under that as an afterthought: Twiggs Tootleloo, doctoral candidate in colormancy.

With significantly more pep in their step, Quint charged back to their office and located their satchel. It was loaded with all that could be needed for detection, from rope to rations to beard oil (no proud dwarf traveled without it). The only thing missing was their axe. The library had a strict "no iron" policy.

Quint's first stop was rare books, where Elsa directed them to a reserved study carrel. The chair still bore a bright-red cardigan.

They could make all sorts of deductions from the simple garment, but there was no need. They knew exactly who it belonged to: the adorable halfling with the button nose and bright eyes who had once put his hand on Quint's biceps so he could brush by them in the stacks. Quint had felt that hand for a week after the touch, searing into them.

A teeny, pink-haired head peeked over the divide of the carrels.

"Are you looking for Twiggs? He said he was going to get a snack, like…" Wide, gemlike eyes blinked sparkling lashes. "I'm not actually sure. I lost track of time around Monday."

"It's Wednesday," Quint told this incarnation of fatigue.

"So that's why my nectar curdled! Huh. Anyway, I thought Twiggs was getting more peanut-butter acorns, but he never came back."

There was only one vending machine in the library that dispensed peanut-butter acorns, and it was in the sub-basements. Twiggs was down there without even his cardigan! Quint carefully folded it and put it into their satchel.

"I swear by the Great Forge that I will return him to you!"

The student blinked slowly. "Thanks?"

Quint sprinted toward the stairs. To be thorough, they stopped on every floor on the way down, winding their way through every aisle. They tripped over a student in the enchantment section who had barricaded themselves in with texts, circumnavigated an amorous couple wedged together in the alchemy shelves, and hacked through the vines that had grown over the fifth-floor exit again, but eventually they made it to the entrance to the sub-basements.

A sign in flowery script over the door read:

Special Collections
The library is not responsible for your
body, mind, or soul past this point.
Have a nice day!

Quint adjusted the strap on their satchel and entered.

The sub-basements wicked away all the bright excitement of the upper levels. They were pervaded with must, dust, and poor lighting, and books were crammed into every nook and cranny. Each sign was yellowed and curling up on itself, as if afraid to make too bold a declaration about what might dwell there.

It was so much like home that Quint rarely visited. It made them long for the damp chill of a cavern. Swept through with homesickness, they picked their way through the first two sub-basements, checking only for signs of life before moving on.

As they headed down to the next level, the last bookcase they passed was labeled:

Not Quite Necromancy,
But You Can't Be Too Careful

Quint desperately missed their axe.

On the landing of the third sub-basement was the peanut-butter acorn vending machine. It emanated a menacing glow, illuminating the single coin lying in front of it.

"Twiggs?" Quint called out. "Hello?"

They moved into the stacks, looking down for some hint or clue.

That's when they were tackled from above.

"Back, fiend!" a small voice cried as arms wrapped around Quint's neck. "You'll never take me!"

Unfortunately for their attacker, Quint significantly out-massed them. Quint rocked back on their heels in surprise, catching their hand on a shelf to steady themselves. Their attacker hung limply around their neck, like a sad scarf.

"Twiggs?" Quint asked carefully. "I'm Detective Quint Guff. I was sent here to find you."

The arms let go and standing before Quint, coming up to their shoulder, was the adorable halfling with the button nose and now dust-speckled brown curls. His homespun linen shirt was askew.

"Oh, thank the Sheep-Mother! I thought I'd be stuck down here for the rest of eternity!" Twiggs said. "Do you know the way back to the stairs?"

They were mere feet from the vending machine that had been in sight of the stairs.

"You...couldn't find them?" Quint asked with a frown. "Did you leave your glasses upstairs?"

"Hilarious," Twiggs growled. That was also really adorable. "All I wanted was a familiar snack. I don't know why I have to come all the way down here to get halfling-friendly food, but whatever. I get my acorns, turn around, and you know what I find?"

"What?" Quint asked, bemused.

"No stairs! I've been walking in circles ever since. I guess I got myself really worked up with all the creepy silence. When I heard you, I thought you were a killer or something. Sorry."

"It's fine," Quint assured him. Maybe Twiggs had had some kind of study-induced breakdown? "Let's get you out of here."

Twiggs gave them a sarcastic *go ahead* gesture. Quint headed for the stairs...

...which were gone. Where there had been a spiraling nightmare of steps was only old wooden flooring that could have been there since Quint's great-grandparents' time.

"I told you," Twiggs said, coming up alongside them. "No stairs!"

Quint stomped hard on the floor. It sounded solid. They looked up to the ceiling, but it was shrouded entirely in a foreboding mist.

Quint frowned. "Was that fog there before?"

Twiggs followed their line of sight. "There was a ceiling there before."

"Maybe we should move away from the demon-summoning books."

"Those are in sub-basement nine," Twiggs said. "These are vaguely-annoying-imp-summoning books."

The mist formed a face with a wicked smile.

"Vaguely annoying is close enough," Quint decided. "The stairs on the higher floors are on the left—let's head that way!"

"...and we're running. Great."

Every time Quint looked over their shoulder, the mist seemed to follow just behind them, no matter how fast they went.

Twiggs pointed. "A door!"

Twiggs latched onto the handle and pulled. It didn't budge. Quint got both hands around it and tugged. When that didn't work, they braced one foot against the wall. Gritting their teeth, they pulled with all their strength, and the door groaned before popping open.

Both of them dove through, and Quint slammed it shut behind them.

They were in a stairwell. But the stairs only went down.

Twiggs's heaving breath echoed. He looked so tired and scared. Quint offered them their battered old canteen. Twiggs snatched it and took a long sip.

"Thank you," he said between gasps. "I think both of us are lost down here now, but I appreciate the rescue attempt."

"We'll get out," Quint said confidently. "The director always says the library is a friendly place."

They both looked down the foreboding stairs.

"I wish I'd gotten more acorns before we ran in terror," Twiggs sighed.

"Do you like jerky?"

Twiggs's eyes went big. "They let you bring in meat?"

"Please don't tell on me!" Quint glanced around like the director might be hiding nearby, though it was difficult to imagine her cheery glitter in the musty, gray stairwell. "If you don't tell, I'll share."

"Tell on you? I haven't had meat in three years, except when I went home for Solstice. Gimme!"

Quint split the chunk of jerky, and they shared it as they headed down the stairs.

"So you're finishing your dissertation?" they asked.

"Is this the time for small talk?" Twiggs asked with a hint of sarcasm.

"We could keep going in grim silence, but in my experience that gets old fast."

"Do you have a lot of experience with this kind of thing?"

"Not exactly," Quint allowed, "but I was an Ore Scout as a kid, and we went on a lot of long walks through less-explored caverns."

The door to the next level opened without complaint. Quint went through first and found only more stacks. The ceiling was clear, and they didn't hear anything, so they gestured at Twiggs to follow them out.

"What now?" Twiggs asked.

"Let's head to the center and look for more stairs. If they're not there, we go around the perimeter and see if they're on the other side."

"Good plan." Twiggs nodded. "Let's do it."

There were no stairs in the center of the floor. Instead of a vending machine, this floor had a water fountain. Quint set their canteen on the water-lily base and waved their hand over it. It reluctantly dispensed a thin stream of water.

"It doesn't make any sense," Twiggs muttered.

"Because this library is a nonsense mine," Quint grumbled, then winced. "I didn't say that."

Understanding passed over Twiggs's face. He asked, "You have a problem with the university?"

"No!" they protested, going red as they screwed the canteen lid back on. "I mean— Don't you—? Never mind."

"You might as well say it," Twiggs prompted.

It was hard to say aloud, stuck behind Quint's teeth. They licked their lips and managed, "I get tired of being the wrong shape."

Twiggs winced. "Back home, I don't really fit in," he admitted. "My friends already have kids and farms to manage. It's rare enough to be a halfling wizard, but the fact that I wanted to go pro? I had to get a full scholarship because my parents wouldn't help me. When I came here, I thought I'd finally fit in somewhere. Some days, I do. Other days, it's so much worse."

"That's exactly it!" Quint cried. "I always wanted to be a detective. My parents thought it was cute, but when I didn't change my mind as I got older, it became 'concerning.' I knew there wasn't a place for me underground. I thought I'd find my people above it."

"And everyone here is so nice." Twiggs leaned closer, eyes keen. "Right? So nice that you feel terrible saying anything bad about anything."

"Yes! They listen to my suggestions, they smile, and then nothing changes!" Quint said. "No one ever complains or thinks a bad thing about anyone."

"Which is good," Twiggs groaned. "Nice."

"Sometimes I want to have a good grumble," Quint said eagerly.

Twiggs grinned. "I love gossip, and no one will gossip with me."

Their eyes met.

"I'm a good detective," Quint told him. "I listen closely. I've got great gossip."

"And I," Twiggs said with a hint of mischief, "have enough complaints to fill a ten-foot scroll."

This was *a moment.*

Quint should say something!

Nothing came to them.

Before they could find a reply, there was a horrible crashing noise. It went on and on, coming from behind them and getting louder.

"What is that?" Twiggs shouted. "It sounds like the gates of the underworld opening!"

"Let's not hang around to find out!"

Quint grabbed Twiggs's hand and took off. They ran to the other side of the floor, hoping for another door. They reached the wall and found nothing.

"Left or right?" Twiggs asked.

The loudest *thud* yet sounded.

"Left!" Quint decided and took off again, still holding on.

They reached a corner, and Quint stopped to let Twiggs catch his breath. The aisle's peeling label read:

Grayish Arts

All was quiet.

"If this is gray," Quint whispered, "what's the dark art section like?"

"Not gray like between dark and light," Twiggs said, panting. "Gray is a good color for places of meditation. But it can also cause low moods, so that's probably why it's not readily available upstairs."

"That's what you're studying?"

His eyes still darting every which way, Twiggs explained, "My doctorate is about the effects of scarlet on productivity in the workplace. I want to have an interior design firm that works with an architecture firm to create calmer and better workspaces."

"I like that," Quint whispered back. "It's a good goal."

Twiggs gave them a tight smile. "Thanks, but it's been deprioritized. The current goal is to escape this library."

"Let's walk for now, until we—"

A new noise creased the air: a rustle of plastic and paper.

"Dust jackets," Twiggs squeaked.

Ordinarily, dust jackets protected books from the wear and tear of being constantly reshelved. Occasionally, though, a few were left too long together without books, and the magic seeped in. The jackets, newly sentient and confused, swarmed together and sought book-shaped things to shield. Unfortunately, nearly everything looked book-shaped to them. The last infestation had taken the director and three librarians two weeks to banish to the midden heap and had left the entire library sticky from the jackets' adhesive corners.

"Count of three, we run for it." Quint tried to keep their voice steady. Calm. Sturdy.

"Okay." Twiggs reached out and took their hand this time.

"One. Two…"

There was no "three." The swarm was upon them.

"Get off!" Twiggs swatted at three jackets trying to hug his face.

Quint kept their hand in front of their own face, smacking some out of the air. They pulled two jackets off Twiggs and stuck them to the floor.

"Put your hands in front of your face!" Quint yelled.

"I'm trying to!"

The sound of a thousand rusty door hinges from earlier started up again, creating a terrifying symphony. Quint's ears filled with creaking, rustling, and Twiggs's muffled screams as they tried to beat back the swarm.

"We have to run!" they cried.

"I can't see!"

"Hold on!" Quint got their arm around Twiggs's waist. "Sorry for touching you without asking!"

"I don't care right now!"

With a grunt, Quint swung Twiggs into their arms and took off running. The stairs weren't far. They could make it.

A sharp *clang* cut through the air.

A terrible, lumpy shadow fell over the end of the aisle. The way was blocked.

Twiggs clutched at Quint's arm. "It's a book cart!"

Quint squinted at the shape.

"You!" they hissed. "You were banished!"

The cart rumbled forward a few inches, the unholy sound echoing all around them.

"You banished a book cart?"

"The director did," Quint explained. "It's the Creakiest Book Cart. No one can think with that noise, so into the midden heap it went with all the other banished things."

The book cart approached, the wheels moaning like the souls of the damned.

"Is it evil?" Twiggs demanded.

"No?"

The cart nudged Quint's foot. They glanced behind them, where the flock of jackets was getting in their own way, their tacky wings sticking to each other and balling up even as they swarmed closer.

"It wants us to ride it," Twiggs declared.

"How do you know that?"

"It's acting like one of the ponies at home," Twiggs said as they wiggled enough that Quint had to set them down.

The cart had three shelves and a central divider to make it two-sided for maximum book-carrying capacity. In a twinkle, Twiggs was sitting on the top shelf, astride the center on his knees. It looked ridiculous and wildly uncomfortable, but the cart didn't try to buck him off.

"I won't fit," Quint protested.

Twiggs looked over Quint's shoulder. "Stand on the bottom shelf and let's go!"

Quint got their feet on the bottom, facing Twiggs, certain that the whole cart would tip over and this would be how they died. At least it would be underground—that would please their parents.

As soon as Quint had a decent grip, the cart took off. It bounded from the jackets, then smacked right into the door to the landing, which flew open, and carried them back into the stairwell.

"We're free!" Twiggs said with a laugh. A laugh which stopped short. "No! No! Bad cart!"

The cart did not slow, bumping its way down the stairs. Quint closed their eyes and prayed to the old gods. They didn't actually believe in them, but it seemed like the thing to do in this situation.

Then there was silence and stillness.

"Are we dead?" Twiggs asked raggedly.

Quint opened their eyes, evaluating the stairwell. There were no more stairs going down.

"No—worse. We're in the last sub-basement."

Twiggs climbed off the cart with a wince. "Why did you take us all the way down?"

The cart creaked.

Quint got off it too, giving it a pat on the handle. "In fairness," they said, "I'm not sure it could go up the stairs."

"True," Twiggs said, giving the cart a once-over. "Why didn't anyone fix it?"

"I'm not sure. They must've tried."

Twiggs squatted and gave the front wheel a poke. The cart squeaked, backing away. "Oh. I see. You wouldn't let anyone look at the problem— like a shy horse. Didn't care for those librarians messing with you, hm?"

"It's a cart," Quint said flatly.

Twiggs gently petted the front of the cart. "A cart like us."

Quint wrinkled their nose. "What do you mean?"

"It didn't fit in. Sometimes a horse knows who to trust, you know? Maybe it sensed kindred spirits in us."

As if in agreement, the cart creaked again.

Twiggs held his hands out and started chanting. Fairy magic usually smelled like flowers, and dwarf magic felt like the heat of the forge. Whatever Twiggs was doing tasted like warm, fresh bread and the smell of good earth. It was amazing, but the wheels cried out again as the cart shuddered.

"What if it doesn't need magic?" Quint asked, feeling a bit foolish for even suggesting it.

"What else would it need?"

"Back home, when something has a squeaky wheel, we oil it."

There was another cacophony as the cart butted against Quint.

"That's brilliant!" Twiggs said, smiling up at them. Quint's stomach clenched. "Too bad we don't have anything that could help."

Quint rifled through their satchel, pulling out the vial of beard oil.

Twiggs barked a laugh. "Why do you have that?"

Quint knelt to gingerly apply the oil to the wheel. "You never know when you're going to have a beard emergency."

"I don't think that's something you have to worry about," Twiggs snorted. "Your hair looks like it was spun from one of those enchanted spinning wheels."

Quint's heart thudded harder in their chest, but they kept their attention on the cart. "There," they said. "Try that."

The cart rattled back. One of the other wheels let out a squeak, but the one Quint had treated slid quietly over the floor.

"Amazing," Twiggs breathed out, then laughed. "Figures. We rely on magic too much."

"Maybe," Quint allowed. "But it *is* magic. I would lean on it too if I could."

"You can't? Huh. I didn't know any non-magical people worked here. Wouldn't it be easier to be a detective somewhere else?"

When Quint's Da had asked them the same thing, they'd said it was the best opportunity. When their friends had asked them, they'd said it would be an adventure.

Neither answer was quite the truth.

"I love magic," Quint admitted. "I thought if I could be close to it, it would be nearly as good as doing it."

"Has it been?"

They met Twiggs's eyes, which didn't twinkle like a fairy's or glitter in the gloom like a dwarf's. The velvet depths regarded them with the warmth of a hearth.

"Yes," they said softly.

"I've had magic my whole life, so I can't really imagine it from the outside. What's it like for you?"

No one had ever asked, but Quint had a ready answer. "It's like music. I can't make it, but that doesn't mean I can't love to listen to it."

"I never thought of it like that." Twiggs smiled at them.

They were both quiet for a moment. Twiggs had his arms wrapped around himself, and with the brief absence of danger, Quint could think clearly again.

"Your cardigan!"

They opened their satchel and produced the red sweater. Twiggs's face lit up as he took it and tugged it back on.

"I'm sorry I didn't remember I had it earlier," Quint said.

"Yes, very rude." Twiggs rolled his eyes. "Especially considering you've only saved my life three times today."

Quint grinned. Sarcasm! They had missed sarcasm so much. "I'll endeavor to be more polite as we enter the pit of infernal summoning."

"See that you do!" Twiggs laughed a little, then sobered as he looked at the door. "Right. Only way out is through."

Quint cracked open the door. The dust was thick in the air, diffusing the light into a murky yellow miasma. The bookcases were sparsely populated; some shelves held only a single text.

"I've never seen shelves this empty here," Quint whispered.

"Dark magic books don't get along with each other," Twiggs whispered back. He stayed behind Quint. The cart rolled forward and nudged under Twiggs's hand. "If you shelve them together, they'll shred each other to bits."

With little choice, Quint started forward.

"Why does the library even have them?"

"Dark magic isn't evil on its own."

"Death magic has to be evil. Doesn't it?"

"Rot and decay are necessary for new things to grow and thrive," Twiggs explained. His voice was thinner, as if the gloom were stretching it out from his mouth. "I requested one of these books last year, and it was no more evil than any of the others upstairs."

"What were you looking for?"

"Blood is scarlet, so I'd be remiss not to cover it." Twiggs slipped the hand not on the cart into Quint's. It happened slowly, as if he hoped Quint wouldn't notice.

Quint definitely noticed.

"That's really thorough of you. What'd you learn?"

"If you paint walls with blood, it smells really bad and attracts bugs," Twiggs said wryly.

"Did you conduct that experiment in a lab?" Quint asked, without much hope.

"Too much waiting time for approval," Twiggs snorted. "Grad students don't have roommates, at least."

"I admire your commitment to your research."

Twiggs laughed. "Do you really?"

The sound bounced around the space, and to Quint's surprise, the lights sprang up a little brighter.

Twiggs rocked on his feet excitedly. "We must've hit some kind of detection spell! Maybe the exit's nearby!"

Escaping was the desired outcome, but Quint's heart sank anyway. This had been the most exciting thing to happen to them in months. Once they were back upstairs, Twiggs would return to his work, finish his dissertation, and go on to some bright future, while Quint plugged away at a job no one wanted them to do.

The floor below them rumbled.

They both froze. The cart halted. Breath held, they waited. A single flap of plastic creased the air, then a few more, then dozens.

"The dust jackets!" Quint shouted.

The swarm was upon them in seconds. Quint threw themselves over Twiggs, shielding him completely. At least one of them might survive to get out of here.

The jackets kept swirling, but nothing touched them. Tentatively, Quint lifted their head. The swarm had made a cone around them and the book cart.

"What are they doing?" they asked breathlessly.

From under Quint's chest, Twiggs's voice was muffled. "If I didn't know better, I'd say they were protecting us."

"From what?"

The cart shuddered. The ground itself was undulating.

"Oh. Oh, no," Twiggs whispered.

"It can't be! The director said they got rid of it!"

Twiggs groaned. "Of course she did. It's just like the cart and the jackets! Everything the director said they sent to the midden heap is here—this *is* the midden heap!"

Beyond the edge of the shield of jackets, the floor exploded. It was hard to make out through the translucent sheets, but the sound of concrete and carpet scraps hitting the jackets was clear enough.

"Do you know any killing spells?" Quint asked desperately.

Twiggs shook his head. "I'm a colormancer!"

They both watched in horror as the bookworm, distorted through the haze of the jackets' wings, reared up. Its body was made from damaged texts, matted dust bunnies, and torn cardigans. Formed from the library's ancient midden heap, the golem made a sound like a dozen toilets flushing as it lunged toward them.

The jackets held strong, resisting the initial blow. For a moment it seemed like their shield would hold, but the worm lunged again, sending a whole phalanx of dust jackets scattering. Quint got Twiggs back on the cart and jumped on themselves just in time to avoid the dark maw of the beast. The cart took off, hurtling down the aisles, the worm in hot pursuit.

"We're going to die down here!" Twiggs moaned.

"No, we're not!" Quint growled. "Not today!" They snatched a book off the shelf and threw it at the worm.

The worm ate it.

"Don't throw any more books!"

"What should I do, then?" Quint demanded.

"I should know some spells for this," Twiggs lamented, the cart going fast enough to whip his curls into a frenzy. "We're going to die because I'm a bad wizard!"

"You're a great wizard!"

"You don't know that."

"Then prove it," Quint challenged. "Show me your best spell!"

As the cart bumped along beneath them, Twiggs put a hand on Quint's shoulder, balancing himself as he turned to face the worm. An incantation tumbled from his lips, and the taste of warm bread filled the air.

A wall rose up behind them, up and up until it touched the ceiling. It was an angry red, so red it burned to look at directly. The worm slammed against it.

"Color swatch," Twiggs said faintly. "I guess any spell can be defensive if you cast it hard enough."

"You're amazing," Quint assured him, watching the wall shake under the worm's assault as they continued to retreat. "You bought us time."

But they were talking to no one: Twiggs had passed out, slumped over the top of the cart, listing toward Quint. Quickly, they got an arm around him so he wouldn't fall off.

Quint couldn't think of a single other thing to do. They had no weapons. It was them and the cart and all the discarded things from the world upstairs versus an enormous, starving worm.

They rolled to a slow stop against a far wall.

"This isn't fair," they said as they gave the cart a gentle pat. "There's no reason we should all be thrown down here to be forgotten because we're not cheery or sweet or floral."

The worm stopped beating against the wall.

Everything fell silent.

Quint was certain to their bones that something larger was listening, in the way they had been when they were very small and their parents were in the other room.

"We deserve the sunlight as much as anything else," they went on, warming to the topic now that they were sure they had something's attention. "Even the worm! Maybe if it was in a nice magical forest or something, it wouldn't be so dangerous. The jackets still want to protect things, and the cart only wanted oil! Twiggs wants to be a good wizard, and I—"

They faltered, and it was as if the world held its breath.

"I want to help people," they whispered, and as they said it, the truth of it burst out of them. "I want to help him! Please, help me save him!"

The cart pulled away from the wall, nearly toppling Quint and Twiggs off it. It slowly gained speed, and Quint had to dash away tears they didn't remember shedding. In the cart's frantic escape, it didn't so much as come to a stop as ram into the center column of the room.

The crash finally did throw Quint off the cart, but at least Twiggs fell right on top of them, cushioned from the fall. A faint throb of red pulsed behind them one last time, then shivered away into pink before fading to nothing.

"What's happening?" Twiggs asked muzzily, eyes fluttering open.

Behind them, there was a gentle *ding*. Elevator doors—that had not been there moments before—materialized and slid open.

"We're getting out of here," Quint told him, scooping him up in their arms and tugging the cart behind them into the elevator.

Off in the stacks, the jackets had coalesced back into a swarm, the worm visible through them.

"We're going to come back for you," Quint told them. "I promise."

One of the jackets darted forward as the elevator doors started to close. It alighted on Quint's shoulder and flapped a little before settling in quietly. Twiggs stared at it.

"What did I miss?"

"I don't actually know," Quint admitted. "I think I talked to the library."

"The whole thing?"

The car carried them up and up, and Twiggs rested his head on Quint's shoulder as they filled him in.

When Twiggs had heard it all, he said, "Maybe the library has been magical long enough to have some thoughts."

Quint frowned. "Maybe so."

"Or you've got your own kind of magic," Twiggs said. "After all, you rescued me."

"I didn't, really."

"You came down there, stuck with me through all of that, and got us out." Twiggs stretched up and kissed the small bare patch of skin between Quint's beard and sideburn. "Thank you."

"I—"

The elevator doors opened.

Director Berrybottom, flying a few feet off the ground, was waiting for them.

"Quinty-dear! You're all right. Did you find the grimoire?"

Quint's stomach flipped over. They had forgotten all about the book.

"Hi." Twiggs gave a little wave, still held in Quint's arms. "The library tried to kill me while I was getting a snack, and Quint saved me, which I think is more important, personally. Which grimoire?"

The cart rumbled out of the elevator, and Quint followed, carrying Twiggs.

"Why, *The Grimoire of Color and Folly*!" The director looked between them.

"I left that in my study carrel," Twiggs said indignantly. "I don't take things out of the rare book room!"

From around the corner, Elsa hurried toward them. "I found it! Another student borrowed it from Twiggs's carrel!"

Quint closed their eyes with a soft groan. Carefully, they set Twiggs on his feet.

"He needs food and rest." They turned on their heel. "I'll go fill out the paperwork."

Adventure over, Quint reentered the elevator. The cart followed them. At least it would be some company as they began the dull business of writing all of this up only to file it somewhere no one would ever read it.

Back at their office, they slung their pack down heavily by the door and started to shed their coat. Before they could get it off, there was a frantic knock at the door.

Quint opened it.

Twiggs stood on the other side, breathing heavily from running up several flights of stairs.

A finger stabbed into their chest. "What do you think you're doing, running away from me?"

"I wasn't," Quint protested. "You should go eat something."

"With you. Obviously."

"Obviously?"

The book jacket still on Quint's shoulder fluttered and took off, winging lazily upward.

"We should stick together." Twiggs reached out and took Quint's hand. "I think we make a pretty good team."

Quint didn't want to argue with those hearth-warm eyes locked onto theirs. The kiss on their cheek still tingled.

"In that case, would you like to get some lunch with me? Dinner? I don't actually know what time it is," Quint said in a rush, words tumbling after each other. "We can gossip and complain."

"I would love that." Twiggs beamed. "And tomorrow, I think we should storm the director's office to have a serious talk about workplace safety."

Quint smiled back. "And stocking snack machines more sensibly."

"You really get me," Twiggs laughed.

The cart bumped against Quint affectionately. They gave it a pat and whispered, "Thanks—I owe you an oiling."

Quint offered their arm, and Twiggs looped his own through it. They stepped out into the bookcases together, shutting the office door firmly behind them.

CAFFEINE AND THE UNSLEEPING

LUCY K. R.

Tags: attraction at first sight, blood drinking, coffee shop, college/ university, customer service representative, flirting, fluff, gay, the grumpy one is soft for the sunshine one, interspecies relationship, m/m, modern with magic, student (graduate), present tense, romance, third person limited (multiple) point of view, vampire

Verse One

There is a boy in the dark and the damp. The mortuary is mostly underground, like a grave itself. The boy brushes the hair of corpses the way some children tend to dolls.

Once, a corpse is sent to them with a book tucked into his inner jacket pocket. The boy keeps the book and traces its words in the dim candlelight.

The boy grows, and then the boy is a man. He dresses the corpses to spare his father's aching back, and sounds out the words of that ancient book in the daylight during scarce moments outside.

A man *should* keep aging. Should change and grow and alter as the world alters him.

The man does not stay a man. He is a whim, and a poor one at that. He is a whim, and he knows it even as the teeth sink into his neck and the blood slides between his lips. He is a whim, and he will be forgotten.

Vampirism is a hobby for the wealthy—an aristocratic pastime, made possible only through wealth and circumstance. Without a castle gate and thick curtains to draw against the poisonous daylight, without the hopeless to prey on, what is a vampire but another beggar?

The vampire learns the age at which corpses can no longer sustain him. He drinks from them in the dark of the cellar where he has always worked, dresses them carefully to cover the wounds, and delicately styles their hair and faces as apology for the indignity.

He wastes candlelight to read his book, so slowly savored through the many years. But without the sun, locked away in the dark and damp, the pages rot until the words are devoured by the wet and the insects, as all things will be in time.

The day the vampire turns one page to find the next illegible is the same day his father starts coughing.

Somewhere in the city is a vampire with a lace collar and a wry smile, who on a whim changed a working man to be like him, then wandered away again.

It takes a long, long time in the dark before the vampire can see that as anything but a curse.

Verse Two

The university was established in the same year he was, and Vladimir cannot pretend that has nothing to do with his choice to attend. He never had a sibling, and truly he is glad for that. It would have been hard to watch them age and grow without him.

The university, however, is like him—not *untouched* by time, not unchanged by it, but steady and still within its flow compared to the lightning lives of humans and beasts alike. It is a comfort to imagine that they are of a kind in that way.

The tunnels crisscrossing campus were installed in deference to the terrible storms and heavy snowfalls of winter, but have been easily converted to accommodate for their "immortals inclusion initiative"—an initiative that appears not to have seen much use, as when Vladimir input his birthdate in an online form, it took down the entire campus's electronic systems for twenty-four hours.

He doesn't mind the lack of fellow immortals. He is far more interested in the presence of his fellow anthropologists, and they, in turn, have some use for him as the eldest among them. Though much of his life was spent in the dark and in the shadows, he knows some of textiles from his work with the dead, and more about burial customs, hairstyles, and makeup through the many, many years.

Even more precious to him are those among his peers who are studying times long before he and the university came into being. One had even utilized the "3D printer" in the library to recreate the ancient skeleton Lucy's skull for his research. Vladimir had held it cupped in both hands, feeling her fangs press lightly into his palm, and had felt a distant kinship echo through millennia.

It was nearly enough for him to forgive the infuriating, though distant, hum of the wretched "printer" churning out plastic waste that had taken up residence in *his* library.

The library, of course, but still, *his library*. Founded the same year he was, and full to bursting with books. Countless books, all crisp and cared for, though many yellowed with age. The library is built on a hill, dry and safe. There are rooms kept dark, even on bright days, but the desk lamps at the reading tables never run out of wax and gutter into uselessness.

The first time Vladimir had attempted an undergraduate degree, even though the library had been far inferior to this one, he had nearly failed his classes because he couldn't stop reading. He'd spent days in there—days and days and days, safely tucked into one of the dark rooms, heedless of the rising and setting sun.

"No, I get it," Anna the librarian had said when he'd apologized for the third time for startling her with his glowing eyes in the darkened room. "You're living, like, the opposite of that Twilight Zone episode. Go for it!"

He'd then rented "that Twilight Zone episode" from the library's media desk, and had reported back to her the day after that it was the most frightening thing he'd seen in hundreds of years.

He still wrote to her often.

That had been at his first college, back in the old country, where he'd found another copy of that ancient book that had been worn away and eaten in his hands by the terrible passage of years.

This copy had been safe and sound, pages still crisp, if somewhat brittle. He had not read it, but had looked down on it in his palms and thought *you're safe here.*

He was aware enough of himself even then to know he was not just talking to the book.

Now, as he gears up for his second year in his doctoral program and the building of his dissertation and defense, he returns to the safety of his library with a spring in his step. He'd been to see the great-great-grand-cousins and their children during summer break and had been delighted to find he had not been away too long this time. The little children were still little children, though old enough that their parents no longer wore dark circles beneath their eyes.

The family resemblance between him and his living kin has worn away bit by bit through the centuries, but it hardly matters. They do not have his pale skin or his limp, dark hair. They are vibrantly, beautifully alive, and he loves them. Their city's library is very fine, and he of course ensures they have all the books they could desire, with reading lights to spare. His first few decades of reconnecting with living family, he had drowned their households in lights until one of his distant cousin's spouses had kindly reminded him that they really only needed one good light to read by, not a dozen.

"Old friend, I've some new stories to tell you," Vladimir murmurs, tracing his fingers across the Latin engraved on the library's moonlit marble entryway.

Littera Scripta Manet, the words read, as ever.

He pushes through the revolving door, and is not greeted by the usual low murmur of voices and turning pages, with the occasional sharp click of a mouse. No, instead he is welcomed with a terrible, oscillating roar like a wildcat howling displeasure, hissing and spitting. A plume of steam arises from the source of the noise like smoke from a mountaintop—a new structure, where at the end of last semester they had blocked off the old help desk.

"Triple-shot vanilla latte?" sings a sweet-voiced man from behind the counter, a knit cap cradling his skull and his deep brown eyes squinted in a heartless smile.

Verse Three

The most beautiful man Ben has ever seen is standing stock-still and staring at him, and has been for a solid three minutes.

Ben knows this because he's been watching the clock while pretending to work on the Point of Sale at the front counter.

He'd been warned that taking on the night shift might mean some weirdos. That's part of the deal in any service industry job. You get some oddballs, and the weirder your hours are, the weirder the oddballs will be.

So far the gorgeous guy hasn't actually *done* anything, so Ben tries to keep an open mind. Sometimes weirdos can be the best customers, and judging by the people he's run into so far during these late library hours, it's likely the guy hasn't slept in thirty-six hours.

It's enough to make him rethink his own long-term plans. At least right now he's only the normal amount of sleep-deprived!

The guy's just so *still*, is the thing. Not still like a stone, but still like an owl. Watching and wild.

The most beautiful man Ben has ever seen finally starts walking as the clock ticks closer to four minutes, though it's more of a stalk than anything. He's got ridiculously long legs, and piercing, predatory eyes, and hair that's falling into his face until he lifts an elegant hand to push it back, joining the perfect coif slicked back over his head.

"Hi," Ben says, his voice coming out fried like the sorority siblings who order from his daytime coworkers. He clears his throat, leans one hand against the counter, and summons up a winning customer service smile. "Coffee?"

"This"—the man's words are clipped, but his "s" hisses between his clenched teeth—"is a *library*, sir. A *sacred* place of learning. A repository and sanctuary for the thoughts of man, amassed and curated through *centuries* of lives and deaths—the culmination of the best our species has to offer in the wretched mess of a world we have made!"

"Y—yeah." Ben leans forward a little more, eyes flicking down to the curl of the stranger's pale lip, revealing startlingly sharp teeth. "Cool, right?"

The man recoils, nostrils flaring.

"Cool. *Cool*, you say, while standing behind the smoking gun at the center of devastation. Alexandria, at least, only *burned*. This is the slow ruin—the creeping death of knowledge—the rotting of worlds. Bad enough when they began to allow the vapid hoards liquid refreshment among such vulnerable creatures as books, but to *encourage* it, to *exacerbate* it—The belching smog of your infernal machines sounds the trumpeting finale of the age of thought over consumption."

Ben stands behind the counter, the gears in his mind turning while making no progress, like bike pedals spinning pell-mell while the chain drags the ground, unmoving. A brief glance at the coffee shop sign, PerkyJolt, then back at the beautiful and clearly *very* angry man before him.

Sir, this is a Wendy's, his mind supplies as he struggles to offer some response to the tirade, but he quickly shuts that thought down.

"Um," he says instead, fiddling with the corner of his mandatory pink-and-orange apron. "Sorry you're feeling that way. I kind of just work here?"

All at once, the fire goes out of the gorgeous man, leaving him looking still lovely, but exhausted rather than spirited. He closes his dark starfield eyes, takes a deep, deliberate inhale, then breathes out in a heavy sigh.

"Yes," he says. "You are at work. I apologize for the outburst."

And then he's gone, stepping away from the line without even asking if Ben knows the Wi-Fi password.

In the wake of him, the library seems impossibly quiet. It's always quiet, sure, but it seems to echo now, hollowed out. The analog clock hanging high on the library wall over the display case of selected sculptures by local elementary schoolers—which get exponentially creepier the later the shift gets—says it's only nine o'clock. The sculptures are hardly even eerie yet.

No one else is in the library's main entry, despite the not-actually-cozy reading nooks and the small selection of café tables. It's just Ben, the sculptures, the books, and the clock. Faintly, he becomes aware of the ticking.

The librarians had drawn the line at music in the café.

He could always backwash the espresso machine again…

"Anyone else met the angry goth guy yet?" he asks in the work group chat while the soft roar of the machine blankets him.

But it's past 9 p.m., and most of his coworkers are students, which means they're all saying "I should be sleeping!" in loud, crowded rooms over screaming vocalists and pounding drums.

Ben puts up the "Brew Right Back!" sign on the counter and slips away to the combination library main desk and security office. Anaya, the woman who occasionally stops by for a triple-shot espresso with a crack of black pepper on top, might have a better chance of answering his question.

And more than that, maybe she can shed some light on the crisp words still lingering in Ben's ears. *At least Alexandria only burned.*

A university is, at heart, a place for learning. And within that heart, if there were blood, it would be the library. Relentless and unstopping, incapable of total rest so long as the university still lives.

That night, for the first time in what feels like ages, Ben learns.

Verse Four

Though it stings, Vladimir has lost safe places before. Over the centuries, comforts have been ripped away from him more than once. That the world has changed for the better for his kind is undoubtable—that he is safer now than ever before is certainly true—that having a library at *all* that he can access at his leisure, safely hidden from the sun for more than an hour at a time, even if there is now a rotten core in the esteemed place of learning…

He cannot avoid the greatest treasure of his many years simply because an awful new tumor has grown within the entryway.

Still, he takes a little longer to return than he should. Professor Jimenez gives him a concerned look when he provides only one new reference to her during their monthly dissertation meeting. Usually he has discovered four to seven materials that either relate to or expand upon his theory.

Steps dragging, he forces his way back to confront the bad new habit his honorary sibling has developed. The light dusting of snow marks where his reluctance scuffs his well-shined shoes against the path. Soon the tunnels will be more crowded during the daytime as heavy snow begins to fall. He does not mind sharing, of course, but it is a different kind of loneliness, to be surrounded by people.

The library doors open before him, wind rushing in to fill the silent space and pushing his hair into wild disarray. He combs it back with one hand, takes a breath, and lifts his eyes.

The young man in the knit beanie is behind the counter of his worst nightmare again—the one whose work Vladimir had interrupted with his tirade before, as though the person staffing such an establishment had any say over its location. Perhaps he should apologize again—perhaps that is why the man's eyes have gone wide in recognition.

There is the sound of water behind the counter, and a trickle of steam rising from the blasted machine. Vladimir clears his throat and nods toward the young man, ready to pretend for the rest of the night that he cannot hear the song of impending doom no matter how high in the library's many floors he climbs.

"You're back!" cries the worker, and Vladimir, already halfway through dragging his gaze away, startles at the intensity of the tone. "Wait one second," the man continues, crouching down to rummage behind his counter. "I have it here—hah! Got it."

He straightens, a plastic binder held in both hands, and offers it out to Vladimir with all the ardent enthusiasm of a suitor with a bouquet of roses.

He has beautiful eyes—hazel and green, bright with delight beneath his full brows. As though in a trance, Vladimir steps forward in one smooth motion, stopping with both hands outstretched to receive whatever he is being offered. He hesitates at the last moment, his fingers curling back toward himself.

"I asked Dr. Anaya over at the main desk—did you know she's a doctor?—anyhow, I asked her about the, uh, about what you said? That the café's bad for the library."

"You did?" Vladimir asks, not yet taking the binder but not looking away. That feels…rare. Precious. Vladimir spoke. This man listened.

"This is the, what did she call it…the impact study! About the café, and the humidity and everything. I didn't really understand it, but I'm not actually a student, so… Anyhow, I thought you might like to look?"

Vladimir's hands do not shake as he closes his fingers gently around the garish purple plastic. Shaking fingers is a privilege of mortals, but what remains of his heart—what there is of his soul and spirit—quake beneath the stranger's hopeful smile.

"Thank you," he says, the words carefully spoken. They taste in his mouth like they might come out wrong—too strong and too soon in the face of this unexpected care. "You did not have to go to the trouble."

"No trouble," lies the stranger, releasing the binder slowly, as if he were reluctant to part from the shared point of contact.

There are many talents Vladimir once had that he has become rusty in through the years. Flirting, however, has never been among their number, but isn't that why he came to school in the first place? To try new things? To broaden his horizons?

"My name is Vladimir," he says, halting and uncertain as he hugs the binder to his chest. "And I would like to apologize again for my outburst."

"Ben," says the man, his lips curving up to reveal a broad grin full of slightly crooked and deeply human teeth. "And honestly, it was just good to have something to think about for the shift. Do you, uh, want a pastry? While you're reading? On the house."

"I thank you for your concern," Vladimir replies. "However I am unable to partake."

"Gluten free?"

"Vampire."

"Ah," says Ben.

A look of consternation clouds his brow, a little pout replacing that smile. He looks down at the tablet before him, poking it with a single finger rather than gazing at him any longer, and Vladimir's ancient, troublesome heart sinks.

"I think we're technically supposed to have blood products, but corporate gets weird about stocking things that don't sell a ton. I'll talk to my manager, though! Not that you *have* to—I mean, it's probably super overpriced through us as opposed to— Actually I don't know *anything* about blood prices. Is it like a grocery store thing? Shit, is this weird to talk about? Plus you don't even like that the café's here, so—"

Vladimir lifts the binder, and Ben falls silent, eyes and attention drawn to it again.

"I will read this first," Vladimir says, "and decide based on the facts presented whether to retract my complaint regarding the café's presence in the library. Regardless of that outcome, I shall also write to your 'corporate' to remind them of the university grant that requires this library to be open such hours for students such as myself, and the stipulations of such grants in regards to equal opportunity and access. Would that be acceptable?"

"Even if you think we shouldn't be here?" Ben asks, a smile ticking at the corner of his pout again.

"I think you should be here," Vladimir says, and then winces at himself. Clumsy words always haunt him when he most wants eloquence. "That is, you have a mind for research, regardless of my feelings toward your place of work."

"I couldn't even understand it," chuckles Ben, glancing to the side and smiling, yes, but not happily.

"You looked," Vladimir says. "You tried. When I first entered a school, as a grown man mind you, I had only read a single book and had never seen a dictionary. Having the mind to learn had not granted me the opportunity."

"Huh." The barista leans forward onto the counter like he had the first day and cups his round cheek in one hand, glancing Vladimir briefly up and down. "And look at you now."

"I— Yes." He hugs the binder tighter to his chest. "Look at me."

The words snag and catch at the moment—a spider's web against beating bird wings, birthing a fraction of a pause. Then the library doors whoosh open once more, the breeze cutting past them both. A group of young women, hurriedly hushing one another as they pass the entrance to the space. Vladimir clears his throat, seeing them angling at once toward the café, and takes a step back.

"Uh." Ben straightens, tugging on the brightly colored apron he wears. "Tell me what you find out?"

"Yes," Vladimir replies. "Will you be here tomorrow?"

"Yeah. I think? Yes. Friday. Yeah, I'll be here."

"As will I."

Verse Five

With the help of his advisors through the years, Vladimir's schedule has been a consistent companion for some time now. He builds a variation upon the familiar with every semester he studies, and iterates upon the basic themes as he walks through his endless days.

This is the first time his schedule has changed of its own accord.

"I've asked my manager to install a dehumidifier, too," Ben says the next night, after Vladimir has summarized the relevant portions of the impact study, which had been filled with the more logistical and finance-based reasoning, and only briefly touched upon his concerns, but which had set him at ease nonetheless.

There were other concerns he had not thought to have. Concerns of "digitization" and declining attendance to make use of the library's many tools. Concerns of funding. Concerns the café has answered.

"You did not have to," Vladimir tells him, but he's smiling when he says it.

"I'd sort of like the white noise," Ben replies with a shrug. "It gets quiet down here."

Not all of Vladimir's research books can be removed from the sections in which they reside. Those that can, he begins to bring downstairs to the seating area around the café, where he can be nearby while Ben chats with other people, makes coffees, or leans on the counter and pokes at his phone.

He does not offer anyone else binders full of answers to their fears, Vladimir notes.

"Do you prefer to stand?" he asks Ben one night, gaze drawn from *Heidelmen's Theory of Mesozoic Vampirism* back to the man behind the counter who is shifting his weight once more.

"Not really," Ben replies.

"Why not sit, then?" Vladimir gestures to the chair across from him.

He means it as an indication that they are surrounded by empty seating, and that at 1 a.m. there is unlikely to be much need of a barista.

That Ben takes it as an invitation to sit across from him and crane his neck to peek at his book is a misunderstanding he welcomes.

"Is this thesis stuff? That's a thing higher-level students do, right?"

"You are correct in the general, though specifically I am working on a dissertation." Vladimir marks his place with a finger so that he can converse appropriately.

"Ah, gotcha… Is it cool to ask about dissertation stuff?" Ben's cheeks curve upward. There is a little stubble left on his jawline—a tiny patch missed by his shaving. It would be rough to the touch. Vladimir tries not to stare at it.

"My secrets are few." He gestures expansively with his free hand, the other still marking the words "viral immortality" in the text.

"Then"—leaning in closer, eyes wide and bright—"what's your dissertation about?"

"You do not know how dangerous a question that is, Ben," Vladimir says in reply, letting warning well in his voice.

"Will you tell me?"

"You may never escape me telling you, should I begin."

Ben looks up at the clock on the wall. He studies it a moment, then turns his bright smile back in Vladimir's direction.

"I've got time."

"The working title is 'Beyond the Predatory: The Historical Role of Vampirism and Other Immortality Diseases in Human Family Groups.'"

"I'm guessing it's about the historical role of vampirism in family groups?" Ben jokes. It stings a little, but Vladimir smiles regardless. "Long title is all," Ben clarifies. "Like an isekai anime."

"Poetry is not a strength of mine," Vladimir says with a shrug.

"I bet it could be, if you wanted. What's the role?"

"Hm?"

"Of vampirism in family groups," Ben clarifies, brows lifted.

"Ah. Well, that is what my research exists to find out. I have a hypothesis, certainly, but whether it holds true in the face of evidence remains to be seen."

Against the faux wood of the table, Vladimir feels his hand looks unbearably pale. There are no blue veins to mark him—only the soap-white curve of his knuckles. Ben places a hand on the table between them as well. It seems wildly full of color in comparison.

When Vladimir looks up, Ben's brows are lifted, waiting. He clears his throat, and for the first time in a long time, to a person outside his expertise, he begins to speak.

Verse Six

"I've been thinking about it a lot," Ben says the next time they meet, after a long weekend apart. Monday night is slightly busier, and they are speaking over the counter rather than huddled at a table. "Your dissertation thingy, that is."

Vladimir tries not to show too blatantly how that affects him. To be thought of in absentia is a gift, and one he had been holding close to his chest in regards to Ben in return.

"What you said about family groups benefiting from people who love the family without, uh...making more? I think it's not just immortals like you it would resonate with. A lot of queer people like me would get it too."

"Like you," Vladimir breathes, the words feeling warm on his tongue.

Ben glances to the side, at the little huddles of study groups feverishly trying to make up for a wasted weekend. He looks nervous, and Vladimir hastens to say, "I have never used that...that particular word, but I am also— Yes. Yes, you are right. I may be bringing personal bias into—"

"Oh, that's not what I meant!" Ben hurries to say, patting Vladimir's hand without seeming to realize he's doing so. "Not that you should worry! I just meant it as in, like...I think there's a lot of value there. In a family that doesn't just look like a mom, a dad, 2.5 kids...y'know?"

Cautiously, carefully, Vladimir turns his hand so he can catch Ben's palm between his own, holding him gently there.

"You should call it something stronger," Ben says, eyes earnest and sincere. "Something like 'Undying Uncles, or The Family Time Won't Take.'"

"Ah," Vladimir purrs, immeasurably pleased and only growing more so as Ben holds his hand in return. "Poetry."

Verse Seven

PerkyJolt's corporate offices eventually relent on the blood supply. It is horrible, overpackaged, and overpriced. Ben buys one for Vladimir anyway, one winter's night after a few weeks of setbacks on his ever-expanding dissertation.

It comes in a little red carton with a sippy straw and a biohazard symbol. Technically Ben is supposed to check people's IDs for Vs before making the sale, in case some frat freak decides to take a swig of human blood on a dare and ends up making headlines featuring the company brand, but he just pushes the "I checked" button and moves on.

It's pretty sad, compared to the frothy delights he whips up for most of his customers. A cold little carton of blood. Ben's asked a lot of people out for coffee in his time, and only when he was dating the juice-cleanse guy had he seen a drink as sad as this one.

He hesitates, then glances slowly over at the espresso machine and its gleaming silver steam wand.

Mistakes happen fast. Ben makes this one in record time. The physical properties of blood are not at *all* what he expected them to be when exposed to heat and steam. And now there's a biohazard in the library. And on his tacky apron, the espresso machine, the coffee cups, the floor, the PoS system, the—

The doors slide open, and Ben looks over wide-eyed. His gaze locks with Vladimir's from across the room, and he sees realization dawn in his dark gaze even as a red light flickers from within his eyes—alien and incredible. Then, far more wonderful, he sees his thin lips part in surprise, then keep parting, baring fangs, then regular teeth beside them, and then opening wide in an enormous, *piercing* laugh.

Worth it, Ben thinks, staring open-mouthed as overpriced blood drips off the espresso machine and onto the counter in an awful coagulated clump, and Vladimir *howls* with laughter. *Worth it, worth it, worth it.*

Vladimir insists on helping with the cleanup after, the halfway-to-threadbare rag going from white to pink through its many trips back and forth between the mess and the bucket of disinfectant.

"Isn't this sort of beneath you?" Ben asks playfully, wringing out his own rag.

"Not in the slightest," Vladimir snaps with a flash of fang before reining himself in. "No man should be above the daily tasks of existence."

"No?" Ben chuckles, shaking his head as he tosses his own square of pink fabric into the trash and picks up some paper towels to finish the job. "Lot of people would disagree with you."

"Plenty of people are wrong." Vladimir scoffs, and then hesitates, mouth twisting, before glancing at Ben again from the corner of his eye. "I like to think the good ones can learn."

"Huh," Ben says, remembering fondly the contrite way Vladimir had apologized for his initial reaction to the café. "I like that."

Verse Eight

"What do you do all night?" Vladimir finally thinks to ask, watching Ben enjoy a stale croissant while he idly sips from his personal flask of blood.

The synthetic stuff sold behind the counter was acceptable in a pinch, but hardly gourmet—the factory-made junk food of the vampire world.

"Mostly lattes," Ben replies, fiddling with something on his device that seems to contain multitudinous little creatures of no discernible use or character.

"Aside from making coffees and talking to me," Vladimir clarifies. "You are here till 4 a.m., are you not?"

"Oh. Yeah, but it's okay. I get things set for the next shift, scroll a little, and it means I've got time to drive my little sister to daycare in the morning."

"...there are scrolls?" Vladimir asks, glancing around the library. *He* has never seen a scroll here, but Ben *is* friends with the rare book librarian Dr. Anaya, so perhaps—

"No, like..." Ben's monsters vanish with a couple of quick taps of the screen and are replaced by the dismal hellscape of some social media platform or another, quickly blurred into an idea by the upward swiping of Ben's finger.

"Scrolling," he repeats, pairing the action with the word, then shrugging in advance of what he surely must know will be Vladimir's disapproval.

"Ben," he says, as kindly as he can muster. "My good, kind friend. You are in a *library*."

"Yeah, but I'm not actually a student, you know? I'm only here to keep the lights on."

"The books neither know nor care," Vladimir insists. "They only require your interest."

"Ah, I dunno. Learning and I didn't get along," Ben says with a shrug. "I'm just a guy who makes coffee."

"I do not think you are 'just' anything," Vladimir replies before he can catch his tongue and rein it into a more suitable turn of phrase. When it earns him a glance from beneath Ben's long eyelashes, he clears his throat and continues, "I think you could be many things, all of them wonderful. I think you already are."

"You can't even enjoy the one thing I do well," gripes Ben, leaning forward to point at Vladimir's chest.

"Do you not see yourself as I see you?" Vladimir asks, soft this time.

It's a Thursday again, late in the night. Somewhere in the library people are studying. Somewhere, the 3D printer is churning, distantly, horribly audible. Somewhere, Dr. Anaya is cataloging an ancient book which Vladimir may or may not have been alive during the binding of.

In the coffee shop in the library lobby, they are alone. Ben, soft and uncertain and hopeful; Vladimir, once again out of his area of expertise and trying nevertheless to move forward.

"You saved my library from my fear," Vladimir tells him. "Or at least saved me from it. You are wonderful, Ben."

"I wish I could take you out for coffee," Ben declares, leaning forward.

"Let's stay in," Vladimir counters, and meets him halfway.

Verse Nine

There is a boy in the library, though not for the usual reasons. He was never clever nor well-studied—never much good at anything, really, aside from loving his little sister and helping his parents out. Libraries like this weren't made for people like him.

He found out recently that this library has a brother, which isn't something a library usually has, but that's not stopping it from being true. The library's brother thinks the boy is smart. He brings him books of poetry from upstairs while he's on shift. The boy reads the good ones aloud, and the library's brother pauses his own work to listen.

"Poetry," the brother breathes in different tones, depending on what the boy has read.

Laughter often follows.

Outside, there are endless bills to pay and mortuaries underground. There are people for whom life, however long, is a pastime, who never clean spilled blood or coffee. There are those who care more about money than books, who would have opened a café even if the steam *had* been a problem.

Outside, it is dark.

Safe in each other's company, they bless that quiet darkness.

Index

About the Authors

Robin S. Blackwood

Robin S. Blackwood has been writing stories since they were a child and has always loved fantasy and science fiction. Their first published original fiction was in the Duck Prints Press anthology *Scholarly Pursuits*, although they'd been writing and posting fanfiction for a while before that. While their fandoms, and their original fiction, range from light-hearted fantasy to space opera to horror, favourite themes will always include non-human perspectives on the world, queerness, and queer non-humans. When they're not writing they enjoy reading, watching (usually old) films, fencing, and playing the guitar. They live in the UK.

E. V. Dean

E. V. Dean is a writer with a decade of fanfiction writing under her belt. She's embarking on her original fiction adventure with the angst tag kept within arm's reach. Her favorite excuse not to write is watching *Jeopardy.*

Eliza J. Fitzwilliam

Eliza is a doctoral student in the humanities who traded rainy England for the even rainier part of Canada. She likes to claim that this is because the rain is better for reading, crafting, and writing (and, on occasion, researching...), but it may just have been a lack of strategic planning on her part.

She has been writing on and off since she was a small child, filling notebooks with stories that she would read out to her family on long car rides. Though she hopes her stories have grown more sophisticated since then, that same sense of joy and wonder is still the main reason she puts pen to paper or keeps typing away.

Today, when not studying, she remains an avid, perhaps even manic, reader; a writer of fan fiction and original works; and a *Dungeons & Dragons* player and DM—all hobbies that allow her to explore her favourite themes of fantasy, sci-fi, magic, history, adventure, and romance. And if you sit still near her for long enough, she will start to tell you about the latest thing she has read.

This is her first published piece of original work.

RHOSYN GOODFELLOW

Rhosyn Goodfellow is an author of queer speculative fiction and romance living with xir spouse and two dogs in the Pacific Northwest, where xe is sad to report that xe has not yet mysteriously disappeared nor encountered any cryptids. Xir hobbies include spoiling the aforementioned dogs, drinking inadvisable amounts of coffee, and running unreasonably long distances very slowly. Xe's secretly just a collection of loosely related stories dressed up in a meat suit.

MARE GRIFFEN

Mare is a writer from the US. When not begrudgingly being employed in a 9–to–5, she spends her time meandering, overthinking, doting on her beloved cat, and writing fanfic. She survives on coffee and distraction.

ZEL HOWLAND

Zel (they/she) is a writer and artist currently living in Los Angeles with their partner. When not writing, they spend their time painting, embroidering, analyzing literature and TV shows, and playing *Dungeons & Dragons*. They are the author of many a fanfiction, as well as the novel *The Shadow of Ophelia Walker*.

ROBIN HUNTINGTON

Robin Huntington (she/her) is a scientist and writer who lives in the eastern US with her spouse and reptile pets. After starting her fiction-writing journey in her teens, she took a twenty-year break only to discover a passion for writing fanfic six years ago that's recently expanded into original fiction as well. Her contribution to this volume is her first published original work. When she's not writing, she can be found birding, cooking, watching TV shows about cooking, or spending time online with fandom friends.

INDIGO J. H.

Indi is a queer, disabled writer in their early 20s, living in Vancouver, BC: the traditional, ancestral, and unceded territories of the Squamish, Musqueam, and Tsleil-Waututh Nations. They've been writing since they were a very small child, though usually those stories were exclusively about puppies. Now, Indi is passionate about writing stories with the disability representation they didn't always have growing up.

When they're not spending their time writing, they like reading, singing in choir, seeing their friends and family, and taking a truly excessive amount of naps during the day.

BETTINA JUSZAK

Originally from Germany, Bettina has (so far) spent time in the US, the UK, and Canada. She is particularly interested in exploring questions of music and language in imaginary worlds, aided by degrees in linguistics and literature. When not writing, she loses herself in hobbies such as archery, cross stitch, attempting to learn yet another language, and complaining about the amount of space her book and notebook collection takes up. Her first published work appeared in the *Upon a Twice Time* anthology published by Air and Nothingness Press, followed by Duck Prints Press's *Aether Beyond the Binary* anthology.

Lucy K. R.

To whom it may concern,

I would like to register a complaint in regards to one "Lucy K. R.," who I understand this press has been publishing. I certainly hope that you are simply unenlightened as to the sordid nature of this individual, and I shall attempt to ensure my concerns are enumerated thoroughly so as to better educate you.

First, it must be said that Lucy K. R., whose pronouns are she/her, chose to forgo publishing under a more common "first initial, middle initial, full last name" moniker simply because she thought the inverse was "funny." Her written works, while often wholesome, have been known to contain concerning amounts of both emotional vulnerability and abject silliness. In addition, she was recently wedded to Tomowowo—another member of your press and infinitely preferable—before immediately requesting that her new bride "give Taekwondo a try," as she herself is thoroughly enamored with the art.

Adding to the appalling facts above, you may take this biography as further complaint! It would have been perfectly simple for Lucy K. R. to write a brief and clear biography with details such as "plays upright bass" or "particularly fond of cats" rather than droning on and on in the form of a complaint written by a posh-but-narrow-minded British woman of some standing.

I shall continue to hope that the wonderful editors and executives at Duck Prints Press, each a jewel and treasure, were simply uninformed of the unsuitableness of Mrs. K. R., and shall now take every appropriate measure to remove her from subsequent anthologies, as well as censoring her currently available works in *A Truth Universally Acknowledged, She*

Wears the Midnight Crown, And Seek (Not) to Alter Me, and *Aim for the Heart*.

Kind regards,
A. Prued Esq.

NICOLA KAPRON

Nicola Kapron has previously been published by Neo-opsis Science Fiction Magazine, Rebel Mountain Press, Soteira Press, All Worlds Wayfarer, Mannison Press, and more. Nicola lives in British Columbia with a hoard of books—mostly fantasy and horror—and an extremely fluffy cat.

CASSIA KING

Cassia King writes sapphic adult fantasy romance. When not crafting word magic, she enjoys collecting trinkets, reading tarot, and lifting weights. Cassia lives in Maryland with her herd of pets. You can connect with her on Instagram (@cassiakingauthor), on Bluesky (@cassiakingauthor.bsky.social), or at www.authorivyljames.com, where she writes queer contemporary romance and poetry as Ivy L. James.

MINA KRAMEK

Mina has been looking through archways and in tree hollows for a portal to another world since she was six years old, and discovered along the way that she loves exploring this world almost as much. The first stories she ever told were fairy-tale retellings, and she still has a soft spot for them. She's been writing fanfiction since long before she knew what it was but finished a story for the first time in 2020 after watching *The Untamed* three times in a row. Since then, she's posted about 750k words worth of stories on AO3 and modded a Big Bang. She would always rather be sipping wine by a river and learning the history of somewhere she's never been before, but staying home with her cats, a book, or the occasional crochet project is pretty good too.

SHANNON LIPPERT

Shannon is a writer of poetry, plays, and prose, a performing artist, a director, and a troublemaker. Hailing from Boston, her/their creative work is joyfully transformative, weaving icons of popular culture and found language into new narratives that challenge the limitations of their original sources. Shannon's transformative works include: *My Immortal*, a karaoke-style performance art piece; and *The Harrys*, a web series; and their stage plays inspired by Shakespeare's *Titus Andronicus, Troilus and Cressida*, and *Cymbeline*. You can find their recent poetry in *What Rough Beast* by Indolent Books and *All Shall Be Well*, an anthology by Amethyst Review.

LYONEL LOY

Lifelong maladaptive daydreamer, finally working up the courage to write those daydreams down. Spends time cosplaying as a Responsible Adult With A Job.

JESSICA MASON

Jessica Mason is known as alocalband in fandom spaces and has previously published stories under the name Jessica Black. She has a BFA in Screenwriting and has spent the majority of her adult life working on assorted film and television projects in Los Angeles, New York, and Puerto Rico. Lately, however, she's been content to settle down in her quiet mountain hometown with her cat, her library, and an ever-growing stationary collection. Hobbies include reading, hiking, tabletop gaming, knitting, and going to hockey games.

MAGGIE PAGE

Maggie Page lives in Texas with family, including her incorrigibly clumsy mom with a green thumb and two silly dogs. Her most recent publications with Duck Prints Press appear in *He Bears the Cape of Stars* and *Add Magic to Taste*. Previously, Maggie has published several poems and a piece of flash fiction with collegiate and independent journals.

Aside from writing, Maggie enjoys music, traveling, camping, creating art of both decent and questionable quality, and torturing her loved ones with ruthless board game victories. Befriending her comes with the hazard of being subjected to fervent media analysis, which is her true favorite pastime. Currently, exposure to Sherlock Holmes and *Dishonored* are risks upon approaching her.

LEE PINI

Lee Pini is a queer author (she/he/they) who has been writing since they could pick up a pencil and has published several contemporary m/m romances. They have lived in England, Northern Ireland, and Florida, and currently live in their home state of Minnesota with their wife, cat, and collection of action figures. Lee studied archaeology at the graduate level but currently uses their degree primarily to chuckle knowingly at classics memes. When they aren't at their day job or writing, they're reading vociferously, listening to music, enjoying nature, or nerding out. Their dream is for someone to one day write fanfiction about their characters.

VEE SLOANE

Vee Sloane has authored a novel, several short stories, some poetry, and twenty-two years worth of fanfic. They live with one lovely spouse, one rambunctious clever child, and one sleepy cat.

Swev

Swev is a European writer and artist in her mid-thirties. She greatly enjoys speculative fiction of all sorts and has dabbled in various fandoms since she was a kid, initially as an artist and later also as a writer. Her favourite punctuation marker is the em-dash—one might consider her usage of it excessive.

Aside from writing and drawing her own pieces, she also enjoys typesetting, moderating events, and petting her cats.

D. E. Towry

D. E. Towry (they/them) is a lifelong writer from Colorado. Their first written work was an enigmatic "dream book" at six years old, and that early attempt to conjure the numinous into the real led to a love of writing fantasy, sci-fi, mysteries, and AU fanfiction. Their story in *Scholarly Pursuits* is their first published work.

When they're not writing, D enjoys reading and hoarding books, playing video games, being storyteller or dungeon master for table-top rpgs, and satisfying an absolutely eldritch appetite for knowledge.

Dei Walker

Dei Walker (she/her) is a queer New Englander abroad, having spent almost half her life overseas. She currently lives with her family in Beijing, China. When she isn't writing, she can be found knitting, scuba diving, or playing games (video or tabletop).

Premium Backers List

About Duck Prints Press, LLC

Duck Prints Press, LLC, is an independent publisher based in New York, USA, on the unceded lands of the Schaghticoke, Haudenosaunee, Mohawk, and Mohican peoples. Our founding vision is to work with fanwork creators to publish their original works. We are particularly dedicated to working with queer creators and publishing stories and artwork featuring characters from across the LGBTQIA+ spectrum.

Become a Duck Prints Press Patron by backing us on Patreon!

Find us online at our website, **duckprintspress.com**, or on social media:
Bluesky: duckprintspress
Dreamwidth: duckprintspress.dreamwidth.org
Instagram: duckprintspress
Mastodon: @dppunforth
Patreon: duckprintspress
Pillowfort: duckprintspress
Pinterest: duckprintspress
TikTok: @duckprintspress
Tumblr: duckprintspress

Goodreads: https://www.goodreads.com/user/show/129902473-duck-prints-press-llc
Storygraph: https://app.thestorygraph.com/profile/unforth